THE JOHN HARVARD LIBRARY

LOOKING BACKWARD 2000–1887

By Edward Bellamy

EDITED BY JOHN L. THOMAS

THE BELKNAP PRESS OF

HARVARD UNIVERSITY PRESS

Cambridge · Massachusetts
London · England

John Harvard Library books are edited
at the Charles Warren Center for Studies
in American History, Harvard University

Library of Congress Catalog Card Number 67-14337
ISBN 0-674-53900-1

Printed in the United States of America

Contents

Introduction

*E*DWARD BELLAMY was a little-known New England journalist and author of pale romances when the publication of his utopian novel, *Looking Backward,* in 1888, propelled him from the literary wings into the middle of the American political stage. Sales of the book, sixty thousand the first year, soared over a hundred thousand the next as editions appeared in England, France, and Germany. From the West Coast came sudden and unaccountable demands for copies, and in the Farm Belt a fifty-cent paperback edition quickly became a bestseller. Overnight Bellamy found himself something of a hero. *The Nation* warned readers that they would return from the year 2000 "haunted by visions of a golden age." Haunted or otherwise disenchanted, millions of Americans—social workers, farmers, businessmen, bankers, and housewives—variously confronted Bellamy's argument for a wholesale rearrangement of their capitalist society. Clergymen took Julian West's conversion to universal brotherhood as their Sunday texts. Reformers and social theorists debated the merits of the industrial army, and practitioners of the strenuous life hailed the advent of a new era of physical and moral hardihood. Theosophists along with retired army officers thought they discerned in the skyline of a future Boston the outlines of permanent social harmony. If the young John Dewey read the novel as a plea for an untried scheme of social engineering, the compilers of the Sweet Home Family Soap Album considered themselves warranted in including Bellamy along with Louisa May Alcott and James Whitcomb Riley as celebrants of traditional American values.

Such a mixture of adulation and serious attention was the

more perplexing because, as Bellamy readily admitted, in undertaking his utopian fantasy he had not envisioned a serious contribution to social thought. *Looking Backward* was initially conceived as a simple fable of social happiness. "There was no thought," he explained, "of contriving a house which practical men might live in, but merely of hanging in mid-air, far out of reach of the sordid and material world of the present, a cloud-palace for an ideal humanity." To supply elbowroom for the imagination he had first unfolded his story in the year 3000 in Asheville, North Carolina, the provincial capital of a world state. The scene opened on an enormous parade of a departmental division in the world industrial army marching toward its annual muster-day ceremony where new recruits took the oath of duty before the world standard and veterans were demobilized with the thanks of humanity. In constructing the scene Bellamy had been impressed by the martial order he described—"each battalion with its appropriate insignia, the triumphal arches, the garlanded streets, the banquets, the music." Then as he reread his description there came one of those moments of insight which change the whole concept of a work. The industrial army, which in the beginning had seemed merely a rhetorical analogy to the military, now appeared as an organizing principle, "a complete working model . . . the unanswerable demonstration of its feasibility drawn from the actual experience of whole nations organized and manoeuvered as armies." His discovery led to a complete recasting of the novel. "Instead of a mere fairy tale of social perfection, it became the vehicle of a definite scheme of industrial reorganization." [1] The time in Bellamy's own experience when Americans had massed and marched as armies was the Civil War, and to that "grand object-lesson in solidarity," as he called it, he instinctively returned for the organizational principle of his utopia. In its revised form *Looking Backward* is an exposition of the ethics of solidarity derived in large part from its author's mystical interpretation of the Civil War.

When the Civil War ended Bellamy was a boy of fifteen, the

[1] "How I Came to Write 'Looking Backward'," *The Nationalist*, I (May, 1889), 1–4.

frail and introspective son of a Baptist minister in Chicopee Falls, Massachusetts. The Reverend Rufus Bellamy traced his lineage to Dr. Joseph Bellamy, friend and disciple of Jonathan Edwards, but the austerities of Calvinist revisionism had been tempered in the grandson's theology by a bland and amiable evangelicalism. Rufus Bellamy fed his flock and raised his family on conventional piety and Emersonian self-reliance. A Calvinist heritage not unduly burdensome to the genial Baptist clergyman nevertheless deeply troubled his son. Although his childhood by his own admission was one of "entire conformity" to the rules of New England propriety, Bellamy remembered growing up with the persistent dread of "a grievous sinner, accursed from God with whom he must make peace or suffer the most terrible consequences." He made his first truce with this adversary at the age of fourteen when he became converted and joined his father's church, an experience he later described in the third person:

He came to feel a sense of intimacy and to enjoy an indescribably close and tender communion with what seemed to him a very real and sublime being. . . . In prayer he took a deep and awful pleasure; it was to him a sensation at once of almost sensuous happiness as of ineffable sublimity when at such times his heart seemed to throb with that of deity and his soul seemed fused and melted in perfect union with the divine. A love more tender and passionate than any which human charms ever moved him seemed then to bind him to the infinite. . . . He saw the world with new eyes.[2]

The mystical apprehension concealed in this piece of conventional religious rhetoric furnished the materials for the central drama in Bellamy's imaginative life, one in which the antagonist was Nemesis, a paralyzing guilt and dread from which he constantly struggled to free himself. Ten years later the young agnostic discarded the specifically Christian meaning of the conversion experience, but the act itself, the sudden miraculous escape from Nemesis, he kept as the core of his new philosophy. When he left his father's church in 1874, he complained that Christianity feminized the believer and that conversion con-

[2] Autobiographical fragment, Unpublished Papers of Edward Bellamy, Houghton Library, Harvard University.

summated a kind of spiritual rape. Nevertheless, the release from guilt in the moment of self-transcendence which formed the psychological foundation of his Religion of Solidarity remained essentially that experienced by the fourteen-year-old boy.

The balance of Bellamy's adolescent emotional capital was spent in imagined "intercourse with heroes and kings" and the indulgence of an insatiable appetite for high adventure and military exploit. In retrospect it seemed to him that the role of outsider was cast for him out of the books in the family library where as an ardent young Napoleon he sat savoring "the intoxicating aroma of glory." Rejected at West Point—he was already suffering from tuberculosis—and undecided on a career, he spent a year of desultory reading at Union College and another in Germany before returning to Springfield to study law in the offices of a local firm. In 1871 he was admitted to the bar, but his first case, an action for eviction, so disgusted him that he quit an unpromising career and settled provisionally on journalism. After a brief stint with William Cullen Bryant's New York *Evening Post* he joined the newly established Springfield *Union* in 1872, an editorial post he continued to hold until 1878 when his health broke down completely and his family dispatched him on a voyage to Hawaii to recover. On his return he made his first venture into independent journalism with the Springfield *Penny News* (later the *Daily News*) which he and his brother Charles established in 1880 and edited jointly for two years. In 1882 he removed his capital from the paper in order to finance a full-time literary career. His first novel, *Six to One: A Nantucket Idyll*, appeared in 1878. A second novel and his best work, *The Duke of Stockbridge*, was published serially in the *Berkshire Courier* (Great Barrington, Massachusetts) a year later. In 1880 came *Dr. Heidenhoff's Process* and in 1884 *Miss Ludington's Sister*. With the publication of *Looking Backward* in 1888 and his decision to enter reform politics, the scene of his activities shifted to Boston where for two years he edited *The New Nation*, the organ of the Nationalist movement, and helped organize the People's Party in Massachusetts. When first his own Nationalist organization and then Populist enthusiasm collapsed in the Panic of 1893, he returned home to finish a last book, *Equality*, before succumbing to the disease which had stalked him all his life. A hurried trip to Colorado in 1897 failed to restore his wasted lungs, and in the spring of 1898 he was brought home to Chicopee Falls to die at the age of forty-eight.

Outwardly his life was uncomplicated and uneventful. The natural man in him, he admitted more than once, was not socially inclined. For many years he lived as a bachelor in the seclusion of his father's house, and after his marriage in 1881 to a young girl whom his parents had adopted, he settled down next door. All his life he was forced to conserve his limited energies carefully. His notebooks contain a private record of his struggle against his disease; the entries are readings of a psychic barometer that registered the fluctuations of a mind "quite out of conceit" with his infirmity. "I think I have got my death," he wrote in 1870 during one of his recurring bouts of illness.

I had always supposed the hour when this conviction impressed itself on my mind would be marked by strange experiences. But I do not find it so. . . . My philosophy I find has not been wholly without fruit. It has at least bred a certain faculty which now stands me in good stead. I may recover from my present ailment but to me it somehow seems almost a foregone conclusion that I shall not. Nor should I much care but for the bitter blow my death would be to my parents. For their sake I shall obstinately fight a disease with which otherwise I should have no serious controversy. The most common tragedy is the fight of a man against disease. Herein is Laocoön daily repeated all about us.[3]

This "realizing sense" of his own precarious hold on life frequently sharpened a vague fear of Nemesis into a Calvinist conviction of imminent catastrophe reminiscent of Joseph Bellamy's world. "What an unutterably funny spectacle we mortal men present," runs another of these entries. "We stroll along side by side gaily disporting, gravely plodding in fine apparel and fine spun refinement of companionship. Yet we cannot see where we put down our feet. We know there will come a step— it may well be the very next—beyond which we shall take no other but of a sudden drop eternal fathoms deep."[4]

[3] Notebooks, Unpublished Papers.
[4] *Ibid.*

Springfield, though it meant a narrowing of intellectual horizons after New York, afforded the security seemingly necessary to Bellamy's apprehensive nature. Diffident and abstracted, he succeeded in masking with a dry humor and an almost professional courtesy a temperament badly out-of-joint with the Gilded Age and an inner life increasingly dominated by fantasy. "Might-have-been-land—" he wrote in one of his periodic attempts at self-appraisal. "Let me reach it by a stair between my real and potential self which produces a parting. Having fully calculated upon and expected a thing, I am so justly disappointed by its failure to come to pass that the balance of my nature goes over to the potential world, and I go to Might-have-been-land." [5] An editorial voice on a solidly Republican newspaper provided only a partial outlet for this sense of alienation from the thermidorean politics of the Gilded Age. Like many of the young intellectuals surveying the moral landscape of post-Civil War America— figures as different as Henry George and Henry Adams, Louis Sullivan and Lillian Wald, Jane Addams and Henry Demarest Lloyd—Bellamy discovered patches of blight in the lush foliage of economic growth, parched islands of waste where prewar values had withered under the blasts of entrepreneurial energy released by the war. The fate of his father's mild evangelicalism he read in the contrasting signs at campground revivals, the flag on the tabernacle proclaiming "The Earth is the Lord's" and the posters of real estate developers beneath announcing "Lots forty by sixty feet, for sale at $250." Self-reliance and self-culture were being buried under layers of counterfeit. Imitation was the vice of the age—the rich wore gold and the poor scrambled for a substitute. Americans built imitation houses in which they lived grandly imitative lives. The whole surface of life in the United States seemed to glitter with a cheap veneer. "How to make people hate shams of all kinds, and demand what they have shall be genuine is one of the great moral questions of the day." [6]

It was easy enough to dismiss the Great Barbecue as an orgy of humbug, but where were the principles with which to build

[5] *Ibid.*
[6] "Imitation," *Springfield Union*, December 14, 1872.

a better society? Bellamy's acute sense of impotence stemmed from his perception of the breakdown of prewar standards, moral absolutes that were no longer relevant to the forces and purposes of an industrial society. The carnage of civil war had damaged beyond repair the sanctity of the private conscience; and the man of exquisite moral sensibility, once a hero in an age of Garrisons and Sumners, now appeared in a different light. Encased in their invulnerable personalities, such sticklers for conscience seemed to have acted less as liberators of the spirit than as noble despots unwilling or unable to sacrifice private certitude for the preservation of the Union. As he watched the failures of Reconstruction, Bellamy began to re-examine the assumptions of Emerson's generation and to assess the temperament which had made them with such confidence. Both of these themes he explored in 'an early short story, "The Boy Orator," an analysis of the perfectionist mind which he never published.[7]

Joseph Claiborne, the boy orator, is an eighteen-year-old Garrisonian abolitionist canvassing western Massachusetts on the eve of Lincoln's election. The son of an antislavery pioneer and the product of a lyceum culture, he is nevertheless a naturally shy and inarticulate disciple who achieves eloquence only in a state of self-hypnosis induced by pondering accounts of the atrocities of Southern slaveowners. Before each lecture he secludes himself and meditates on horror tales of mutilation and violent death until, sympathizing abstractly with the slave victims, he is filled with a poetry of denunciation. About politics he knows and cares nothing. "I know slavery and that's all I know," he tells his host, a political abolitionist who has been questioning him closely on Lincoln's chances. His sponsor pronounces him a fool and dismisses him, but Joseph, like his perfectionist teachers, thrives on antagonism. "The surest way to demoralize him was to prophesy his success in his hearing, but a contemptuous reference to his size and powers turned his nerves to steel and insured a brilliant display. His electricity required the opposition of a negative body to discharge itself." With the self-assurance of the morally innocent he retires to his room to

[7] Unpublished Papers.

prepare his performance, unaware that he is about to make a terrifying discovery that will change his life.

Joseph's favorite atrocity tale concerns a degenerate white boy his own age who brutally whipped his slave companion, pausing now and then to force his victim to his knees to beg forgiveness for an unnamed crime. Something in the gratuitous nature of the act always gives Joseph a keener sense of the enormity of slavery than even more violent accounts. This time, however, his experience is alarmingly different: instead of identifying with the black victim he feels an almost sexual thrill of absolute power along with the white tormentor.

. . . the very intensity with which he sympathized with the slave heightened the sweet voluptuousness that thrilled through his shuddering nerves at fancying himself the master and tyrant. It was as if a devilish plant had sprung out of the very hotbed of his indignation and pity [and] by subtle chemistry had now transformed their bitter and fiery juices into sensuous intoxicating fumes. The brutal reveries held him by irresistible fascination till the new abhorrent lust had flowed through every vein.

Joseph rushes horrified to the mirror to confront the devil but sees only a pale frightened face staring back "as if he had been turned outside himself and saw demons looking out of his windows." His terror gradually subsides, and by a desperate act of will he rallies his principles which have been scattered "by this sudden appearance of a traitor in the center of the camp." That evening on the platform he surpasses all his previous performances. To his listeners, who are already converted and have come to witness a spectacle, he appears to be wrestling with an invisible demon. "His antagonist was himself, out of whom with fiery invective, argument, illustrations, appeal he was striving with frantic earnestness to cast out the lust of slavery." He finishes to tumultuous applause but aware, now that the circuit to the divine has been broken, that he is a fraud who all along has hungered for absolute power without knowing it. "Never so much as tonight had he given himself up to the pleasures of gratified vanity." He has been betrayed by the discovery of evil in himself.

At this point the narrative thread is broken, and the story resumes ten years later—five years after Appomattox—in a shabby boardinghouse in Pittsfield where Joseph, now thoroughly corrupted by self-knowledge, is preparing to leave for Brazil, the last refuge of slavery in the Western Hemisphere. He is taking with him thirty-five hundred dollars with which to indulge his perverted taste for tyranny. To his friend, an ex-Confederate who has accepted defeat and emancipation, he explains that unfortunately Southerners born into a slave system and inhibited by economic interest had never truly savored the intoxicating pleasures of absolute ownership of human beings. "No sir, a man must be born and bred in a free land, in a turbulent angular democracy like this Massachusetts of ours, to enjoy with a keen palate the rich cloying sweetness of exercising pure despotism over his fellows." His conversion to satanism, Joseph continues, is not difficult to understand. Abstract sympathy such as he felt for the slaves hides a potential tyranny. "There is only a very narrow margin between a morbid aversion for a thing and a morbid attraction to it. One is always in danger of passing from one extreme to the other. A man's feelings, you know, are subject to the law of the see-saw." The balance of his own nature has been permanently tipped towards the demonic, and he is off to Brazil to seek immolation for his former perfectionist self by buying a slave.

In this unfinished sketch Bellamy was reassessing the psychology of reform of the prewar generation, both the moment of divine revelation and the inadequate premises on which it rested. In its transcendental and evangelical version the moment of revelation provided momentary insight into the beneficent order of the universe. The isolated sensibility experienced a brief but complete union with all being and in so doing discovered new capacities for good. Through communication with the divine the irreducible self was galvanized to moral action, its regenerative powers unleashed by the mystical moment. The role of the isolated self as a mediator between God and the world of appearances was not deemed a particularly arduous one so long as it was assumed, as Emerson's generation tended to pre-

suppose, that inconsistencies and ambiguities were merely il-
lusory and could be resolved on the plane of the ideal through
intuition. An Emersonian universe was thus a simple universe
held in balance by a philosophical dualism which did not require great introspection or careful probing of the relation of the
inner self to the world outside. Bellamy rejected this specifically
transcendental dualism as incomplete. What Joseph Claiborne
sees staring back at him from the mirror is the evil side of his
own nature, a demonic presence too strong to overcome. His lust
for power is revealed to him when he suddenly realizes that
just as the white boy in the atrocity tale craved unlimited command so he seeks dominion over his audiences and revels in the
unchecked manipulation of others. His is an abstract and therefore false identification with the victims of evil. The moment of
revelation which in transcendental and evangelical Christian doctrine disclosed a benevolent universe is inverted by Bellamy in
an insight closer to the dark imaginings of Edwards and Hawthorne than to the optimism of Emerson or Parker. Joseph Claiborne is disarmed by his realization that abstract sympathy
unsupported by suffering or sacrifice ends in a perverted desire
for power. It is this truth of inner experience, Bellamy believed,
that the prewar generation much to its cost failed to comprehend.

Bellamy never finished this story, perhaps because he sensed
in his melodramatic handling of the theme of initiation into evil
a philosophical dilemma of his own making. In a world where
pure sympathy inevitably breeds pure tyranny no moral action
is possible. In the context of an egocentric universe the problem
of the truly moral act seemed insoluble. Yet if he found ambiguities in the motives of the abolitionists and prewar reformers,
Bellamy did not deplore the fact of the Civil War or minimize
its achievement in freeing the slave. For him, however, the real
meaning of the war lay in the escape it offered from the labyrinth
of the self-enclosed personality. The key to its significance was
sacrifice, not the imaginary subjection of self to other individuals
which was simply another form of slavery but the complete
surrender to an ideal that ended in true freedom. He developed
this theme of sacrifice as the lesson of the Civil War again and

again in his novels and stories, but he gave it fullest treatment in a short story entitled "An Echo of Antietam." [8]

Like all his fiction, "An Echo of Antietam" suffers from a surface sentimentality and is redeemed only in part by the argument hidden beneath the imagery. In a small town in upstate New York a young lieutenant in the Union Army is taking leave of his fiancée as his regiment prepares to march off in support of McClellan. A successful young lawyer, he has only reluctantly concluded to offer his services to the Union. His fiancée is equally reluctant to accept his decision, and after a private farewell embellished with hot tears and heart throbs, she follows him at a distance to the nearby city for one last glimpse of him as his regiment marches to the depot. The soldiers come wheeling around the corner, and she tries in vain to single out her lover.

As the blue river sweeps along, the row of polished bayonets, rising and falling with the swinging tread of the men, are like interminable foam-crested waves rolling in upon the shore. The imposing mass, with its rhythmic movement, gives the impression of a single organism. One forgets to look for the individuals in it, forgets that there are individuals. Even those who have brothers, sons, lovers there, for a moment forget them in the impression of a mighty whole. The mind is slow to realize that this great dragon, so terrible in its beauty, emitting light as it moves from a thousand burnished scales, with flaming crest proudly waving in the van, is but an aggregation of men singly so feeble.

Cluttered though it is with conflicting images, the scene presents a conception of solidarity remarkably similar to the opening description in the first version of *Looking Backward*. The merging of self with the whole, Bellamy argues in both the story and the novel, is the beginning of salvation for the individual and society alike. On the eve of the battle, standing alone above the Union and Confederate camps, the lieutenant meditates on the heroic instinct of humanity which is proof "deeper than reason, that man is greater than his seeming self." In an artistic

[8] "An Echo of Antietam" first appeared in the *Century Magazine*, July, 1889, and was subsequently reprinted in *The Blindman's World and Other Stories* (Boston, 1898).

lapse betraying his essentially moralistic nature Bellamy supplies the lesson: "What a pity it truly is that the tonic air of the battlefields—the air that Philip breathed at Antietam—cannot be gathered up and preserved as a precious elixir to reinvigorate the atmosphere in times of peace when men grow faint and cowardly and quake at the thought of death." Unlike Joseph Claiborne who was unable to renounce self, the heroine in "An Echo of Antietam" makes the sacrificial gesture which is the instrument of her salvation. Her sacrifice gives her a mystical prescience which tells her of the death of her lover before the official news reaches the town. His body is brought home, funeral services are held, and her agony ends only when she becomes fully aware of the meaning of her surrender.

. . . the piteous thing she had dreaded, the feeling now when it was forever too late, that it would have been better if she had kept her love back, found no place in her heart. There was, indeed, had she known it, no danger at all that she would be left to endure that, so long as she dreaded it, for the only prayer that never is unanswered is the prayer to be lifted above self. So to pray and so to wish is but to cease to resist the divine gravitations ever pulling at the soul. As the minister discoursed of the mystic gain of self-sacrifice, the mystery of which he spoke was fulfilled in her heart. She appeared to stand in some place overarching life and death, and there was made partaker of an exultation whereof if religion and philosophy might but catch and hold the secret their ancient quest were over.

A godlike freedom is the reward of those who through renunciation rise above self and seek incorporation in the universal.

Bellamy frequently experienced the dissociation of personality which he described in this story. In 1874 when he left his father's church there began a period of "profound anxiety and longing almost to sickness," as he described his search for a substitute for inherited Christian doctrine. He developed the habit of jotting his ideas down haphazardly in notebooks which are filled with plot outlines, sketches, and fragments of philosophizing and which, taken together, provide an index to his emerging Religion of Solidarity. The principal theme to which he kept returning was the dual nature of the self, its divisibility into what he called the "personal" and the "impersonal." In one

entry he speaks of the "comparative infinitesimality" of the individual and all purely personal conceptions. Every man consists
of two parts or sides, a transient and unimportant personality
composed of bodily appetites and selfish interests and another
side that is infinite and eternal, the only true and important self.
"The mind of man becomes conscious of this infinite side of his
being by actual experience of states of feeling in which he rises
into the realm of infinity and impersonality. . . ." The exact
nature and meaning of this mystical apprehension Bellamy found
it impossible to explain though he never stopped trying. Sometimes he changed the terminology, referring to the "self" and
the "not-self" in the hope of finding precision in greater objec-
tivity. Or he constructed dialogues with an imaginary friend
who asks: "Is then, this conscious yet impersonal being whom
you claim as the real essence of every man the one God and
Sovereign of the Universe?" And receives this answer: "I can
only guess at that. To my apprehension this, my true self, has
the aspect of infinity and seems to be all." [9] In still another mood
and style suggestive of Emerson he would urge himself to "seek
a home, a center, a more ultimate ego in the universe" and to
"cultivate a habit of regarding the experiences of the individual
from that standpoint." The world of the mind, he became convinced, awaited a Copernican revolution to free the psychic
faculties for a leap to a new level of consciousness.

Gradually these musings took shape, and in 1874 he assembled
them in an essay which he entitled "The Religion of Solidarity." [10]
Although he later criticized the crudeness and redundancy of
the essay, which was never published in his lifetime, he admitted
that it contained the germ of his new philosophy. "The Religion of
Solidarity" forms the focal point on which all of his fiction
converges and, more important, describes in detail the psychological substructure on which the utopian society in *Looking
Backward* is built.

The basic premise in Bellamy's religious philosophy is the

---

[9] Notebooks, Unpublished Papers.
[10] The most readily available version of "The Religion of Solidarity" is
in Joseph Schiffman, ed., *Edward Bellamy: Selected Writings on Religion
and Society* (New York, 1955).

human instinct for perfect communion with the infinite, a psychic drive to break through the barriers of time and circumstance which prevent the individual soul from merging with the universe. This drive, he believed, can be found at one time or another in all people. In some it takes the form of a "veritable orgasm" of impersonal desire; in others memory offers a momentary release from the self "shut up in today." Constantly agitating the individual man is a second self in search of the ultimate. Restless and discontented, this part of the psyche tries to snap the slender ties attaching it to its twin and break away into freedom. "It is homesick for a vaster mansion than the personality affords." The inference to be drawn from this observation is that people have more in common with the universal life toward which they are mysteriously directed than with their own "narrow, isolated and incommodious" personalities. At any time they may experience an ecstatic moment when they are "out of the body" only to be returned with a wrench to their separate conditions.

Such is the real double nature of man: as an individual he is dissatisfied with his limited scope and meager powers; as part of the universal he is at peace. Mistakenly people conceive of the larger life as vague and insubstantial, somehow less real than the partial self, whereas if they only stopped to consider, they would recognize in these impersonal moods the pull of a deeper reality. Because the mystical perception is broken and incomplete—"rising and falling, wavering, undulating, ever glowing and fading, ebbing and flowing"—we fail to read its meaning which is that individuality, personality, and partiality spell segregation, partition, and confinement. As yet men have been too timid to cultivate these moments of insight and have turned back shuddering from what seems to them a void. But genius, the partaking of solidarity, welcomes the appearance of a second soul, "an inner and passionless ego, which regards the experiences of the individual with a superior curiosity, as it were, a half-pity." In the past such experiences have been considered abnormal; in the future they will be regarded as natural.

How is the ephemeral impression of solidarity to be caught and held? Bellamy pointed to several "doorways" to the mystical experience: the "sexual relation" with its resolution of mutual antagonisms; a related "sex of the intellect" or confluence of souls; and the life of the family in which the rough edges of personality are worn away by time and intimacy. In all cases the impersonal mood is affected and to a certain extent determined by physical factors—states of exaltation or fatigue—and can be induced artificially by music or narcotics. Above all, Bellamy was persuaded, solidarity was a moral state to be compassed by purposeful endeavor. "Be not careful, then, of your goings and comings," he advised himself. "Be not deluded into magnifying their importance. Live with a certain calm abandon, a serene and generous recklessness. We should hold our lives loosely, and not with the convulsive grip of one who counts his personal life his all."

The life of solidarity, then, could be planned and sustained by cultural habit. "It remains for us, by culture of our spiritual cognitions, by education, drawing forth of our partially latent universal instincts, to develop into a consciousness as coherent, definite, and indefeasible as that of our individual lives, the all-identical life of the universe within us." The new life thus opened would include both action and contemplation. Neither the Indian mystic nor the American go-getter could serve as the model of behavior in the society Bellamy envisioned, but only the man who viewed life both miscroscopically and tele-scopically. Instead of Alexanders and Napoleons, Savanarolas and Saint Teresas, the world of the future would contain serene and selfless citizens moved by the instinct for cohesion which "manifested in men . . . takes the form of loyalty or patriotism, philanthropy or sympathy." The prospects for a future impersonal civilization, Bellamy believed, were particularly bright in America where democracy by completing the break-up of castes and classes fostered the growth of impersonality through the expansion of an external equality. If culture could be consciously directed toward the discovery of a new spiritual dimension to life, then for the first time utopia was distinctly possible.

In "The Religion of Solidarity" Bellamy's revolt against romantic egocentricity ends in a retreat into mysticism. He had come to suspect the romantic rebel with his tendency "to take refuge in the bundle of mental and physical experiences which he calls himself as the only thing of which he is absolutely sure." In Europe the romantic revolt had culminated in the "mad self-assertion" of a Byron or a Baudelaire; in America where its range was narrower it had produced a morality of "inexpressible loneliness." In both cases, however, the unbridled expression of self had led to wild and purposeless rebellion against "subordination or coherency in anything." The resultant moral instability of the Gilded Age Bellamy found intolerable. The romantic idealists, certain of their central position in a benevolent universe, had turned outward for an uncritical assessment of the cosmos. Such self-assurance seemed to Bellamy both unwarranted and unprofitable. The coincidence of the Civil War and the arrival of a mechanistic and morally neutral view of the universe had upset the balance which the transcendentalists had assumed permanent. The analytical mind—in this case Bellamy's own—could only turn in on itself and with a concentration which the transcendentalists could never quite muster explore its own recesses in the hope that newly discovered psychological techniques would of themselves uncover a coherent philosophy. This was to be Bellamy's method from now on: probing the depths of the inner life and trying to assemble the intuitions thus disclosed into a cohesive ethical system. There would be no place for tragedy in such a design, no room for the monomania of a Captain Ahab or the diabolism of a Chillingworth. The life of solidarity as he envisioned it ten years before *Looking Backward* was to be pastoral comedy set in utopia where universal harmony reigns and there is no guilt or sorrow, deprivation, loneliness or death. This is the "good place" which Julian West discovers in the year 2000.

II

"The Religion of Solidarity" reflected Bellamy's growing discontent with a materialist American society and at the same time a deepening uncertainty as to the advantages of piecemeal reform. Both of these doubts found expression in his editorials which from the beginning showed a genuine concern with the problems of industrialism and a sympathy for the deprived. Chief among the victims of rapid industrialization were children driven from the schoolhouse to the factory. Like Horace Mann and the earlier generation of educational reformers, Bellamy saw a system of free compulsory education as a panacea, but to their individualistic humanitarian arguments he added a new solicitude for the state. Universal education, he predicted, would expand the economy, strengthen the American community and, most important, create a new type of citizen who could be relied upon in times of national danger. He also supported labor's holding action against the forces of the new capitalism. In general he approved the aims and aspirations of the American workingman though not the theory of class war preached by Marxists nor the power lodged in the First International whose demise he noted with satisfaction. Cooperatives modelled on British experiments rather than strikes and boycotts betraying class militancy seemed to him the only sensible way to avoid industrial warfare. To close the dangerous rift between capital and labor Americans would have to acquire new values and perfect new techniques for realizing them.

An outsider's sensitivity and compassion was checked by the persistence of a tenacious Christian conservatism which was already directing Bellamy toward the idea of the managed society. If his analysis of the American political scene was correct, what the country needed was a new leadership invested with powers of control and restraint. The American jury system, for example, operated with neither efficiency nor impartiality. The mock trial of Boss Tweed in New York only confirmed the impotency of the law as administered by a corrupt people. An appointive judiciary, a greatly strengthened executive power, moral management of politics by enlightened stewards—these and other ingredients in the Mugwump prescription for a wholesome society flavored Bellamy's editorials. "Fellow citizens," ran one such admonition, "let us put on the brakes." [11] In case Americans were not so inclined he would have to find a way to translate his

[11] "Trial by Jury," December 19, 1872; unsigned editorial comment, August 17, 1872, *Springfield Union*.

Religion of Solidarity into acceptable political terms. These terms first outlined in his editorials for the Springfield *Union* spelled order, simplicity, restraint, and discipline.

The demand for order and efficiency constituted the rallying cry of a number of young intellectuals in the Gilded Age. In medicine and science, social work and reform, even within the government itself there appeared a younger generation, intellectual heirs of the Civil War, who in a more or less concerted revolt against the undirected humanitarianism of their elders were striking out in new directions in search of the rational, scientifically organized society. A few of the rebels, following the lead of Comte, conceived of a "National Intellect," the creation of which was to be the work of a scientific elite. Others like the civil service reformers looked to a revitalized patrician leadership standing above the political battle. In the case of John Wesley Powell, Clarence King, and Lester Ward, government service offered new opportunities to put their managerial talents in the service of rational social control. For men like these new techniques complemented new ideals: statistics, planning, and experimentation reinforced their interest in economy, function, and system. Determining the values of the new class of professionals was a toughness of mind and a corrective philosophy of half-a-loaf that revealed the length of their departure from the amateur idealism of the prewar generation. In their view the strenuous life was not to be sought in a retreat, however brief, to Walden Pond but at the center of American society where all victories were necessarily partial but where a group of trained professionals under fire from public and politicians alike could prove the utility of their concepts.[12]

Insofar as his contemporaries had found a voice or accepted a role Bellamy envied them, for it often seemed to him that his own emphasis on social control stemmed from inner doubts and that his concern for a public order was simply a means of resolving private confusions. He admitted to himself that most of the

[12] For an illuminating discussion of the impact of the Civil War on American intellectuals see George M. Frederickson, *The Inner Civil War: Northern Intellectuals and the Crisis of the Union* (New York, 1965).

time his interior world was filled with "a vast crowd of unsolved insoluble problems" threatening to ambush him in a "felt darkness." Every step in this interior realm—"and immobility is impossible"—had to be taken provisionally and under protest in threading his way between troops of great questions looming like monstrous shapes. "In writing," he confessed, "I am infinitely plagued by a sense of the insecurity of foundations. . . . This is the bane of my literary labors. Continued refinement of my ideas in search of the ultimate generality." [13]

Self-preoccupation led him to minimize the importance of environment in shaping personality. "Of the causes which determine the tone of a man's disposition," he noted in his journal, "his natural temperament is immensely the preponderant one. His circumstances, adverse or fortunate, are of very inferior importance." [14] Insistent on the limitations of environment, he was naturally uncertain as to the wisdom of tinkering with it. For the most part reformers appeared content to demand equal opportunity and a fair start in the race for wealth, rules which he found meaningless. Any social arrangement was intolerable that allowed one man to climb on another's back. As for an equal start—"What difference does it make to you that your oppressor is a self-made man risen from the ranks? His rod is even heavier than the born rich man's." The doctrine of self-help offered no solution to the problem of suffering.

As in most of his social attitudes, Bellamy was of two minds about personal suffering. On the one hand, he supposed it an initiatory rite of manhood, a stern testing of the masculine qualities and the necessary price of self-transcendence. This was a view particularly congenial to a people who had just witnessed the organized butchery of a four-year civil war, and in the less sensitive portions of the American public it could breed an extraordinary callousness toward the deprived and the destitute. On the other hand, Bellamy knew from experience the tragic waste of human energies caused by suffering. Part of his mind was already occupied with the invention of a society without suffering or the guilt and remorse it entailed.

[13] Notebooks, Unpublished Papers.   [14] *Ibid.*

Meanwhile the buccaneering tactics of the Goulds, Cookes, and Rockefellers threatened to overturn a social order based on *laissez-faire* and private philanthropy. Could American society halt their drive to power? As yet Bellamy was not sure. He read widely in socialist literature but was by no means convinced that socialism in any form could work. Unlimited freedom to acquire wealth seemed to him essential in providing ambition and incentive, yet the very possession of wealth bred selfishness and corruption. The desire for wealth, as he analyzed it, consisted of three distinct motives: an appetite for comforts and luxuries, a hunger for distinction, and a longing for power. The problem for society was to secure for everyone the first condition by indulging the universal appetite for material abundance while at the same time curbing the individual's drive for distinction and power. Perhaps an effective manipulation of motives could prevent recourse to socialism.

This scheme of a future so bright is not arrogant in its claims, demands no impracticable conditions, will not abrogate even the institution of property. It recognizes its utility, its necessity—the healthful development it provides to human instincts, the zest it adds to human life. The individuality it impresses upon men without which their society would be intolerable. If true reform would correct the abuses not destroying the existence of the institution, would confine its normal office of promoting individuality of a majority of human lives, not permit its baleful perversion to the most potent instrument of despotism.[15]

In constructing the society of the future the true reformer should serve as the disinterested steward of wealth sharing his riches with the less fortunate and thereby preventing an appeal to more drastic measures. A recurring theme in the notebooks and an idea that continued to fascinate him concerned the new hero with his "modern magic wand," the impersonal philanthropist who distributes his money out of sheer impulse and primarily with a view to his own amusement. "Of course he will do good rather than evil, but it is in the fun to be gotten out of the experiment with their lives rather than by the mere true busi-

[15] Notebooks, Unpublished Papers.

ness of almsgiving that he is to find satisfaction and reward." In a subsequent comment he supplied the moral: "How the romance of fairy land would return if rich men did likewise."

The modern magic wand was only one of the metaphors with which Bellamy traced his design of "a sudden transformation of an otherwise hopeless situation." Almost all of his stories and novels center on the retrieval from imminent disaster or escape from Nemesis through magic. "Abracadabra, the conquering word," he wrote in explaining his method of composition.[16] Magic in his fiction takes various forms: a fantastic science fiction machine for blotting out memory; flashes of extrasensory perception transfiguring loneliness into intimacy; a mysterious psychical alchemy turning despair into hope. The formula later used to project Julian West into the twenty-first century appears in one guise or another in all of Bellamy's work—"Let an apparently inevitable and highly tragical situation be carefully developed, to be happily solved by showing the supposed fatal fact, or element, all along supposed by the parties to be real, is imaginary." [17] The meaning for social reform as it emerges from Bellamy's early fiction is unmistakable—solidarity through thaumaturgy.

In an early short story, "The Cold Snap," magic functions as the mystical regeneration of the spirit through the ritual of family prayer.[18] The narrator and his wife have just returned to the family home in a small New England village when a "cold snap," as they first think it, sends the temperature plummeting far below zero. Dimly the narrator senses "how wholly by sufferance it is that man exists at all on earth," but his fears are forgotten in the temporary exhilaration of suspended routine. Slowly, however, as the cold deepens into catastrophe and the old farmhouse fills with a glacial silence, bravado gives way to anxiety and then to paralysis of will until the family unit has disintegrated under the stupefying effects of the cold. Communication with the outside world is cut off; the members of the family

---

[16] *Ibid.*   [17] *Ibid.*

[18] "The Cold Snap" was first published in *Scribners Monthly,* September, 1875, and is reprinted in *The Blindman's World.*

are imprisoned by nature which is inexorably undermining their wills. "Other forces of nature have in them something of the spirit a man can sympathize with, as the wind, the waves, the sun; but there is something terribly inhuman about the cold . . . a congenial principle brooding over the face of chaos in the aeons before light was." The cold, by now a terrifying hint of a cosmic heat-death, also threatens the death of the heart. There are some inflictions, the narrator muses, which strengthen the will to endure, "but to cold succumb soul and mind." With a seemingly diabolical indifference the cold detaches the family one by one from a life-sustaining communion and quietly awaits the capitulation of each individual will to live. Suddenly, in a last desperate act of defiance, the family comes together for prayer. Always before, the narrator reflects, praying had seemed merely "a fit and graceful ceremony" from which no one expected anything in particular. "But now the meaning so long latent became eloquent. . . . There was a familiar strangeness, which touched us all." It is not divine intervention that saves the family but the mystical renewal of affections and with it the will to live which ritual effects. "Owing to the sustaining power there is in habit, the participation in family devotions proved strengthening to us all. In emergencies we get back from our habits the mental and moral vigor that first went to their formation." The rediscovery of habit in the ceremonial act brings the family back from the margins of dissolution and death, and the next day the cold snap breaks.

In "The Cold Snap" magic brings the recovery of communal habit. In a story entitled "At Pinney's Ranch" magic is mixed with melodrama and mindreading to accomplish a rescue from a fate worse than death. John Lansing is one of Bellamy's heroes pursued by Nemesis, the familiar fugitive who "while absolutely guiltless" is nevertheless caught "in one of those nets of circumstance which no foresight can avoid."[19] Though innocent of a charge of murder, he runs away leaving his wife and children to believe that he has drowned in making his escape. Under a new name he works his way west to the silver mines of Colorado

[19] Notebooks, Unpublished Papers.

where he earns a fortune but finds the life of an exile not worth living. Then comes word that the real murderer has been caught but that his wife, thinking him dead, has decided "for the sake of the children" to marry a man she does not love. The Colorado ranch is a hundred miles from the nearest telegraph. What to do? Long ago, we are told, Lansing and his wife practiced mind reading with no little success. Clearly it is time to try again if he is to save her. Sitting in an empty room at Pinney's ranch, Lansing attempts the impossible.

. . . as a wrestler strains against a mighty antagonist, his will strained and tugged in supreme stress against the impalpable obstruction of space. . . . Finally . . . there came a sense of efficiency, the feeling of achieving something. . . . The outflow of energy lost the tendency to dissipation, and became steady. . . . Fainter far, as much finer as is mind than matter, yet not less mistakable, was the thrill which told the man, agonizing on that lonely mountain of Colorado, that the will which he had sent forth to touch the mind of another, a thousand miles away, had found a resting place, and the chain between them was complete. No longer projected at random into the void, but as if sent along an established medium of communication, his will now seemed to work upon hers not uncertainly and with difficulty, but as if in immediate contact. Simultaneously, also, its mood changed. No more appealing, agonizing, desperate, it became insistent, imperious, demanding.[20]

Standing at the altar, his wife gets the message in the form of an instant aversion to the unoffending bridegroom. She shrieks her refusal, the ceremony is disrupted, the marriage cancelled, and a few days later husband and wife are happily reunited.

These samples of his short stories, typical in their melodramatic handling of theme, betray Bellamy as a moralist rather than an artist. His method is seen most clearly in a reminder in the notebooks to write a book "not so much with view to being an interesting story as a digest of philosophy of life but with enough of narrative to avoid dulness." Seldom did his ideas come to him through observation. They appear first in the notebooks as ab-

[20] "At Pinney's Ranch" was first published in the *Atlantic Monthly*, December, 1887, and is reprinted in *The Blindman's World*.

stract propositions or situations requiring further elaboration or argument.

Story. Case of a rich miser caught himself in a burglar trap in his own vaults, starving to death, welcomes approach of burglar as his only chance for life.

"Scaling the Heights." Title of the subjective-objective story of the man who sought to raise himself to the divine state by attaining the combination of subjective-objective in himself.

Story of coming race. How pessimism had so theorized on the evil condition of the race that suicide was the fashion, and a school of thugs was established. The most cultured of the race also as solemn duty took life whenever they could out of sheer compassion. A convention called, which declares that the pessimists are right as the world stands, but if men were physically, morally, mentally what they ought to be, life would be more enjoyable. They also decide that none of the reforms, political or social, which have been agitated since the beginning as means of ameliorating the race, have any chance of success until men are more moral and intelligent. The experiment of stirpiculture is attempted. Hope is born again among men. They see a future for the race and devote themselves with enthusiasm to the new cult.[21]

To a mind engrossed in abstractions the romance is more congenial than the novel. With the exception of *The Duke of Stockbridge,* also labeled a "romance" but in fact a realistically rendered historical novel, Bellamy's fiction is the transmutation of moral abstractions into fable or fantasy. There is a foreground in his novels and stories—the thinly disguised village life of Chicopee Falls, simple and familiar—and in the distance clouds charged with moral mysteries hang heavy and portentous over the pastoral scene. But the middle ground of social life, the rendering of character and drama, is conspicuously lacking. Action and character function chiefly as devices for explicating ethical problems which Bellamy's village types carry about with them like so many placards. Where the gap between conception and execution is widest the result is sentimentality which pro-

---

[21] Notebooks, Unpublished Papers.

vides an escape hatch from the ambiguities and confusions of the Religion of Solidarity. His first novel, *Six to One: A Nantucket Idyll*, is a case in point. The rhapsodical language of "The Religion of Solidarity" could not entirely obscure for Bellamy the disturbing complexities of the impersonal life. Were there undiscovered perils in the mystical experience? Was the hunger for identity with the universal a life-force or a death-wish? Did the discovery of the dual nature of the self destroy or create illusion? All of these questions figure in *Six to One* which despite the inept treatment of the dramatic materials is an intriguing discussion of the meaning of the Religion of Solidarity.[22]

Six to One is more directly autobiographical than Bellamy's other fiction. The "one" is Frank Edgerton, a New York newspaperman suffering from a nervous breakdown who comes to Nantucket to recuperate. The "six" comprise a band of feminine healers of the spirit for whom the arrival of an eligible male is an occasion of merriment and matchmaking. Edgerton is restored to health by their combined ministrations which include clambakes, sailing expeditions, and hours of mawkish conversation. He falls in love with one of the girls, rescues her from drowning, and marries her with the intention of saving her from a lonely life by the sea. The tale is a simple reverie peopled with all-too-charming types dawdling toward a predictable conclusion.

From the outset, however, it is clear that Edgerton and Addie Follett, his sea-bride, are projections of the author's dual consciousness, the one an intended representative of the personal, the other of the impersonal state of mind. In this sense the story with its dialogue framed as debate and the action determined by opposing philosophical points of view is a dramatization of Bellamy's controversy with himself. Edgerton by his own definition is a "broken-down man," a victim of recurrent fits of depression. As a reporter he has been engrossed in the personal, "transmitting the sensations of a world through his nerves every day" until he realizes that its hectic pace and lack of meaning has made him a "mental invalid." He needs the restorative power

[22] *Six to One: A Nantucket Idyll* (New York, 1878).

which only the sea can provide. Addie Follett is a "nun of the sea" who has renounced the world and devoted herself to the cultivation of the impersonal. "There are personal and impersonal eyes," Edgerton reflects, "personal eyes that are full of an importunate individuality, and impersonal eyes that are serene meeting-places of souls. When you looked into this young lady's eyes you did not see her at all; she seemed to leave her self behind to come and meet you there." Unlike the other girls, Addie is content with her island existence. The sea, she tells Edgerton, confesses and shrives her. "The suggestions of boundless space, of immeasurable strength, of eternal patience, of motion that had not paused or rested since the impulse of creation, raised her thoughts to a plane whither personal preoccupations could not follow." Edgerton prefers his nature domesticated and companionable. The sea, he counters, is as incomprehensible as the modern God while rivers and lakes are like demi-gods and lesser divinities with a touch of humanity in them. "You complain," replies Addie, "that the sea doesn't care a rap whether we live or die, but that's precisely the key to the highest sort of sympathy we mortals have with it, for it is an impersonal sympathy, in which we as much forget our personalities as it ignores them."

At first the sea seems to Edgerton a source of spiritual renewal, its incomprehensible vastness soothing his shattered nerves. "His eyes felt as his muscles would, were the attraction of gravitation suddenly annulled and the body made weightless. . . . He seemed resting on the heaving bosom of infinity. . . ." The dominant impression of impersonality, however, is undercut by Bellamy's indulgence in the pathetic fallacy. Edgerton also senses in it a jealous rival dominating the girl with its capricious moods, its waves "sullenly" feeling their way through the darkness to enclose her and "moaning" and "muttering" on the beach. Then in a return to his favorite figure Bellamy attributes to the sea a martial valor and stoic selflessness from which men can learn the meaning of life.

The waves sweeping across the unbroken breadth of the Atlantic, tripped and fell thunderously at their feet. The hemispherical journey of each of them represented an achievement of Titanic power that gave a startling impression of the prodigality of force in nature. With such momentum the interminable succession of rollers came on, that the word of God seemed freshly needed to stay each one with its 'thus far and no further.' The invisible reins of Omnipotence must needs have been upon the necks of these mighty white-maned coursers to curb them at the critical moment.

The meaning of the scene is lost on neither readers nor spectators, one of whom exclaims: "The sight of these brave waves pouring so steadily on to certain destruction, one after another in endless ranks, merely to wash away a mile or two of land in a century—what an example of self-sacrifice it is. If I were a general, I'd bring my army down on the beach before leading them into battle." To which another of Edgerton's harem replies: "And they die so gayly; that's what I like. Your sour heroes I never could fancy. To my notion nothing ought to be gayer than heroism." It is left to Edgerton to summarize the lesson: "Surely death is after all the supreme function of life, its consummate act. And yet in what a shabby, broken-spirited, draggle-tail fashion most people die." When it comes his turn to die with Addie after failing to drag her out of the undertow, he decides that it would be manlier to die voluntarily rather than wait for utter exhaustion. In Bellamy's magic realm, however, the moment of submission is instantly followed by providential rescue. Just as Edgerton gives up the struggle, a boat arrives and he and his sea-bride are snatched from impersonal death.

Rescue takes still another form in *Dr. Heidenhoff's Process*, a science-fiction fable of guilt and redemption woven like *Looking Backward* around the dream.[23] In the opening scene the hero and heroine, Henry Burr and Madeline Brand, are enjoying the somnolent piety of a Sunday evening prayer meeting when the service is interrupted by the appearance of another of Bellamy's fugitives from Nemesis, the guilt-ridden sinner in search of solace who, in an anguished outburst to the congregation, states the theme of the story which the subsequent tale of fated lovers develops in detail.

[23] *Dr. Heidenhoff's Process* (New York, 1880).

Just think how blessed a thing for men it would be . . . if their memories could be cleaned and disinfected at the same time their hearts were purified. Then the most disgraced and ashamed might live good and happy lives again. Men would be redeemed from their sins in fact, and not merely in name. The figurative promises of the gospel would become literally true. But this is idle dreaming.

The proposition thus stated, Bellamy turns to the main story by way of illustration. The central section of the novel tells the tale of humble Henry's unrequited love for the proud Madeline. Outmaneuvered by the villain, Henry goes off to Boston and a new job while the unwary Madeline is disgraced by the loss of her virtue. Presently she appears in Boston, and Henry finds that his love now elevated by pity is greater than ever. But Madeline is consumed with guilt. While she languishes in the "noxious shadows" of the "poison-tree" of shame, Henry grows desperate to the point of madness at his inability to free her. Late one evening after a painful interview punctuated by a farewell kiss, he returns to his lodging, takes a large dose of sleeping-powder, and falls into a deep sleep.

The next day Henry seemingly discovers the magic formula for redemption in a newspaper advertisement announcing an "Extirpation of Thought Process" invented by one Dr. Heidenhoff. A visit to the doctor reveals that he has indeed solved the mysteries of "galvano-therapeutics" or mechanical brainwashing. Much discussion follows concerning apodes, cathodes, catelectrotonus, and anelectrotonus as the doctor explains how this electrical shock treatment obliterates the "obnoxious train of recollections" with little more damage to the patient than a "momentary slight confusion." The trifling discomfiture incident to the loss of memory is more than offset by a new freedom from shame and remorse which heretofore have "wielded their cruel scepters over human lives." Henry produces a willing Madeline for experimentation, ·the operation is performed, and while she recovers on the couch the doctor expatiates on the moral implications of his invention which is clearly Bellamy's central concern. Thought-extirpation, the doctor assures Henry, will bring a moral revolution. First to disappear will be crime and revenge, for without memory of wrongdoing neither the perpetrator nor the victim will have sufficient motive for antisocial behavior. Friendship, now constantly threatened and often damaged beyond repair, will be preserved by the removal of remembered slights and disservices. Eventually, Dr. Heidenhoff explains while Madeline stirs on the couch, his memory-extirpation process will result in a new understanding of the essentially discontinuous nature of the personality. "Can the man of to-day," he asks, "prevent or affect what he did yesterday, let me say, rather, what the man did out of whom he has grown. . . ?" On the contrary, consciousness exists only in the present moment, and it is in that moment only that the individual really exists. In an eternal present true solidarity will at last be possible. Meanwhile his invention helps those unfortunate people who cannot attain a state of social solidarity by their own efforts. I break for the weak the chains of memory which hold them to the past; but stronger souls are independent of me. They can unloose the iron links and free themselves. Would that more had the needful wisdom and strength thus serenely to put their past behind them, leaving the dead to bury their dead, and go blithely forward, taking each new day as a life by itself, and reckoning themselves daily newborn, even as they verily are!

Someday, the doctor predicts, there will come a whole society of *ubermensch* who can accept the fact of discontinuity of personality and exchange bondage to the past for the freedom of utopia.

Henry Burr and Madeline Brand, however, have not reached utopia. Her cure is the product of a morphine dream, and Henry awakes to see in the hands of his watch lying on the bedside table the "clear, hard lines of reality" emerging from the "vague contours of dream-land." A note arrives from Madeline telling him of her decision not to marry him for fear that his happiness would be contaminated by her guilt. "Is it only when death touches our bodies that we are called?" she asks. "Oh, I am called, I am called indeed!" The magical liberation disappears with the dream.

The discontinuity of personality which is one of the main psychological features of the utopian society in *Looking Backward* also serves as the exploratory theme in the last of Bellamy's early fantasies, *Miss Ludington's Sister* subtitled *A Romance of Immortality*.[24] Here situation is determined by the longing, not to forget the past but to capture and hold it. Miss Ida Ludington is a middle-aged spinster who as a beautiful young girl suffered from a disfiguring disease which left her hideously seamed and scarred. Craving some kind of external permanence to compensate for her lost beauty, she is forced to witness the destruction of her pastoral village of Hilton by the forces of industrialism. She leaves the town and with her sizable inheritance buys a large plot of land on rural Long Island where she builds a replica of the Hilton of her childhood complete to the last brick and nail. There in lonely splendor she relives her childhood, visiting the schoolhouse, sitting in the back of the church and wandering the elm-shaded green of the duplicate town. The reigning princess of her fantasy world is the young girl in the portrait hanging over the mantelpiece, the seventeen-year-old Ida Ludington who, so the aging spinster believes, governs the dispossessed spirits of her neighbors, in real life long dead.

Miss Ludington is joined in her nostalgic haven by the son of a distant relative, Paul De Riemer, whom she adopts and raises in her ghost town. The boy falls in love with the girl in the picture whose history and secret life Miss Ludington relates to him. He grows to manhood and goes off to college but returns with no serious thoughts of a vocation, seemingly content wih this passion for the "spirit Ida." To justify his devotion he invents a philosophy of immortality which he explains to Miss Ludington. People take for granted the indivisibility of the individual personality, he tells her, whereas the truth is otherwise. What we consider as simply stages of growth are really distinct personalities in themselves. Thus Miss Ludington's former self—the lovely lost Ida of her childhood—is not really lost at all but is as immortal as her present self. Belief in immortality necessarily means belief in the multiplicity of selves, each one deathless in its own right.

[24] *Miss Ludington's Sister: A Romance of Immortality* (Boston, 1884).

So obsessed is Paul with proving his theory that he gives himself completely to the worship of the "spirit-child" Ida and eagerly awaits the reunion that death will bring. Throughout the maudlin affair there are striking parallels between Bellamy's own life and the imagined life of his hero: a prolonged vocational crisis; the anguished search for emotional security; an excessive "ideality" dictating the life of a recluse; and a self-induced and self-justifying impotence. As Paul becomes increasingly dissatisfied with his emasculating love of the spirit Ida, he and Miss Ludington hear of a famous medium in New York who has had great success with "materializations." They visit her, she produces the youthful Ida briefly in spirit form, and Paul receives confirmation of the truth of his philosophy. At a subsequent materialization the medium, who conveniently suffers from a weak heart, dies in the midst of the translation, and her life passes into the spirit-form of Ida who promptly steps forth from the shades and into the life at Hilton.

The rest of this sentimental mishmash involves Paul's painful extrication of himself from the trammels of adoration. He succumbs to a desire for the flesh-and-blood Ida but is properly confused as to the correct mode of approach. Finally he declares himself whereupon the all-too-full-bodied young lady runs away leaving a letter in which she confesses the hoax. Alas, she is not what he had supposed her—the whole affair has been a monstrous trick perpetrated on the credulous pair. Undaunted by this exposure of fraud, Paul rushes after her, wins her, and after the timely death of Miss Ludington, marries her. In a last speech Miss Ludington tells Ida: "I like to fancy, and I know it is Paul's belief, that the spirit of my Ida influenced you to come to us just as you came, that under her form Paul might fall in love with you." Readers along with the characters have had the best of both possible worlds.

Bellamy's approach to fiction, as these unsuccessful forays in the field of romance indicate, was narrowly constrained by his belief that it should be the vehicle for the moral sensibility in search of norms. At the center of all these romances lies a cluster of propositions derived from the Religion of Solidarity which

Bellamy later reassembled in *Looking Backward.* The flight from the past into an eternal present, the multiplicity of selves finally reunited in absolute harmony, deeper levels of perception and extra-sensory communication—all of these themes figure prominently in utopia of the twenty-first century. But how could a dream world made with magic be related to the materialistic selfish world of the Gilded Age, the world he worked in and criticized in his editorials? Given the social myopia of most Americans and their contaminated political system, how was the transition to a more rational and humane social order to be effected? In short, assuming the potential reality of the utopia prefigured in these early romances, how did one get there?

III

By 1880 Bellamy's editorial inspection of the American industrial record had led him to agree with Henry George and Henry Demarest Lloyd that the problem of the age was social rather than political and that its chief component was a rapidly growing inequality. The symptoms which George defined as parallel tendencies toward progress and poverty, and Lloyd as the conflicting interests of wealth and commonwealth, Bellamy identified as the contradictory principles of oligarchy and democracy. All three concurred in their diagnosis of what Bellamy called "a deep disease in our civilization."

In a general way their analysis appeared to underscore the "scientific" conclusions of the Marxists. The industrial revolution had initiated a seemingly irreversible trend toward the concentration of wealth. Ever greater amounts of economic power rested in fewer and fewer hands. Economic power in turn furnished political control to the capitalists who hired the state as their policeman. The tremendous resources, both economic and political, enjoyed by the wealthy classes enabled them to exploit the workers and farmers in a more efficient and ruthless way than ever before in history. "The very rich," Bellamy observed in one of his editorials, "can make their own terms with the agents of their work, and they do it, as a rule, so as to realize excessive profits." When workers tried to organize or retaliate with strikes and boycotts, the capitalist owners of America simply tightened their grip on the weapons of government and turned them against the people. Should they ever succeed in gaining complete control—a not unlikely prospect—then American democracy would become just another of the discards of history.[25]

Bellamy and his fellow social analysts departed from the Marxist model, however, in rejecting the premise of inevitability derived from economic determinism. The ethical factors which the Marxists relegated to the scrap-heap of bourgeois illusions figured as independent determinants for Bellamy, Lloyd, and George, and it was just their preoccupation with the ethical dimension of capitalism that gave a catastrophic cast to their thought and a moral stridency to their tone. All three were intrigued with the theme of moral degeneration prefiguring a fatal lapse into barbarism and kept returning for illustrations to the example of the republics of the ancient world. There was little likelihood, Bellamy admitted, that the United States would ever relinquish the name of a republic, but the substance had already dwindled alarmingly. If Americans wanted to learn how republics perished, they had only to shut up their history books and look about them.

Never had prospects for social reform seemed bleaker than in the wake of the Panic of 1873. As the industrial crisis deepened Bellamy grew less and less confident in the ability of radical reformers and purveyors of native-brand communitarian schemes to halt the regression into oligarchy. Incredible as it seemed, a time of unprecedented suffering and deprivation was also the heyday of the cranks and one-idea men preaching delusion. Reform itself had become a business and idealism a commodity. Socialists, communists, and the other radical re-

[25] For Bellamy's editorial criticism of capitalism in the *Springfield Union* see "Over-Production and Over-Trading," July 20, 1875; "A Reform Worth Having," July 13, 1876; "Overworked Children in Our Mills," June 5, 1873; "Riches and Rottenness," November 14, 1877; "Wastes and Burdens of Society," November 15, 1877; "The Condition of Business Prosperity," August 16, 1876.

formers, he was convinced, made three cardinal mistakes common to all radicals: the mistake of abusing the rich as individuals; the mistake of threatening to overturn society; and the mistake of confusing true social reform with the gains of the labor movement. Collectivist plans for government ownership he dismissed as no more realistic than the panaceas of the Greenbackers or the Single-Taxers. Less than ten years before the publication of *Looking Backward* he wrote an editorial entitled "Communism Boiled Down" in which he raised the same objections to collectivism that would later be made against his own plan for an industrial army.

The cure-all for our labor and capital frictions and smash-ups seems, then, to be this, to put into the hands of the government all the carrying, transfer, exchange, productive industry of the country, its manufactures, agriculture, trade, and its entire use of capital; permitting no private employment of this for personal profits. . . . Now go to, ye dreamers, and find the material for a government equal to such an administration of this or any other country, in intelligence and honesty. Here we should have a civil service to stagger the immortals! No such material exists on the face of the globe. And if it did, how are we going to get this machine on the track and set it running? Well may the answer come back—'we don't know!' You might as well fly from the haystack to the moon. For a man to neglect his business and his family to study up such a scheme as this, is lunacy or worse.[26]

The more closely he examined industrial conditions, the more convinced Bellamy became that genuine reform would have to be the work of a class of disinterested and high-minded citizens resolved on a counterrevolution to check the anarchical tendencies of finance capitalism. Such dispossessed patriots—middling ranks of decent men—were the carriers of Montesquieu's "virtue" without which no republic could long survive. Hemmed in by the selfish ambitions of the wealthy classes on the one side and the unreasoning envy of the poor on the other, they still might conceivably hold the balance of power which they could throw into the scale against the revolutionary might of the new rich.

[26] *Springfield Union,* August 3, 1877.

They alone possessed the impartiality and freedom from self-interest needed to save the country: they were at once centurions at the gate of an older ideal republic and acolytes at the altar of the Religion of Solidarity. Once before they had fought to save the Union. Were they to sit by now or could they organize effectively? In 1877, the year of the strikes, the discontent of American workingmen, smoldering since the Panic four years earlier, suddenly erupted in a series of explosions that sounded to Bellamy like the first shots in a class war. The following year during his voyage to Hawaii he sketched out an idea for a story which shows how deeply impressed he had been by the violence of the previous year yet how reluctant he remained to throw in his lot with the reformers. "Story illustrating ideas of liberty, equality, fraternity and rights of labor," he wrote. "Scene taken from the late riots. Plenty of incident. One of the characters man who is finishing great book and has fear of death before it is finished which makes him a coward though naturally brave." [27] *The Duke of Stockbridge* was not the great book he intended to write some day, nor did it deal directly with the "late riots" but with the incidents of Shays' Rebellion nearly a century before. The work was nevertheless conceived as a commentary on the contemporary social scene and its hero as the prototype of the modern patriot with whom Bellamy's hopes for the future lay. In the novel Bellamy was really canvassing at an historical distance the possibilities for effective action in his own day. His conclusions were not encouraging. On the surface the novel is the story of a revolution that failed, but in a deeper sense it is the story of the failure of politics.[28]

The Duke of Stockbridge recounts the revolutionary misadventures of the Shaysites in western Massachusetts in 1786. Subtitled "A Romance of Shays' Rebellion," it nevertheless marks a departure from Bellamy's earlier work in that genre, because of its vernacular rendering of character and situation in a realistic historical setting. There are three classes in Bellamy's

[27] Hawaiian Notebook, Unpublished Papers.
[28] *The Duke of Stockbridge: A Romance of Shays' Rebellion* [1900], ed. Joseph Schiffman (Cambridge, 1962).

Stockbridge: the gentry or court party, the yeomanry made up of small farmers and artisans of the town, and a nascent proletariat consisting of foundry workers and landless war veterans. The gentry rules the town through an alliance of leading families cemented by marriage. Like their counterparts a century later, they are *nouveaux riches* with all the social myopia of their class. Squire Woodbridge summarizes their ambitions in a simile which Bellamy was to use again even more effectively in *Looking Backward*. The Squire thinks of the common people as a team of horses he has been driving. "There had been a little runaway, and he had been pitched out on his head. Let him once get his grip on the lines again, and the whip in his hand, and there should be some fine dancing among the leaders, or his name was not Jahleel Woodbridge, Esquire, and the whipping post on the green was nothing but a rosebush." Power has hardened the gentry into self-centered oligarchs who flaunt their unearned superiority and manage the affairs of the town with a contemptuous disregard of the common good. Like the Robber Barons of a later age, they are disposed to exploit the habit of deference but are unable to fulfill their roles as natural rulers.

Arrayed against the gentry in Stockbridge are the unhappy yeoman farmers and artisans who have watched the golden days of war prosperity darken into hard times. Only a generation or two removed from the English peasant, they still cling to "the inherited instincts of servility." Uneducated, politically inarticulate, without leaders and lacking social vision, they seem at first poor revolutionary material. "They had thought little and vaguely, but had felt much and keenly, and it was evident the man who could voice their feelings, however partially, however perversely, and for his own ends, would be master of their actions." The yeomanry too is blinded by self-interest. Nostalgically the farmers recall the edenic war years when, as one of them explains, "rich folks and poor folks lived together kinder neighborly . . . an' 'cordin tew scripter," but they have neither the wit nor inclination to discover the cause of their present plight. Patient, docile, long-suffering, they are also potentially surly, mean-spirited, and dangerous if driven too far into personal hardship. Honesty in the governed, Bellamy makes clear, is no substitute for honor among the governors.

Stockbridge also contains an embryonic proletariat in the iron foundry workers and unemployed veterans whose army service has served to "exasperate them against the pretentions of the superior class, without availing to eradicate their inbred instincts of servility in the presence of the very men they hated." Their leader is a demagogue named Hubbard, clearly intended as the forerunner of the modern labor agitator, who can teach them to destroy but not to create. Hubbard's philosophy is a primitive Machiavellianism. "It's all in a nutshell," he tells them. "If we don't give them the devil, they'll give us the devil. Take your choice." No true community will be forthcoming from Hubbard and his myrmidons for all his efforts to mould them into "good insurrectionary material."

Into a post-Revolutionary society riddled with class conflict comes Bellamy's hero, Perez Hamlin, the patriot who has fought the war, not in local skirmishes with the militia, but in the great battles with Washington's army where he has learned the lessons of patriotism. As he rides into Stockbridge after an absence of ten years, his buff uniform faded and threadbare but with the habit of authority written on his face, it is evident that here is a man apart. Army service, that "school of democratic ideas," has transformed the son of a poor farmer into a leader of men.

It was not . . . alone any details of dress, but a certain distinction in air and bearing about Perez, which had struck them. The discipline of military responsibility, and the officer's constant necessity of maintaining an aspect of authority and dignity, before his men, had left refining marks upon his face, which distinguished it as a different sort from the countenances about him with their expressions of pathetic stolidity, or boorish shrewdness.

Perez Hamlin is at once recognizable as the archetype of the Mugwump hero, a figure particularly congenial to a displaced New England intellectual elite after the Civil War. He appears in various attitudes in the fictional portraits of Bellamy's contemporaries. In the novels of John Hay, Edward Everett Hale,

Thomas Higginson, and Thomas Bailey Aldrich, samples of wish fulfillment, he is given the role of victor over the forces of political corruption, a moral champion who triumphs through example. As Carrington in Henry Adams' *Democracy* and as Basil Ransome in Henry James's *The Bostonians* his range is circumscribed and his principles neutralized by political impotence. Whatever the scope assigned him, the Mugwump hero is an embodiment of a patrician ideal of the natural aristocrat whose virtue and personal magnetism lift him above the reach of petty politicians. He is the leader who while wielding power remains uncontaminated by it and who stoops to play politics only to make politics in the last analysis superfluous. Bellamy's version of the Mugwump hero is colored by a pessimistic appraisal of democratics politics similar to that of Adams and James. As a leader without a following Perez Hamlin is doomed to failure.

The course of the revolution traced by Bellamy follows an all but predetermined sequence from the collapse of the old regime though a rule of the moderates to a reign of terror, thermidorean reaction, and, finally, restoration. The reduced scope imposed by provincial rebellion does not significantly alter the pattern first discerned by the Romantic historians of the French Revolution: Berkshire County is peopled with Irreconcilables, native Girondins and *Enragés*, and even the inevitable Man on Horseback. The action rises from the first hesitant steps of the rebels, gains momentum with their early successes, falters as the revolutionary party splits, resumes with the appearance of the plebiscitary leader, and is dramatically reversed with the success of the counterrevolution and the return to power of a repressive legitimacy. The scale of *The Duke of Stockbridge* is miniature backcountry rebellion, the narrative compass accommodated to a rustic Puritanism, but the informing design and dramatic point are those of Carlyle. Bellamy's diagnosis is likewise a moral one. There is little doubt that if the people are to be delivered from themselves, Perez Hamlin will be their savior.

After the premature attempt at counterrevolution collapses

the nerve of the court party fails and Perez rules by force. Nominally a member of a triumvirate Committee of Correspondence, he is in fact the single figure of authority in the town, incorporating in himself executive, judicial, administrative, and police functions. Government is reduced to its simplest terms, and Perez, like the administrators of the utopian state in *Looking Backward*, works with directness, efficiency, and a roughhewn justice. For the moment complex forms of law are unnecessary because the spirit of equity is embodied in him. Soon, however, it becomes apparent that the Duke lacks a permanent power base. With the gentry temporarily subdued, the rebels split into two factions, a smaller party of rural Girondins who are convinced that matters have gone far enough, and a larger group of Jacobins "without a stake in the community" who lack the initiative or incentive to get out of debt. "As a fever awakes to virulent activity the germs of disease in the body, so revolution in the political system develops the latent elements of anarchy." The discontented element forms a band of "regulators" who threaten to reorganize property interests but spend most of their time lounging on the village green and consuming Squire Edwards' supply of rum. The Duke is trapped between the rabble and a resurgent gentry impatiently awaiting the arrival of Governor Bowdoin's troops and the opportunity of stringing him up. When the government in Boston offers conciliatory terms and dispatches troops to secure their enforcement, the revolution stalls. The Duke is faced with dethronement, if not at the hands of the gentry, then by the more dangerous forces of irresponsible radicalism.

The blame for Shays' Rebellion, Bellamy suggests with the industrial upheavals of the Seventies clearly in mind, lay with an atomistic society which by fostering greed in the ruling class inexorably drove the masses to revolt. In his resolve to fix final responsibility, however, Bellamy overlooked the ambiguity in his depiction of the military life. If Perez Hamlin's training as a soldier is the obvious source of his patriotism and selfless devotion to justice, it is just as surely the cause in the many more veterans of a fatal disinclination to accept the demands and responsibilities of peacetime. Bellamy's failure to acknowledge this double side of military life would lead him, first to overvalue the concept of the industrial army in *Looking Backward* and then, when he had considered its implications for democracy more carefully, to discard it as perilous.

For the Shaysites as for all revolutionaries ultimate defeat is inescapable. The court party organizes an expeditionary force of local *jeunesse dorée*, drives the Duke into exile, and kills him. His death signals the beginning of the restoration. The tax collector makes his rounds as before, the red flag flies from the ridgepoles of farmhouses condemned for taxes, and the sound of the sheriff's whip is heard on the village green. The revolution is over.

The Duke of Stockbridge is Bellamy's statement on the impossibility of revolution: the failure of the Shaysites is plainly intended as a lesson for a post-Civil War generation. Bellamy's fictional anatomy of revolution discloses the futility of class politics and force employed on a class basis. When the natural leaders of society become so hardened by wealth and power that they ignore the sufferings of the people and turn to repressive measures, a revolution is virtually inevitable. Yet mass opposition cannot be successfully focussed without leadership which is not to be found in the popular ranks. The only hope for revolution rests on the command of an outsider—the independent classless man of virtue and impersonal justice. Such a leader is able to secure the temporary allegiance of the revolutionaries through superior personal force, but unless he can succeed in converting them to his own lofty standards of impersonality, he cannot hold their loyalty. The Perez Hamlins cannot finally win, Bellamy insists, because the people, like their rulers, act from motives of malice and class prejudice. Once the destructive phase of revolution is over, they have no moral foundation on which to build a better society, no impersonal devotion to the common good on which to unite. They too become corrupted, betray the revolution, and destroy their leader. Though not always fully aware of his redemptive role, the leader wants to save the people by the power of his example and train them to help build the just society. He tries to raise them above class interest and political chicanery, but they fail to understand him. In the end the revolutionary leader is abandoned to his heroic but suicidal gesture. Revolutions cannot succeed.

Utopia as a model in the mind rather than a program for revolution offered Bellamy the alternative to politics which he sought. The late nineteenth century inherited two related but distinguishable utopian traditions.[29] There was first of all the classical concept of utopia, most fully developed by Sir Thomas More, as the "good place" which is also "no place," that is, a nonhistorical or transhistorical fiction to be contemplated but never realized. The classical concept furnished neither directives nor blueprints but offered instead a Platonic ideal in the form of a myth by which to measure the achievements and short-comings of real societies. It is just this sharp contrast between the imagined ideal and an imperfect reality that gives the classical utopian exercise its aura of melancholy oppressing the reader with the conviction that the not-impossible is yet highly improbable. A second distinguishing feature of classical utopia is the fact of its discovery rather than creation. The classical convention provided an actual *locus,* an undiscovered country or uncharted isle upon which the traveller stumbles and from which he returns with wondrous tales of social harmony. Insofar as utopia is understood to have been built it is usually described as the handiwork of a mythical King Utopus in the dim recesses of prehistory. The traveller who uncovers the lost civilization is an observer rather than an actor: he records the habits and customs of the utopian inhabitants and studies their laws and technology, but on his return to the known world is unable to apply the lessons he has learned. In similar fashion the reader returns from his imaginary voyage with the disturbing sense of the disjunction of the real and the ideal.

The Enlightenment and the democratic revolutions of the

[29] For excellent brief discussions of the changes in utopian thinking since the sixteenth century, from which this account is taken, see Frank E. Manuel, "Toward a Psychological History of Utopias"; Judith Shklar, "The Political Theory of Utopia: From Melancholy to Nostalgia"; Northrop Frye, "Varieties of Literary Utopias" in *Daedalus,* Spring, 1965.

eighteenth century made deep inroads into the territory of classical utopia and left the landscape dotted with signposts. Democratic ideology culminating in the French Revolution seemingly closed the breach between the desirable and the attainable, and utopia suddenly appeared as a distinct possibility. As the great discoveries depleted the stock of usable geographical conventions and science introduced new concepts of time which issued in new theories of history and progress, *utopia,* the "good place," came to be thought of as *euchronia,* the "good time coming." With the discovery of the temporal dimension of civilization came the philosopher of history—Vico, Condorcet, Fourier, Marx, and Comte—who transplanted the model of utopia into a predictable future. In the post-Enlightenment utopia contemplation gives way to action, the descriptive becomes the prescriptive, and the classical observer turns actor. Throughout the nineteenth century the older convention continued to provide materials for hundreds of Icarian voyages and fictional discoveries, but the vital interest in utopia shifted to a concern with the prediction, the blueprint, and the model. Whether the utopian vehicle was Marx's proletarian revolution or the contagious experimentalism of the communitarians, the democratic objectives of the romantic utopians nurtured a millenarian expectation of an end to prehistory and the imminent arrival of a final state of social harmony. Replacing the classical utopian state apparatus in the minds of nineteenth-century utopian theorists was the concept of the self-regulating community in which organized political force is no longer needed. Both in the Marxist dream of the classless society and in the less coherent prophecies of the communitarians the state evaporates leaving a residue of social habit as the sole cohesive substance in a new order of freedom and individual self-fulfillment. Mankind transcends politics and power and miraculously enters the threshold of utopia.

In the United States before the Civil War this second strand of romantic utopianism unravelled in hundreds of experimental communities which left a legacy, however diminished by the war itself, for Bellamy and the social reformers of the late nineteenth century. The communitarians traded vigorously in blueprints and models and were concerned above all with the precise means of building utopia. As perfectionists they believed devoutly in the educative example and invested heavily in a variety of model communities. All of their experiments were enveloped in an atmosphere of social urgency rising from their conviction that America could be made over by the multiplication of the right social model. However varied in detail and accomplishment, the utopian communities rested on the related assumptions that self-culture could be expanded and applied to groups and that private concerns could be made to equal a greater public good if only the correct formula were found. The Civil War dispelled the optimum mood of the communitarians just as the accompanying industrial revolution appeared to discredit their methods, and Bellamy though he studied the history of the prewar communities carefully found it difficult to believe that such isolated and ill-organized experiments competing for acceptance in the open market of a *laissez-faire* economy could ever change American society by the power of example. Of the two available traditions he preferred, at least in the beginning, the classical literary tradition of utopia as an aid to reflection.

Nineteenth-century American writers had not mined the literary utopian vein with conspicuous success. Even James Fenimore Cooper, a critic sufficiently alienated from Jacksonian Democracy to work the utopian lode with the tools of the classical convention, found the yield meager. Cooper's *The Crater* (1847) is an imaginary record of the displacement of a patrician class and the subsequent despoiling of a pastoral island colony by demagogues. Despite its exotic South Sea setting complete with guano and seaweed the novel remains too close to the world of Dodge and Bragg to make a significant contribution to the literature of utopia. Sylvester Judd's *Margaret* (1845) and Edward Everett Hale's *Sybaris* (1869), both products of limited Unitarian imaginations, recreate Christian utopias reminiscent of New England village life at the turn of the nineteenth century. Judd's Mons Christi is erected by a ministerial husband-and-wife team with charity and the gospel of self-help. Hale's Sybaris, as rediscovered by a son of the Granite State in the service of

Garibaldi, is not the antique haven of voluptuaries known to history but an idealized New England planted in the Mediterranean and filled with patriotic citizens who practice conservation and economy under the aegis of freely chosen but perpetually ruling patricians. Like the Crater, Sybaris seems more a retreat for the politically dispossessed than an outpost on the frontiers of technological utopia.

Technology as the creature of industrialism figures prominently in the novels of two other precursors of Bellamy, *The Crystal Button* (1890) by Chauncey Thomas and *The Diothas* (1883) by John Macnie. Thomas was a carriagemaker from Howland, Maine, who set up shop in Boston and used his earnings to finance his utopian novel. He finished *The Crystal Button* some time between 1872 and 1878 but did not publish it until the sales of *Looking Backward* convinced him that there was a profitable market for literary utopias. Macnie was an acerbic Scotch mathematician who came to this country after the Civil War and spent twenty years teaching in boys' schools in the East before moving on to the newly established University of North Dakota where he taught mathematics, physics, ancient and modern languages, and literature. In addition to writing two widely used treatises on algebra and geometry and acquiring a considerable reputation as a classical scholar, Macnie, who seems to have been an intellectual jack-of-all-trades, took time out in 1883 to write *The Diothas* under the pseudonym of Ismar Thiusen. Seven years later, also on the strength of the sales of *Looking Backward,* he reissued the novel under the title *A Far Look Ahead.*

The world of the future described by Thomas is a technocrat's paradise. His city of Tone—Boston in the year 4872—is a metropolis of pyramidal apartment houses with huge glass facings, subways operated by compressed air, traffic tunnels for trains traveling at two hundred miles an hour, and a huge harbor filled with aluminum ships driven by electricity. Power is supplied by gigantic wind generators, industry and agriculture have been completely automated, and consumer goods are distributed, as in Bellamy's Boston of the future, through pneumatic tubes.

The alphabet has been abolished and replaced with a universal language of symbols. Macnie's world of the ninety-seventh century suffers even more acutely from technological malnutrition. Here too we find dirigibles, telephones, radios, syntopticons, and a new mathematics with a base twelve, but the city of Nuiroc in A.D. 9600 is the already familiar warehouse abandoned by prosperous citizens for outlying garden cities. As prophets of a new technology both Macnie and Thomas are afflicted with an imaginative astigmatism, one of the hazards of writing utopian fiction. Most of their predictions fall far short of levels of technological achievement attained scarcely half a century later, and many of their seemingly extravagant conjectures are already relics of an early stage of industrial automation. The technological poverty of their societies suggests that the real center of interest in utopia lies beneath its science-fiction surface in the sociological and psychological substructure.

At the structural level these two forerunners of *Looking Backward* differ markedly. The social happiness enjoyed by the inhabitants of Tone in the forty-ninth century was won for them early in the twentieth by the evangelical cult of the Crystal Button whose members swore "to be true and honest" and with their oath gradually and painlessly transformed the earth. They were first the prophets and then the engineers of utopia, patiently building the gospel of brotherhood into the social framework until the whole world came under a self-perpetuating Government of Settled Forms based on a Code of Common Sense and disencumbered of laws, legislatures, politics, and parties. Macnie's society, on the other hand, is the work of "a great military genius" who seizes power only after long centuries of devastating wars between Absolutists and ineffectual Liberals. Before he abdicates, the military dictator teaches the people of the world the two maxims with which to manage their utopia: "Resist the beginnings of evil," and "Mercy to the bad is cruelty to the good." In place of Thomas' society run by ritualized habit Macnie envisions a spartan state resting on plebescitary dictatorship, a rigorously enforced censorship, and programs of sterilization, prohibition, and repression.

The striking differences between Thomas' utopia, which in certain respects closely resembles Bellamy's, and the compulsive order of Macnie's dystopia are of more than passing interest because Bellamy was accused of plagiarizing from *The Diothas.* There is no direct evidence that Bellamy knew Macnie, although surface similarities suggest that he may have read Macnie's book. In both novels hypnotism provides the vehicle for entering utopia. In both the heroes undergo the same disconcerting experience of cherishing young ladies to whom they are at once lover and ancestor. There is also a general similarity of technological detail. Beyond this rather unimpressive internal evidence there is only a brief biographical portrait of "E——" in the preface of the first edition of *The Diothas,* too indistinct for a positive identification of Bellamy. These fragments were enough for a handful of Bellamy's critics to recall rumors from the North Dakota campus of Macnie's supposed displeasure at reading *Looking Backward* and finding in it some of his own ideas. The charge of plagiarism, however, is difficult to sustain. Hypnotism and states of suspended animation were common devices for solving the problem of utopian entry and re-entry. Moreover, scientific and popular predictions of radio, television, airships, and other technological paraphernalia of the twentieth century were equally commonplace in the 1880's. Then there is the fact that Macnie's hero returns to the nineteenth century via a waterfall while Julian West settles permanently in his utopia. Most crucial, however, is the disagreement between Bellamy and Macnie over the evolution and operation of utopia. Macnie locates his transformation seventy-five-hundred years in the future; Bellamy sets his evolutionary process at work soon after the turn of the twentieth century. Macnie's society is administered by law which is rigorously enforced by an elite; Bellamy's is run chiefly by ritualized habit which supposedly minimizes the need for sanctions. In its idealized setting for the Religion of Solidarity and its blending of themes long contemplated, *Looking Backward* is the product of a dream which Bellamy owed to no one.

Such ideas for his new book as Bellamy shared with anyone

he discussed with his younger brother Charles, his partner on the *Penny News*. While he examined the industrial crisis from the vantage point of Shays' Rebellion, Charles was reaching similar pessimistic conclusions in a novel of his own. *The Breton Mills*, published the same year as *The Duke of Stockbridge*, records the failure of paternalism and good intentions. A young millowner, sensitive to the callous treatment accorded the employees by his father, attempts to introduce company stores and profit sharing only to be thwarted by the opposition of the owners and the ingratitude of the workers. Although the social import of the novel is obscured by a romantic subplot offering the triumph of true love as dubious compensation for the defeat of reform, Charles Bellamy's analysis confirms his brother's gloomy predictions. In 1884, two years after their partnership ended, Charles published a second book, *The Way Out*, in which he made moderate proposals for social insurance, antimonopoly legislation, an eight-hour law, and the nationalizing of land.

Bellamy was less interested in his brother's partial reforms than with the outline of the utopian society that was assuming definite form in his mind. In a note in the journals at this time he sketched the political arrangements for a mythical state of Antononna where competition for power was unknown. "The men most eminent in their several professions of medicine, great inventors, and men who in any way had worthily served the State constituted a class of eligibles, from whom the governors were chosen by lot in order to avoid all possibility of emulation and self-seeking. . . ." [30] The journals also contain references to eugenics and "stirpiculture"—"an enlightened sort of stock raising"—with which a future society might breed a superior race. Another comment concerns a society where "thought-reading" is the only means of communication, an idea he was later to develop into a short story.[31] Always more urgent to him than

[30] Notebooks, Unpublished Papers.

[31] "To Whom This May Come," which was published in *Harpers Monthly*, February, 1889, and reprinted in *The Blindman's World*, concerns a lost race of mind readers and their "power of direct mind-to-mind vision, whereby pictures of the total mental state were communicated, instead of the imperfect descriptions of single thoughts. . . ." The utopian possibilities of

political matters of administration and allocation of power were tentative solutions to the problem of personal demands and social claims that so disrupted his own life. He was sure, for example, that in the society of the future love would lose its tragic undertones and that family life would grow marvelously depersonalized.

. . . not only will the family relations involve vastly less in important respects, no dependence of one upon another, and of forced constant association, but from having less friends. . . .

Men and women will be broader and less intense correspondingly in their relations to one another, while a thousandfold more than now occupied with nature and the next steps of the race, i.e., that which is at present called super-human.

The heart of man will (as is obviously rational and philosophical) be set less and less on the transitory and the perishable and more and more on the spiritual and the infinite toward which man now tends.

So shall passions, the strongest in man's nature, which have hitherto been chiefly directed to his preservation by their divisions into sexuality and the family relations . . . be directed to the general advancement and elevation of the human type.[32]

Interspersed with these speculative passages are thematic keys and ideas for plots.

---

mind reading as a product of the Religion of Solidarity, only suggested in *Looking Backward,* are fully developed here. "But think what health and soundness there must be for souls among a people who see in every face a conscience which, unlike their own, they cannot sophisticate, who confess one another with a glance and shrive with a smile! Ah friends, let me now predict, though ages may elapse before the slow event shall justify me, that in no way will the mutual vision of minds, when at last it shall be perfected, so enhance the blessedness of mankind as by rending the veil of self, and leaving no spot of darkness in the mind for lies to hide in. Then shall the soul no longer be a coal smoking among ashes, but a star set in a crystal sphere." The title story in *The Blindman's World* develops the related theme of the power of "foresight" given to a race of Martians. "They for whom the future has no mystery can, of course, know neither hope nor fear. Moreover, every one being assured what he shall attain to and what not, there can be no such thing as rivalship, or emulation, or any sort of competition in any respect; and therefore all the brood of heart-burnings and hatreds, engendered on Earth by the strife of man with man, is unknown. . . ."

[32] Notebooks, Unpublished Papers.

How with a clever physician for accomplice a man or woman might escape complicated situation by simulating death and being buried and resurrected. . . .

Case of a man who was supposed to have died, and after being mourned by a whole community for several days came to life and returned, How unwelcome he was!

To describe the mood . . . as escaping from a narrow place into a large one that the close impression of story shall not be pacific but exhilarating.[33]

Gradually and as yet with no clear sense of purpose Bellamy was beginning to combine the dramatic and the speculative ingredients of *Looking Backward.*

For years now he had been working on sections of what was to be an autobiographical novel. The events and crises in his own life appear heightened but essentially unchanged in the different versions of the story of Eliot Carson, the recluse-turned-reformer. Bellamy invented a variety of professional roles for his hero in the several versions of the narrative, but in each of them Carson makes the same decision to turn his back on a false world and become a hermit spending his life fishing and philosophizing. Eliot Carson is a prophet without disciples until he meets a beautiful girl, marries her, and has children. Bellamy's brief notes for a concluding section of the novel which he never finished have the force of a confessional. "Then his child came, not anticipated with much pleasure. Submitted to. With it comes a revelation of his oneness with mankind. He cannot thenceforward bear the thought of leaving his children, any man's, anybody's children to struggle in such a horrid world as this. Cured once for all of Hermitism and self-absorption, he plunges with enthusiasm, with tremendous earnestness into the study of social conditions and develops nationalism."

Bellamy married in 1882; two years later his son was born and in 1886 a daughter, "evangels who have taught me more . . . than I ever learned before of what is truly important." He began drafting the story of *Looking Backward* in the winter of

[33] *Ibid.*

1886 while he was still unsure of his reform bearings. "I had never, previous to the publication of the work, any affiliations with any class or sect of industrial or social reformers," he later explained, "nor, to make my confession complete, any particular sympathy with undertakings of the sort." In the beginning his only problem was to make his perfect society of the thirtieth century internally consistent. Then he re-examined the idea of the industrial army, and the analogy which "had been floating in my mind, for a year or two" underwent a transformation.

The form of a romance was retained, although with some impatience, in the hope of inducing the more to give it a reading. Barely enough story was left to decently drape the skeleton of the argument and not enough, I fear, in spots for even that purpose. A great deal of merely fanciful matter concerning the manners, customs, social and political institutions, mechanical contrivances, and so forth of the people of the thirtieth century, which had been intended for the book, was cut out for fear of diverting the attention of readers from the main theme. Instead of the year A.D. 3000, that of A.D. 2000 was fixed upon as the date of the story. Ten centuries had at first seemed to me none too much to allow for the evolution of anything like an ideal society, but with my new belief as to the part which the national organization of industry is to play in bringing the good time coming, it appeared to me reasonable to suppose that by the year 2000 the order of things which we look forward to will already have become an exceedingly old story.[34]

By the time the manuscript had been revised in the autumn of 1887, Bellamy's purpose had completely changed. After years of indecision and self-doubt he had become a reformer, and the book which Ticknor and Company published in January, 1888, was to serve as the manifesto of a singular kind of American reform movement.

IV

Looking Backward is a religious fable. At first glance it seems to consist of two different and unrelated stories—the fantastic

[34] "How I Came to Write 'Looking Backward'."

tale of Julian West's resurrection in the year 2000 and the account furnished Julian by his host Doctor Leete of the creation and management of utopia. Bellamy encouraged this compartmentalized reading by emphasizing his growing impatience with the contrivances and "other whimsies" of Julian's story once he had discovered his reform purpose. He continued to regard Julian's transformation simply as a "fanciful device" designed to give color to an argument which in itself was "as little fanciful as possible." Even with the model industrial army the two parts of the book seemed to conflict, and recasting involved the sacrifice of details and "interesting effects" to the lessons derived from "the rigid application of the democratic formula to the social problem." The impression left by his subsequent explanation is one of unresolved tension between the formal requirements of fantasy and the expository demands of what had become a plan for industrial reform.

Yet Bellamy retained the fantasy form not merely, as he said, in the hope of winning readers with a sugarcoated argument but because it provided the framework for the psychological drama of conversion which was the means to his utopia. As he first plotted it the story was told in the third person with Julian West treated objectively as one of the several characters. In the revised version Julian is made narrator, and the story he tells is of his own conversion to the Religion of Solidarity culminating in his miraculous relocation in utopia. At the end of the novel Julian's utopian surroundings coincide with his new inner state. His reward for the spiritual trials of conversion is permanent transposition to the heaven on earth shown him by Doctor Leete. In this sense Julian earns his way into utopia in precisely the same way it was first created by the inhabitants who welcome him.

In the supposedly real world of Boston in 1887 Julian West is a prisoner of his own selfishness. A wealthy and privileged Brahmin, he is wholly engrossed in his personal affairs centering on his impending marriage to Edith Bartlett and a frustrating series of strikes in the building trades which has delayed the completion of his luxurious new house. He spends his last evening before entering his trance at the home of his fiancée joining in the general denunciation of the working class. From the outset it is clear that the industrial and social crisis has resulted from the compounded smugness of Julian's class. He leaves for home filled with loathing for the workers and convinced that the country is about to take a header into chaos.

Julian suffers from insomnia, a symptom of repressed guilt, and on reaching his house in the fashionable quarter of the city he retires into his sealed sleeping chamber in the cellar which serves as a retreat for his self-enclosed personality. Above are the noises of a city gripped by social crisis, the disturbing cries of distress and suffering. "But to this subterranean room no murmur from the upper world ever penetrated. When I had entered it and closed the door, I was surrounded by the silence of the tomb." In fact Julian is spiritually dead, shut up in a burial vault of his own invention from which he is miraculously resurrected through the offices of a hypnotist and the marvel of suspended animation.

Julian's escape from the prison of self is accomplished in a painful trauma that is the necessary condition for his moral rebirth. He awakes one hundred and thirteen years later to see his new freedom mirrored in the splendor and expanse of the city spread out before him. The view of urban utopia and the sense of ventilation and spaciousness immediately affects his mood. Never before has he been more alert and intellectually acute. In this new state of mental intoxication he feels genuine sympathy for people for the first time and is able to "banish artificiality" in his relations with his host, Doctor Leete, and his family.

The initial excitement of his escape from subjectivity, however, quickly gives way to a growing terror as Julian begins to understand what has happened to him. With his discovery that he is now totally isolated in an alien world his agony begins and reaches a climax in the terrifying recognition that his identity has dissolved into a weird psychic duality.

There are no words for the mental torture I endured during this helpless, eyeless groping for myself in a boundless void. No other experience of the mind gives probably anything like the sense of absolute intellectual arrest from the loss of a mental fulcrum, a starting point of thought, which comes during such momentary obscuration of the sense of one's identity. I trust I may never know what it is again.

Loneliness and psychic devastation bring Julian to the verge of insanity—". . . all had broken loose . . . all had dissolved . . . seething together in apparently irretrievable chaos." Then he realizes that his identity is really double, that he is two persons— a remembered self and this new objective and dispassionate superego standing outside and above experience. Thematically the scene is the focal point of the book and the center of Bellamy's religious philosophy. In "The Religion of Solidarity" he had defined the individual consciousness as comprising a personal and an impersonal self and had reduced the social question to the problem of attaining solidarity through the cultivation of impersonality. Julian West succeeds in making this leap of consciousness but at considerable psychological cost. He is saved by the love of Doctor Leete's daughter Edith and quickly recovers his emotional stability. Bellamy's handling of the love story here as elsewhere is inept: Julian West and Edith Leete are conventional Victorian lovers unfolding their passion in episodes pasted together with sentiment. If the execution betrays Bellamy's taste for the mawkish, the conception of Julian's conversion from unconcern to commitment is nevertheless compelling. Under Edith's tutelage he learns to approximate the impersonal mood without anguish and to recall his old life with equanimity, "for all the world like a man who has permitted an injured limb to lie motionless under the impression that it is exquisitely sensitive, and on trying to move it finds that it is paralyzed." Julian has found that freedom from a guilty past promised by Dr. Heidenhoff and his memory-extirpation machine.

Once he has recovered his mental balance Julian is ready for his education in solidarity or "Nationalism," as it is called in utopia. Doctor Leete prepares his pupil with low-keyed lectures filled with parables and homilies. Julian accepts his indoctrination gratefully, listening to his tutor's account of the coming of utopia, accompanying him on tours of the city, inspecting the social machinery and analyzing the simple religion of brotherhood which makes it work. He is an observer passively absorbing an education in utopian ethics but still troubled by his lack of standing in his new world. "I am outside the system," he tells Edith, "and don't see how I can get in; there seems no way to get in, except to be born in or to come in as an emigrant from some other system." He can only await the end of his initiation. The main section of the book dramatizes the period of preparation or "justification" and is formally concluded by Doctor Barton's radio sermon on the real meaning of the miracle Julian has witnessed. Extending to society as a whole the conversion process Julian has experienced, the minister marvels at the suddenness of the transformation which has given humanity a new freedom. "We are merely stripped for the race; no more. We are like a child which has just learned to stand upright and walk. . . . humanity has entered on a new phase of spiritual development, an evolution of the higher faculties. . . . Humanity has burst its chrysalis. The heavens are before it."

Julian carries this millennial prophecy with him on his hallucinatory pilgrimage back into the nineteenth century. His nightmare journey through the Boston of 1887 is a final ordeal of faith after his indoctrination, his first positive act in behalf of the utopian order. In his dream he returns as a Saint John in an urban wilderness, wandering the streets and registering the suffering on the faces of the damned—the worried scowls of State Street bankers, the hysterical grins on Washington Street merchants, and the gaping brutalized stares of the poor in the South End. Gazing from one death's head to another, he suddenly stands convicted and feels the guilt which is necessary for his salvation.

I was moved with contrition as with a strong agony, for I had been one of those who had endured that these things should be. . . . Therefore now I found upon my garments the blood of this great multitude of strangled souls of my brothers. The voice of their blood cried out against me from the ground. Every stone of the reeking pavement, every brick of the pestilential rookeries, found tongue and called after me as I fled: What hast thou done with thy brother Abel?

Julian stumbles to the Bartlett's home on Commonwealth Avenue, rushes into the dining room where the guests are dining in complacent splendor, and announces that he has just been to Golgotha and seen humanity hanging on a cross. Unmoved, the publicans denounce him as a fanatic as he tries to convince them of their crime.

Still I strove with them. Tears poured from my eyes. In my vehemence I became inarticulate. I panted, I sobbed, I groaned, and immediately afterward found myself sitting upright in bed in my room in Doctor Leete's house, and the morning sun shining through the open window into my eyes.

The magic of conversion—Bellamy's favorite device—has saved the repentant sinner. Julian realizes in a final ecstatic moment that his return to a sinful past was only an illusion and his deliverance to utopia the ultimate reality.

The story of Julian's redemption is joined to the descriptive account of utopia by a parallel. Utopia, explains Doctor Leete, has come to the late twentieth century just as it did to Julian West—through a change of heart. In the historical recreation of capitalist America, Julian's situation in 1887 is simply multiplied to account for the social crisis. The American people, he is told, could find no way out of their dilemma. Strikes, lock-outs, Pinkertons, unemployment, slums, and starvation were the signs of an industrial civilization on the verge of collapse. So long as most Americans like Julian remained class-bound and blind to the truth of brotherhood, all their inventions and increased efficiency only made their problem the more insoluble. To recognize the simple, self-evident solution the American people had first to be converted through circumstance and revelation to the ideal of solidarity. Neither labor unions nor employers' associations, radical reformers nor the defenders of the competitive system recognized the need for a higher ethical basis for civilization. It remained for the "national party" with its standard of solidarity to discover the truth on which utopia was built. In the beginning simply a handful of prophets disillusioned with class appeals, the regenerate spread the gospel of benevolent nationalism, the idea of a whole people bound together "not as

an association of men for certain merely political functions . . .
but as a family, a vital union, a common life, a mighty heaven-
touching tree whose leaves are its people, fed from its veins,
and feeding it in turn." The National party grew almost overnight from a small band of evangelists into a potent counter-
revolutionary force that checked the destructive forces of
capitalist greed and proletarian envy.

The triumph of solidarity made all things simple. Solutions to
the great problem of social reorganization heretofore elusive
now lay within easy grasp. The social act of conversion only
helped the people to accept the inevitable. "In fact, to speak
by the book," Doctor Leete tells Julian, "it was not necessary for
society to solve the riddle at all. The solution came as a result
or process of industrial evolution which could not have terminated
otherwise. All that society had to do was to recognize and
cooperate. . . ." Bellamy used the transparent explanations of
his utopian spokesman to combine an economic determinism
similar to Marxism and the traditional American doctrine of
progress. Social development from a state of ruthless competition
to one of peaceful cooperation, he argued through Doctor Leete,
is inevitable and therefore natural and simple. The citizens of
utopia are much concerned to remove the impression that there
is any mystery about the process of evolution. Yet the mystery
remains hidden in the revelation of a higher ethical principle
without which progress is impossible. Once this revelation is
bestowed on the people then and only then can they cooperate
intelligently with history. Julian West's contemporaries could not
anticipate the great transformation and hasten its arrival because
they insisted on a perverse individualism. The change of heart
brought by Nationalism, however, illuminated once and for all
the processes of history. The great transformation, Julian is told,
was accomplished without violence. Converted by the missionary
work of the early Nationalists, the American public readily accepted the lessons of solidarity. The nation became the one great
trust, absorbing all the business of the country and employing
all the citizens who shared equally in its profits. The epoch of
monopolies produced the one great monopoly, and the people

finally came into their own. Significantly, it is the clergyman Doctor Barton who describes the miraculous changes wrought by the last and greatest of the prehistorical revolutions. "In the time of one generation men laid aside the social traditions and practices of barbarians, and assumed a social order worthy of rational and human beings." Utopia, then, originates in collective redemption, the social equivalent of Julian West's conversion. Revelation reduces the complexities of social reorganization to a self-evident proposition: the larger the business the simpler the principles to be applied to it. And what could be simpler than to recruit the whole body of the American people into one gigantic industrial army?

Bellamy's industrial army, as the name suggests, is a strictly military organization staffed by officers and filled with rank-and-file workers who are the foot soldiers of the nation's industrial forces. Its purpose is twofold: first, to attain the necessary high standards of production, distribution, and service; second, and more important, to guarantee the well-being of all citizens by providing them with meaningful work. His utopia is oriented toward work and the assumed inclination of men to perform it willingly. Although leisure has been secured to everyone through increased efficiency and technological improvement, its management and direction in the last year of the twentieth century is not considered a problem. Bellamy's citizens employ their leisure to suit themselves, and constant supervision of their working hours in no way disables them for private enjoyment of rest. It is nevertheless clear that utopians find the real meaning of their lives in working for the common good.

The explanation for the efficiency of the industrial army lies in the exact correspondence of the labor market with consumer needs, the nearly perfect balance of jobs to be filled and men to fill them. Only a rudimentary administrative apparatus is required. In cases where a temporary imbalance exists it is the task of the administrative staff of the industrial army to correct it, not according to any theory or "*a priori* rule" but strictly on an *ad hoc* basis. "The administration, in taking burdens off one class of workers and adding them to other classes, simply follows the fluctuation of opinion among the workers themselves as indicated in the rate of volunteering." Thus what might be thought an impossibly complicated bureaucratic snarl turns out to be a model of simple efficiency.

If Bellamy envisions a primitive kind of industrial management in the manipulation of incentives, it is nevertheless clear that there are limits to the procedure and that ultimately the success of industrial reorganization depends on an appeal to a new type of citizenship and the espousal of the Religion of Solidarity. Emulation still figures prominently as a motive for work, but it does not concern the "nobler" citizens who respond to an inner directive. They are the true patriots who enjoy a new interior freedom and who therefore measure their duties according to their talents and set about them with serene selflessness. Even in the last year of the twentieth century, however, not all the utopians have reached this level of sacrifice, and for those who have not emulation "of the keenest edge" is still needed. Until the Religion of Solidarity has won complete acceptance the principal business of the general staff of the industrial army is fostering the ritual habit of work through incentives and sanctions which will be discarded once the preference for socially useful labor becomes automatic. "The sense of possession of inward freedom," Bellamy noted in his journal, "reconciles us to outward constraint and tyranny." [35] In the final analysis the successful performance of his industrial army depends entirely on the universal applicability of this private conjecture.

To reconcile its citizens to outward constraint Bellamy's society, like all utopias, relies heavily on the power of education. A system of universal free education operates as efficiently as the industrial army itself because the same expanded scale facilitates enormous social savings. Bellamy's specific proposals as disclosed in the educational system of utopia were neither radical nor advanced. At a time when increasing numbers of Americans were demanding a more "practical" education his suggestions appeared to reinforce an excessive concern with utilitarian goals. His utopians take as their primary responsibility the training of

[35] Notebooks, Unpublished Papers.

their young in the industrial and professional skills needed to maintain an economy of abundance. To this end they have established schools of technology, medicine, and the arts which remain open to any qualified citizen up to the age of thirty. The extended period of enrollment constitutes a moratorium that prevents costly mistakes in selecting a vocation. Education is linked to a national program of rigorous physical training on the theory, increasingly popular in Bellamy's day, that sound bodies make sound minds. Utopia nurtures a cult of the strenuous life that in turn perpetuates a race of "stalwart young men and fresh, vigorous maidens."

Notwithstanding his seemingly narrow functional program of mass education Bellamy was deeply concerned with the problem of preserving individualism in an organic society. His educational system is tailored to the "whole man" and eliminates invidious distinctions between mental and physical labor. The best education possible is considered essential for the average utopian "merely to live, without reference to any kind of work he may do." As the citizens cultivate waste land into public parks and gardens so they seek to develop intelligence as a natural social environment. In the reckoning of utopians individual benefit and social advantage are equated in a definition of functional freedom. True individuality, Bellamy argues persuasively, becomes possible only in a rational social order that systematically leads the individual to an acknowledgment of his dependence on others. In this sense education is not a by-product but an integral function of the good society, a way of life in itself extending beyond the province of technological maintenance to a realm of non-material values. The power of education lifts the people of utopia to a higher plane of existence where questions of power and political management can be forgotten.

By the year 2000 several of the limbs of nineteenth-century American government have already withered away. Nearly all the purposes for which a complex federal government once existed have been erased by the triumph of Nationalism. The United States needs no army or navy, no departments of state or treasury, no revenue service or permanent legislative body. The scope of government has been reduced to the twin spheres of executive and judicial, both equipped with extensive enforcement powers. Congress is convened annually but acts chiefly as a rubber stamp for executive orders. Since the fundamentals of society have long since been agreed upon the people are easily maneuvered away from direct involvement with the decision-making process which formerly required legislation. Doctor Leete describes the situation exactly when he tells Julian that now there is nothing left to make laws about. Government has ceased to be deliberative and is now purely managerial.

Bellamy gives to the industrial army the directive control in utopia. His original concept of a society organized *like* an army is replaced in the revised version by the notion of an industrial army *as the government*. As the double titles of each rank suggest, industrial and administrative functions have been combined. The line of promotion runs from assistant foreman or lieutenant to foreman or captain to superintendent or colonel. Then come the major generals who are also heads of the bureaus representing their trades, and above them the lieutenant generals or chiefs of the ten great departments comprising allied trades and guilds. These departmental commanders form an executive council from which the Commander-in-Chief or President of the United States is chosen.

Presidential power is buttressed by a highly organized police power and a pliant judiciary. Yet neither of these agencies would suffice to maintain order were it not for the unwavering patriotic spirit of the citizenry. "Now that industry of whatever sort is no longer self-service, but service to the nation, patriotism, passion for humanity, impel the worker as in your day they did the soldier." The industrial army is an army not simply by virtue of its organization but also in the devotion and self-denial it inculcates. Lest we miss the full significance of the military display Bellamy raises the example of Prussia. The utopian working force, Dr. Leete announces proudly, can best be compared to the "fighting machine" of the German army in the time of Von Moltke. Here, it would seem, is militarism with a vengeance!

Bellamy was not the first nor the most outspoken of his generation of social observers, many of them New Englanders, to prescribe martial virtue as a cure for the ills of society or to recommend the lessons of the Civil War as a means of renewing national vigor. Within a decade Theodore Roosevelt would invoke the strenuous life inherited from veterans of Grant's and Sherman's campaigns in support of a "splendid little war." The historian Francis Parkman and the philosopher William James both drew heavily on their memories of the War for the Union, Parkman in calling for a new manliness to invigorate the patricians, James as a directive in his search for a moral equivalent for war based on the martial values of "obedience" and "intrepidity." In the years after 1880 Francis A. Walker, Thomas Wentworth Higginson, and Oliver Wendell Holmes, Jr.—all veterans of the Civil War and sons of New England acutely conscious of its heritage of nationalism—elaborated new concepts of the "useful citizen" and the "soldier's faith" derived from experiences on Civil War battlefields.

For all of Bellamy's solemnizing of the martial life his dream of a totalitarian society was vitiated by an even deeper commitment to the partriarchal principle. For Roosevelt and his disciples of moral athleticism military virtue was an *enchiridion* to be buckled on for open combat against a flabby materialism. Even the patrician-minded Mugwumps hoped for an eventual return to power of a temporarily dispossessed natural aristocracy. Bellamy's purpose, on the contrary, was determined not by a drive for power but by the desire to renounce it, and the result in his ideal society is not the accession of the people to control but their abdication in favor of a rule of elders purified by age and experience of corrupting ambition. "In devouring I seem to conquer," he once wrote in explaining his own inner migration, "but the thing devoured transforms me. Nothing is really ever conquered."[36] This personal maxim is the rule which the citizens of his utopia must learn, and not until they have accepted it are they entrusted with responsibility. The power structure in utopia is designed to remove the decision-making process from the grasp of the young and headstrong and vest it in a com-

[36] Notebooks, Unpublished Papers.

munity of patriarchs supposedly immune to the contamination of selfishness. The President of the United States is not eligible for office until he has reached the age of fifty. The heads of departments who form his cabinet and from whom he is chosen do not arrive at positions of authority until they are forty and then undergo a mandatory retirement before becoming eligible for the presidential office. Within the army itself promotion depends in large measure on the attainment of selflessness and impartiality which age and experience presumably supply. The moratorium granted to the young is intended as a last holiday for the self, a purge of the personal aspects of character and necessary preparation for assuming the duties of impersonality and solidarity.

The capstone of Bellamy's patriarchal structure is an electoral system disfranchising the active workers in the industrial army whose limited loyalties might prove dangerous to its discipline. The generals of the guilds as well as other higher officers are elected by "honorary members" of the army, those veterans who have been honorably discharged. Organized into an industrial G.A.R., they supervise the performance of the active workers with a benign detachment and choose their leaders for them. The "old fellows" like Doctor Leete are so zealous of the national interest that younger aspirants to leadership must be thoroughly competent in order to pass inspection. Indeed, the doctor offers the opinion that no previous form of society has ever developed an electorate "so ideally adapted to their office, as regards absolute impartiality, knowledge of the special qualifications and record of the candidates, solicitude for the best result, and complete absence of self-interest." The ideal political form dictated by the Religion of Solidarity allows for a plebescite of the patriarchs without unwarranted interference of the citizenry. This division between thought and action is made complete by a special provision for the professional classes who are organized in separate self-regulating guilds managed by retired "regents." Since the professionals by virtue of their training can be expected to behave judiciously they are given the vote but are not themselves eligible for office. Thus the intent as well as the effect of Bellamy's political scheme is to secure the resignation of the very class to which he belonged. In order to assure the tranquility essential to inner freedom his imaginary colleagues renounce the uses of the wisdom they are engaged in pursuing. It comes as a surprise only to Julian and Doctor Leete to discover that the origin of the system was the government by alumni—"a board of fairly sensible men"—with which nineteenth-century colleges and universities were conducted.

The rule of the patriarchs which tempers the theoretical harshness of Bellamy's utopia also accentuates the curious affectlessness of his people. His picture of the coming order with its disconcerting lack of textures and chiaroscuro reveals the narrowing of a social vision to the private world of a recluse. In at least one of its perspectives his utopia is the dream of an anchorite conserving a religious principle by minimizing direct contact with the outside world. Long before he began to write *Looking Backward* he filled his notebooks with imagined escapes of the mind from emotional attachment to other people. "These intense emotions, whether of pain or pleasure," he wrote in one such mood, "we do not want them."

We look for a placid race that shall not alternate between honey and vinegar, but live on mild ambrosia ever. It will be part of the plan of a future and wiser society to discourage the overgrowth of the affections, recognizing as indisputable that more misery results from excess of affectional development than from deficiency. . . .

Another entry in the journals proposes a reorganization of society "to extinguish sorrow" by outlawing parental control. "Society having arranged to provide that [welfare] better than the parents possibly could, the parental love is but an aching root of a tooth no longer useful." In still another conjecture he predicted the coming of a new form of love without tragic overtones —"cheerful comradeship only of people who suit but do not adore each other." In such a world there would be no excessive dependence or "forced constant association" and therefore no bereavement or despair. Men and women would live less intimately with one another and more involved with the universal.

The impersonal life foreshadowed in the notebooks and the

early fiction emerges in full clarity in Doctor Leete's family circle. The doctor is clearly Bellamy's archetype of the truly civilized man, yet he remains an oddly disquieting figure, politic, genteel to a fault, but also remote and dispassionate. He is the supremely rational man so dominated by the ideal of impersonality as nearly to lose his identity. Each day Julian finds him unchanged, an affable but detached observer of the world about him which he analyzes with clinical precision. Seldom does the tone of his conversation rise above the level of moral earnestness. Family life is correspondingly disengaged. Father, mother, and daughter move through each other's lives without collision. There are no quarrels or moments of communion because none of their lives impinge directly on the sensibilities of others. The household is harmonious because passion has been banished. Though "strangely daunted" at first, Julian soon grows accustomed to this new affectless state and accepts Edith's love knowing it for a form of pity. The book ends with his eager return to the state of detachment that has replaced family life.

Nor are the conditions of utopian life measurably different outside the Leete household. Bellamy's is a society of renewable abundance in which production is divorced from consumption, work from leisure, result from process, involvement with materials from enjoyment of "things." In spite of his gestures in the direction of a unified sensibility Bellamy really regarded work as a lower form of activity, an obligation to society which once fulfilled is to be rewarded with the gift of leisure. Doctor Leete states the utopian position exactly when he tells Julian that work is "a necessary duty to be discharged before we can fully devote ourselves to the higher exercise of our faculties, the intellectual enjoyment and pursuits which alone mean life." Leisure in utopia provides the means of recapturing an original freedom that has been surrendered to society, the recovery of a "birthright" necessarily diminished by society. With the worker's discharge from the industrial army comes "the period when we shall first really attain our majority and become enfranchised from discipline and control, with the fee of our lives vested in ourselves." Presumably the reclamation of the true self is accomplished by the sense of social interdependence which maturity brings, yet if Dr. Leete is typical, the utopian citizen remains remarkably self-contained. There is no mention of a single character outside the family circle. At a time when sociologists and social workers were just beginning to experiment with new ideas of the social creation of personality and new concepts of role-playing Bellamy remained a prisoner of an older concept of American individualism which the Religion of Solidarity had supposedly negated.

The split between production and consumption, long a familiar feature of the mass industrial society, is given peculiar emphasis in *Looking Backward*. Goods and services are provided anonymously: manufacturing and processing are carried on in huge centralized complexes, and shopping has become a simple and unexciting business of ordering samples in mammoth showrooms. Services are supplied by faceless functionaries performing with the disinterested air of soldiers on duty. The individual, Julian is informed, never regards himself as the servant of others. "It is always the nation which he is serving." Neither the waiter in the public dining room nor the clerk in the government store confronts in any direct way those whom they serve. Yet in spite of the impersonality of Bellamy's system it is remarkable how few of the nineteenth-century middle-class amenities have been sacrificed. Domestic servants are still available, the family table remains an alternative to public dining, and domesticity is still carried on in private homes and apartments.

The setting for domestic life in utopia, however, is sharply austere, and the Leete household echoes to an aesthetic emptiness which is quickly explained by the host. A constantly renewed supply of consumer goods has done away with the old habits of saving and collecting. No one feels the need of possessions. On the other hand, public life expressing the ideal of solidarity is rich and ornate. Citizens discard their personal belongings which have ceased to express their personalities and invest instead in architecture, sculpture, landscape gardens, and other public symbols. Although Boston is a garden city carved into neighborhoods furnished with clubhouses and dining halls, there is no actual sign of social interchange. The people of utopia apparently carry over into public life the reserve and self-sufficiency that characterizes their domestic arrangements. Bellamy's description of the public dining hall, its marble staircases, fountains, and statuary suggesting a set for a Hollywood musical, is peopled not with individuals or groups but with a "stream" of diners flooding up the staircase and down spacious corridors into appointed compartments.

Utopian culture is also depersonalized. Its chief medium is the radio. Instead of attending church, concerts, and other public functions the utopians simply tune in their choice with a flip of the switch. Included in the daily cultural fare is a supply of music which Edith Leete likens to a banquet. She declines to play or sing for Julian with the explanation that "it was these difficulties in the way of commanding really good music which made you endure so much playing and singing in your homes by people who had only the rudiments of the art." Amateurism has fallen before professionalism, the spontaneous has given way to the programmed. Utopian culture is offered as a commodity to be used but not absorbed, its content badly eroded by the demands of solidarity. Thus Julian West, marveling at the plot of a late twentieth-century novel, is struck "not so much by what was in the book as what was left out"—all contrasts between rich and poor, strong and weak, coarseness and refinement, contentment and misery. Utopia, he concludes, has succeeded admirably in avoiding the "sordid anxieties" of life. With irrepressible sensations of relief we welcome the temporary exchange of this state of emotional paralysis for Julian's nightmare world of conflict.

If the dystopian features of Bellamy's ideal society, like his technological predictions, have become commonplace less than a century later, they are also detachable from the central argument of the book, its moral indictment of capitalism. It is in his arraignment of the American capitalist system that Bellamy comes closest to assuming the reformer's stance he had criticized for so long. Although he could not foresee the lengths to which his censure would take him in an attempt to found a new party, the chapters in *Looking Backward* recounting the collapse of capitalism and its replacement by Nationalism show his utopian vision shading into a theory of reform. In time this theory would force him to repair the foundations of his utopia and adjust them to the shifting industrial terrain of the 1890's. Then he would find many of his original assumptions—not the least of them his scheme for an industrial army—entirely inadequate as a basis for effective reform. In the analytical sections of *Looking Backward*, however, he formulated a moral case against capitalism which he never modified.

Capitalism, he argued, promotes four different kinds of waste: the waste of competition and duplication; the waste of misdirected undertakings; the waste of periodic gluts and panics; and, finally, the tragic waste of idle labor. In the final sum these add up to financial chaos, misuse of human energies, and widespread suffering. Bellamy's solution is the increased efficiency which only the nationalizing of production and distribution can provide. The main instrumentality in his plan for nationalizing the economy is a science of statistics. Statistics supply his utopians with a simple administrative tool, unavailable under capitalism, for measuring resources, estimating needs, and allocating work. As capitalism evolves into Nationalism through progressive phases of consolidation and concentration, it creates a gigantic industrial machine "so logical in its principles and direct and simple in its workings" that it all but runs itself. This happy outcome has already been realized by the year 2000. The industrial machine fed like a computer with the right statistics automatically produces at full capacity and provides the abundance of material goods which is the precondition for utopia. With the disappearance of capitalism goes its rationale, a forced economy of scarcity. Nationalization brings a "large surplus" of staples and consumer goods with which to correct fluctuations in supply and demand. In the few areas of the nationalized economy where scarcity cannot be wholly eliminated it is equalized by price-fixing according to a primitive labor theory of value. Such is the simple mechanism at the core of Bellamy's plan for transcending the conflicts of capitalism.

Ultimately it was the waste of human resources under capitalism that most alarmed Bellamy, the inability of profit-minded entrepreneurs to employ the natural aptitudes of people in any rational and humane way. In a capitalist America the vast majority of men though nominally free were in fact victims of forces they were taught to believe beyond their control. For millions of misdirected and exploited Americans capitalism amounted to slavery. At this point in his indictment Bellamy shifted his attack from capitalism to materialism and the twin devils of competition and commercialism. Discovering the real enemy, he abandoned the unfamiliar field of economics for the realm of ethics where he launched his major attack on "the land of Ishmael." He denounced commercialism as the most vicious strain of antisocial behavior, "absolutely inconsistent with mutual benevolence and disinterestedness." Its motto was the huckster's pitch: "Never mind the rest. They are frauds. . . . Buy of me." In place of the false standards of commercialism *Looking Backward* offered the simple communist precept: "The amount of the effort alone is pertinent to the question of desert." That is, all men who do their best are entitled to the same reward. Only when his essentially Christian communism was universally accepted, Bellamy insisted, would the final spiritualization of mankind be consummated.

Ironically, material abundance in *Looking Backward* is the precondition for the utopian spiritual quest. Capitalism made parsimony a necessity, but since the arrival of Nationalism individual needs and expectations can be instantly fulfilled. The result is a profound change in social habits. No longer are frugality and self-denial considered virtues to be cultivated with Puritan intensity. Anxiety, the great American Nemesis, has at last been destroyed. "No man any more has care for the morrow, either for himself or his children, for the nation guarantees the nurture, education, and comfortable maintenance of every citizen from the cradle to the grave." Assured for the first time in history of a surfeit of material goods, mankind turns away from the feast for the pursuit of higher things. Human nature has not changed, Doctor Leete explains, but the changed environment has released a latent altruism in people which had been ruthlessly suppressed by capitalism. The deliverance of the world is at hand.

In *Looking Backward,* then, it is the vision rather than the theory which finally concerns Bellamy who was less an engineer than a prophet. For him the problem of means logically followed the question of ends. "Until we have a clear idea of what we want and are sure we want it," he wrote in defense of the book, "it would be a waste of time to discuss how we are to get it." *Looking Backward* contemplates an irreversible change in the human condition made possible by a massive shift of psychic energies to a spiritual pole. This is what Bellamy meant when he described the coming change in the United States as "an indistinct revolution . . . more radical than if it had been political." His revolution creates an affluent and abundant society, but more important, it brings an intensified psychic awareness similar to the "noosphere" or "noosystem" of Teilhard de Chardin and Julian Huxley. Just as life has passed from inorganic to organic forms, Bellamy believed, it would now pass from separate to integrated consciousness. In his Christian version of evolution the end of the process is "lost in light" in the moment when the human race returns to God and "the divine secret hidden in the germ shall be perfectly unfolded." Utopia, after all, was the palace in the clouds which he had first imagined it. For the moment, however, it appeared differently to him and to those readers of *Looking Backward* who thought they saw in his picture of the perfect society a house for practical men.

V

The publication of *Looking Backward* reversed the direction of Bellamy's life. After fifteen years of disengagement he decided to join the cause of social reform. "If you will kindly sell 50,000 copies of *Looking Backward* for me," he wrote to his first publisher Benjamin Ticknor, "I will engage to give the voters of 1892 a platform worth voting for, and furnish the voters." [37] To

[37] Bellamy to Benjamin Ticknor, June 15, 1888, Unpublished Papers.

Horace Scudder, the editor of the *Atlantic Monthly*, he admitted that he was tempted to return to the "psychologic studies and speculations" of his earlier work. "But since my eyes have been opened to the evils and faults of our social state and I have begun to cherish a clear hope of better things, I simply 'can't get my consent' to write or think of anything else." As a literary man he feared he was "a goner" and past praying for. "There is one life which I would like to lead, and another which I must lead. If I had only been twins!" [38] Two years of constant writing and revising, however, had exhausted him. He worried a good deal about his health and privately began timing the intervals between fits of coughing while experimenting with a variety of medicines. He was forced to give up the idea of a lecture tour and spent most of his time in his study at home conscientiously answering the letters of congratulation and inquiry that poured in. For the moment it was clear that if Nationalism was to be more than a literary pipe dream, initiative would have to come from his readers.

The original idea for a Nationalist organization was advanced by two Boston newspapermen, Sylvester Baxter of the *Globe* and Cyrus Field Willard, the labor editor on the *Herald*. The two men wrote to Bellamy in the summer of 1888 asking his permission. "Go ahead by all means, if you can find anybody to associate with," he replied in giving particular approval to their plan for approaching the "cultured and cultivated classes." [39] Before Baxter and Willard could set their plan in motion another group of Bostonians, fully qualified both as to culture and social standing, formed a Bellamy Club in the fall of 1888 to spread the gospel of Nationalism. The Boston founders of the Nationalist movement made a curious assortment of visionaries. The nucleus of this cluster of litterateurs and political mavericks was a group of retired army officers whose reading of *Looking Backward* had convinced them that there was no grander or more patriotic cause to enlist in than Bellamy's industrial army. Gen-

---

[38] Bellamy to Horace Scudder, August 25, 1890, Typed Copy, Unpublished Papers.

[39] Bellamy to Cyrus Field Willard, July 4, 1888, Unpublished Papers.

eral A. F. Devereux had fought in the War of the Rebellion; Captain Charles E. Bowers had won distinction at Gettysburg; Colonel Thomas Wentworth Higginson and Captain Edward S. Huntington still carried old campaign wounds. For these aging warriors Bellamy's ideas recalled distant years of service in defense of the nation and kindled hopes for new days of discipline and duty. Militarism retreated before mysticism in the minds of the theosophist converts to Nationalism, John Storer Cobb, Henry Austin, and John Ransome Bridge. For Edward Everett Hale and William Dean Howells the Nationalist idea seemed an offshoot of Lincoln Republicanism transplanted in a social gospel garden. W. D. P. Bliss and Vida Scudder, less enthusiastic about military efficiency than spiritual uplift, saw Nationalism as a variety of Christian socialism. A somewhat more chastened liberalism dictated the cooperation if not the strict allegiance of the Irish Catholic novelist-reformer John Boyle O'Reilley and his friend and editor of the *Pilot* James Jeffrey Roche. A final ingredient of Boston Nationalism was an amalgam of high feminism and cultural radicalism provided by Mary Livermore, Abby Morton Diaz, Agnes Chevaillier, and the sculptress Anne Whitney. In December of 1888, with Bellamy in attendance, Boston's fourth estate was joined to theosophism, Christian socialism, business conservatism, and military ardor in the first Nationalist Club in the country. After a spirited debate the majority of twenty-five members agreed to shun politics and concentrate their talents in a Nationalist Educational Association which would publish a monthly magazine.

At first Bellamy approved the decision to avoid political involvement. A deep distrust of the professional led him to overrate the powers of the gentleman. To Higginson, who also feared that the Nationalists might engage in ill-considered agitation, he confided his theory of reform as counterrevolution. One or two participants of Higginson's stripe, he explained, would be worth more to the cause than a host of ordinary recruits, for only the intellectual class could take reform "up out of the plane of the beer saloons and out of the hands of blasphemous demagogues and get it before the sober and morally minded masses of the American people." The untutored millions needed leaders they could trust.

I am sure that you will agree with me that in view of the impending industrial revolution and the necessity that the American people should be properly instructed as to its nature and possible outcome, a profound responsibility is upon the men who have the public ear and confidence. No doubt somehow or other the Revolution will get itself carried out but it will make a vast difference as to the ease or peril of the change whether or not it is led and guided by the natural leaders of the community, or left to the demagogues. It was the peculiar felicity of our countrymen in their revolt of 1776 that their natural leaders, the men of education and position, led it. I hope and confidently trust that the same felicity may attend them in the coming industrial and social revolution and assure an equally prosperous course and issue for this transformation. As for our politicians they of course will only follow not lead public opinion. It belongs to the literary class to create, arouse and direct that opinion. It is their opportunity. . . . [40]

Bellamy saw a sample of literary Nationalism when the first issue of *The Nationalist* appeared in May, 1889. In a poem entitled "The Heirs of Time" Higginson described "the patient armies of the poor" as tomorrow's "myriad monarchs" who "without a trumpet's call" would secure their title-deeds to life and liberty. Under the heading "Freedom's Last War-Cry" General Devereux invoked patriotism and self-sacrifice to meet the challenge of industrial barons. Sylvester Baxter assured readers that Nationalists merely followed the course of a spiralling evolutionary process to a new plane of freedom where the individual in transacting with the state would only be dealing with himself in a higher aspect. Henry Austin depicted Nationalist pioneers as armed with thoughts rather than swords. The theosophist John Ransome Bridge employed a tenderer image: "It is when a civilization is in its flower and before the petals loosen that there seems to come a crisis, a moment of opportunity, which, if taken advantage of, would ultimately lead to a new order of social life—the full fruitage after the blossom." Bellamy's re-

[40] Bellamy to Thomas Wentworth Higginson, December 28, 1889, Unpublished Papers.

minder that fifty years would see the complete accomplishment of the Nationalist program hit the only discordant note in this medley of Nationalist lyrics.

It was not long before he began to chafe under the self-imposed restraints of the Nationalist founders. Impatiently he wrote to Higginson, "It will not do too long to put the people off with generalities when they begin to ask what to do." [41] If his movement were to survive the competition of socialists and radicals, it would have to come to grips with the problem of means. His growing dissatisfaction was aggravated by the formation of a Second Nationalist Club in Boston composed of men who shared his impatience. The leaders of the second club were businessmen-politicians like Henry Legate and reform editors like Mason Green, a former staffer on Samuel Bowles's *Springfield Republican*. While members of the parent club concentrated almost exclusively on the speculative aspects of Nationalist doctrine, the new group tackled questions of municipal ownership, five-dollar coal, and cheap transportation. In their rooms overlooking the Common the founders listened to discourses on the solidarity of the race and the coming enthusiasm of humanity while their counterparts across town debated the question of first steps—nationalization of the railroads, utility franchises, and municipal tenement houses. As Nationalist clubs sprang up all over the country—some five hundred by 1890—most of them were similarly divided between amateur social theorists content with armchair discussions and political activists determined to bring a program of nationalization before the voters. On the surface Nationalism seemed to be a repository for malcontents of every description—prohibitionists, woman's-righters, antimonopoly men, die-hard communitarians, socialists, and disgruntled small businessmen. The same issue of their magazine could carry an article defining Nationalism as true conservatism in harmony with "the principles of Political Economy as laid down by the English School" and another calling for the destruction of the bourgeois state. A few Nationalists believed that trade unions

[41] Bellamy to Thomas Wentworth Higginson, June 20, 1889, Unpublished Papers.

should be the instruments of the great reform, but a great many more planned a back-to-the-people movement aimed at the purification of politics. In the welter of conflicting nostrums and panaceas the main question remained unanswered as to whether Nationalism meant a new brand of politics or more of that old-time religion. For men like Legate and Green in Boston, Jesse Cox and Clarence Darrow in Chicago, Max Georgii in Washington and, for a time, Daniel DeLeon in New York the lever of Nationalism was a program for municipal socialism and the progressive nationalizing of utilities, mines, and railroads. Bellamy took his cue from them. When *The Nationalist* quietly expired in 1891, he disregarded his doctor's orders and agreed to take over the editorship of *The New Nation*, a weekly paper advocating the substitution of industrial cooperation for capitalism "as rapidly as practicable." He spent the next three years commuting to the editorial offices at No. 15 Winter Street in Boston, the headquarters of what he hoped would soon be a great political organization.

Perhaps the most important factor in Bellamy's decision to turn to practical politics was the pressure of hostile criticism of his utopian model. The generally unperceptive comments of Social Darwinists and conservative evangelicals he met with effective rejoinders, but one critical survey of the book forced him to reconsider his plan for an industrial army. This was a lengthy critique in the *Atlantic Monthly* for February, 1890, by General Francis A. Walker. Walker had enjoyed a long and distinguished public service, first as a brevet-brigadier general in the Union Army and subsequently as the head of the Bureau of Statistics and superintendent of the Ninth Census, professor of political economy at Yale's Sheffield School, and now President of Massachusetts Institute of Technology. The bulk of his review of *Looking Backward* consisted of supposedly "practical" objections to utopia so popular with Social Darwinists. On the way to demolishing the concept of the industrial army, however, he stopped to call attention to the author's "false notion" that military discipline applied to the American economy would work miracles. "In sooth, Mr. Bellamy did not turn to the military system of organization because he was a socialist. He became a socialist because he had been moon-struck with a fancy for the military organization and discipline itself. So that, in a sense, militarism is, with him, an end rather than a means."

Bellamy realized that Walker's shaft had struck uncomfortably close to the truth, and in his reply he shifted his defense of the industrial army to different grounds. He readily admitted to an admiration of the soldier's life but pointed out that an ounce of fact was worth a pound of theory. His actual model for social reorganization, he now realized, was "the several thousand clerks employed in the governmental departments in Washington" whose circumstances were "very similar to those which will obtain in the coming industrial army." In other words, the skeleton force of the army was already in operation as the Civil Service. Not militarism but organicism, the view of society "not as an accidental conglomeration of mutually independent molecules, but in its totality only," formed the real basis for Nationalism. No doubt an industrial army would be the agent of social solidarity, but no one could predict its organization and operation in detail. What could be forecast with some certainty, however, were the definite steps to be taken in gradually extending national control over the forces of production and distribution: federal assumption of the telegraph, telephone, railroads, and mines and municipal assumption of lighting, heat, and transit facilities. Measures like these would immediately create a national body of over a million workers to provide along with the Civil Service the nucleus of an industrial force "organized on a thoroughly humane basis of steady employment, reasonable hours, pensions for sickness, accident, and age, with liability to discharge only for fault or incompetence after a fair hearing." This revised definition with its emphasis on social insurance and fair labor standards signalized the beginning of Bellamy's retreat from the military model which he had once thought essential.[42] As he saw the actual uses to which military force was

[42] " 'Looking Backward' Again," *The North American Review,* CL (March, 1890), 351–363. See also "Progress of Nationalism in the United States," *The North American Review,* CLIV (June, 1892), 742-752.

put at Homestead and elsewhere in breaking strikes and unions, he became less and less sure of the advantages of his original idea.

To modify his initial hypothesis Bellamy developed a theory of Nationalist evolution that gave his movement a sharper focus and a more positive program. In his editorials for *The New Nation*, in speeches and articles for the *North American Review*, *The Forum*, and *The Dawn* he explained Nationalism as a purely American program rooted in the political equalitarianism of the American Revolution. According to his new reading of the American past, the United States had been founded in a condition of general economic equality. The coming of the Industrial Revolution and unprecedented economic growth had brought an end to this equality of condition. A philosophy of moral and economic *laissez-faire* congenial to the entrepreneurial temperament had facilitated and then justified the tremendous increase in wealth and power which was rapidly siphoned off into a new class of plutocrats. Only a handful of Americans before the Civil War—in particular the communitarians—had seen where this unprecedented concentration of economic power was leading, and their attempts to construct alternative types of communities while premature and often ill-considered made them the true precursors of the Nationalists. Not until after Appomattox, however, were the costs of headlong industrialization made unmistakably clear in agrarian distress, the rise of monopolies, and the appearance of an American proletariat. Slowly the people began to understand the nature if not the cause of their plight as first one group and then another felt the oppressive hand of the new class of capitalist owners. The Seventies saw the appearance of pioneer reformers, the Greenbackers, Single-Taxers, and the Knights of Labor, but in the meantime the industrial barons strengthened their grip on the economy, consolidating small concerns into giant networks, rigging the market, diverting huge profits to their own unregulated use, driving out the independent businessman, and exploiting the American workingman. The new capitalists, Bellamy concluded, were the real revolutionaries who were trying to overthrow the republic and would soon succeed if no counterforce were interposed.

The Nationalists, on the contrary, were the legitimate heirs of the equalitarian tradition of the American Revolution now threatened by materialist greed and love of power. For the Nationalists the problem was not one of dreaming up new political forms but of maintaining and conserving the original purposes of the republican contract. Seen in this light, they were the conservatives. "We are the true conservative party," Bellamy told his followers at the first anniversary meeting of the Boston Nationalists in 1890, "because we are devoted to the maintenance of republican institutions against the revolution now being effected by the money power. We propose no revolution, but that the people shall resist a revolution. We oppose those who are overthrowing the republic. Let no mistake be made here. We are not revolutionists, but counterrevolutionists." Nationalists, it seemed, could achieve their defensive aims constitutionally by educating the American people and helping them to elect leaders who would change the laws. In other words, Nationalists would have to play politics.

Was not a nationalized economy really socialism, and were not the Nationalists unwitting agents of a socialist revolution? Bellamy denied the charge. Like most Americans of his generation he considered socialism a license for bomb throwing and inflammatory speechmaking by bearded radicals. If not all socialists were Marxists calling openly for violence, they were nevertheless advocates of a materialist philosophy that justified class-based agitation. Socialism was an import from Europe where class prejudice was instinctive, and furthermore its proponents ignored the national state which was the only true moral organism. "The European socialists," he wrote in *The Forum* (March, 1894), "or a large part of them do not insist upon economic equality, but allow economic variations in the ideal State. This is because they do not, like the Nationalists, deduce their conclusion by the rigid application of the democratic idea to the economic system." Nationalism, on the other hand, was a purely American philosophy promising not simply an equitable but an *equal* distribution of wealth guaranteed by the nation. "The nationalist not only believes in socialized industries but that socialization should be on the already established lines of national organism in its various grades of the municipal, state, and general administration. According to the nationalist the solution of the industrial question will result strictly from the evolution into industry of the national idea, which is that of a collective administration of the common affairs of citizens in the equal interest of all." Nationalism, as distinguished from socialism, was a citizens movement appealing equally to all classes to join in abolishing class.

Bellamy's objection to the trade-union theory of socialism argued by Laurence Gronlund in *The Cooperative Commonwealth* was grounded in the same fear of economic pluralism. As he understood their program, the trade unionists proposed a loose federation of organized trades whereas Nationalists envisioned an integral body of trade unions comprising the national organism. The partial remedies suggested by the trade unionists resulted from their imperfect understanding of the industrial problem. "No mere organizations of labor, useful as they are, will alone solve the problems of securing permanent employment on favorable terms." To obtain a guarantee of that sort capital as well as labor would have to be organized, and this only Nationalism could do.

Notwithstanding a middle-class antipathy to the supposedly divisive character of socialist thought Bellamy retained a number of socialist premises without troubling to square them with the tenets of his National evangelism. Although he rejected the Marxist law of inevitable class conflict as a sophism, he did agree that class antagonism would disappear only with the transcendence of the capitalist state and that in the meantime the middle class was rapidly becoming proletarianized and the working class driven below subsistence level. He further agreed with socialists in discounting the purely political power of the state under capitalism to restrain the exploitative activities of the money power. His closest approximation of the socialist position was made in his introduction to the American edition of the *Fabian Essays* in which he defined Nationalists as socialists "who, holding all that socialists agree on, go further, and hold also that the distribution of the cooperative product . . . must be not merely equitable, whatever that term may mean, but must be always and absolutely equal." Equality as a moral imperative and an American ideal drove him to define Nationalism as a religion and to demand from his followers a sense of consecration. Nationalism, he insisted, rested on sound economic law and on the Christian principle of cooperation, "but the latter is so much more the important consideration that even if a brotherly relation with our fellowmen could only be attained by the sacrifice of wealth, not the less would the true Nationalist seek it." It was this conviction that he stood in the vanguard of a great moral crusade which turned him away from theorizing toward Populism.

His determination to enter politics after years of irresolution was due in large measure to the industrial disorders and agrarian discontent after 1890 which seemed to offer the radical reformers their last chance. "I am more hopelessly gone on social reform than ever and have to own a total lack of interest in anything else," he wrote to Horace Scudder declining an invitation to write for the *Atlantic*.[43] Nothing else mattered now but securing a hearing for Nationalism. With the first issue of *The New Nation* in January, 1891, he opened a campaign to make Nationalism the ideological spearhead of the Populist attack on the two major parties. By the time of the Cincinnati Convention he had tied his hopes and the fortune of his paper to a third party distinctly pledged to radical reform.

Bellamy saw in Populism a new kind of revivalistic politics preparing the way for utopia, the politics of morality played by a different set of rules and judged by another set of standards than those of traditional American politics. According to the traditional rules the object of parties and the function of politicians is to win elections and secure office. In order to do this parties must appeal to a variety of voters who are presumed to have differing and even conflicting interests. Platforms, therefore, must be lofty but vague and wholly subordinated to the business of finding attractive candidates to run on them. Divisive issues and firm commitments are to be avoided wherever possible and

[43] Bellamy to Horace Scudder, September 15, 1893, Unpublished Papers.

at the very least neutralized by compromise and concession. The test of a party's strength—and the only test—is the number of votes it wins on election day. While a political party and its leaders may be said to have certain educative tasks, these are clearly secondary to the main job of putting the party in power and keeping it there. Thus conducted, traditional politics in the United States is considered by the great majority of Americans as a wholesome occupation, a normal and indeed necessary part of a healthy democratic society.

The revivalistic politics which Bellamy practiced in *The New Nation* in behalf of Populism reversed every one of these assumptions. Political parties, he insisted, are corrupt by definition. ("Politics now largely means a combination of votes to protect certain private interests. Patriotism is dying at the seat of power." March 21, 1891.) A Populist victory will destroy a debased political system. ("The advent of the people's party means not only the overthrow of one or both of the existing parties, but the political death of a whole crop of demagogues, whose trade it has been to keep the people apart, and take the bribes of politicians." May 30, 1891.) Nationalists will help the Populists conduct a new kind of campaign. ("To nationalists, principles are more important than men, and the platform than the candidates." July 9, 1892.) The financial and organizational poverty of Populism, far from being a liability, is a blessing in disguise. ("If they have a moral principle back of them, they do not need money to win." July 4, 1891.) Since the primary function of the People's Party is educative, it scarcely matters how many votes it wins. (". . . whether the vote of the people's party proves to be a handsome one or barely visible, will make no difference to the members or their future policy." November 7, 1891.) Purity is better than power. ("We believe the prospects of this party or any that succeed it, will be good in proportion as it lays aside compromise. . . ." November 14, 1891.) Should the Populists gain the balance of power in Congress, however, the American people may expect momentous changes in the conduct of public affairs. (". . . we may look to see the beginning of a new heroic period in our parliamentary history, recalling the days when the

champions of North and South in the decade before 1860, prel-
uded with arguments the mighty struggle that was coming."
October 15, 1892.) Total victory for Populism will bring true
national unity and the end of an imperfect electoral system.
("It is to be hoped that men will in time cease the folly of
electing a whole Congress or Parliament at a time, or a president
for a fixed term." November 12, 1892.)

For two years in spite of his rapidly failing health Bellamy
poured all his efforts and the slender resources of his paper into
the Populist cause. He helped organize the party in Massachusetts, spoke in support of the state ticket, and wrote dozens of
editorials advocating Populism as the first step toward complete
nationalization. The fortunes of the party and his paper rose
and fell together. In 1892 General Weaver carried six states
with twenty-two electoral votes, and *The New Nation* reached
the peak of its limited circulation. Soon thereafter both Populist
and Nationalist ranks were decimated by the Panic of 1893.
Neither *The New Nation* nor a third party committed even
provisionally to nationalization survived the depression that followed. Without money to keep his paper going and worn out
by two years of commuting, Bellamy closed up shop and retired
to his study at home convinced that in some measure he had
saved his Nationalist cause from becoming "dissipated into a
vague and foggy philanthropy." Since Nationalism now had its
thousand standard-bearers he could turn to "other lines of work
promising possibly a larger service to the cause."

In reality he was simply putting the best face on his disillusion-
ment. At best the effect of Nationalist propaganda on the People's
Party had been minimal. Nationalists had attended the conventions at Cincinnati and Omaha but with no very impressive results. Measures proposed by Nationalists as first steps seemed to
most Populists desperate alternatives to be considered only after
more moderate measures had failed. Nor had Bellamy made
support of Populism officially binding on his followers, believing
as he did that they ought not to compromise the purity of their
principles. His hopes for a serviceable political vehicle for the
Religion of Solidarity, intense while they lasted, were nevertheless

short-lived and in a deeper sense partial. Until the election of 1896 he considered Populism a practical testing of his ideas and a way of educating the American people to the truths of Nationalism. The fusion of Populists and Democrats on a free silver ticket, however, and their defeat by the Republicans left no doubt that Nationalism had been rejected. McKinley's election smashed beyond repair Bellamy's dream of a triumphant revivalistic politics. "While we are left practically without a party," he wrote to the equally disconsolate Henry Demarest Lloyd in the aftermath of defeat, "it is good riddance, seeing that the organization has fallen into bad hands." [44] The campaign of 1896 had done much to break up the political soil and prepare the people for radical reform. What the country needed now was a "manifesto" which a new party now or later could take up, "a complete set of propositions" proving the inevitability and the practicality of Nationalism. Already he was at work on his own manifesto, *Equality*, a sequel to *Looking Backward* and his final set of directions for building utopia.

Equality, which was finished in 1896 and published a year later, is both a less integrated and a less interesting book than *Looking Backward*. The fable has entirely disappeared, and though the contrast between the utopia of the year 2000 and the chaos of the last years of the nineteenth century is as vivid as before, it is presented in swollen expository chapters. There is little dramatic interest beyond the repeated discoveries of the perfections of utopia. Bellamy is more concerned with technological extrapolation than in *Looking Backward*, and utopia is more clearly delineated here as a consumer society based on calculated waste. There are also new details on the economic system, industrial management, the scale of governmental intervention, the rights of property and inheritance, and the operation of a social fund. Education is treated in tedious detail, both the formal educational procedures in the classroom and the rigorous physical education of utopian youth. All of these matters are collected in random fashion as though Bellamy, already aware of his failing

[44] Bellamy to Henry Demarest Lloyd, December 5, 1896, Unpublished Papers.

powers, had hastily gathered up his leftover ideas and crammed them between the covers.

His main concern in *Equality* lay in the attempt to synthesize the American political tradition of equality and the American religious tradition of revivalism. If the utopian society exhibited in *Looking Backward* and anticipated, as he believed, in the Populist movement were ever to be more than a blueprint, then Americans had to be convinced of the morality of absolute equality. This meant capturing for Nationalism the tradition of the Declaration of Independence and combining it with the equally vital principle of Christian evangelicalism in a theory of American history. He approached his task by first defining economic equality as the logical consequence of the political ideals of the American Revolution. Like all actors in history, the signers of the Declaration of Independence had not been fully aware of the implications of the document they approved. "Nothing is more certain than that the signers of the immortal Declaration had no idea that democracy meant anything more than a device for getting along without kings." The seed of economic equality first planted in the American Revolution had required a whole century to take root and grow. The growth of equality proceeded through two phases, the first a negative one in which the democratic system was thought of primarily as a substitute for royalty. Throughout the nineteenth century democracy remained, in effect, simply a protest against previous forms of government without any vital principle of its own. Then at the end of the nineteenth century the idea of equality entered a second positive phase, and democracy was suddenly seen as something more than a mere check on the power of rulers. Finally the people realized that "the main use and function of popular government was . . . the use of the power of the social organization to raise the material and moral welfare of the whole body of the sovereign people to the highest point . . . that is to say, an equal level." Then came the Great Revolution initiated by the Nationalists and carried out by all the people. The second revolution was only the fulfillment of the promises of the first, a completion of the principle of equality embodied in the Declaration of Independence. To describe its course Bellamy returned to his favorite military figure.

In conquering the political power formerly exercised by the king, the people had but taken the outworks of the fortress of tyranny. The economic system which was the citadel and commanded every part of the social structure remained in possession of private and irresponsible rulers, and so long as it was so held, the possession of the outworks was of no use to the people, and only retained by the sufferance of the garrison of the citadel. The Revolution came when the people saw that they must either take the citadel or evacuate the outworks.

Like the democratic idea itself, the Great Revolution was divided into two stages, the first lasting from the close of the Civil War to the end of the century, "a time of terror and tumult, of confused and purposeless agitation, and a Babel of contradictory clamor," the second the result of a sudden spiritual reawakening which brought order and rationality. In the first phase the revolutionaries, mostly farmers and laborers, were unable to recognize the cause of their distress and wasted their ammunition in minor sorties against the capitalist order. Their mistakes followed directly from their failure to realize that concentration and consolidation of power were inevitable results of the natural evolution of capitalism. They marched against the course of history instead of with it. Disorganized and confused, the early revolutionaries utterly failed to agree on a realistic program and get it before the American people. Then just as the Revolution seemed doomed to failure a group of farsighted Nationalists proposed a new front in the war on capitalism. "Fight forward, not backward!" they cried. "March with the course of economic evolution, not against it." Once their idea of progressive nationalization had been accepted the scene was set for the central event of the Revolution, the Great Revival, a self-generating flood of enthusiasm for social rather than personal salvation, "the general awakening of the people of America . . . to the profoundly ethical and truly religious character and claims of the movement for an industrial system which should guarantee the economic equality of all the people." As it swept across the country the Great Revival awakened the truly religious nature of Americans and brought home to them Christ's message of universal brotherhood. Thus was the Great Revolution made peaceful and permanent.

From the revival we date the beginning of the era of modern religion—a religion which has dispensed with the rites and ceremonies, creeds and dogmas, and banished from life fear and concern for the meaner self; a religion of life and conduct dominated by an impassioned sense of the solidarity of humanity and of man with God; the religion of a race that knows itself divine and fears no evil, either now or hereafter. . . .

In the final pages of *Equality* the Religion of Solidarity which had first imprisoned Bellamy in fantasy and then released him for an unsuccessful experiment in reform returns once again to seize him with its promise of a mysterious revelation. A year later he was dead of tuberculosis at the age of forty-eight.

VI

For half a century after his death Bellamy's reputation proved remarkably durable. *Looking Backward* received dozens of reprintings and was translated into nearly as many languages. It appeared regularly on lists of the Ten Great Books compiled by American publishers and reviewers and was enthusiastically read by a Progressive generation responsive to its prediction of radical change without social upheaval. In the early years of the Depression it was revived briefly by the Edward Bellamy Association of New York, which included as honorary members John Dewey, Upton Sinclair, Clarence Darrow, and Roger Baldwin, but quickly dropped when a more pragmatic generation of reformers discovered and rejected its implicit totalitarianism. Subsequently, the appeal of the book, like that of the utopian mode itself, has declined until today an affluent society based on deficit spending and credit cards, familiar with the techniques of brainwashing and just beginning to experiment with the social possibilities of hallucinogenic drugs, finds little to admire in Bellamy's primitive controls and much to deplore in the loss of cultural vitality incident to applying them. Less than a century after its publication *Looking Backward* seems less valuable for its insights into the problem of utopian engineering than in its accidental disclosure of the trials of the religious temperament faced with the challenge of mass industrial society.

It is tempting to reduce *Looking Backward* to an idiosyncratic perspective. Inevitably Bellamy's picture of an ideal world reflected his private demands for an ordered life. It was no doubt natural for a recluse to imagine an affectless society where direct human contact is drastically curtailed. A victim of a wasting disease and a semi-invalid, Bellamy was the more easily reconciled to an exchange of freedom of action for a quiet freedom of the mind, and his utopians follow his example. Essentially a non-political observer of the American scene, he found it difficult to think clearly about the function of politics in a democracy, and his utopia suffers accordingly from his dismissal of the fundamental problems of power and decision-making. Even the utopian obsession with physical hardihood can be traced to his concern with a robust life which was denied him. Nationalism, the industrial army, the Great Revolution—all were attempts at translating a private Religion of Solidarity into a comprehensive public message. Both the strengths and the weaknesses of his utopian vision derive from the intensely personal qualities of the book.

The initial popularity of *Looking Backward,* however, raises larger questions of its meaning for Bellamy's contemporaries, and the varied reception accorded it by different segments of the American public suggests the complexities involved in measuring its impact. It can nonetheless be said that despite the radical disjunctions inherent in the utopian device itself *Looking Backward* is a piece of social conservatism fashioned to reinforce accepted American values and traditions. It reaffirmed belief in a specifically American doctrine of progress which it strengthened with a new organicism and historicism. The book reasserted even as it modified the primacy of moral reform as the American Way and helped to connect the evangelical perfectionism of the pre-Civil War reformers with the moralistic prospect of the Progressives. As a central text in the social gospel movement it underscored in a peculiarly forceful way the Christian content of American social thought and more particularly the notion of reform as a moral enterprise directed toward conversion and regeneration. In so doing it revived the sense of an American Mission and renewed a confidence in a muscular national purpose drawing its strength from spiritual sources. For a vast number of American readers *Looking Backward* was a moral restorative, a tonic not so different from the patent-medicine panaceas of the day guaranteed to cure every ailment. Like the gaudy advertisements he so deplored, Bellamy promised something for everybody.

There were also more judicious and discriminating readers of *Looking Backward,* however, who caught an enthusiasm for reform from Bellamy which they carried over into their various Progressive roles. Judge Ben Lindsay later recalled an "idealistic kid" who ranked Bellamy with Saint Francis of Assisi as great lovers of mankind. Norman Thomas remembered *Looking Backward* as his introduction to socialism. Roger Baldwin grew up in a family that numbered Bellamy along with Emerson and Ingersoll as its intellectual heroes. Vida Scudder, social worker and friend of Jane Addams, credited Bellamy and his book with playing a "major role" in awakening the American middle class to the "brutalities and stupidities of the capitalist order." Upton Sinclair considered Bellamy not just a "noble personality" but a "real thinker." For the most part the Progressives did not mistake *Looking Backward* for a blueprint. It was not his model of utopia but his indictment of the capitalist system "through imagination," as John Dewey put it, that led them to consider alternative social values and devise ways of achieving them. Writing in the midst of a later crisis, Dewey credited Bellamy with having been the first to popularize the instrumentalist hypothesis that unequal distribution of material goods in a modern interlocking industrial economy will inevitably produce undesirable social consequences.

. . . Bellamy has given the unanswerable reply to those moralists who unwittingly defend the existing order by making a sharp separation between the material on the one side and the ethical on the other. Bellamy's communism rests on an ethical basis rather than upon a view that is sometimes called 'scientific' because of its abstraction from considerations of human well-being. But his ethical principle always takes cognizance of the dependence of human life and its supreme values upon equal access to and control over material things.[45]

Bellamy was neither the first nor the most persuasive of his generation of critics to relate ethics and economics in an instrumental equation, but his arraignment of an unregulated capitalist system and his prophecy of peaceful change contributed significantly to the objectives if not to the techniques of Progressivism. In many ways he exemplified the moderate man of good will whom he and later the Progressives sought to convert—the competent citizen, conservative in his social habits, resistant to ideas of class, skeptical of ideology and distrustful of reformers, yet increasingly sensitive to the inequities and injustices of unchecked competition. The difference between them was that in belatedly recognizing and correcting these wrongs Bellamy's average citizen was responding to the change in outlook which *Looking Backward* helped to formulate.

[45] "A Great American Prophet," *Common Sense*, April, 1934.

A Note on the Text

The first edition of *Looking Backward* was published by Ticknor and Company in January, 1888. Later that year Houghton, Mifflin and Company bought out Ticknor and made new plates from the corrected manuscript which Bellamy had prepared for a German translation. This second edition is the one selected for reprinting here. In revising the text Bellamy made numerous changes in spelling, capitalization, punctuation, and paragraphing. In addition to these minor changes Bellamy also made a number of substantive alterations. These are marked with asterisks in the text of the present edition; the original version is supplied in the bracketed footnotes. Technical changes also, where they affect the meaning, are indicated in the notes. All quotations from Bellamy's unpublished papers appear by permission of Mrs. Marion Bellamy Earnshaw and the Harvard College Library.

Looking Backward 2000–1887

Preface

Historical Section Shawmut College, Boston, December 26,* 2000

*L*IVING as we do in the closing year of the twentieth century, enjoying the blessings of a social order at once so simple and logical that it seems but the triumph of common sense, it is no doubt difficult for those whose studies have not been largely historical to realize that the present organization of society is, in its completeness, less than a century old. No historical fact is, however, better established than that till nearly the end of the nineteenth century it was the general belief that the ancient industrial system, with all its shocking social consequences, was destined to last, with possibly a little patching, to the end of time. How strange and wellnigh incredible does it seem that so prodigious a moral and material transformation as has taken place since then could have been accomplished in so brief an interval! The readiness with which men accustom themselves, as matters of course, to improvements in their condition, which, when anticipated, seemed to leave nothing more to be desired, could not be more strikingly illustrated. What reflection could be better calculated to moderate the enthusiasm of reformers who count for their reward on the lively gratitude of future ages!

The object of this volume is to assist persons who, while desiring to gain a more definite idea of the social contrasts between the nineteenth and twentieth centuries, are daunted by the formal aspect of the histories which treat the subject. Warned by a teacher's experience that learning is accounted a weariness to the flesh,

* [In the first edition the date is December 28, 2000.]

the author has sought to alleviate the instructive quality of the book by casting it in the form of a romantic narrative, which he would be glad to fancy not wholly devoid of interest on its own account.

The reader, to whom modern social institutions and their underlying principles are matters of course, may at times find Dr. Leete's explanations of them rather trite,—but it must be remembered that to Dr. Leete's guest they were not matters of course, and that this book is written for the express purpose of inducing the reader to forget for the nonce that they are so to him. One word more. The almost universal theme of the writers and orators who have celebrated this bimillennial epoch has been the future rather than the past, not the advance that has been made, but the progress that shall be made, ever onward and upward, till the race shall achieve its ineffable destiny. This is well, wholly well, but it seems to me that nowhere can we find more solid ground for daring anticipations of human development during the next one thousand years, than by "Looking Backward" upon the progress of the last one hundred.

That this volume may be so fortunate as to find readers whose interest in the subject shall incline them to overlook the deficiencies of the treatment is the hope in which the author steps aside and leaves Mr. Julian West to speak for himself.

Chapter I

I FIRST saw the light in the city of Boston in the year 1857. "What!" you say, "eighteen fifty-seven? That is an odd slip. He means nineteen fifty-seven, of course." I beg pardon, but there is no mistake. It was about four in the afternoon of December the 26th, one day after Christmas, in the year 1857, not 1957, that I first breathed the east wind of Boston, which, I assure the reader, was at that remote period marked by the same penetrating quality characterizing it in the present year of grace, 2000.

These statements seem so absurd on their face, especially when I add that I am a young man apparently of about thirty years of age, that no person can be blamed for refusing to read another word of what promises to be a mere imposition upon his credulity. Nevertheless I earnestly assure the reader that no imposition is intended, and will undertake, if he shall follow me a few pages, to entirely convince him of this. If I may, then, provisionally assume, with the pledge of justifying the assumption, that I know better than the reader when I was born, I will go on with my narrative. As every schoolboy knows, in the latter part of the nineteenth century the civilization of to-day, or anything like it, did not exist, although the elements which were to develop it were already in ferment. Nothing had, however, occurred to modify the immemorial division of society into the four classes, or nations, as they may be more fitly called, since the differences between them were far greater than those between any nations nowadays, of the rich and the poor, the educated and the ignorant. I myself was rich and also educated, and possessed, therefore, all the elements of happiness enjoyed by the most fortunate in that age. Living in luxury, and occupied only with the pursuit of the pleasures and refinements of life,

I derived the means of my support from the labor of others, rendering no sort of service in return. My parents and grand-parents had lived in the same way, and I expected that my descendants, if I had any, would enjoy a like easy existence.

But how could I live without service to the world? you ask. Why should the world have supported in utter idleness one who was able to render service? The answer is that my great-grand-father had accumulated a sum of money on which his descendants had ever since lived. The sum, you will naturally infer, must have been very large not to have been exhausted in supporting three generations in idleness. This, however, was not the fact. The sum had been originally by no means large. It was, in fact, much larger now that three generations had been supported upon it in idleness, than it was at first. This mystery of use without consumption, of warmth without combustion, seems like magic, but was merely an ingenious application of the art now happily lost but carried to great perfection by your ancestors, of shifting the burden of one's support on the shoulders of others. The man who had accomplished this, and it was the end all sought, was said to live on the income of his investments. To explain at this point how the ancient methods of industry made this possible would delay us too much. I shall only stop now to say that interest on investments was a species of tax in perpetuity upon the product of those engaged in industry which a person possessing or inheriting money was able to levy. It must not be supposed that an arrangement which seems so unnatural and preposterous according to modern notions was never criticised by your an-cestors. It had been the effort of lawgivers and prophets from the earliest ages to abolish interest, or at least to limit it to the smallest possible rate. All these efforts had, however, failed, as they necessarily must so long as the ancient social organizations prevailed. At the time of which I write, the latter part of the nineteenth century, governments had generally given up trying to regulate the subject at all.

By way of attempting to give the reader some general impres-sion of the way people lived together in those days, and espe-cially of the relations of the rich and poor to one another, perhaps I cannot do better than to compare society as it then was to a prodigious coach which the masses of humanity were harnessed to and dragged toilsomely along a very hilly and sandy road. The driver was hunger, and permitted no lagging, though the pace was necessarily very slow. Despite the difficulty of drawing the coach at all along so hard a road, the top was covered with passengers who never got down, even at the steepest ascents. These seats on top were very breezy and comfortable. Well up out of the dust, their occupants could enjoy the scenery at their leisure, or critically discuss the merits of the straining team. Naturally such places were in great demand and the competition for them was keen, every one seeking as the first end in life to secure a seat on the coach for himself and to leave it to his child after him. By the rule of the coach a man could leave his seat to whom he wished, but on the other hand there were many accidents by which it might at any time be wholly lost. For all that they were so easy, the seats were very insecure, and at every sudden jolt of the coach persons were slipping out of them and falling to the ground, where they were instantly compelled to take hold of the rope and help to drag the coach on which they had before ridden so pleasantly. It was naturally regarded as a terrible misfortune to lose one's seat, and the apprehension that this might happen to them or their friends was a constant cloud upon the happiness of those who rode.

But did they think only of themselves? you ask. Was not their very luxury rendered intolerable to them by comparison with the lot of their brothers and sisters in the harness, and the knowledge that their own weight added to their toil? Had they no compassion for fellow beings from whom fortune only distinguished them? Oh, yes; commiseration was frequently expressed by those who rode for those who had to pull the coach, especially when the vehicle came to a bad place in the road, as it was constantly doing, or to a particularly steep hill. At such times, the desperate straining of the team, their agonized leaping and plunging under the pitiless lashing of hunger, the many who fainted at the rope and were trampled in the mire, made a very distressing spectacle, which often called forth highly creditable displays of feeling on the top of the coach. At such times the passengers would call down encouragingly to the toilers of the rope, exhorting them to patience, and holding out hopes of possible compensation in another world for the hardness of their lot, while others contributed to buy salves and liniments for the crippled and injured. It was agreed that it was a great pity that the coach should be so hard to pull, and there was a sense of general relief when the specially bad piece of road was gotten over. This relief was not, indeed, wholly on account of the team, for there was always some danger at these bad places of a general overturn in which all would lose their seats.

It must in truth be admitted that the main effect of the spectacle of the misery of the toilers at the rope was to enhance the passengers' sense of the value of their seats upon the coach, and to cause them to hold on to them more desperately than before. If the passengers could only have felt assured that neither they nor their friends would ever fall from the top, it is probable that, beyond contributing to the funds for liniments and bandages, they would have troubled themselves extremely little about those who dragged the coach.

I am well aware that this will appear to the men and women of the twentieth century as incredible inhumanity, but there are two facts, both very curious, which partly explain it. In the first place, it was firmly and sincerely believed that there was no other way in which Society could get along, except the many pulled at the rope and the few rode, and not only this, but that no very radical improvement even was possible, either in the harness, the coach, the roadway, or the distribution of the toil. It had always been as it was, and it always would be so. It was a pity, but it could not be helped, and philosophy forbade wasting compassion on what was beyond remedy.

The other fact is yet more curious, consisting in a singular hallucination which those on the top of the coach generally shared, that they were not exactly like their brothers and sisters who pulled at the rope, but of finer clay, in some way belonging to a higher order of beings who might justly expect to be drawn. This seems unaccountable, but, as I once rode on this very coach and shared that very hallucination, I ought to be believed. The strangest thing about the hallucination was that those who had but just climbed up from the ground, before they had outgrown the marks of the rope upon their hands, began to fall under its influence. As for those whose parents and grandparents before them had been so fortunate as to keep their seats on the top, the conviction they cherished of the essential difference between their sort of humanity and the common article was absolute. The effect of such a delusion in moderating fellow feeling for the sufferings of the mass of men into a distant and philosophical compassion is obvious. To it I refer as the only extenuation I can offer for the indifference which, at the period I write of, marked my own attitude toward the misery of my brothers.

In 1887 I came to my thirtieth year. Although still unmarried, I was engaged to wed Edith Bartlett. She, like myself, rode on the top of the coach. That is to say, not to encumber ourselves further with an illustration which has, I hope, served its purpose of giving the reader some general impression of how we lived then, her family was wealthy. In that age, when money alone commanded all that was agreeable and refined in life, it was enough for a woman to be rich to have suitors; but Edith Bartlett was beautiful and graceful also.

My lady readers, I am aware, will protest at this. "Handsome she might have been," I hear them saying, "but graceful never, in the costumes which were the fashion at that period, when the head covering was a dizzy structure a foot tall, and the almost incredible extension of the skirt behind by means of artificial contrivances more thoroughly dehumanized the form than any former device of dressmakers. Fancy any one graceful in such a costume!" The point is certainly well taken, and I can only reply that while the ladies of the twentieth century are lovely demonstrations of the effect of appropriate drapery in accenting feminine graces, my recollection of their great-grandmothers enables me to maintain that no deformity of costume can wholly disguise them.

Our marriage only waited on the completion of the house which I was building for our occupancy in one of the most desirable parts of the city, that is to say, a part chiefly inhabited by the rich. For it must be understood that the comparative desirability of different parts of Boston for residence depended then, not on natural features, but on the character of the neighboring population. Each class or nation lived by itself, in quarters of its own. A rich man living among the poor, an educated man among the uneducated, was like one living in isolation among a jealous and alien race. When the house had been begun, its completion by the winter of 1886 had been expected. The spring of the following year found it, however, yet incomplete, and my marriage still a thing of the future. The cause of a delay calculated to be particularly exasperating to an ardent lover was a series of strikes, that is to say, concerted refusals to work on the part of the brick-layers, masons, carpenters, painters, plumbers, and other trades concerned in house building. What the specific causes of these strikes were I do not remember. Strikes had become so common at that period that people had ceased to inquire into their particular grounds. In one department of industry or another, they had been nearly incessant ever since the great business crisis of 1873. In fact it had come to be the exceptional thing to see any class of laborers pursue their avocation steadily for more than a few months at a time.

The reader who observes the dates alluded to will of course recognize in these disturbances of industry the first and incoherent phase of the great movement which ended in the establishment of the modern industrial system with all its social consequences. This is all so plain in the retrospect that a child can understand it, but not being prophets, we of that day had no clear idea what was happening to us. What we did see was that industrially the country was in a very queer way. The relation between the workingman and the employer, between labor and capital, appeared in some unaccountable manner to have become dislocated. The working classes had quite suddenly and very generally become infected with a profound discontent with their condition, and an idea that it could be greatly bettered if they only knew how to go about it. On every side, with one accord, they preferred demands for higher pay, shorter hours, better dwellings, better educational advantages, and a share in the refinements and luxuries of life, demands which it was impossible to see the way to granting unless the world were to become a great deal richer than it then was. Though they knew something of what they wanted, they knew nothing of how to accomplish it, and the eager enthusiasm with which they thronged about any one who seemed likely to give them any light on the subject lent sudden reputation to many would-be leaders, some of whom had little enough light to give. However chimerical the aspirations of the laboring classes might be deemed, the devotion with which they supported one another in the strikes, which were their chief weapon, and the sacrifices which they underwent to carry them out left no doubt of their dead earnestness.

As to the final outcome of the labor troubles, which was the phrase by which the movement I have described was most commonly referred to, the opinions of the people of my class differed according to individual temperament. The sanguine argued very forcibly that it was in the very nature of things impossible that the new hopes of the workingmen could be satisfied, simply because the world had not the wherewithal to satisfy them. It was only because the masses worked very hard and lived on short commons that the race did not starve outright, and no considerable improvement in their condition was possible while the world, as a whole, remained so poor. It was not the capitalists whom the laboring men were contending with, these maintained, but the iron-bound environment of humanity, and it was merely a question of the thickness of their skulls when they would discover the fact and make up their minds to endure what they could not cure.

The less sanguine admitted all this. Of course the workingmen's aspirations were impossible of fulfillment for natural reasons, but there were grounds to fear that they would not discover this fact until they had made a sad mess of society. They had the votes and the power to do so if they pleased, and their leaders meant they should. Some of these desponding observers went so far as to predict an impending social cataclysm. Humanity, they argued, having climbed to the top round of the ladder of civilization, was about to take a header into chaos, after which it would doubtless pick itself up, turn round, and begin to climb again. Repeated experiences of this sort in historic and prehistoric times possibly accounted for the puzzling bumps on the human cranium. Human history, like all great movements, was cyclical, and returned to the point of beginning. The idea of indefinite progress in a right line was a chimera of the imagination, with no analogue in nature. The parabola of a comet was perhaps a yet better illustration of the career of humanity. Tending upward and sunward from the aphelion of barbarism, the race attained the perihelion of civilization only to plunge downward once more to its nether goal in the regions of chaos.

This, of course, was an extreme opinion, but I remember serious men among my acquaintances who, in discussing the signs of the times, adopted a very similar tone. It was no doubt the common opinion of thoughtful men that society was approaching a critical period which might result in great changes. The labor troubles, their causes, course, and cure, took lead of all other topics in the public prints, and in serious conversation.

The nervous tension of the public mind could not have been more strikingly illustrated than it was by the alarm resulting from the talk of a small band of men who called themselves anarchists, and proposed to terrify the American people into adopting their ideas by threats of violence, as if a mighty nation which had but just put down a rebellion of half its own numbers, in order to maintain its political system, were likely to adopt a new social system out of fear.

As one of the wealthy, with a large stake in the existing order of things, I naturally shared the apprehensions of my class. The particular grievance I had against the working classes at the time of which I write, on account of the effect of their strikes in postponing my wedded bliss, no doubt lent a special animosity to my feeling toward them.

Chapter II

T HE thirtieth day of May, 1887, fell on a Monday. It was one of the annual holidays of the nation in the latter third of the nineteenth century, being set apart under the name of Decoration Day, for doing honor to the memory of the soldiers of the North who took part in the war for the preservation of the union of the States. The survivors of the war, escorted by military and civic processions and bands of music, were wont on this occasion to visit the cemeteries and lay wreaths of flowers upon the graves of their dead comrades, the ceremony being a very solemn and touching one. The eldest brother of Edith Bartlett had fallen in the war, and on Decoration Day the family was in the habit of making a visit to Mount Auburn, where he lay.

I had asked permission to make one of the party, and, on our return to the city at nightfall, remained to dine with the family of my betrothed. In the drawing-room, after dinner, I picked up an evening paper and read of a fresh strike in the building trades, which would probably still further delay the completion of my unlucky house. I remember distinctly how exasperated I was at this, and the objurgations, as forcible as the presence of the ladies permitted, which I lavished upon workmen in general, and these strikers in particular. I had abundant sympathy from those about me, and the remarks made in the desultory conversation which followed, upon the unprincipled conduct of the labor agitators, were calculated to make those gentlemen's ears tingle. It was agreed that affairs were going from bad to worse very fast, and that there was no telling what we should come to soon. "The worst of it," I remember Mrs. Bartlett's saying, "is that the working classes all over the world seem to be going crazy at once. In Europe it is far worse even than here. I'm sure I should not dare to live there at all. I asked Mr. Bartlett the other day where we should emigrate to if all the terrible things took place which those socialists threaten. He said he did not know any place now where society could be called stable except Greenland, Patagonia, and the Chinese Empire." "Those Chinamen knew what they were about," somebody added, "when they refused to let in our western civilization. They knew what it would lead to better than we did. They saw it was nothing but dynamite in disguise."

After this, I remember drawing Edith apart and trying to persuade her that it would be better to be married at once without waiting for the completion of the house, spending the time in travel till our home was ready for us. She was remarkably handsome that evening, the mourning costume that she wore in recognition of the day setting off to great advantage the purity of her complexion. I can see her even now with my mind's eye just as she looked that night. When I took my leave she followed me into the hall and I kissed her good-by as usaul. There was no circumstance out of the common to distinguish this parting from previous occasions when we had bade each other good-by for a night or a day. There was absolutely no premonition in my mind, or I am sure in hers, that this was more than an ordinary separation.

Ah, well!

The hour at which I had left my betrothed was a rather early one for a lover, but the fact was no reflection on my devotion. I was a confirmed sufferer from insomnia, and although otherwise perfectly well had been completely fagged out that day, from having slept scarcely at all the two previous nights. Edith knew this and had insisted on sending me home by nine o'clock, with strict orders to go to bed at once.

The house in which I lived had been occupied by three generations of the family of which I was the only living representative in the direct line. It was a large, ancient wooden mansion, very elegant in an old-fashioned way within, but situated in a quarter that had long since become undesirable for residence from its invasion by tenement houses and manufactories. It was not a house to which I could think of bringing a bride, much less so dainty a one as Edith Bartlett. I had advertised it for sale, and meanwhile merely used it for sleeping purposes, dining at my club. One servant, a faithful colored man by the name of Sawyer, lived with me and attended to my few wants. One feature of the house I expected to miss greatly when I should leave it, and this was the sleeping chamber which I had built under the foundations. I could not have slept in the city at all, with its never ceasing nightly noises, if I had been obliged to use an upstairs chamber. But to this subterranean room no murmur from the upper world ever penetrated. When I had entered it and closed the door, I was surrounded by the silence of the tomb. In order to prevent the dampness of the subsoil from penetrating the chamber, the walls had been laid in hydraulic cement and were very thick, and the floor was likewise protected. In order that the room might serve also as a vault equally proof against violence and flames, for the storage of valuables, I had roofed it with stone slabs hermetically sealed, and the outer door was of iron with a thick coating of asbestos. A small pipe, communicating with a wind-mill on the top of the house, insured the renewal of air.

It might seem that the tenant of such a chamber ought to be able to command slumber, but it was rare that I slept well, even there, two nights in succession. So accustomed was I to wakefulness that I minded little the loss of one night's rest. A second night, however, spent in my reading chair instead of my bed, tired me out, and I never allowed myself to go longer than that without slumber, from fear of nervous disorder. From this statement it will be inferred that I had at my command some artificial means for inducing sleep in the last resort, and so in fact I had. If after two sleepless nights I found myself on the approach of the third without sensations of drowsiness, I called in Dr. Pillsbury.

He was a doctor by courtesy only, what was called in those days an "irregular" or "quack" doctor. He called himself a "Professor of Animal Magnetism." I had come across him in the course of some amateur investigations into the phenomena of animal magnetism. I don't think he knew anything about medicine, but he was certainly a remarkable mesmerist. It was for the purpose of being put to sleep by his manipulations that I used to send for him when I found a third night of sleeplessness impending. Let my nervous excitement or mental preoccupation be however great, Dr. Pillsbury never failed, after a short time, to leave me in a deep slumber, which continued till I was aroused by a reversal of the mesmerizing process. The process for awaking the sleeper was much simpler than that for putting him to sleep, and for convenience I had made Dr. Pillsbury teach Sawyer how to do it.

My faithful servant alone knew for what purpose Dr. Pillsbury visited me, or that he did so at all. Of course, when Edith became my wife I should have to tell her my secrets. I had not hitherto told her this, because there was unquestionably a slight risk in the mesmeric sleep, and I knew she would set her face against my practice. The risk, of course, was that it might become too profound and pass into a trance beyond the mesmerizer's power to break, ending in death. Repeated experiments had fully convinced me that the risk was next to nothing if reasonable precautions were exercised, and of this I hoped, though doubtingly, to convince Edith. I went directly home after leaving her, and at once sent Sawyer to fetch Dr. Pillsbury. Meanwhile I sought my subterranean sleeping chamber, and exchanging my costume for a comfortable dressing-gown, sat down to read the letters by the evening mail which Sawyer had laid on my reading table.

One of them was from the builder of my new house, and confirmed what I had inferred from the newspaper item. The new strikes, he said, had postponed indefinitely the completion of the contract, as neither masters nor workmen would concede the point at issue without a long struggle. Caligula wished that the Roman people had but one neck that he might cut it off, and as I read this letter I am afraid that for a moment I was capable of wishing the same thing concerning the laboring classes of America. The return of Sawyer with the doctor interrupted my gloomy meditations.

It appeared that he had with difficulty been able to secure his services, as he was preparing to leave the city that very night. The doctor explained that since he had seen me last he had learned of a fine professional opening in a distant city, and decided to take prompt advantage of it. On my asking, in some panic, what I was to do for some one to put me to sleep, he gave me the names of several mesmerizers in Boston who, he averred, had quite as great powers as he.

Somewhat relieved on this point, I instructed Sawyer to rouse me at nine o'clock next morning, and, lying down on the bed in my dressing-gown, assumed a comfortable attitude, and surrendered myself to the manipulations of the mesmerizer. Owing, perhaps, to my unusually nervous state, I was slower than common in losing consciousness, but at length a delicious drowsiness stole over me.

Chapter III

*H*E is going to open his eyes. He had better see but one of us at first."

"Promise me, then, that you will not tell him."

The first voice was a man's, the second a woman's, and both spoke in whispers.

"I will see how he seems," replied the man.

"No, no, promise me," persisted the other.

"Let her have her way," whispered a third voice, also a woman.

"Well, well, I promise, then," answered the man. "Quick, go! He is coming out of it."

There was a rustle of garments and I opened my eyes. A fine looking man of perhaps sixty was bending over me, an expression of much benevolence mingled with great curiosity upon his features. He was an utter stranger. I raised myself on an elbow and looked around. The room was empty. I certainly had never been in it before, or one furnished like it. I looked back at my companion. He smiled.

"How do you feel?" he inquired.

"Where am I?" I demanded.

"You are in my house," was the reply.

"How came I here?"

"We will talk about that when you are stronger. Meanwhile, I beg you will feel no anxiety. You are among friends and in good hands. How do you feel?"

"A bit queerly," I replied, "but I am well, I suppose. Will you tell me how I came to be indebted to your hospitality? What has happened to me? How came I here? It was in my own house that I went to sleep."

"There will be time enough for explanations later," my unknown host replied, with a reassuring smile. "It will be better to avoid agitating talk until you are a little more yourself. Will you oblige me by taking a couple of swallows of this mixture? It will do you good. I am a physician."

I repelled the glass with my hand and sat up on the couch, although with an effort, for my head was strangely light.

"I insist upon knowing at once where I am and what you have been doing with me," I said.

"My dear sir," responded my companion, "let me beg that you will not agitate yourself. I would rather you did not insist upon explanations so soon, but if you do, I will try to satisfy you, provided you will first take this draught, which will strengthen you somewhat."

I thereupon drank what he offered me. Then he said, "It is not so simple a matter as you evidently suppose to tell you how you came here. You can tell me quite as much on that point as I can tell you. You have just been roused from a deep sleep, or, more properly, trance. So much I can tell you. You say you were in your own house when you fell into that sleep. May I ask you when that was?"

"When?" I replied, "when? Why, last evening, of course, at about ten o'clock. I left my man Sawyer orders to call me at nine o'clock. What has become of Sawyer?"

"I can't precisely tell you that," replied my companion, regarding me with a curious expression, "but I am sure that he is excusable for not being here. And now can you tell me a little more explicitly when it was that you fell into that sleep, the date, I mean?"

"Why, last night, of course; I said so, didn't I? that is, unless I have overslept an entire day. Great heavens! that cannot be possible; and yet I have an odd sensation of having slept a long time. It was Decoration Day that I went to sleep."

"Decoration Day?"

"Yes, Monday, the 30th."

"Pardon me, the 30th of what?"

"Why, of this month, of course, unless I have slept into June, but that can't be."

"This month is September."

"September! You don't mean that I've slept since May! God in heaven! Why, it is incredible."

"We shall see," replied my companion; "you say that it was May 30th when you went to sleep?"

"Yes."

"May I ask of what year?"

I stared blankly at him, incapable of speech, for some moments.

"Of what year?" I feebly echoed at last.

"Yes, of what year, if you please? After you have told me that I shall be able to tell you how long you have slept."

"It was the year 1887," I said.

My companion insisted that I should take another draught from the glass, and felt my pulse.

"My dear sir," he said, "your manner indicates that you are a man of culture, which I am aware was by no means the matter of course in your day it now is. No doubt, then, you have yourself made the observation that nothing in this world can be truly said to be more wonderful than anything else. The causes of all phenomena are equally adequate, and the results equally matters of course. That you should be startled by what I shall tell you is to be expected; but I am confident that you will not permit it to affect your equanimity unduly. Your appearance is that of a young man of barely thirty, and your bodily condition seems not greatly different from that of one just roused from a somewhat too long and profound sleep, and yet this is the tenth day of September in the year 2000, and you háve slept exactly one hundred and thirteen years, three months, and eleven days."

Feeling partially dazed, I drank a cup of some sort of broth at my companion's suggestion, and, immediately afterward becoming very drowsy, went off into a deep sleep.

When I awoke it was broad daylight in the room, which had been lighted artificially when I was awake before. My mysterious host was sitting near. He was not looking at me when I opened my eyes, and I had a good opportunity to study him and meditate upon my extraordinary situation, before he observed that I was awake. My giddiness was all gone, and my mind perfectly clear.

The story that I had been asleep one hundred and thirteen years, which, in my former weak and bewildered condition, I had accepted without question, recurred to me now only to be rejected as a preposterous attempt at an imposture, the motive of which it was impossible remotely to surmise.

Something extraordinary had certainly happened to account for my waking up in this strange house with this unknown companion, but my fancy was utterly impotent to suggest more than the wildest guess as to what that something might have been. Could it be that I was the victim of some sort of conspiracy? It looked so, certainly; and yet, if human lineaments ever gave true evidence, it was certain that this man by my side, with a face so refined and ingenuous, was no party to any scheme of crime or outrage. Then it occurred to me to question if I might not be the butt of some elaborate practical joke on the part of friends who had somehow learned the secret of my underground chamber and taken this means of impressing me with the peril of mesmeric experiments. There were great difficulties in the way of this theory; Sawyer would never have betrayed me, nor had I any friends at all likely to undertake such an enterprise; nevertheless the supposition that I was the victim of a practical joke seemed on the whole the only one tenable. Half expecting to catch a glimpse of some familiar face grinning from behind a chair or curtain, I looked carefully about the room. When my eyes next rested on my companion, he was looking at me.

"You have had a fine nap of twelve hours," he said briskly, "and I can see that it has done you good. You look much better. Your color is good and your eyes are bright. How do you feel?"

"I never felt better," I said, sitting up.

"You remember your first waking, no doubt," he pursued, "and your surprise when I told you how long you had been asleep?"

"You said, I believe, that I had slept one hundred and thirteen years."

"Exactly."

"You will admit," I said, with an ironical smile, "that the story was rather an improbable one."

"Extraordinary, I admit," he responded, "but given the proper conditions, not improbable nor inconsistent with what we know of the trance state. When complete, as in your case, the vital functions are absolutely suspended, and there is no waste of the tissues. No limit can be set to the possible duration of a trance when the external conditions protect the body from physical injury. This trance of yours is indeed the longest of which there is any positive record, but there is no known reason wherefore, had you not been discovered and had the chamber in which we found you continued intact, you might not have remained in a state of suspended animation till, at the end of indefinite ages, the gradual refrigeration of the earth had destroyed the bodily tissues and set the spirit free."

I had to admit that, if I were indeed the victim of a practical joke, its authors had chosen an admirable agent for carrying out their imposition. The impressive and even eloquent manner of this man would have lent dignity to an argument that the moon was made of cheese. The smile with which I had regarded him as he advanced his trance hypothesis did not appear to confuse him in the slightest degree.

"Perhaps," I said, "you will go on and favor me with some particulars as to the circumstances under which you discovered this chamber of which you speak, and its contents. I enjoy good fiction."

"In this case," was the grave reply, "no fiction could be so strange as the truth. You must know that these many years I have been cherishing the idea of building a laboratory in the large garden beside this house, for the purpose of chemical experiments for which I have a taste. Last Thursday the excavation for the cellar was at last begun. It was completed by that night, and Friday the masons were to have come. Thursday night we had a tremendous deluge of rain, and Friday morning I found my cellar a frog-pond and the walls quite washed down. My daughter, who had come out to view the disaster with me, called my attention to a corner of masonry laid bare by the crumbling away of one of the walls. I cleared a little earth from it, and, finding that it seemed part of a large mass, determined to investigate it. The workmen I sent for unearthed an oblong vault some eight feet below the surface, and set in the corner of what had evidently been the foundation walls of an ancient house. A layer of ashes and charcoal on the top of the vault showed that the house above had perished by fire. The vault itself was perfectly intact, the cement being as good as when first applied. It had a door, but this we could not force, and found entrance by removing one of the flagstones which formed the roof. The air which came up was stagnant but pure, dry and not cold. Descending with a lantern, I found myself in an apartment fitted up as a bedroom in the style of the nineteenth century. On the bed lay a young man. That he was dead and must have been dead a century was of course to be taken for granted; but the extraordinary state of preservation of the body struck me and the medical colleagues whom I had summoned with amazement. That the art of such embalming as this had ever been known we should not have believed, yet here seemed conclusive testimony that our immediate ancestors had possessed it. My medical colleagues, whose curiosity was highly excited, were at once for undertaking experiments to test the nature of the process employed, but I withheld them. My motive in so doing, at least the only motive I now need speak of, was the recollection of something I once had read about the extent to which your contemporaries had cultivated the subject of animal magnetism. It had occurred to me as just conceivable that you might be in a trance, and that the secret of your bodily integrity after so long a time was not the craft of an embalmer, but life. So extremely fanciful did this idea seem, even to me, that I did not risk the ridicule of my fellow physicians by mentioning it, but gave some other reason for postponing their experiments. No sooner, however, had they left me, than I set on foot a systematic attempt at resuscitation, of which you know the result."

Had its theme been yet more incredible, the circumstantiality of this narrative, as well as the impressive manner and personality of the narrator, might have staggered a listener, and I had begun to feel very strangely, when, as he closed, I chanced to catch a glimpse of my reflection in a mirror hanging on the wall of the room. I rose and went up to it. The face I saw was the face to a hair and a line and not a day older than the one I had looked at as I tied my cravat before going to Edith that Decoration Day, which, as this man would have me believe, was celebrated one hundred and thirteen years before. At this, the colossal character of the fraud which was being attempted on me, came over me afresh. Indignation mastered my mind as I realized the outrageous liberty that had been taken.

"You are probably surprised," said my companion, "to see that, although you are a century older than when you lay down to sleep in that underground chamber, your appearance is unchanged. That should not amaze you. It is by virtue of the total arrest of the vital functions that you have survived this great period of time. If your body could have undergone any change during your trance, it would long ago have suffered dissolution."

"Sir," I replied, turning to him, "what your motive can be in reciting to me with a serious face this remarkable farrago, I am utterly unable to guess; but you are surely yourself too intelligent to suppose that anybody but an imbecile could be deceived by it. Spare me any more of this elaborate nonsense and once for all tell me whether you refuse to give me an intelligible account of where I am and how I came here. If so, I shall proceed to ascertain my whereabouts for myself, whoever may hinder."

"You do not, then, believe that this is the year 2000?"

"Do you really think it necessary to ask me that?" I returned.

"Very well," replied my extraordinary host. "Since I cannot convince you, you shall convince yourself. Are you strong enough to follow me upstairs?"

"I am as strong as I ever was," I replied angrily, "as I may have to prove if this jest is carried much farther."

"I beg, sir," was my companion's response, "that you will not allow yourself to be too fully persuaded that you are the victim of a trick, lest the reaction, when you are convinced of the truth of my statements, should be too great."

The tone of concern, mingled with commiseration, with which he said this, and the entire absence of any sign of resentment at my hot words, strangely daunted me, and I followed him from the room with an extraordinary mixture of emotions. He led the way up two flights of stairs and then up a shorter one, which landed us upon a belvedere on the house-top. "Be pleased to look around you," he said, as we reached the platform, "and tell me if this is the Boston of the nineteenth century."

At my feet lay a great city. Miles of broad streets, shaded by trees and lined with fine buildings, for the most part not in continuous blocks but set in larger or smaller inclosures, stretched in every direction. Every quarter contained large open squares filled with trees, among which statues glistened and fountains flashed in the late afternoon sun. Public buildings of a colossal size and an architectural grandeur unparalleled in my day raised their stately piles on every side. Surely I had never seen this city nor one comparable to it before. Raising my eyes at last towards the horizon, I looked westward. That blue ribbon winding away to the sunset, was it not the sinuous Charles? I looked east; Boston harbor stretched before me within its headlands, not one of its green islets missing.

I knew then that I had been told the truth concerning the prodigious thing which had befallen me.

Chapter IV

I DID not faint, but the effort to realize my position made me very giddy, and I remember that my companion had to give me a strong arm as he conducted me from the roof to a roomy apartment on the upper floor of the house, where he insisted on my drinking a glass or two of good wine and partaking of a light repast.

"I think you are going to be all right now," he said cheerily "I should not have taken so abrupt a means to convince you of your position if your course, while perfectly excusable under the circumstances, had not rather obliged me to do so. I confess," he added laughing, "I was a little apprehensive at one time that I should undergo what I believe you used to call a knockdown in the nineteenth century, if I did not act rather promptly. I remembered that the Bostonians of your day were famous pugilists, and thought best to lose no time. I take it you are now ready to acquit me of the charge of hoaxing you."

"If you had told me," I replied, profoundly awed, "that a thousand years instead of a hundred had elapsed since I last looked on this city, I should now believe you."

"Only a century has passed," he answered, "but many a millennium in the world's history has seen changes less extraordinary."

"And now," he added, extending his hand with an air of irresistible cordiality, "let me give you a hearty welcome to the Boston of the twentieth century and to this house. My name is Leete, Dr. Leete they call me."

"My name," I said as I shook his hand, "is Julian West."

"I am most happy in making your acquaintance, Mr. West," he responded. "Seeing that this house is built on the site of your own, I hope you will find it easy to make yourself at home in it."

After my refreshment Dr. Leete offered me a bath and a change of clothing, of which I gladly availed myself.

It did not appear that any very startling revolution in men's attire had been among the great changes my host had spoken of, for, barring a few details, my new habiliments did not puzzle me at all.

Physically, I was now myself again. But mentally, how was it with me, the reader will doubtless wonder. What were my intellectual sensations, he may wish to know, on finding myself so suddenly dropped as it were into a new world. In reply let me ask him to suppose himself suddenly, in the twinkling of an eye, transported from earth, say, to Paradise or Hades. What does he fancy would be his own experience? Would his thoughts return at once to the earth he had just left, or would he, after the first shock, wellnigh forget his former life for a while, albeit to be remembered later, in the interest excited by his new surroundings? All I can say is, that if his experience were at all like mine in the transition I am describing, the latter hypothesis would prove the correct one. The impressions of amazement and curiosity which my new surroundings produced occupied my mind, after the first shock, to the exclusion of all other thoughts. For the time the memory of my former life was, as it were, in abeyance.

No sooner did I find myself physically rehabilitated through the kind offices of my host, than I became eager to return to the house-top; and presently we were comfortably established there in easy-chairs, with the city beneath and around us. After Dr. Leete had responded to numerous questions on my part, as to the ancient landmarks I missed and the new ones which had replaced them, he asked me what point of the contrast between the new and the old city struck me most forcibly.

"To speak of small things before great," I responded, "I really think that the complete absence of chimneys and their smoke is the detail that first impressed me."

"Ah!" ejaculated my companion with an air of much interest, "I had forgotten the chimneys, it is so long since they went out of use. It is nearly a century since the crude method of combustion on which you depended for heat became obsolete."

"In general," I said, "what impresses me most about the city is the material prosperity on the part of the people which its magnificence implies."

"I would give a great deal for just one glimpse of the Boston of your day," replied Dr. Leete. "No doubt, as you imply, the cities of that period were rather shabby affairs. If you had the taste to make them splendid, which I would not be so rude as to question, the general poverty resulting from your extraordinary industrial system would not have given you the means. Moreover, the excessive individualism which then prevailed was inconsistent with much public spirit. What little wealth you had seems almost wholly to have been lavished in private luxury. Nowadays, on the contrary, there is no destination of the surplus wealth so popular as the adornment of the city, which all enjoy in equal degree."

The sun had been setting as we returned to the house-top, and as we talked night descended upon the city.

"It is growing dark," said Dr. Leete. "Let us descend into the house; I want to introduce my wife and daughter to you."

His words recalled to me the feminine voices which I had heard whispering about me as I was coming back to conscious life; and, most curious to learn what the ladies of the year 2000 were like, I assented with alacrity to the proposition. The apartment in which we found the wife and daughter of my host, as well as the entire interior of the house, was filled with a mellow light, which I knew must be artificial, although I could not discover the source from which it was diffused. Mrs. Leete was an exceptionally fine looking and well preserved woman of about her husband's age, while the daughter, who was in the first blush of womanhood, was the most beautiful girl I had ever seen. Her face was as bewitching as deep blue eyes, delicately tinted complexion, and perfect features could make it, but even had her countenance lacked special charms, the faultless luxuriance of her figure would have given her place as a beauty among the women of the nineteenth century. Feminine softness and delicacy were in this lovely creature deliciously combined with an appearance of health and abounding physical vitality too often lacking in the maidens with whom alone I could compare her. It was a coincidence trifling in comparison with the general strangeness of the situation, but still striking, that her name should be Edith.

The evening that followed was certainly unique in the history of social intercourse, but to suppose that our conversation was peculiarly strained or difficult would be a great mistake. I believe indeed that it is under what may be called unnatural, in the sense of extraordinary, circumstances that people behave most naturally, for the reason, no doubt, that such circumstances banish artificiality. I know at any rate that my intercourse that evening with these representatives of another age and world was marked by an ingenuous sincerity and frankness such as but rarely crown long acquaintance. No doubt the exquisite tact of my entertainers had much to do with this. Of course there was nothing we could talk of but the strange experience by virtue of which I was there, but they talked of it with an interest so naive and direct in its expression as to relieve the subject to a great degree of the element of the weird and the uncanny which might so easily have been overpowering. One would have supposed that they were quite in the habit of entertaining waifs from another century, so perfect was their tact.

For my own part, never do I remember the operations of my mind to have been more alert and acute than that evening, or my intellectual sensibilities more keen. Of course I do not mean that the consciousness of my amazing situation was for a moment out of mind, but its chief effect thus far was to produce a feverish elation, a sort of mental intoxication.[1]

Edith Leete took little part in the conversation, but when several times the magnetism of her beauty drew my glance to her face, I found her eyes fixed on me with an absorbed intensity, almost like fascination. It was evident that I had excited her interest to an extraordinary degree, as was not astonishing, sup-

[1] In accounting for this state of mind it must be remembered that, except for the topic of our conversations, there was in my surroundings next to nothing to suggest what had befallen me. Within a block of my home in the old Boston I could have found social circles vastly more foreign to me. The speech of the Bostonians of the twentieth century differs even less from that of their cultured ancestors of the nineteenth than did that of the latter from the language of Washington and Franklin, while the differences between the style of dress and furniture of the two epochs are not more marked than I have known fashion to make in the time of one generation.

posing her to be a girl of imagination. Though I supposed curiosity was the chief motive of her interest, it could but affect me as it would not have done had she been less beautiful.

Dr. Leete, as well as the ladies, seemed greatly interested in my account of the circumstances under which I had gone to sleep in the underground chamber. All had suggestions to offer to account for my having been forgotten there, and the theory which we finally agreed on offers at least a plausible explanation, although whether it be in its details the true one, nobody, of course, will ever know. The layer of ashes found above the chamber indicated that the house had been burned down. Let it be supposed that the conflagration had taken place the night I fell asleep. It only remains to assume that Sawyer lost his life in the fire or by some accident connected with it, and the rest follows naturally enough. No one but he and Dr. Pillsbury either knew of the existence of the chamber or that I was in it, and Dr. Pillsbury, who had gone that night to New Orleans, had probably never heard of the fire at all. The conclusion of my friends, and of the public, must have been that I had perished in the flames. An excavation of the ruins, unless thorough, would not have disclosed the recess in the foundation walls connecting with my chamber. To be sure, if the site had been again built upon, at least immediately, such an excavation would have been necessary, but the troublous times and the undesirable character of the locality might well have prevented rebuilding. The size of the trees in the garden now occupying the site indicated, Dr. Leete said, that for more than half a century at least it had been open ground.

Chapter V

W HEN, in the course of the evening the ladies retired, leaving Dr. Leete and myself alone, he sounded me as to my disposition for sleep, saying that if I felt like it my bed was ready for me; but if I was inclined to wakefulness nothing would please him better than to bear me company. "I am a late bird, myself," he said, "and, without suspicion of flattery, I may say that a companion more interesting than yourself could scarcely be imagined. It is decidedly not often that one has a chance to converse with a man of the nineteenth century."

Now I had been looking forward all the evening with some dread to the time when I should be alone, on retiring for the night. Surrounded by these most friendly strangers, stimulated and supported by their sympathetic interest, I had been able to keep my mental balance. Even then, however, in pauses of the conversation I had had glimpses, vivid as lightning flashes, of the horror of strangeness that was waiting to be faced when I could no longer command diversion. I knew I could not sleep that night, and as for lying awake and thinking, it argues no cowardice, I am sure, to confess that I was afraid of it. When, in reply to my host's question, I frankly told him this, he replied that it would be strange if I did not feel just so, but that I need have no anxiety about sleeping; whenever I wanted to go to bed, he would give me a dose which would insure me a sound night's sleep without fail. Next morning, no doubt, I would awake with the feeling of an old citizen.

"Before I acquire that," I replied, "I must know a little more about the sort of Boston I have come back to. You told me when we were upon the house-top that though a century only had elapsed since I fell asleep, it had been marked by greater changes in the conditions of humanity than many a previous millennium. With the city before me I could well believe that, but I am very curious to know what some of the changes have been. To make a beginning somewhere, for the subject is doubtless a large one, what solution, if any, have you found for the labor question? It was the Sphinx's riddle of the nineteenth century, and when I dropped out the Sphinx was threatening to devour society, because the answer was not forthcoming. It is well worth sleeping a hundred years to learn what the right answer was, if, indeed, you have found it yet."

"As no such thing as the labor question is known nowadays," replied Dr. Leete, "and there is no way in which it could arise, I suppose we may claim to have solved it. Society would indeed have fully deserved being devoured if it had failed to answer a riddle so entirely simple. In fact, to speak by the book, it was not necessary for society to solve the riddle at all. It may be said to have solved itself. The solution came as the result of a process of industrial evolution which could not have terminated otherwise. All that society had to do was to recognize and coöperate with that evolution, when its tendency had become unmistakable."

"I can only say," I answered, "that at the time I fell asleep no such evolution had been recognized."

"It was in 1887 that you fell into this sleep, I think you said."

"Yes, May 30th, 1887."

My companion regarded me musingly for some moments. Then he observed, "And you tell me that even then there was no general recognition of the nature of the crisis which society was nearing? Of course, I fully credit your statement. The singular blindness of your contemporaries to the signs of the times is a phenomenon commented on by many of our historians, but few facts of history are more difficult for us to realize, so obvious and unmistakable as we look back seem the indications, which must also have come under your eyes, of the transformation about to come to pass. I should be interested, Mr. West, if you would give me a little more definite idea of the view which you and men of your grade of intellect took of the state and prospects of society in 1887. You must, at least, have realized that the widespread industrial and social troubles, and the underlying dissatisfaction of all classes with the inequalities of society, and the general misery of mankind, were portents of great changes of some sort."

"We did, indeed, fully realize that," I replied. "We felt that society was dragging anchor and in danger of going adrift. Whither it would drift nobody could say, but all feared the rocks."

"Nevertheless," said Dr. Leete, "the set of the current was perfectly perceptible if you had but taken pains to observe it, and it was not toward the rocks, but toward a deeper channel."

"We had a popular proverb," I replied, "that 'hindsight is better than foresight,' the force of which I shall now, no doubt, appreciate more fully than ever. All I can say is, that the prospect was such when I went into that long sleep that I should not have been surprised had I looked down from your house-top to-day on a heap of charred and moss-grown ruins instead of this glorious city."

Dr. Leete had listened to me with close attention and nodded thoughtfully as I finished speaking. "What you have said," he observed, "will be regarded as a most valuable vindication of Storiot, whose account of your era has been generally thought exaggerated in its picture of the gloom and confusion of men's minds. That a period of transition like that should be full of excitement and agitation was indeed to be looked for; but seeing how plain was the tendency of the forces in operation, it was natural to believe that hope rather than fear would have been the prevailing temper of the popular mind."

"You have not yet told me what was the answer to the riddle which you found," I said. "I am impatient to know by what contradiction of natural sequence the peace and prosperity which you now seem to enjoy could have been the outcome of an era like my own."

"Excuse me," replied my host, "but do you smoke?" It was not till our cigars were lighted and drawing well that he resumed. "Since you are in the humor to talk rather than to sleep, as I certainly am, perhaps I cannot do better than to try to give you enough idea of our modern industrial system to dissipate at least the impression that there is any mystery about the process of its evolution. The Bostonians of your day had the reputation of being great askers of questions, and I am going to show my descent by asking you one to begin with. What should you name as the most prominent feature of the labor troubles of your day?"

"Why, the strikes, of course," I replied.

"Exactly; but what made the strikes so formidable?"

"The great labor organizations."

"And what was the motive of these great organizations?"

"The workmen claimed they had to organize to get their rights from the big corporations," I replied.

"That is just it," said Dr. Leete; "the organization of labor and the strikes were an effect, merely, of the concentration of capital in greater masses than had ever been known before. Before this concentration began, while as yet commerce and industry were conducted by innumerable petty concerns with small capital, instead of a small number of great concerns with vast capital, the individual workman was relatively important and independent in his relations to the employer. Moreover, when a little capital or a new idea was enough to start a man in business for himself, workingmen were constantly becoming employers and there was no hard and fast line between the two classes. Labor unions were needless then, and general strikes out of the question. But when the era of small concerns with small capital was succeeded by that of the great aggregations of capital, all this was changed. The individual laborer, who had been relatively important to the small employer, was reduced to insignificance and powerlessness over against the great corporation, while at the same time the way upward to the grade of employer was closed to him. Self-defense drove him to union with his fellows.

"The records of the period show that the outcry against the concentration of capital was furious. Men believed that it threatened society with a form of tyranny more abhorrent than it had ever endured. They believed that the great corporations were preparing for them the yoke of a baser servitude than had ever been imposed on the race, servitude not to men but to soulless machines incapable of any motive but insatiable greed. Looking back, we cannot wonder at their desperation, for certainly humanity was never confronted with a fate more sordid and hideous than would have been the era of corporate tyranny which they anticipated.

"Meanwhile, without being in the smallest degree checked by the clamor against it, the absorption of business by ever larger monopolies continued. In the United States there was not, after the beginning of the last quarter of the century, any opportunity whatever for individual enterprise in any important field of industry, unless backed by a great capital.* During the last decade of the century, such small businesses as still remained were fast-failing survivals of a past epoch, or mere parasites on the great corporations, or else existed in fields too small to attract the great capitalists. Small businesses, as far as they still remained, were reduced to the condition of rats and mice, living in holes and corners, and counting on evading notice for the enjoyment of existence. The railroads had gone on combining till a few great syndicates controlled every rail in the land. In manufactories, every important staple was controlled by a syndicate. These syndicates, pools, trusts, or whatever their name, fixed prices and crushed all competition except when combinations as vast as themselves arose. Then a struggle, resulting in a still greater consolidation, ensued. The great city bazar crushed its country rivals with branch stores, and in the city itself absorbed its smaller rivals till the business of a whole quarter was concentrated under one roof, with a hundred former proprietors of shops serving as clerks. Having no business of his own to put his money in, the small capitalist, at the same time that he took service under the corporation, found no other investment

---

* [In the first edition this sentence reads: "In the United States, where this tendency was later in developing than in Europe, there was not, after the beginning of the last quarter of the century, any opportunity whatever for individual enterprise in any important field of industry, unless backed by a great capital."]

for his money but its stocks and bonds, thus becoming doubly dependent upon it.

"The fact that the desperate popular opposition to the consolidation of business in a few powerful hands had no effect to check it proves that there must have been a strong economical reason for it. The small capitalists, with their innumerable petty concerns, had in fact yielded the field to the great aggregations of capital, because they belonged to a day of small things and were totally incompetent to the demands of an age of steam and telegraphs and the gigantic scale of its enterprises. To restore the former order of things, even if possible, would have involved returning to the day of stage-coaches. Oppressive and intolerable as was the régime of the great consolidations of capital, even its victims, while they cursed it, were forced to admit the prodigious increase of efficiency which had been imparted to the national industries, the vast economies effected by concentration of management and unity of organization, and to confess that since the new system had taken the place of the old the wealth of the world had increased at a rate before undreamed of. To be sure this vast increase had gone chiefly to make the rich richer, increasing the gap between them and the poor; but the fact remained that, as a means merely of producing wealth, capital had been proved efficient in proportion to its consolidation. The restoration of the old system with the subdivision of capital, if it were possible, might indeed bring back a greater equality of conditions, with more individual dignity and freedom, but it would be at the price of general poverty and the arrest of material progress.

"Was there, then, no way of commanding the services of the mighty wealth-producing principle of consolidated capital without bowing down to a plutocracy like that of Carthage? As soon as men began to ask themselves these questions, they found the answer ready for them. The movement toward the conduct of business by larger and larger aggregations of capital, the tendency toward monopolies, which had been so desperately and vainly resisted, was recognized at last, in its true significance, as a process which only needed to complete its logical evolution to open a golden future to humanity.

"Early in the last century the evolution was completed by the final consolidation of the entire capital of the nation. The industry and commerce of the country, ceasing to be conducted by a set of irresponsible corporations and syndicates of private persons at their caprice and for their profit, were intrusted to a single syndicate representing the people, to be conducted in the common interest for the common profit. The nation, that is to say, organized as the one great business corporation in which all other corporations were absorbed; it became the one capitalist in the place of all other capitalists, the sole employer, the final monopoly in which all previous and lesser monopolies were swallowed up, a monopoly in the profits and economies of which all citizens shared. The epoch of trusts had ended in The Great Trust.* In a word, the people of the United States concluded to assume the conduct of their own business, just as one hundred odd years before they had assumed the conduct of their own government, organizing now for industrial purposes on precisely the same grounds that they had then organized for political purposes. At last, strangely late in the world's history, the obvious fact was perceived that no business is so essentially the public business as the industry and commerce on which the people's livelihood depends, and that to entrust it to private persons to be managed for private profit is a folly similar in kind, though vastly greater in magnitude, to that of surrendering the functions of political government to kings and nobles to be conducted for their personal glorification."

"Such a stupendous change as you describe," said I, "did not, of course, take place without great bloodshed and terrible convulsions."

"On the contrary," replied Dr. Leete, "there was absolutely no violence. The change had been long foreseen. Public opinion had become fully ripe for it, and the whole mass of the people was behind it. There was no more possibility of opposing it by force than by argument. On the other hand the popular sentiment toward the great corporations and those identified with them had ceased to be one of bitterness, as they came to realize their necessity as a link, a transition phase, in the evolution of

* [This sentence was added in the second edition.]

the true industrial system. The most violent foes of the great private monopolies were now forced to recognize how invaluable and indispensable had been their office in educating the people up to the point of assuming control of their own business. Fifty years before, the consolidation of the industries of the country under national control would have seemed a very daring experiment to the most sanguine. But by a series of object lessons, seen and studied by all men, the great corporations had taught the people an entirely new set of ideas on this subject. They had seen for many years syndicates handling revenues greater than those of states, and directing the labors of hundreds of thousands of men with an efficiency and economy unattainable in smaller operations. It had come to be recognized as an axiom that the larger the business the simpler the principles that can be applied to it; that, as the machine is truer than the hand, so the system, which in a great concern does the work of the master's eye in a small business, turns out more accurate results. Thus it came about that, thanks to the corporations themselves, when it was proposed that the nation should assume their functions, the suggestion implied nothing which seemed impracticable even to the timid. To be sure it was a step beyond any yet taken, a broader generalization, but the very fact that the nation would be the sole corporation in the field would, it was seen, relieve the undertaking of many difficulties with which the partial monopolies had contended."

Chapter VI

D R. LEEETE ceased speaking, and I remained silent, endeavoring to form some general conception of the changes in the arrangements of society implied in the tremendous revolution which he had described.

Finally I said, "The idea of such an extension of the functions of government is, to say the least, rather overwhelming."

"Extension!" he repeated, "where is the extension?"

"In my day," I replied, "it was considered that the proper functions of government, strictly speaking, were limited to keeping the peace and defending the people against the public enemy, that is, to the military and police powers."

"And, in heaven's name, who are the public enemies?" exclaimed Dr. Leete. "Are they France, England, Germany, or hunger, cold, and nakedness? In your day governments were accustomed, on the slightest international misunderstanding, to seize upon the bodies of citizens and deliver them over by hundreds of thousands to death and mutilation, wasting their treasures the while like water; and all this oftenest for no imaginable profit to the victims. We have no wars now, and our governments no war powers, but in order to protect every citizen against hunger, cold, and nakedness, and provide for all his physical and mental needs, the function is assumed of directing his industry for a term of years. No, Mr. West, I am sure on reflection you will perceive that it was in your age, not in ours, that the extension of the functions of governments was extraordinary. Not even for the best ends would men now allow their governments such powers as were then used for the most maleficent."

"Leaving comparisons aside," I said, "the demagoguery and

corruption of our public men would have been considered, in my day, insuperable objections to any assumption by government of the charge of the national industries. We should have thought that no arrangement could be worse than to entrust the politicians with control of the wealth-producing machinery of the country. Its material interests were quite too much the football of parties as it was."

"No doubt you were right," rejoined Dr. Leete, "but all that is changed now. We have no parties or politicians, and as for demagoguery, and corruption, they are words having only an historical significance."

"Human nature itself must have changed very much," I said.

"Not at all," was Dr. Leete's reply, "but the conditions of human life have changed, and with them the motives of human action. The organization of society with you was such that officials were under a constant temptation to misuse their power for the private profit of themselves or others. Under such circumstances it seems almost strange that you dared entrust them with any of your affairs. Nowadays, on the contrary, society is so constituted that there is absolutely no way in which an official, however ill-disposed, could possibly make any profit for himself or any one else by a misuse of his power. Let him be as bad an official as you please, he cannot be a corrupt one. There is no motive to be. The social system no longer offers a premium on dishonesty. But these are matters which you can only understand as you come, with time, to know us better." *

"But you have not yet told me how you have settled the labor problem. It is the problem of capital which we have been discussing," I said. "After the nation had assumed conduct of the mills, machinery, railroads, farms, mines, and capital in general of the country, the labor question still remained. In assuming the responsibilities of capital the nation had assumed the difficulties of the capitalist's position."

---

* [The passage beginning "The organization of society. . . ." was expanded in the second edition. The first edition reads: "The organization of society no longer offers a premium on baseness. But these are matters which you can only understand as you come, with time, to know us better."]

"The moment the nation assumed the responsibilities of capital those difficulties vanished," replied Dr. Leete. "The national organization of labor under one direction was the complete solution of what was, in your day and under your system, justly regarded as the insoluble labor problem. When the nation became the sole employer, all the citizens, by virtue of their citizenship, became employees, to be distributed according to the needs of industry."

"That is," I suggested, "you have simply applied the principle of universal military service, as it was understood in our day, to the labor question."

"Yes," said Dr. Leete, "that was something which followed as a matter of course as soon as the nation had become the sole capitalist. The people were already accustomed to the idea that the obligation of every citizen, not physically disabled, to contribute his military services to the defense of the nation was equal and absolute. That it was equally the duty of every citizen to contribute his quota of industrial or intellectual services to the maintenance of the nation was equally evident, though it was not until the nation became the employer of labor that citizens were able to render this sort of service with any pretense either of universality or equity. No organization of labor was possible when the employing power was divided among hundreds or thousands of individuals and corporations, between which concert of any kind was neither desired, nor indeed feasible. It constantly happened then that vast numbers who desired to labor could find no opportunity, and on the other hand, those who desired to evade a part or all of their debt could easily do so."

"Service, now, I suppose, is compulsory upon all," I suggested.

"It is rather a matter of course than of compulsion," replied Dr. Leete. "It is regarded as so absolutely natural and reasonable that the idea of its being compulsory has ceased to be thought of. He would be thought to be an incredibily contemptible person who should need compulsion in such a case. Nevertheless, to speak of service being compulsory would be a weak way to state its absolute inevitableness. Our entire social order is so wholly based upon and deduced from it that if it were conceivable that a man could escape it, he would be left with no possible way to provide for his existence. He would have excluded himself from the world, cut himself off from his kind, in a word, committed suicide."

"Is the term of service in this industrial army for life?"

"Oh, no; it both begins later and ends earlier than the average working period in your day. Your workshops were filled with children and old men, but we hold the period of youth sacred to education, and the period of maturity, when the physical forces begin to flag, equally sacred to ease and agreeable relaxation. The period of industrial service is twenty-four years, beginning at the close of the course of education at twenty-one and terminating at forty-five. After forty-five, while discharged from labor, the citizen still remains liable to special calls, in case of emergencies causing a sudden great increase in the demand for labor, till he reaches the age of fifty-five, but such calls are rarely, in fact almost never, made. The fifteenth day of October of every year is what we call Muster Day, because those who have reached the age of twenty-one are then mustered into the industrial service, and at the same time those who, after twenty-four years' service, have reached the age of forty-five, are honorably mustered out. It is the great day of the year with us, whence we reckon all other events, our Olympiad, save that it is annual."

Chapter VII

*I*T is after you have mustered your industrial army into service,"
I said, "that I should expect the chief difficulty to arise, for
there its analogy with a military army must cease. Soldiers have
all the same thing, and a very simple thing, to do, namely, to
practice the manual of arms, to march and stand guard. But
the industrial army must learn and follow two or three hundred
diverse trades and avocations. What administrative talent can
be equal to determining wisely what trade or business every
individual in a great nation shall pursue?"

"The administration has nothing to do with determining that
point."

"Who does determine it, then?" I asked.

"Every man for himself in accordance with his natural aptitude, the utmost pains being taken to enable him to find out
what his natural aptitude really is. The principle on which our
industrial army is organized is that a man's natural endowments,
mental and physical, determine what he can work at most
profitably to the nation and most satisfactorily to himself. While
the obligation of service in some form is not to be evaded, voluntary election, subject only to necessary regulation, is depended
on to determine the particular sort of service every man is to
render. As an individual's satisfaction during his term of service
depends on his having an occupation to his taste, parents and
teachers watch from early years for indications of special aptitudes in children. A thorough study of the National industrial
system, with the history and rudiments of all the great trades,
is an essential part of our educational system. While manual
training is not allowed to encroach on the general intellectual
culture to which our schools are devoted, it is carried far enough

to give our youth, in addition to their theoretical knowledge of the national industries, mechanical and agricultural, a certain familiarity with their tools and methods. Our schools are constantly visiting our workshops, and often are taken on long excursions to inspect particular industrial enterprises. In your day a man was not ashamed to be grossly ignorant of all trades except his own, but such ignorance would not be consistent with our idea of placing every one in a position to select intelligently the occupation for which he has most taste. Usually long before he is mustered into service a young man has found out the pursuit he wants to follow, has acquired a great deal of knowledge about it, and is waiting impatiently the time when he can enlist in its ranks."

"Surely," I said, "it can hardly be that the number of volunteers for any trade is exactly the number needed in that trade. It must be generally either under or over the demand."

"The supply of volunteers is always expected to fully equal the demand," replied Dr. Leete. "It is the business of the administration to see that this is the case. The rate of volunteering for each trade is closely watched. If there be a noticeably greater excess of volunteers over men needed in any trade, it is inferred that the trade offers greater attractions than others. On the other hand, if the number of volunteers for a trade tends to drop below the demand, it is inferred that it is thought more arduous. It is the business of the administration to seek constantly to equalize the attractions of the trades, so far as the conditions of labor in them are concerned, so that all trades shall be equally attractive to persons having natural tastes for them. This is done by making the hours of labor in different trades to differ according to their arduousness. The lighter trades, prosecuted under the most agreeable circumstances, have in this way the longest hours, while an arduous trade, such as mining, has very short hours. There is no theory, no *a priori* rule, by which the respective attractiveness of industries is determined. The administration, in taking burdens off one class of workers and adding them to other classes, simply follows the fluctuations of opinion among the workers themselves as indicated by the rate of men volunteering. The principle is that no man's work ought to be, on the whole, harder for him than any other man's for him, the workers themselves to be the judges. There are no limits to the application of this rule. If any particular occupation is in itself so arduous or so oppressive that, in order to induce volunteers, the day's work in it had to be reduced to ten minutes, it would be done. If, even then, no man was willing to do it, it would remain undone. But of course, in point of fact, a moderate reduction in the hours of labor, or addition of other privileges, suffices to secure all needed volunteers for any occupation necessary to men. If, indeed, the unavoidable difficulties and dangers of such a necessary pursuit were so great that no inducement of compensating advantages would overcome men's repugnance to it, the administration would only need to take it out of the common order of occupations by declaring it 'extra hazardous,' and those who pursued it especially worthy of the national gratitude, to be overrun with volunteers. Our young men are very greedy of honor, and do not let slip such opportunities. Of course you will see that dependence on the purely voluntary choice of avocations involves the abolition in all of anything like unhygienic conditions or special peril to life and limb. Health and safety are conditions common to all industries. The nation does not maim and slaughter its workmen by thousands, as did the private capitalists and corporations of your day."

"When there are more who want to enter a particular trade than there is room for, how do you decide between the applicants?" I inquired.

"Preference is given to those who have acquired the most knowledge of the trade they wish to follow. No man, however, who through successive years remains persistent in his desire to show what he can do at any particular trade, is in the end denied an opportunity. Meanwhile, if a man cannot at first win entrance into the business he prefers, he has usually one or more alternative preferences, pursuits for which he has some degree of aptitude, although not the highest. Every one, indeed, is expected to study his aptitudes so as to have not only a first choice as to occupation, but a second or third, so that if, either at the outset of his career or subsequently, owing to the progress of invention or changes in demand, he is unable to follow his first vocation, he can still find reasonably congenial employment. This principle of secondary choices as to occupation is quite important in our system. I should add, in reference to the counter-possibility of some sudden failure of volunteers in a particular trade, or some sudden necessity of an increased force, that the administration, while depending on the voluntary system for filling up the trades as a rule, holds always in reserve the power to call for special volunteers, or draft any force needed from any quarter. Generally, however, all needs of this sort can be met by details from the class of unskilled or common laborers." *

"How is this class of common laborers recruited?" I asked. "Surely nobody voluntarily enters that."

"It is the grade to which all new recruits belong for the first three years of their service. It is not till after this period, during which he is assignable to any work at the discretion of his superiors, that the young man is allowed to elect a special avocation. These three years of stringent discipline none are exempt from, and very glad our young men are to pass from this severe school into the comparative liberty of the trades. If a man were so stupid as to have no choice as to occupation, he would simply remain a common laborer; but such cases, as you may suppose, are not common."

"Having once elected and entered on a trade or occupation," I remarked, "I suppose he has to stick to it the rest of his life."

"Not necessarily," replied Dr. Leete; "while frequent and

* [In the first edition the preceding paragraph reads: "Preference is given to those with the best general records in their preliminary service as unskilled laborers, and as youths in their educational course. No man, however, who through successive years remains persistent in his desire to show what he can do at any particular trade, is in the end denied an opportunity. I should add, in reference to the counter-possibility of some sudden failure of volunteers in a particular trade, or some sudden necessity of an increased force, that the administration, while depending on the voluntary system for filling up the trades as a rule, holds always in reserve the power to call for special volunteers, or draft any force needed from any quarter. Generally, however, all needs of this sort can be met by details from the class of unskilled or common laborers."]

merely capricious changes of occupation are not encouraged or even permitted, every worker is allowed, of course, under certain regulations and in accordance with the exigencies of the service, to volunteer for another industry which he thinks would suit him better than his first choice. In this case his application is received just as if he were volunteering for the first time, and on the same terms. Not only this, but a worker may likewise, under suitable regulations and not too frequently, obtain a transfer to an establishment of the same industry in another part of the country which for any reason he may prefer. Under your system a discontented man could indeed leave his work at will, but he left his means of support at the same time, and took his chances as to future livelihood. We find that the number of men who wish to abandon an accustomed occupation for a new one, and old friends and associations for strange ones, is small. It is only the poorer sort of workmen who desire to change even as frequently as our regulations permit. Of course transfers or discharges, when health demands them, are always given." *

"As an industrial system, I should think this might be extremely efficient," I said, "but I don't see that it makes any provision for the professional classes, the men who serve the nation with brains instead of hands. Of course you can't get along without the brain-workers. How, then, are they selected from those who are to serve as farmers and mechanics? That must require a very delicate sort of sifting process, I should say."

"So it does," replied Dr. Leete; "the most delicate possible test is needed here, and so we leave the question whether a man shall be a brain or hand worker entirely to him to settle. At the end of the term of three years as a common laborer, which every man must serve, it is for him to choose, in accordance to his natural tastes, whether he will fit himself for an art or profession, or be a farmer or mechanic. If he feels that he can do better work with his brains than his muscles, he finds every facility provided for testing the reality of his supposed

* [The preceding one-and-one-half paragraphs, beginning with "These three years of stringent discipline none are exempt from," were added in the second edition.]

bent, of cultivating it, and if fit, of pursuing it as his avocation. The schools of technology, of medicine, of art, of music, of histrionics, and of higher liberal learning are always open to aspirants without condition."

"Are not the schools flooded with young men whose only motive is to avoid work?"

Dr. Leete smiled a little grimly.

"No one is at all likely to enter the professional schools for the purpose of avoiding work, I assure you," he said. "They are intended for those with special aptitude for the branches they teach, and any one without it would find it easier to do double hours at his trade than try to keep up with the classes. Of course many honestly mistake their vocation, and, finding themselves unequal to the requirements of the schools, drop out and return to the industrial service; no discredit attaches to such persons, for the public policy is to encourage all to develop suspected talents which only actual tests can prove the reality of. The professional and scientific schools of your day depended on the patronage of their pupils for support, and the practice appears to have been common of giving diplomas to unfit persons, who afterwards found their way into the professions. Our schools are national institutions, and to have passed their tests is a proof of special abilities not to be questioned.

"This opportunity for a professional training," the doctor continued, "remains open to every man till the age of thirty* is reached, after which students are not received, as there would remain too brief a period before the age of discharge in which to serve the nation in their professions. In your day young men had to choose their professions very young, and therefore, in a large proportion of instances, wholly mistook their vocations. It is recognized nowadays that the natural aptitudes of some are later than those of others in developing, and therefore, while the choice of profession may be made as early as twenty-four, it remains open for six years longer."†

A question which had a dozen times before been on my lips

* [In the first edition the age is "thirty-five."]

† [The first edition reads: "for eleven years longer. I should add that the right of transfer, under proper restrictions, from a trade first chosen to one preferred later in life, also remains open to a man till thirty-five."]

now found utterance, a question which touched upon what, in my time, had been regarded the most vital difficulty in the way of any final settlement of the industrial problem. "It is an extraordinary thing," I said, "that you should not yet have said a word about the method of adjusting wages. Since the nation is the sole employer, the government must fix the rate of wages and determine just how much everybody shall earn, from the doctors to the diggers. All I can say is, that this plan would never have worked with us, and I don't see how it can now unless human nature has changed. In my day, nobody was satisfied with his wages or salary. Even if he felt he received enough, he was sure his neighbor had too much, which was as bad. If the universal discontent on this subject, instead of being dissipated in curses and strikes directed against innumerable employers, could have been concentrated upon one, and that the government, the strongest ever devised would not have seen two pay days."

Dr. Leete laughed heartily.

"Very true, very true," he said, "a general strike would most probably have followed the first pay day, and a strike directed against a government is a revolution."

"How, then, do you avoid a revolution every pay day?" I demanded. "Has some prodigious philosopher devised a new system of calculus satisfactory to all for determining the exact and comparative value of all sorts of service, whether by brawn or brain, by hand or voice, by ear or eye? Or has human nature itself changed, so that no man looks upon his own things but 'every man on the things of his neighbor?' One or the other of these events must be the explanation."

"Neither one nor the other, however, is," was my host's laughing response. "And now, Mr. West," he continued, "you must remember that you are my patient as well as my guest, and permit me to prescribe sleep for you before we have any more conversation. It is after three o'clock."

"The prescription is, no doubt, a wise one," I said; "I only hope it can be filled."

"I will see to that," the doctor replied, and he did, for he gave me a wineglass of something or other which sent me to sleep as soon as my head touched the pillow.

Chapter VIII

WHEN I awoke I felt greatly refreshed, and lay a considerable time in a dozing state, enjoying the sensation of bodily comfort. The experiences of the day previous, my waking to find myself in the year 2000, the sight of the new Boston, my host and his family, and the wonderful things I had heard, were a blank in my memory. I thought I was in my bed-chamber at home, and the half-dreaming, half-waking fancies which passed before my mind related to the incidents and experiences of my former life. Dreamily I reviewed the incidents of Decoration Day, my trip in company with Edith and her parents to Mount Auburn, and my dining with them on our return to the city. I recalled how extremely well Edith had looked, and from that fell to thinking of our marriage; but scarcely had my imagination begun to develop this delightful theme than my waking dream was cut short by the recollection of the letter I had received the night before from the builder announcing that the new strikes might postpone indefinitely the completion of the new house. The chagrin which this recollection brought with it effectually roused me. I remembered that I had an appointment with the builder at eleven o'clock, to discuss the strike, and opening my eyes, looked up at the clock at the foot of my bed to see what time it was. But no clock met my glance, and what was more, I instantly perceived that I was not in my room. Starting up on my couch, I stared wildly round the strange apartment.

I think it must have been many seconds that I sat up thus in bed staring about, without being able to regain the clew to my personal identity. I was no more able to distinguish myself from pure being during those moments than we may suppose a soul in the rough to be before it has received the ear-marks, the individualizing touches which make it a person. Strange that the sense of this inability should be such anguish! but so we are constituted. There are no words for the mental torture I endured during this helpless, eyeless groping for myself in a boundless void. No other experience of the mind gives probably anything like the sense of absolute intellectual arrest from the loss of a mental fulcrum, a starting point of thought, which comes during such a momentary obscuration of the sense of one's identity. I trust I may never know what it is again.

I do not know how long this condition had lasted,—it seemed an interminable time,—when, like a flash, the recollection of everything came back to me. I remembered who and where I was, and how I had come here, and that these scenes as of the life of yesterday which had been passing before my mind concerned a generation long, long ago mouldered to dust. Leaping from bed, I stood in the middle of the room clasping my temples with all my might between my hands to keep them from bursting. Then I fell prone on the couch, and, burying my face in the pillow, lay without motion. The reaction which was inevitable, from the mental elation, the fever of the intellect that had been the first effect of my tremendous experience, had arrived. The emotional crisis which had awaited the full realization of my actual position, and all that it implied, was upon me, and with set teeth and laboring chest, gripping the bedstead with frenzied strength, I lay there and fought for my sanity. In my mind, all had broken loose, habits of feeling, associations of thought, ideas of persons and things, all had dissolved and lost coherence and were seething together in apparently irretrievable chaos. There were no rallying points, nothing was left stable. There only remained the will, and was any human will strong enough to say to such a weltering sea, "Peace, be still"? I dared not think. Every effort to reason upon what had befallen me, and realize what it implied, set up an intolerable swimming of the brain. The idea that I was two persons, that my identity was double, began to fascinate me with its simple solution of my experience.

I knew that I was on the verge of losing my mental balance. If I lay there thinking, I was doomed. Diversion of some sort I must have, at least the diversion of physical exertion. I sprang up, and, hastily dressing, opened the door of my room and went down-stairs. The hour was very early, it being not yet fairly light, and I found no one in the lower part of the house. There was a hat in the hall, and, opening the front door, which was fastened with a slightness indicating that burglary was not among the perils of the modern Boston, I found myself on the street. For two hours I walked or ran through the streets of the city, visiting most quarters of the peninsular part of the town. None but an antiquarian who knows something of the contrast which the Boston of to-day offers to the Boston of the nineteenth century can begin to appreciate what a series of bewildering surprises I underwent during that time. Viewed from the house-top the day before, the city had indeed appeared strange to me, but that was only in its general aspect. How complete the change had been I first realized now that I walked the streets. The few old landmarks which still remained only intensified this effect, for without them I might have imagined myself in a foreign town. A man may leave his native city in childhood, and return fifty years later, perhaps, to find it transformed in many features. He is astonished, but he is not bewildered. He is aware of a great lapse of time, and of changes likewise occurring in himself mean-while. He but dimly recalls the city as he knew it when a child. But remember that there was no sense of any lapse of time with me. So far as my consciousness was concerned, it was but yes-terday, but a few hours, since I had walked these streets in which scarcely a feature had escaped a complete metamorphosis. The mental image of the old city was so fresh and strong that it did not yield to the impression of the actual city, but contended with it, so that it was first one and then the other which seemed the more unreal. There was nothing I saw which was not blurred in this way, like the faces of a composite photograph.

Finally, I stood again at the door of the house from which I had come out. My feet must have instinctively brought me back to the site of my old home, for I had no clear idea of returning thither. It was no more homelike to me than any other spot in this city of a strange generation, nor were its inmates less utterly and necessarily strangers than all the other men and women now on the earth. Had the door of the house been locked, I should have been reminded by its resistance that I had no object in entering, and turned away, but it yielded to my hand, and advancing with uncertain steps through the hall, I entered one of the apartments opening from it. Throwing myself into a chair, I covered my burning eyeballs with my hands to shut out the horror of strangeness. My mental confusion was so intense as to produce actual nausea. The anguish of those moments, during which my brain seemed melting, or the abjectness of my sense of helplessness, how can I describe? In my despair I groaned aloud. I began to feel that unless some help should come I was about to lose my mind. And just then it did come. I heard the rustle of drapery, and looked up. Edith Leete was standing before me. Her beautiful face was full of the most poignant sympathy.

"Oh, what is the matter, Mr. West?" she said. "I was here when you came in. I saw how dreadfully distressed you looked, and when I heard you groan, I could not keep silent. What has happened to you? Where have you been? Can't I do something for you?"

Perhaps she involuntarily held out her hands in a gesture of compassion as she spoke. At any rate I had caught them in my own and was clinging to them with an impulse as instinctive as that which prompts the drowning man to seize upon and cling to the rope which is thrown him as he sinks for the last time. As I looked up into her compassionate face and her eyes moist with pity, my brain ceased to whirl. The tender human sympathy which thrilled in the soft pressure of her fingers had brought me the support I needed. Its effect to calm and soothe was like that of some wonder-working elixir.

"God bless you," I said, after a few moments. "He must have sent you to me just now. I think I was in danger of going crazy if you had not come." At this the tears came into her eyes.

"Oh, Mr. West!" she cried. "How heartless you must have thought us! How could we leave you to yourself so long! But it is over now, is it not? You are better, surely."

"Yes," I said, "thanks to you. If you will not go away quite yet, I shall be myself soon."

"Indeed I will not go away," she said, with a little quiver of her face, more expressive of her sympathy than a volume of words. "You must not think us so heartless as we seemed in leaving you so by yourself. I scarcely slept last night, for thinking how strange your waking would be this morning; but father said you would sleep till late. He said that it would be better not to show too much sympathy with you at first, but to try to divert your thoughts and make you feel that you were among friends."

"You have indeed made me feel that," I answered. "But you see it is a good deal of a jolt to drop a hundred years, and although I did not seem to feel it so much last night, I have had very odd sensations this morning." While I held her hands and kept my eyes on her face, I could already even jest a little at my plight.

"No one thought of such a thing as your going out in the city alone so early in the morning," she went on. "Oh, Mr. West, where have you been?"

Then I told her of my morning's experience, from my first waking till the moment I had looked up to see her before me, just as I have told it here. She was overcome by distressful pity during the recital, and, though I had released one of her hands, did not try to take from me the other, seeing, no doubt, how much good it did me to hold it. "I can think a little what this feeling must [have] been like," she said. "It must have been terrible. And to think you were left alone to struggle with it! Can you ever forgive us?"

"But it is gone now. You have driven it quite away for the present," I said.

"You will not let it return again," she queried anxiously.

"I can't quite say that," I replied. "It might be too early to say that, considering how strange everything will still be to me."

"But you will not try to contend with it alone again, at least," she persisted. "Promise that you will come to us, and let us sympathize with you, and try to help you. Perhaps we can't do much, but it will surely be better than to try to bear such feelings alone."

"I will come to you if you will let me," I said.

"Oh yes, yes, I beg you will," she said eagerly. "I would do anything to help you that I could."

"All you need do is to be sorry for me, as you seem to be now," I replied.

"It is understood, then," she said, smiling with wet eyes, "that you are to come and tell me next time, and not run all over Boston among strangers."

This assumption that we were not strangers seemed scarcely strange, so near within these few minutes had my trouble and her sympathetic tears brought us.

"I will promise, when you come to me," she added, with an expression of charming archness, passing, as she continued, into one of enthusiasm, "to seem as sorry for you as you wish, but you must not for a moment suppose that I am really sorry for you at all, or that I think you will long be sorry for yourself. I know, as well as I know that the world now is heaven compared with what it was in your day, that the only feeling you will have after a little while will be one of thankfulness to God that your life in that age was so strangely cut off, to be returned to you in this."

Chapter IX

D R. and Mrs. Leete were evidently not a little startled to learn, when they presently appeared, that I had been all over the city alone that morning, and it was apparent that they were agreeably surprised to see that I seemed so little agitated after the experience.

"Your stroll could scarcely have failed to be a very interesting one," said Mrs. Leete, as we sat down to table soon after. "You must have seen a good many new things."

"I saw very little that was not new," I replied. "But I think what surprised me as much as anything was not to find any stores on Washington Street, or any banks on State. What have you done with the merchants and bankers? Hung them all, perhaps, as the anarchists wanted to do in my day?"

"Not so bad as that," replied Dr. Leete. "We have simply dispensed with them. Their functions are obsolete in the modern world."

"Who sells you things when you want to buy them?" I inquired.

"There is neither selling nor buying nowadays; the distribution of goods is effected in another way. As to the bankers, having no money we have no use for those gentry."

"Miss Leete," said I, turning to Edith, "I am afraid that your father is making sport of me. I don't blame him, for the temptation my innocence offers must be extraordinary. But, really, there are limits to my credulity as to possible alterations in the social system."

"Father has no idea of jesting, I am sure," she replied, with a reassuring smile.

The conversation took another turn then, the point of ladies' fashions in the nineteenth century being raised, if I remember rightly, by Mrs. Leete, and it was not till after breakfast, when the doctor had invited me up to the house-top, which appeared to be a favorite resort of his, that he recurred to the subject.

"You were surprised," he said, "at my saying that we got along without money or trade, but a moment's reflection will show that trade existed and money was needed in your day simply because the business of production was left in private hands, and that, consequently, they are superfluous now."

"I do not at once see how that follows," I replied.

"It is very simple," said Dr. Leete. "When innumerable different and independent persons produced the various things needful to life and comfort, endless exchanges between individuals were requisite in order that they might supply themselves with what they desired. These exchanges constituted trade, and money was essential as their medium. But as soon as the nation became the sole producer of all sorts of commodities, there was no need of exchanges between individuals that they might get what they required. Everything was procurable from one source, and nothing could be procured anywhere else. A system of direct distribution from the national storehouses took the place of trade, and for this money was unnecessary."

"How is this distribution managed?" I asked.

"On the simplest possible plan," replied Dr. Leete. "A credit corresponding to his share of the annual product of the nation is given to every citizen on the public books at the beginning of each year, and a credit card issued him with which he procures at the public storehouses, found in every community, whatever he desires whenever he desires it. This arrangement, you will see, totally obviates the necessity for business transactions of any sort between individuals and consumers. Perhaps you would like to see what our credit-cards are like.

"You observe," he pursued as I was curiously examining the piece of pasteboard he gave me, "that this card is issued for a certain number of dollars. We have kept the old word, but not the substance. The term, as we use it, answers to no real thing, but merely serves as an algebraical symbol for comparing the values of products with one another. For this purpose they are all priced in dollars and cents, just as in your day. The value of what I procure on this card is checked off by the clerk, who pricks out of these tiers of squares the price of what I order."

"If you wanted to buy something of your neighbor, could you transfer part of your credit to him as consideration?" I inquired.

"In the first place," replied Dr. Leete, "our neighbors have nothing to sell us, but in any event our credit would not be transferable, being strictly personal. Before the nation could even think of honoring any such transfer as you speak of, it would be bound to inquire into all the circumstances of the transaction, so as to be able to guarantee its absolute equity. It would have been reason enough, had there been no other, for abolishing money, that its possession was no indication of rightful title to it. In the hands of the man who had stolen it or murdered for it, it was as good as in those which had earned it by industry. People nowadays interchange gifts and favors out of friendship, but buying and selling is considered absolutely inconsistent with the mutual benevolence and disinterestedness which should prevail between citizens and the sense of community of interest which supports our social system. According to our ideas, buying and selling is essentially anti-social in all its tendencies. It is an education in self-seeking at the expense of others, and no society whose citizens are trained in such a school can possibly rise above a very low grade of civilization."

"What if you have to spend more than your card in any one year?" I asked.

"The provision is so ample that we are more likely not to spend it all," replied Dr. Leete. "But if extraordinary expenses should exhaust it, we can obtain a limited advance on the next year's credit, though this practice is not encouraged, and a heavy discount is charged to check it. Of course if a man showed himself a reckless spendthrift he would receive his allowance monthly or weekly instead of yearly, or if necessary not be permitted to handle it all." [*]

"If you don't spend your allowance, I suppose it accumulates?"

"That is also permitted to a certain extent when a special out-

[*] [This sentence was added in the second edition.]

lay is anticipated. But unless notice to the contrary is given, it is presumed that the citizen who does not fully expend his credit did not have occasion to do so, and the balance is turned into the general surplus."

"Such a system does not encourage saving habits on the part of citizens," I said.

"It is not intended to," was the reply. "The nation is rich, and does not wish the people to deprive themselves of any good thing. In your day, men were bound to lay up goods and money against coming failure of the means of support and for their children. This necessity made parsimony a virtue. But now it would have no such laudable object, and, having lost its utility, it has ceased to be regarded as a virtue. No man any more has any care for the morrow, either for himself or his children, for the nation guarantees the nurture, education, and comfortable maintenance of every citizen from the cradle to the grave."

"That is a sweeping guarantee!" I said. "What certainty can there be that the value of a man's labor will recompense the nation for its outlay on him? On the whole, society may be able to support all its members, but some must earn less than enough for their support, and others more; and that brings us back once more to the wages question, on which you have hitherto said nothing. It was at just this point, if you remember, that our talk ended last evening; and I say again, as I did then, that here I should suppose a national industrial system like yours would find its main difficulty. How, I ask once more, can you adjust satisfactorily the comparative wages or remuneration of the multitude of avocations, so unlike and so incommensurable, which are necessary for the service of society? In our day the market rate determined the price of labor of all sorts, as well as of goods. The employer paid as little as he could, and the worker got as much. It was not a pretty system ethically, I admit; but it did, at least, furnish us a rough and ready formula for settling a question which must be settled ten thousand times a day if the world was ever going to get forward. There seemed to us no other practicable way of doing it."

"Yes," replied Dr. Leete, "it was the only practicable way

under a system which made the interests of every individual antagonistic to those of every other; but it would have been a pity if humanity could never have devised a better plan, for yours was simply the application to the mutual relations of men of the devil's maxim, 'Your necessity is my opportunity.' The reward of any service depended not upon its difficulty, danger, or hardship, for throughout the world it seems that the most perilous, severe, and repulsive labor was done by the worst paid classes; but solely upon the strait of those who needed the service."

"All that is conceded," I said. "But, with all its defects, the plan of settling prices by the market rate was a practical plan; and I cannot conceive what satisfactory substitute you can have devised for it. The government being the only possible employer, there is of course no labor market or market rate. Wages of all sorts must be arbitrarily fixed by the government. I cannot imagine a more complex and delicate function than that must be, or one, however performed, more certain to breed universal dissatisfaction."

"I beg your pardon," replied Dr. Leete, "but I think you exaggerate the difficulty. Suppose a board of fairly sensible men were charged with settling the wages for all sorts of trades under a system which, like ours, guaranteed employment to all, while permitting the choice of avocation. Don't you see that, however unsatisfactory the first adjustment might be, the mistakes would soon correct themselves? The favored trades would have too many volunteers, and those discriminated against would lack them till the errors were set right. But this is aside from the purpose, for, though this plan would, I fancy, be practicable enough, it is no part of our system."

"How, then, do you regulate wages?" I once more asked.

Dr. Leete did not reply till after several moments of meditative silence. "I know, of course," he finally said, "enough of the old order of things to understand just what you mean by that question; and yet the present order is so utterly different at this point that I am a little at loss how to answer you best. You ask me how we regulate wages; I can only reply that there is no idea in the modern social economy which at all corresponds with what was meant by wages in your day."

"I suppose you mean that you have no money to pay wages in," said I. "But the credit given the worker at the government storehouse answers to his wages with us. How is the amount of the credit given respectively to the workers in different lines determined? By what title does the individual claim his particular share? What is the basis of allotment?"

"His title," replied Dr. Leete, "is his humanity. The basis of his claim is the fact that he is a man."

"The fact that he is a man!" I repeated incredulously. "Do you possibly mean that all have the same share?"

"Most assuredly."

The readers of this book never having practically known any other arrangement, or perhaps very carefully considered the historical accounts of former epochs in which a very different system prevailed, cannot be expected to appreciate the stupor of amazement into which Dr. Leete's simple statement plunged me.

"You see," he said, smiling, "that it is not merely that we have no money to pay wages in, but, as I said, we have nothing at all answering to your idea of wages."

By this time I had pulled myself together sufficiently to voice some of the criticisms which, man of the nineteenth century as I was, came uppermost in my mind, upon this to me astounding arrangement. "Some men do twice the work of others!" I exclaimed. "Are the clever workmen content with a plan that ranks them with the indifferent?"

"We leave no possible ground for any complaint of injustice," replied Dr. Leete, "by requiring precisely the same measure of service from all."

"How can you do that, I should like to know, when no two men's powers are the same?"

"Nothing could be simpler," was Dr. Leete's reply. "We require of each that he shall make the same effort; that is, we demand of him the best service it is in his power to give."

"And supposing all do the best they can," I answered, "the

amount of the product resulting is twice greater from one man than from another."

"Very true," replied Dr. Leete; "but the amount of the resulting product has nothing whatever to do with the question, which is one of desert. Desert is a moral question, and the amount of the product a material quantity. It would be an extraordinary sort of logic which should try to determine a moral question by a material standard. The amount of the effort alone is pertinent to the question of desert. All men who do their best, do the same. A man's endowments, however godlike, merely fix the measure of his duty. The man of great endowments who does not do all he might, though he may do more than a man of small endowments who does his best, is deemed a less deserving worker than the latter, and dies a debtor to his fellows. The Creator sets men's tasks for them by the faculties he gives them; we simply exact their fulfillment."

"No doubt that is a very fine philosophy," I said; "nevertheless it seems hard that the man who produces twice as much as another, even if both do their best, should have only the same share."

"Does it, indeed, seem so to you?" responded Dr. Leete. "Now, do you know, that seems very curious to me? The way it strikes people nowadays is, that a man who can produce twice as much as another with the same effort, instead of being rewarded for doing so, ought to be punished if he does not do so. In the nineteenth century, when a horse pulled a heavier load than a goat, I suppose you rewarded him. Now, we should have whipped him soundly if he had not, on the ground that, being much stronger, he ought to. It is singular how ethical standards change." The doctor said this with such a twinkle in his eye that I was obliged to laugh.

"I suppose," I said, "that the real reason that we rewarded men for their endowments, while we considered those of horses and goats merely as fixing the service to be severally required of them, was that the animals, not being reasoning beings, naturally did the best they could, whereas men could only be induced to do so by rewarding them according to the amount of their product. That brings me to ask why, unless human nature has mightily changed in a hundred years, you are not under the same necessity."

"We are," replied Dr. Leete. "I don't think there has been any change in human nature in that respect since your day. It is still so constituted that special incentives in the form of prizes, and advantages to be gained, are requisite to call out the best endeavors of the average man in any direction."

"But what inducement," I asked, "can a man have to put forth his best endeavors when, however much or little he accomplishes, his income remains the same? High characters may be moved by devotion to the common welfare under such a system, but does not the average man tend to rest back on his oar, reasoning that it is of no use to make a special effort, since the effort will not increase his income, nor its withholding diminish it?"

"Does it then really seem to you," answered my companion, "that human nature is insensible to any motives save fear of want and love of luxury, that you should expect security and equality of livelihood to leave them without possible incentives to effort? Your contemporaries did not really think so, though they might fancy they did. When it was a question of the grandest class of efforts, the most absolute self-devotion, they depended on quite other incentives. Not higher wages, but honor and the hope of men's gratitude, patriotism and the inspiration of duty, were the motives which they set before their soldiers when it was a question of dying for the nation, and never was there an age of the world when those motives did not call out what is best and noblest in men. And not only this, but when you come to analyze the love of money which was the general impulse to effort in your day, you find that the dread of want and desire of luxury was but one of several motives which the pursuit of money represented; the others, and with many the more influential, being desire of power, of social position, and reputation for ability and success. So you see that though we have abolished poverty and the fear of it, and inordinate luxury with the hope of it, we have not touched the greater part of the motives which underlay the love of money in former times, or any of those which prompted the supremer sorts of effort. The coarser motives, which no longer move us, have been replaced by higher motives wholly unknown to the mere wage earners of your age. Now that industry of whatever sort is no longer self-service, but service of the nation, patriotism, passion for humanity, impel the worker as in your day they did the soldier. The army of industry is an army, not alone by virtue of its perfect organization, but by reason also of the ardor of self-devotion which animates its members.

"But as you used to supplement the motives of patriotism with the love of glory, in order to stimulate the valor of your soldiers, so do we. Based as our industrial system is on the principle of requiring the same unit of effort from every man, that is, the best he can do, you will see that the means by which we spur the workers to do their best must be a very essential part of our scheme. With us, diligence in the national service is the sole and certain way to public repute, social distinction, and official power. The value of a man's services to society fixes his rank in it. Compared with the effect of our social arrangements in impelling men to be zealous in business, we deem the object-lessons of biting poverty and wanton luxury on which you depended a device as weak and uncertain as it was barbaric. The lust of honor even in your sordid day notoriously impelled men to more desperate effort than the love of money could." *

"I should be extremely interested," I said, "to learn something of what these social arrangements are."

"The scheme in its details," replied the doctor, "is of course very elaborate, for it underlies the entire organization of our industrial army; but a few words will give you a general idea of it."

At this moment our talk was charmingly interrupted by the emergence upon the aerial platform where we sat of Edith Leete. She was dressed for the street, and had come to speak to her father about some commission she was to do for him.

"By the way, Edith," he exclaimed, as she was about to leave

* [This sentence was added in the second edition.]

us to ourselves, "I wonder if Mr. West would not be interested in visiting the store with you? I have been telling him something about our system of distribution, and perhaps he might like to see it in practical operation."

"My daughter," he added, turning to me, "is an indefatigable shopper, and can tell you more about the stores than I can."

The proposition was naturally very agreeable to me, and Edith being good enough to say that she should be glad to have my company, we left the house together.

Chapter X

"IF I am going to explain our way of shopping to you," said my companion, as we walked along the street, "you must explain your way to me. I have never been able to understand it from all I have read on the subject. For example, when you had such a vast number of shops, each with its different assortment, how could a lady ever settle upon any purchase till she had visited all the shops? for, until she had, she could not know what there was to choose from."

"It was as you suppose; that was the only way she could know," I replied.

"Father calls me an indefatigable shopper, but I should soon be a very fatigued one if I had to do as they did," was Edith's laughing comment.

"The loss of time in going from shop to shop was indeed a waste which the busy bitterly complained of," I said; "but as for the ladies of the idle class, though they complained also, I think the system was really a godsend by furnishing a device to kill time."

"But say there were a thousand shops in a city, hundreds, perhaps, of the same sort, how could even the idlest find time to make their rounds?"

"They really could not visit all, of course," I replied. "Those who did a great deal of buying, learned in time where they might expect to find what they wanted. This class had made a science of the specialties of the shops, and bought at advantage, always getting the most and best for the least money. It required, however, long experience to acquire this knowledge. Those who were too busy, or bought too little to gain it, took their chances and were generally unfortunate, getting the least and worst for

the most money. It was the merest chance if persons not experienced in shopping received the value of their money."

"But why did you put up with such a shockingly inconvenient
arrangement when you saw its faults so plainly?" Edith asked me.

"It was like all our social arrangements," I replied. "You can
see their faults scarcely more plainly than we did, but we saw
no remedy for them."

"Here we are at the store of our ward," said Edith, as we
turned in at the great portal of one of the magnificent public
buildings I had observed in my morning walk. There was nothing
in the exterior aspect of the edifice to suggest a store to a representative of the nineteenth century. There was no display of
goods in the great windows, or any device to advertise wares,
or attract custom. Nor was there any sort of sign or legend on
the front of the building to indicate the character of the business
carried on there; but instead, above the portal, standing out from
the front of the building, a majestic life-size group of statuary, the
central figure of which was a female ideal of Plenty, with her
cornucopia. Judging from the composition of the throng passing
in and out, about the same proportion of the sexes among shop-
pers obtained as in the nineteenth century. As we entered, Edith
said that there was one of these great distributing establishments
in each ward of the city, so that no residence was more than
five or ten minutes' walk from one of them. It was the first interior
of a twentieth-century public building that I had ever beheld,
and the spectacle naturally impressed me deeply. I was in a
vast hall full of light, received not alone from the windows on
all sides, but from the dome, the point of which was a hundred
feet above. Beneath it, in the centre of the hall, a magnificent
fountain played, cooling the atmosphere to a delicious freshness
with its spray. The walls and ceiling were frescoed in mellow
tints, calculated to soften without absorbing the light which
flooded the interior. Around the fountain was a space occupied
with chairs and sofas, on which many persons were seated con-
versing. Legends on the walls all about the hall indicated to
what classes of commodities the counters below were devoted.
Edith directed her steps towards one of these, where samples

of muslin of a bewildering variety were displayed, and proceeded to inspect them.

"Where is the clerk?" I asked, for there was no one behind the counter, and no one seemed coming to attend to the customer.

"I have no need of the clerk yet," said Edith; "I have not made my selection."

"It was the principal business of clerks to help people to make their selections in my day," I replied.

"What! To tell people what they wanted?"

"Yes; and oftener to induce them to buy what they didn't want."

"But did not ladies find that very impertinent?" Edith asked, wonderingly. "What concern could it possibly be to the clerks whether people bought or not?"

"It was their sole concern," I answered. "They were hired for the purpose of getting rid of the goods, and were expected to do their utmost, short of the use of force, to compass that end."

"Ah, yes! How stupid I am to forget!" said Edith. "The storekeeper and his clerks depended for their livelihood on selling the goods in your day. Of course that is all different now. The goods are the nation's. They are here for those who want them, and it is the business of the clerks to wait on people and take their orders; but it is not the interest of the clerk or the nation to dispose of a yard or a pound of anything to anybody who does not want it." She smiled as she added, "How exceedingly odd it must have seemed to have clerks trying to induce one to take what one did not want, or was doubtful about!"

"But even a twentieth-century clerk might make himself useful in giving you information about the goods, though he did not tease you to buy them," I suggested.

"No," said Edith, "that is not the business of the clerk. These printed cards, for which the government authorities are responsible, give us all the information we can possibly need."

I saw then that there was fastened to each sample a card containing in succinct form a complete statement of the make and materials of the goods and all its qualities, as well as price, leaving absolutely no point to hang a question on.

"The clerk has, then, nothing to say about the goods he sells?" I said.

"Nothing at all. It is not necessary that he should know or profess to know anything about them. Courtesy and accuracy in taking orders are all that are required of him."

"What a prodigious amount of lying that simple arrangement saves!" I ejaculated.

"Do you mean that all the clerks misrepresented their goods in your day?" Edith asked.

"God forbid that I should say so!" I replied, "for there were many who did not, and they were entitled to especial credit, for when one's livelihood and that of his wife and babies depended on the amount of goods he could dispose of, the temptation to deceive the customer—or let him deceive himself—was wellnigh overwhelming. But, Miss Leete, I am distracting you from your task with my talk."

"Not at all. I have made my selections." With that she touched a button, and in a moment a clerk appeared. He took down her order on a tablet with a pencil which made two copies, of which he gave one to her, and enclosing the counterpart in a small receptacle, dropped it into a transmitting tube.

"The duplicate of the order," said Edith as she turned away from the counter, after the clerk had punched the value of her purchase out of the credit card she gave him, "is given to the purchaser, so that any mistakes in filling it can be easily traced and rectified."

"You were very quick about your selections," I said. "May I ask how you knew that you might not have found something to suit you better in some of the other stores? But probably you are required to buy in your own district."

"Oh, no," she replied. "We buy where we please, though naturally most often near home. But I should have gained nothing by visiting other stores. The assortment in all is exactly the same, representing as it does in each case samples of all the varieties produced or imported by the United States. That is why one can decide quickly, and never need visit two stores."

"And is this merely a sample store? I see no clerks cutting off goods or marking bundles."

"All our stores are sample stores, except as to a few classes of articles. The goods, with these exceptions, are all at the great central warehouse of the city, to which they are shipped directly from the producers. We order from the sample and the printed statement of texture, make, and qualities. The orders are sent to the warehouse, and the goods distributed from there."

"That must be a tremendous saving of handling," I said. "By our system, the manufacturer sold to the wholesaler, the wholesaler to the retailer, and the retailer to the consumer, and the goods had to be handled each time. You avoid one handling of the goods, and eliminate the retailer altogether, with his big profit and the army of clerks it goes to support. Why, Miss Leete, this store is merely the order department of a wholesale house, with no more than a wholesaler's complement of clerks. Under our system of handling the goods, persuading the customer to buy them, cutting them off, and packing them, ten clerks would not do what one does here. The saving must be enormous."

"I suppose so," said Edith, "but of course we have never known any other way. But, Mr. West, you must not fail to ask father to take you to the central warehouse some day, where they receive the orders from the different sample houses all over the city and parcel out and send the goods to their destinations. He took me there not long ago, and it was a wonderful sight. The system is certainly perfect; for example, over yonder in that sort of cage is the dispatching clerk. The orders, as they are taken by the different departments in the store, are sent by transmitters to him. His assistants sort them and enclose each class in a carrier-box by itself. The dispatching clerk has a dozen pneumatic transmitters before him answering to the general classes of goods, each communicating with the corresponding department at the warehouse. He drops the box of orders into the tube it calls for, and in a few moments later it drops on the proper desk in the warehouse, together with all the orders of the same sort from the other sample stores. The orders are read off, recorded, and sent to be filled, like lightning. The filling I thought the most interesting part. Bales of cloth are placed on spindles and turned by machinery, and the cutter, who also has a machine, works right through one bale after another till exhausted, when another man takes his place; and it is the same with those who fill the orders in any other staple. The packages are then delivered by larger tubes to the city districts, and thence distributed to the houses. You may understand how quickly it is all done when I tell you that my order will probably be at home sooner than I could have carried it from here."

"How do you manage in the thinly settled rural districts?" I asked.

"The system is the same," Edith explained; "the village sample shops are connected by transmitters with the central county warehouse, which may be twenty miles away. The transmission is so swift, though, that the time lost on the way is trifling. But, to save expense, in many counties one set of tubes connect several villages with the warehouse, and then there is time lost waiting for one another. Sometimes it is two or three hours before goods ordered are received. It was so where I was staying last summer, and I found it quite inconvenient.[1]

"There must be many other respects also, no doubt, in which the country stores are inferior to the city stores," I suggested.

"No," Edith answered, "they are otherwise precisely as good. The sample shop of the smallest village, just like this one, gives you your choice of all the varieties of goods the nation has, for the county warehouse draws on the same source as the city warehouse."

As we walked home I commented on the great variety in the size and cost of the houses. "How is it," I asked, "that this difference is consistent with the fact that all citizens have the same income?"

"Because," Edith explained, "although the income is the same, personal taste determines how the individual shall spend it. Some like fine horses; others, like myself, prefer pretty clothes; and still others want an elaborate table. The rents which the nation receives for these houses vary, according to size, elegance, and location, so that everybody can find something to suit. The larger houses are usually occupied by large families, in which there

---

[1] I am informed since the above is in type that this lack of perfection in the distributing service of some of the country districts is to be remedied, and that soon every village will have its own set of tubes.

are several to contribute to the rent; while small families, like ours, find smaller houses more convenient and economical. It is a matter of taste and convenience wholly. I have read that in old times pople often kept up establishments and did other things which they could not afford for ostentation, to make people think them richer than they were. Was it really so, Mr. West?"

"I shall have to admit that it was," I replied.

"Well, you see, it could not be so nowadays; for everybody's income is known, and it is known that what is spent one way must be saved another."

Chapter XI

W HEN we arrived home, Dr. Leete had not yet returned, and Mrs. Leete was not visible. "Are you fond of music, Mr. West?" Edith asked.

I assured her that it was half of life, according to my notion.

"I ought to apologize for inquiring," she said. "It is not a question that we ask one another nowadays; but I have read that in your day, even among the cultured class, there were some who did not care for music."

"You must remember, in excuse," I said, "that we had some rather absurd kinds of music."

"Yes," she said, "I know that; I am afraid I should not have fancied it all myself. Would you like to hear some of ours now, Mr. West?"

"Nothing would delight me so much as to listen to you," I said.

"To me!" she exclaimed, laughing. "Did you think I was going to play or sing to you?"

"I hoped so, certainly," I replied.

Seeing that I was a little abashed, she subdued her merriment and explained. "Of course, we all sing nowadays as a matter of course in the training of the voice, and some learn to play instruments for their private amusement; but the professional music is so much grander and more perfect than any performance of ours, and so easily commanded when we wish to hear it, that we don't think of calling our singing or playing music at all. All the really fine singers and players are in the musical service, and the rest of us hold our peace for the main part. But would you really like to hear some music?"

I assured her once more that I would.

"Come, then, into the music room," she said, and I followed

her into an apartment finished, without hangings, in wood, with a floor of polished wood. I was prepared for new devices in musical instruments, but I saw nothing in the room which by any stretch of imagination could be conceived as such. It was evident that my puzzled appearance was affording intense amusement to Edith.

"Please look at to-day's music," she said, handing me a card, "and tell me what you would prefer. It is now five o'clock, you will remember."

The card bore the date "September 12, 2000," and contained the longest programme of music I had ever seen. It was as various as it was long, incuding a most extraordinary range of vocal and instrumental solos, duets, quartettes, and various orchestral combinations. I remained bewildered by the prodigious list until Edith's pink finger-tip indicated a particular section of it, where several selections were bracketed, with the words "5 P.M." against them; then I observed that this prodigious programme was an all-day one, divided into twenty-four sections answering to the hours. There were but a few pieces of music in the "5 P.M." section, and I indicated an organ piece as my preference.

"I am so glad you like the organ," said she. "I think there is scarcely any music that suits my mood oftener."

She made me sit down comfortably, and, crossing the room, so far as I could see, merely touched one or two screws, and at once the room was filled with the music of a grand organ anthem; filled, not flooded, for, by some means, the volume of melody had been perfectly graduated to the size of the apartment. I listened, scarcely breathing, to the close. Such music, so perfectly rendered, I had never expected to hear.

"Grand!" I cried, as the last great wave of sound broke and ebbed away into silence. "Bach must be at the keys of that organ; but where is the organ?"

"Wait a moment, please," said Edith; "I want to have you listen to this waltz before you ask any questions. I think it is perfectly charming;" and as she spoke the sound of violins filled the room with the witchery of a summer night. When this had also ceased, she said: "There is nothing in the least mysterious about the music, as you seem to imagine. It is not made by fairies or genii, but by good, honest, and exceedingly clever human hands. We have simply carried the idea of labor-saving by coöperation into our musical service as into everything else. There are a number of music rooms in the city, perfectly adapted acoustically to the different sorts of music. These halls are connected by telephone with all the houses of the city whose people care to pay the small fee, and there are none, you may be sure, who do not. The corps of musicians attached to each hall is so large that, although no individual performer, or group of performers, has more than a brief part, each day's programme lasts through the twenty-four hours. There are on that card for to-day, as you will see if you observe closely, distinct programmes of four of these concerts, each of a different order of music from the others, being now simultaneously performed, and any one of the four pieces now going on that you prefer, you can hear by merely pressing the button which will connect your house-wire with the hall where it is being rendered. The programmes are so coördinated that the pieces at any one time simultaneously proceeding in the different halls usually offer a choice, not only between instrumental and vocal, and between different sorts of instruments; but also between different motives from grave to gay, so that all tastes and moods can be suited."

"It appears to me, Miss Leete," I said, "that if we could have devised an arrangement for providing everybody with music in their homes, perfect in quality, unlimited in quantity, suited to every mood, and beginning and ceasing at will, we should have considered the limit of human felicity already attained, and ceased to strive for further improvements."

"I am sure I never could imagine how those among you who depended at all on music managed to endure the old-fashioned system for providing it," replied Edith. "Music really worth hearing must have been, I suppose, wholly out of the reach of the masses, and attainable by the most favored only occasionally, at great trouble, prodigious expense, and then for brief periods, arbitrarily fixed by somebody else, and in connection with all sorts of undesirable circumstances. Your concerts, for instance, and operas! How perfectly exasperating it must have been, for the sake of a piece or two of music that suited you, to have to sit for hours listening to what you did not care for! Now, at a dinner one can skip the courses one does not care for. Who would ever dine, however hungry, if required to eat everything brought on the table? and I am sure one's hearing is quite as sensitive as one's taste. I suppose it was these difficulties in the way of commanding really good music which made you endure so much playing and singing in your homes by people who had only the rudiments of the art."

"Yes," I replied, "it was that sort of music or none for most of us."

"Ah, well," Edith sighed, "when one really considers, it is not so strange that people in those days so often did not care for music. I dare say I should have detested it, too."

"Did I understand you rightly," I inquired, "that this musical programme covers the entire twenty-four hours? It seems to on this card, certainly; but who is there to listen to music between say midnight and morning?"

"Oh, many," Edith replied. "Our people keep all hours; but if the music were provided from midnight to morning for no others, it still would be for the sleepless, the sick, and the dying. All our bedchambers have a telephone attachment at the head of the bed by which any person who may be sleepless can command music at pleasure, of the sort suited to the mood."

"Is there such an arrangement in the room assigned to me?"

"Why, certainly; and how stupid, how very stupid, of me not to think to tell you of that last night! Father will show you about the adjustment before you go to bed to-night, however; and with the receiver at your ear, I am quite sure you will be able to snap your fingers at all sorts of uncanny feelings if they trouble you again."

That evening Dr. Leete asked us about our visit to the store, and in the course of the desultory comparison of the ways of the nineteenth century and the twentieth, which followed, something raised the question of inheritance. "I suppose," I said, "the inheritance of property is not now allowed."

"On the contrary," replied Dr. Leete, "there is no interference with it. In fact, you will find, Mr. West, as you come to know us, that there is far less interference of any sort with personal liberty nowadays than you were accustomed to. We require, indeed, by law that every man shall serve the nation for a fixed period, instead of leaving him his choice, as you did, between working, stealing, or starving. With the exception of this fundamental law, which is, indeed, merely a codification of the law of nature—the edict of Eden—by which it is made equal in its pressure on men, our system depends in no particular upon legislation, but is entirely voluntary, the logical outcome of the operation of human nature under rational conditions. This question of inheritance illustrates just that point. The fact that the nation is the sole capitalist and land-owner of course restricts the individual's possessions to his annual credit, and what personal and household belongings he may have procured with it. His credit, like an annuity in your day, ceases on his death, with the allowance of a fixed sum for funeral expenses. His other possessions he leaves as he pleases."

"What is to prevent, in course of time, such accumulations of valuable goods and chattels in the hands of individuals as might seriously interfere with equality in the circumstances of citizens?" I asked.

"That matter arranges itself very simply," was the reply. "Under the present organization of society, accumulations of personal property are merely burdensome the moment they exceed what adds to the real comfort. In your day, if a man had a house crammed full with gold and silver plate, rare china, expensive furniture, and such things, he was considered rich, for these things represented money, and could at any time be turned into it. Nowadays a man whom the legacies of a hundred relatives, simultaneously dying, should place in a similar position, would be considered very unlucky. The articles, not being salable, would be of no value to him except for their actual use or the enjoyment of their beauty. On the other hand, his income remaining the same, he would have to deplete his credit to hire houses to store the goods in, and still further to pay for the service of those who took care of them. You may be very sure that such a man would lose no time in scattering among his friends possessions which only made him the poorer, and that none of those friends would accept more of them than they could easily spare room for and time to attend to. You see, then, that to prohibit the inheritance of personal property with a view to prevent great accumulations would be a superfluous precaution for the nation. The individual citizen can be trusted to see that he is not overburdened. So careful is he in this respect, that the relatives usually waive claim to most of the effects of deceased friends, reserving only particular objects. The nation takes charge of the resigned chattels, and turns such as are of value into the common stock once more."

"You spoke of paying for service to take care of your houses," said I; "that suggests a question I have several times been on the point of asking. How have you disposed of the problem of domestic service? Who are willing to be domestic servants in a community where all are social equals? Our ladies found it hard enough to find such even when there was little pretense of social equality."

"It is precisely because we are all social equals whose equality nothing can compromise, and because service is honorable, in a society whose fundamental principle is that all in turn shall serve the rest, that we could easily provide a corps of domestic servants such as you never dreamed of, if we needed them," replied Dr. Leete. "But we do not need them."

"Who does your house-work, then?" I asked.

"There is none to do," said Mrs. Leete, to whom I had addressed this question. "Our washing is all done at public laundries at excessively cheap rates, and our cooking at public kitchens. The making and repairing of all we wear are done outside in public shops. Electricity, of course, takes the place of all fires and lighting. We choose houses no larger than we need, and furnish them so as to involve the minimum of trouble to keep them in order. We have no use for domestic servants."

"The fact," said Dr. Leete, "that you had in the poorer classes a boundless supply of serfs on whom you could impose all sorts of painful and disagreeable tasks, made you indifferent to devices to avoid the necessity for them. But now that we all have to do in turn whatever work is done for society, every individual in the nation has the same interest, and a personal one, in devices for lightening the burden. This fact has given a prodigious impulse to labor-saving inventions in all sorts of industry, of which the combination of the maximum of comfort and minimum of trouble in household arrangements was one of the earliest results.

"In case of special emergencies in the household," pursued Dr. Leete, "such as extensive cleaning or renovation, or sickness in the family, we can always secure assistance from the industrial force."

"But how do you recompense these assistants, since you have no money?"

"We do not pay them, of course, but the nation for them. Their services can be obtained by application at the proper bureau, and their value is pricked off the credit card of the applicant."

"What a paradise for womankind the world must be now!" I exclaimed. "In my day, even wealth and unlimited servants did not enfranchise their possessors from household cares, while the women of the merely well-to-do and poorer classes lived and died martyrs to them."

"Yes," said Mrs. Leete, "I have read something of that; enough to convince me that, badly off as the men, too, were in your day, they were more fortunate than their mothers and wives."

"The broad shoulders of the nation," said Dr. Leete, "bear now like a feather the burden that broke the backs of the women of your day. Their misery came, with all your other miseries, from that incapacity for coöperation which followed from the individualism on which your social system was founded, from your inability to perceive that you could make ten times more profit out of your fellow men by uniting with them than by contending with them. The wonder is, not that you did not live more comfortably, but that you were able to live together at all, who were all confessedly bent on making one another your servants, and securing possession of one another's goods."

"There, there, Father. If you are so vehement, Mr. West will think you are scolding him," laughingly interposed Edith.

"When you want a doctor," I asked, "do you simply apply to the proper bureau and take any one that may be sent?"

"That rule would not work well in the case of physicians," replied Dr. Leete. "The good a physician can do a patient depends largely on his acquaintance with his constitutional tendencies and condition. The patient must be able, therefore, to call in a particular doctor, and he does so just as patients did in your day. The only difference is that, instead of collecting his fee for himself, the doctor collects it for the nation by pricking off the amount, according to a regular scale for medical attendance, from the patient's credit card."

"I can imagine," I said, "that if the fee is always the same, and a doctor may not turn away patients, as I suppose he may not, the good doctors are called constantly and the poor doctors left in idleness."

"In the first place, if you will overlook the apparent conceit of the remark from a retired physician," replied Dr. Leete, with a smile, "we have no poor doctors. Anybody who pleases to get a little smattering of medical terms is not now at liberty to practice on the bodies of citizens, as in your day. None but students who have passed the severe tests of the schools, and clearly proved their vocation, are permitted to practice. Then, too, you will observe that there is nowadays no attempt of doctors to build up their practice at the expense of other doctors. There would be no motive for that. For the rest, the doctor has to render regular reports of his work to the medical bureau, and if he is not reasonably well employed, work is found for him."

Chapter XII

T HE questions which I needed to ask before I could acquire even an outline acquaintance with the institutions of the twentieth century being endless, and Dr. Leete's good-nature appearing equally so, we sat up talking for several hours after the ladies left us. Reminding my host of the point at which our talk had broken off that morning, I expressed my curiosity to learn how the organization of the industrial army was made to afford a sufficient stimulus to diligence in the lack of any anxiety on the worker's part as to his livelihood.

"You must understand in the first place," replied the doctor, "that the supply of incentives to effort is but one of the objects sought in the organization we have adopted for the army. The other, and equally important, is to secure for the file-leaders and captains of the force, and the great officers of the nation, men of proven abilities, who are pledged by their own careers to hold their followers up to their highest standard of performance and permit no lagging. With a view to these two ends the industrial army is organized. First comes the unclassified grade of common laborers, men of all work, to which all recruits during their first three years belong. This grade is a sort of school, and a very strict one, in which the young men are taught habits of obedience, subordination, and devotion to duty. While the miscellaneous nature of the work done by this force prevents the systematic grading of the workers which is afterwards possible, yet individual records are kept, and excellence receives distinction corresponding with the penalties that negligence incurs. It is not, however, policy with us to permit youthful recklessness or indiscretion, when not deeply culpable, to handicap the future careers of young men, and all who have passed through the unclassified grade without serious disgrace have an equal opportunity to choose the life employment they have most liking for. Having selected this, they enter upon it as apprentices. The length of the apprenticeship naturally differs in different occupations. At the end of it the apprentice becomes a full workman, and a member of his trade or guild. Now not only are the individual records of the apprentices for ability and industry strictly kept, and excellence distinguished by suitable distinctions, but upon the average of his record during apprenticeship the standing given the apprentice among the full workmen depends.

"While the internal organizations of different industries, mechanical and agricultural, differ according to their peculiar conditions, they agree in a general division of their workers into first, second, and third grades, according to ability, and these grades are in many cases subdivided into first and second classes. According to his standing as an apprentice a young man is assigned his place as a first, second, or third grade worker. Of course only young men of unusual ability pass directly from apprenticeship into the first grade of the workers. The most fall into the lower grades, working up as they grow more experienced, at the periodical regradings. These regradings take place in each industry at intervals corresponding with the length of the apprenticeship to that industry, so that merit never need wait long to rise, nor can any rest on past achievements unless they would drop into a lower rank. One of the notable advantages of a high grading is the privilege it gives the worker in electing which of the various branches or processes of his industry he will follow as his specialty. Of course it is not intended that any of these processes shall be disproportionately arduous, but there is often much difference between them, and the privilege of election is accordingly highly prized. So far as possible, indeed, the preferences even of the poorest workmen are considered in assigning them their line of work, because not only their happiness but their usefulness is thus enhanced. While, however, the wish of the lower grade man is consulted so far as the exigencies of the service permit, he is considered only after the upper grade men have been provided for, and often he has to put up with second or third choice, or even with an arbitrary assignment when help is needed. This privilege of election attends every regrading, and when a man loses his grade he also risks having to exchange the sort of work he likes for some other less to his taste. The results of each regrading, giving the standing of every man in his industry, are gazetted in the public prints, and those who have won promotion since the last regrading receive the nation's thanks and are publicly invested with the badge of their new rank."

"What may this badge be?" I asked.

"Every industry has its emblematic device," replied Dr. Leete, "and this, in the shape of a metallic badge so small that you might not see it unless you knew where to look, is all the insignia which the men of the army wear, except where public convenience demands a distinctive uniform. This badge is the same in form for all grades of industry, but while the badge of the third grade is iron, that of the second grade is silver, and that of the first is gilt.

"Apart from the grand incentive to endeavor afforded by the fact that the high places in the nation are open only to the highest class men, and that rank in the army constitutes the only mode of social distinction for the vast majority who are not aspirants in art, literature, and the professions, various incitements of a minor, but perhaps equally effective, sort are provided in the form of special privileges and immunities in the way of discipline, which the superior class men enjoy. These, while intended to be as little as possible invidious to the less successful, have the effect of keeping constantly before every man's mind the great desirability of attaining the grade next above his own.*

---

* [The description of the industrial army beginning with the sentence "With a view to these two ends. . . . " on p. 123 was revised and expanded in the second edition. The first edition reads: "With a view to these two ends, the whole body of members of the industrial army is divided into four general classes. First, the unclassified grade, of common laborers, assigned to any sort of work, usually the coarser kinds to this all recruits during their first three years belong. Second, the apprentices, as the men are called in the first year after passing from the unclassified grade, while they are mastering

"It is obviously important that not only the good but also the indifferent and poor workmen should be able to cherish the ambition of rising. Indeed, the number of the latter being so much greater, it is even more essential that the ranking system should not operate to discourage them than that it should stimulate the others. It is to this end that the grades are divided into classes. The grades as well as the classes being made numerically equal at each regrading, there is not at any time, counting out

---

the first elements of their chosen avocations. Third, the main body of the full workers, being men between twenty-five and forty-five. Fourth, the officers from the lowest who have charge of the men to the highest. These four classes are all under a different form of discipline. The unclassified workers, doing miscellaneous work, cannot of course be so rigidly graded as later. They are supposed to be in a sort of school, learning industrial habits. Nevertheless they make their individual records, and excellence receives distinction and helps in the after career, something as academic standing added to the prestige of men in your day. The year of apprenticeship follows. The apprentice is given the first quarter of it to learn the rudiments of his avocation, but is marked on the last three quarters with a view to determine which grade among the workers he shall be enrolled in on becoming a full workman. It may seem strange that the term of apprenticeship should be the same in all trades, but this is done for the sake of uniformity in the system, and practically works precisely as if the terms of apprenticeship varied according to the difficulty of acquiring the trade. For, in the trades in which one cannot become proficient in a year, the result is that the apprentice falls into the lower grades of the full workmen, and works upward as he grows in skill. This is indeed what ordinarily happens in most trades. The full workmen are divided into three grades, according to efficiency, and each grade into a first and second class, so that there are in all six classes, into which the men fall according to their ability.

"To facilitate the testing of efficiency, all industrial work, whenever by any means, and even at some inconvenience, it is possible, is conducted by piece-work, and if this is absolutely out of the question, the best possible substitute for determining ability is adopted. The men are regraded yearly, so that merit never need wait long to rise, nor can any rest on past achievements, unless they would drop into a lower rank. The results of each annual regrading, giving the standing of every man in the army, are gazetted in the public prints.

"Apart from the grand incentive to endeavor afforded by the fact that the high places in the nation are open only to the highest class men, various incitements of a minor, but perhaps equally effective, sort are provided in the form of special privileges and immunities in the way of discipline, which the superior class men enjoy. These, while not in the aggregate important, have the effect of keeping constantly before every man's mind the desirability of attaining the grade next above his own."]

the officers and the unclassified and apprentice grades, over one-ninth of the industrial army in the lowest class, and most of this number are recent apprentices, all of whom expect to rise. Those who remain during the entire term of service in the lowest class are but a trifling fraction of the industrial army, and likely to be as deficient in sensibility to their position as in ability to better it.†

"It is not even necessary that a worker should win promotion to a higher grade to have at least a taste of glory. While promotion requires a general excellence of record as a worker, honorable mention and various sorts of prizes are awarded for excellence less than sufficient for promotion, and also for special feats and single performances in the various industries. There are many minor distinctions of standing, not only within the grades but within the classes, each of which acts as a spur to the efforts of a group.* It is intended that no form of merit shall wholly fail of recognition.

"As for actual neglect of work, positively bad work, or other overt remissness on the part of men incapable of generous motives, the discipline of the industrial army is far too strict to allow anything whatever of the sort. A man able to do duty, and persistently refusing, is sentenced to solitary imprisonment on bread and water till he consents.¶

† [In the first edition the passage beginning "The grades as well as the classes. . . . " reads: "The classes being numerically equal, there is not at any time, counting out the officers and the unclassified and apprentice grades, over one-eighth of the industrial army in the lowest class, and most of this number are recent apprentices, all of whom expect to rise. Still further to encourage those of no great talents to do their best, a man who, after attaining a higher grade, falls back into a lower, does not lose the fruit of his effort, but retains, as a sort of brevet, his former rank. The result is that those under our ranking system who fail to win any prize, by way of solace to their pride, remaining during the entire term of service in the lowest class, are but a trifling fraction of the industrial army, and likely to be as deficient in sensibility to their position as in ability to better it."]

* [This sentence was added in the second edition.]

¶ [In the first edition this paragraph reads: "As for actual neglect of work, positively bad work, or other overt remissness on the part of men incapable of generous motives, the discipline of the industrial army is far too strict to allow much of that. A man able to do duty, and persistently refusing, is cut off from all human society."]

"The lowest grade of the officers of the industrial army, that of assistant foremen or lieutenants, is appointed out of men who have held their place for two years in the first class of the first grade. Where this leaves too large a range of choice, only the first group of this class are eligible. No one thus comes to the point of commanding men until he is about thirty years old. After a man becomes an officer, his rating of course no longer depends on the efficiency of his own work, but on that of his men. The foremen are appointed from among the assistant foremen, by the same exercise of discretion limited to a small eligible class. In the appointments to the still higher grades another principle is introduced, which it would take too much time to explain now.

"Of course such a system of grading as I have described would have been impracticable applied to the small industrial concerns of your day, in some of which there were hardly enough employees to have left one apiece for the classes. You must remember that, under the national organization of labor, all industries are carried on by great bodies of men, many of your farms or shops being combined as one. It is also owing solely to the vast scale on which each industry is organized, with coördinate establishments in every part of the country, that we are able by exchanges and transfers to fit every man so nearly with the sort of work he can do best.*

"And now, Mr. West, I will leave it to you, on the bare outline of its features which I have given, if those who need special incentives to do their best are likely to lack them under our system. Does it not seem to you that men who found themselves obliged, whether they wished or not, to work, would under such a system be strongly impelled to do their best?" †

I replied that it seemed to me the incentives offered were, if any objection were to be made, too strong; that the pace set

---

* [In the first edition the passage beginning "You must remember. . . . " reads: "You must remember that, under the national organization of labor, all industries are carried on by great bodies of men, a hundred of your farms or shops being combined as one. The superintendent, with us, is like a colonel, or even a general, in one of your armies."]

† [This sentence was added in the second edition.]

for the young men was too hot; and such, indeed, I would add with deference, still remains my opinion, now that by longer residence among you I have become better acquainted with the whole subject.

Dr. Leete, however, desired me to reflect, and I am ready to say that it is perhaps a sufficient reply to my objection, that the worker's livelihood is in no way dependent on his ranking, and anxiety for that never embitters his disappointments; that the working hours are short, the vacations regular, and that all emulation ceases at forty-five, with the attainment of middle life.

"There are two or three other points I ought to refer to," he added, "to prevent your getting mistaken impressions. In the first place, you must understand that this system of preferment given the more efficient workers over the less so, in no way contravenes the fundamental idea of our social system, that all who do their best are equally deserving, whether that best be great or small. I have shown that the system is arranged to encourage the weaker as well as the stronger with the hope of rising, while the fact that the stronger are selected for the leaders is in no way a reflection upon the weaker, but in the interest of the common weal.

"Do not imagine, either, because emulation is given free play as an incentive under our system, that we deem it a motive likely to appeal to the nobler sort of men, or worthy of them. Such as these find their motives within, not without, and measure their duty by their own endowments, not by those of others. So long as their achievement is proportioned to their powers, they would consider it preposterous to expect praise or blame because it chanced to be great or small. To such natures emulation appears philosophically absurd, and despicable in a moral aspect by its substitution of envy for admiration, and exultation for regret, in one's attitude toward the successes and the failures of others.

"But all men, even in the last year of the twentieth century, are not of this high order, and the incentives to endeavor requisite for those who are not must be of a sort adapted to their inferior natures. For these, then, emulation of the keenest edge is provided as a constant spur. Those who need this motive will feel it. Those who are above its influence do not need it.

"I should not fail to mention," resumed the doctor, "that for those too deficient in mental or bodily strength to be fairly graded with the main body of workers, we have a separate grade, unconnected with the others,—a sort of invalid corps, the members of which are provided with a light class of tasks fitted to their strength. All our sick in mind and body, all our deaf and dumb, and lame and blind and crippled, and even our insane, belong to this invalid corps, and bear its insignia. The strongest often do nearly a man's work, the feeblest, of course, nothing; but none who can do anything are willing quite to give up. In their lucid intervals, even our insane are eager to do what they can."

"That is a pretty idea of the invalid corps," I said. "Even a barbarian from the nineteenth century can appreciate that. It is a very graceful way of disguising charity, and must be grateful to the feelings of its recipients."

"Charity!" repeated Dr. Leete. "Did you suppose that we consider the incapable class we are talking of objects of charity?"

"Why, naturally," I said, "inasmuch as they are incapable of self-support."

But here the doctor took me up quickly.

"Who is capable of self-support?" he demanded. "There is no such thing in a civilized society as self-support. In a state of society so barbarous as not even to know family coöperation, each individual may possibly support himself, though even then for a part of his life only; but from the moment that men begin to live together, and constitute even the rudest sort of society, self-support becomes impossible. As men grow more civilized, and the subdivision of occupations and services is carried out, a complex mutual dependence becomes the universal rule. Every man, however solitary may seem his occupation, is a member of a vast industrial partnership, as large as the nation, as large as humanity. The necessity of mutual dependence should imply the duty and guarantee of mutual support; and that it did not in your day constituted the essential cruelty and unreason of your system."

"That may all be so," I replied, "but it does not touch the case of those who are unable to contribute anything to the product of industry."

"Surely I told you this morning, at least I thought I did," replied Dr. Leete, "that the right of a man to maintenance at the nation's table depends on the fact that he is a man, and not on the amount of health and strength he may have, so long as he does his best."

"You said so," I answered, "but I supposed the rule applied only to the workers of different ability. Does it also hold of those who can do nothing at all?"

"Are they not also men?"

"I am to understand, then, that the lame, the blind, the sick, and the impotent, are as well off as the most efficient, and have the same income?"

"Certainly," was the reply.

"The idea of charity on such a scale," I answered, "would have made our most enthusiastic philanthropists gasp."

"If you had a sick brother at home," replied Dr. Leete, "unable to work, would you feed him on less dainty food, and lodge and clothe him more poorly, than yourself? More likely far, you would give him the preference; nor would you think of calling it charity. Would not the word, in that connection, fill you with indignation?"

"Of course," I replied; "but the cases are not parallel. There is a sense, no doubt, in which all men are brothers; but this general sort of brotherhood is not to be compared, except for rhetorical purposes, to the brotherhood of blood, either as to its sentiment or its obligations."

"There speaks the nineteenth century!" exclaimed Dr. Leete. "Ah, Mr. West, there is no doubt as to the length of time that you slept. If I were to give you, in one sentence, a key to what may seem the mysteries of our civilization as compared with that of your age, I should say that it is the fact that the solidarity of the race and the brotherhood of man, which to you were but fine phrases, are, to our thinking and feeling, ties as real and as vital as physical fraternity.

"But even setting that consideration aside, I do not see why it so surprises you that those who cannot work are conceded the full right to live on the produce of those who can. Even in your day, the duty of military service for the protection of the nation, to which our industrial service corresponds, while obligatory on those able to discharge it, did not operate to deprive of the privileges of citizenship those who were unable. They stayed at home, and were protected by those who fought, and nobody questioned their right to be, or thought less of them. So, now, the requirement of industrial service from those able to render it does not operate to deprive of the privileges of citizenship, which now implies the citizen's maintenance, him who cannot work. The worker is not a citizen because he works, but works because he is a citizen. As you recognize the duty of the strong to fight for the weak, we, now that fighting is gone by, recognize his duty to work for him.

"A solution which leaves an unaccounted-for residuum is no solution at all; and our solution of the problem of human society would have been none at all had it left the lame, the sick, and the blind outside with the beasts, to fare as they might. Better far have left the strong and well unprovided for than these burdened ones, toward whom every heart must yearn, and for whom ease of mind and body should be provided, if for no others. Therefore it is, as I told you this morning, that the title of every man, woman, and child to the means of existence rests on no basis less plain, broad, and simple than the fact that they are fellows of one race—members of one human family. The only coin current is the image of God, and that is good for all we have.

"I think there is no feature of the civilization of your epoch so repugnant to modern ideas as the neglect with which you treated your dependent classes. Even if you had no pity, no feeling of brotherhood, how was it that you did not see that you were robbing the incapable class of their plain right in leaving them unprovided for?"

"I don't quite follow you there," I said. "I admit the claim of this class to our pity, but how could they who produced nothing claim a share of the product as a right?"

"How happened it," was Dr. Leete's reply, "that your workers were able to produce more than so many savages would have done? Was it not wholly on account of the heritage of the past knowledge and achievements of the race, the machinery of society, thousands of years in contriving, found by you ready-made to your hand? How did you come to be possessors of this knowledge and this machinery, which represent nine parts to one contributed by yourself in the value of your product? You inherited it, did you not? And were not these others, these unfortunate and crippled brothers whom you cast out, joint inheritors, co-heirs with you? What did you do with their share? Did you not rob them when you put them off with crusts, who were entitled to sit with the heirs, and did you not add insult to robbery when you called the crusts charity?

"Ah, Mr. West," Dr. Leete continued, as I did not respond, "what I do not understand is, setting aside all considerations either of justice or brotherly feeling toward the crippled and defective, how the workers of your day could have had any heart for their work, knowing that their children, or grand-children, if unfortunate, would be deprived of the comforts and even necessities of life. It is a mystery how men with children could favor a system under which they were rewarded beyond those less endowed with bodily strength or mental power. For, by the same discrimination by which the father profited, the son, for whom he would give his life, being perchance weaker than others, might be reduced to crusts and beggary. How men dared leave children behind them, I have never been able to understand."

NOTE. — Although in his talk on the previous evening Dr. Leete had emphasized the pains taken to enable every man to ascertain and follow his natural bent in choosing an occupation, it was not till I learned that the worker's income is the same in all occupations that I realized how absolutely he may be counted on to do so, and thus, by selecting the harness which sets most lightly on himself, find that in which he can pull best. The failure of my age in any systematic or effective way to develop and utilize the natural aptitudes of men for the industries and intellectual avocations was one of the great wastes, as well as one of the most common causes of unhappiness in that time. The vast majority of my contemporaries, though nominally free to do so, never really chose their occupations at all, but were forced by circumstances into work for which they were relatively inefficient, because not naturally fitted for it. The rich, in this respect, had little advantage over the poor. The latter, indeed, being generally deprived of education, had no opportunity even to ascertain the natural aptitudes they might have, and on account of their poverty were unable to develop them by cultivation even when ascertained. The liberal and technical professions, except by favorable accident, were shut to them, to their own great loss and that of the nation. On the other hand, the well-to-do, although they could command education and opportunity, were scarcely less hampered by social prejudice, which forbade them to pursue manual avocations, even when adapted to them, and destined them, whether fit or unfit, to the professions, thus wasting many an excellent handicraftsman. Mercenary considerations, tempting men to pursue money-making occupations for which they were unfit, itstead of less remunerative employments for which they were fit, were responsible for another vast perversion of talent. All these things now are changed. Equal education and opportunity must needs bring to light whatever aptitudes a man has, and neither social prejudices nor mercenary considerations hamper him in the choice of his life work.

Chapter XIII

A s Edith had promised he should do, Dr. Leete accompanied me to my bedroom when I retired, to instruct me as to the adjustment of the musical telephone. He showed how, by turning a screw, the volume of the music could be made to fill the room, or die away to an acho so faint and far that one could scarcely be sure whether he heard or imagined it. If, of two persons side by side, one desired to listen to music and the other to sleep, it could be made audible to one and inaudible to another.

"I should strongly advise you to sleep if you can to-night, Mr. West, in preference to listening to the finest tunes in the world," the doctor said, after explaining these points. "In the trying experience you are just now passing through, sleep is a nerve tonic for which there is no substitute."

Mindful of what had happened to me that very morning, I promised to heed his counsel.

"Very well," he said, "then I will set the telephone at eight o'clock."

"What do you mean?" I asked.

He explained that, by a clock-work combination, a person could arrange to be awakened at any hour by the music.

It began to appear, as has since fully proved to be the case, that I had left my tendency to insomnia behind me with the other discomforts of existence in the nineteenth century; for though I took no sleeping draught this time, yet, as the night before, I had no sooner touched the pillow than I was asleep.

I dreamed that I sat on the throne of the Abencerrages in the banqueting hall of the Alhambra, feasting my lords and generals, who next day were to follow the crescent against the Christian dogs of Spain. The air, cooled by the spray of fountains, was heavy with the scent of flowers. A band of Nautch girls, round-limbed and luscious-lipped, danced with voluptuous grace to the music of brazen and stringed instruments. Looking up to the latticed galleries, one caught a gleam now and then from the eye of some beauty of the royal harem, looking down upon the assembled flower of Moorish chivalry. Louder and louder clashed the cymbals, wilder and wilder grew the strain, till the blood of the desert race could no longer resist the martial delirium, and the swart nobles leaped to their feet; a thousand scimetars were bared, and the cry, "Allah il Allah!" shook the hall and awoke me, to find it broad daylight, and the room tingling with the electric music of the "Turkish Reveille."

At the breakfast-table, when I told my host of my morning's experience, I learned that it was not a mere chance that the piece of music which awakened me was a reveille. The airs played at one of the halls during the waking hours of the morning were always of an inspiring type.

"By the way," I said, "I have not thought to ask you anything about the state of Europe. Have the societies of the Old World also been remodeled?"

"Yes," replied Dr. Leete, "the great nations of Europe as well as Australia, Mexico, and parts of South America, are now organized industrially like the United States, which was the pioneer of the evolution. The peaceful relations of these nations are assured by a loose form of federal union of world-wide extent. An international council regulates the mutual intercourse and commerce of the members of the union and their joint policy toward the more backward races, which are gradually being educated up to civilized institutions. Complete autonomy within its own limits is enjoyed by every nation."

"How do you carry on commerce without money?" I said. "In trading with other nations, you must use some sort of money, although you dispense with it in the internal affairs of the nation."

"Oh, no; money is as superfluous in our foreign as in our internal relations. When foreign commerce was conducted by private enterprise, money was necessary to adjust it on account of the multifarious complexity of the transactions; but nowadays it is a function of the nations as units. There are thus only a dozen or so merchants in the world, and their business being supervised by the international council, a simple system of book accounts serves perfectly to regulate their dealings. Customs duties of every sort are of course superfluous. A nation simply does not import what its government does not think requisite for the general interest.* Each nation has a bureau of foreign exchange, which manages its trading. For example, the American bureau, estimating such and such quantities of French goods necessary to America for a given year, sends the order to the French bureau, which in turn sends its order to our bureau. The same is done mutually by all the nations."

"But how are the prices of foreign goods settled, since there is no competition?"

"The price at which one nation supplies another with goods," replied Dr. Leete, "must be that at which it supplies its own citizens. So you see there is no danger of misunderstanding. Of course no nation is theoretically bound to supply another with the product of its own labor, but it is for the interest of all to exchange some commodities. If a nation is regularly supplying another with certain goods, notice is required from either side of any important change in the relation."

"But what if a nation, having a monopoly of some natural product, should refuse to supply it to the others, or to one of them?"

"Such a case has never occurred, and could not without doing the refusing party vastly more harm than the others," replied Dr. Leete. "In the first place, no favoritism could be legally† shown. The law requires that each nation shall deal with the others, in all respects, on exactly the same footing. Such a course as you suggest would cut off the nation adopting it from the remainder of the earth for all purposes whatever. The contingency is one that need not give us much anxiety."

"But," said I, "supposing a nation, having a natural monopoly

* [This sentence and the one immediately preceding were added in the second edition.]

† [The word "legally" was added in the second edition.]

in some product of which it exports more than it consumes, should put the price away up, and thus, without cutting off the supply, make a profit out of its neighbors' necessities? Its own citizens would of course have to pay the higher price on that commodity, but as a body would make more out of foreigners than they would be out of pocket themselves."

"When you come to know how prices of all commodities are determined nowadays, you will perceive how impossible it is that they could be altered, except with reference to the amount or arduousness of the work required respectively to produce them," was Dr. Leete's reply. "This principle is an international as well as a national guarantee; but even without it the sense of community of interest, international as well as national, and the conviction of the folly of selfishness, are too deep nowadays to render possible such a piece of sharp practice as you apprehend. You must understand that we all look forward to an eventual unification of the world as one nation. That, no doubt, will be the ultimate form of society, and will realize certain economic advantages over the present federal system of autonomous nations. Meanwhile, however, the present system works so nearly perfectly that we are quite content to leave to posterity the completion of the scheme. There are, indeed, some who hold that it never will be completed, on the ground that the federal plan is not merely a provisional solution of the problem of human society, but the best ultimate solution."

"How do you manage," I asked, "when the books of any two nations do not balance? Supposing we import more from France than we export to her."

"At the end of each year," replied the doctor, "the books of every nation are examined. If France is found in our debt, probably we are in the debt of some nation which owes France, and so on with all the nations. The balances that remain after the accounts have been cleared by the international council should not be large under our system. Whatever they may be, the council requires them to be settled every few years, and may require their settlement at any time if they are getting too large; for it is not intended that any nation shall run largely in debt to another, lest feelings unfavorable to amity should be engendered. To guard further against this, the international council inspects the commodities interchanged by the nations, to see that they are of perfect quality."

"But what are the balances finally settled with, seeing that you have no money?"

"In national staples; a basis of agreement as to what staples shall be accepted, and in what proportions, for settlement of accounts, being a preliminary to trade relations."

"Emigration is another point I want to ask you about," said I. "With every nation organized as a close industrial partnership, monopolizing all means of production in the country, the emigrant, even if he were permitted to land, would starve. I suppose there is no emigration nowadays."

"On the contrary, there is constant emigration, by which I suppose you mean removal to foreign countries for permanent residence," replied Dr. Leete. "It is arranged on a simple international arrangement of indemnities. For example, if a man at twenty-one emigrates from England to America, England loses all the expense of his maintenance and education, and America gets a workman for nothing. America accordingly makes England an allowance. The same principle, varied to suit the case, applies generally. If the man is near the term of his labor when he emigrates, the country receiving him has the allowance. As to imbecile persons, it is deemed best that each nation should be responsible for its own, and the emigration of such must be under full guarantees of support by his own nation. Subject to these regulations, the right of any man to emigrate at any time is unrestricted."

"But how about mere pleasure trips; tours of observation? How can a stranger travel in a country whose people do not receive money, and are themselves supplied with the means of life on a basis not extended to him? His own credit card cannot, of course, be good in other lands. How does he pay his way?"

"An American credit card," replied Dr. Leete, "is just as good in Europe as American gold used to be, and on precisely the same condition, namely, that it be exchanged into the currency of the country you are traveling in. An American in Berlin takes his credit card to the local office of the international council, and receives in exchange for the whole or part of it a German credit card, the amount being charged against the United States in favor of Germany on the international account."

"Perhaps Mr. West would like to dine at the Elephant to-day," said Edith, as we left the table.

"That is the name we give to the general dining-house of our ward," explained her father. "Not only is our cooking done at the public kitchens, as I told you last night, but the service and quality of the meals are much more satisfactory if taken at the dining-house. The two minor meals of the day are usually taken at home, as not worth the trouble of going out; but it is general to go out to dine. We have not done so since you have been with us, from a notion that it would be better to wait till you had become a little more familiar with our ways. What do you think? Shall we take dinner at the dining-house to-day?"

I said that I should be very much pleased to do so.

Not long after, Edith came to me, smiling, and said:—

"Last night, as I was thinking what I could do to make you feel at home until you came to be a little more used to us and our ways, an idea occurred to me. What would you say if I were to introduce you to some very nice people of your own times, whom I am sure you used to be well acquainted with?"

I replied, rather vaguely, that it would certainly be very agreeable, but I did not see how she was going to manage it.

"Come with me," was her smiling reply, "and see if I am not as good as my word."

My susceptibility to surprise had been pretty well exhausted by the numerous shocks it had received, but it was with some wonderment that I followed her into a room which I had not before entered. It was a small, cosy apartment, walled with cases filled with books.

"Here are your friends," said Edith, indicating one of the cases, and as my eye glanced over the names on the backs of the volumes, Shakespeare, Milton, Wordsworth, Shelley, Tennyson, Defoe, Dickens, Thackeray, Hugo, Hawthorne, Irving, and a score of other great writers of my time and all time, I understood her meaning. She had indeed made good her promise in a sense compared with which its literal fulfillment would have been a disappointment. She had introduced me to a circle of friends whom the century that had elapsed since last I communed with them had aged as little as it had myself. Their spirit was as high, their wit as keen, their laughter and their tears as contagious, as when their speech had whiled away the hours of a former century. Lonely I was not and could not be more, with this goodly companionship, however wide the gulf of years that gaped between me and my old life.

"You are glad I brought you here," exclaimed Edith, radiant, as she read in my face the success of her experiment. "It was a good idea, was it not, Mr. West? How stupid in me not to think of it before! I will leave you now with your old friends, for I know there will be no company for you like them just now; but remember you must not let old friends make you quite forget new ones!" and with that smiling caution she left me.

Attracted by the most familiar of the names before me, I laid my hand on a volume of Dickens, and sat down to read. He had been my prime favorite among the book-writers of the century,— I mean the nineteenth century,—and a week had rarely passed in my old life during which I had not taken up some volume of his works to while away an idle hour. Any volume with which I had been familiar would have produced an extraordinary impression, read under my present circumstances, but my exceptional familiarity with Dickens, and his consequent power to call up the associations of my former life, gave to his writings an effect no others could have had, to intensify, by force of contrast, my appreciation of the strangeness of my present environment. However new and astonishing one's surroundings, the tendency is to become a part of them so soon that almost from the first the power to see them objectively and fully measure their strangeness, is lost. That power, already dulled in my case, the pages of Dickens restored by carrying me back through their associations to the standpoint of my former life. With a clearness which I had not been able before to attain, I saw now the past and present, like contrasting pictures, side by side.

The genius of the great novelist of the nineteenth century, like that of Homer, might indeed defy time; but the setting of his pathetic tales, the misery of the poor, the wrongs of power, the pitiless cruelty of the system of society, had passed away as utterly as Circe and the sirens, Charybdis and Cyclops.

During the hour or two that I sat there with Dickens open before me, I did not actually read more than a couple of pages. Every paragraph, every phrase, brought up some new aspect of the world-transformation which had taken place, and led my thoughts on long and widely ramifying excursions. As meditating thus in Dr. Leete's library I gradually attained a more clear and coherent idea of the prodigious spectacle which I had been so strangely enabled to view, I was filled with a deepening wonder at the seeming capriciousness of the fate that had given to one who so little deserved it, or seemed in any way set apart for it, the power alone among his contemporaries to stand upon the earth in this latter day. I had neither foreseen the new world nor toiled for it, as many about me had done regardless of the scorn of fools or the misconstruction of the good. Surely it would have been more in accordance with the fitness of things had one of those prophetic and strenuous souls been enabled to see the travail of his soul and be satisfied; he, for example, a thousand times rather than I, who, having beheld in a vision the world I looked on, sang of it in words that again and again, during these last wondrous days, had rung in my mind:—

For I dipt into the future, far as human eye could see,
Saw the vision of the world, and all the wonder that would be;

Till the war-drum throbbed no longer, and the battle-flags were
   furled.
In the Parliament of man, the federation of the world.

Then the common sense of most shall hold a fretful realm in awe,
And the kindly earth shall slumber, lapt in universal law.

For I doubt not through the ages one increasing purpose runs,
And the thoughts of men are widened with the process of the sums.

What though, in his old age, he momentarily lost faith in his own prediction, as prophets in their hours of depression and doubt generally do; the words had remained eternal testimony to the seership of a poet's heart, the insight that is given to faith.

I was still in the library when some hours later Dr. Leete sought me there. "Edith told me of her idea," he said, "and I thought it an excellent one. I had a little curiosity what writer you would first turn to. Ah, Dickens! You admired him, then! That is where we moderns agree with you. Judged by our standards, he overtops all the writers of his age, not because his literary genius was highest, but because his great heart beat for the poor, because he made the cause of the victims of society his own, and devoted his pen to exposing its cruelties and shams. No man of his time did so much as he to turn men's minds to the wrong and wretchedness of the old order of things, and open their eyes to the necessity of the great change that was coming, although he himself did not clearly foresee it."

Chapter XIV

A HEAVY rainstorm came up during the day, and I had concluded that the condition of the streets would be such that my hosts would have to give up the idea of going out to dinner, although the dining-hall I had understood to be quite near. I was much surprised when at the dinner hour the ladies appeared prepared to go out, but without either rubbers or umbrellas.

The mystery was explained when we found ourselves on the street, for a continuous waterproof covering had been let down so as to inclose the sidewalk and turn it into a well lighted and perfectly dry corridor, which was filled with a stream of ladies and gentlemen dressed for dinner. At the corners the entire open space was similarly roofed in. Edith Leete, with whom I walked, seemed much interested in learning what appeared to be entirely new to her, that in the stormy weather the streets of the Boston of my day had been impassable, except to persons protected by umbrellas, boots, and heavy clothing. "Were sidewalk coverings not used at all?" she asked. They were used, I explained, but in a scattered and utterly unsystematic way, being private enterprises. She said to me that at the present time all the streets were provided against inclement weather in the manner I saw, the apparatus being rolled out of the way when it was unnecessary. She intimated that it would be considered an extraordinary imbecility to permit the weather to have any effect on the social movements of the people.

Dr. Leete, who was walking ahead, overhearing something of our talk, turned to say that the difference between the age of individualism and that of concert was well characterized by the fact that, in the nineteenth century, when it rained, the people of Boston put up three hundred thousand umbrellas over as

many heads, and in the twentieth century they put up one umbrella over all the heads.

As we walked on, Edith said, "The private umbrella is father's
favorite figure to illustrate the old way when everybody lived
for himself and his family. There is a nineteenth century paint-
ing at the Art Gallery representing a crowd of people in the
rain, each one holding his umbrella over himself and his wife,
and giving his neighbors the drippings, which he claims must
have been meant by the artist as a satire on his times."

We now entered a large building into which a stream of people
was pouring. I could not see the front, owing to the awning, but,
if in correspondence with the interior, which was even finer than
the store I visited the day before, it would have been magnificent.
My companion said that the sculptured group over the entrance
was especially admired. Going up a grand staircase we walked
some distance along a broad corridor with many doors opening
upon it. At one of these, which bore my host's name, we turned
in, and I found myself in an elegant dining-room containing a
table for four. Windows opened on a courtyard where a fountain
played to a great height and music made the air electric.

"You seem at home here," I said, as we seated ourselves at table,
and Dr. Leete touched an annunciator.

"This is, in fact, a part of our house, slightly detached from
the rest," he replied. "Every family in the ward has a room set
apart in this great building for its permanent and exclusive use
for a small annual rental. For transient guests and individuals
there is accommodation on another floor. If we expect to dine
here, we put in our orders the night before, selecting anything
in market, according to the daily reports in the papers. The meal
is as expensive or as simple as we please, though of course everything is vastly cheaper as well as better than it would be if
prepared at home. There is actually nothing which our people
take more interest in than the perfection of the catering and
cooking done for them, and I admit that we are a little vain of
the success that has been attained by this branch of the service.
Ah, my dear Mr. West, though other aspects of your civilization
were more tragical, I can imagine that none could have been

more depressing than the poor dinners you had to eat, that is, all of you who had not great wealth."

"You would have found none of us disposed to disagree with you on that point," I said.

The waiter, a fine-looking young fellow, wearing a slightly distinctive uniform, now made his appearance. I observed him closely, as it was the first time I had been able to study particularly the bearing of one of the enlisted members of the industrial army. This young man, I knew from what I had been told, must be highly educated, and the equal, socially and in all respects, of those he served. But it was perfectly evident that to neither side was the situation in the slightest degree embarrassing. Dr. Leete addressed the young man in a tone devoid, of course, as any gentleman's would be, of superciliousness, but at the same time not in any way deprecatory, while the manner of the young man was simply that of a person intent on discharging correctly the task he was engaged in, equally without familiarity or obsequiousness. It was, in fact, the manner of a soldier on duty, but without the military stiffness. As the youth left the room, I said, "I cannot get over my wonder at seeing a young man like that serving so contentedly in a menial position."

"What is that word 'menial'? I never heard it," said Edith.

"It is obsolete now," remarked her father. "If I understand it rightly, it applied to persons who performed particularly disagreeable and unpleasant tasks for others, and carried with it an implication of contempt. Was it not so, Mr. West?"

"That is about it," I said. "Personal service, such as waiting on tables, was considered menial, and held in such contempt, in my day, that persons of culture and refinement would suffer hardship before condescending to it."

"What a strangely artificial idea," exclaimed Mrs. Leete, wonderingly.

"And yet these services had to be rendered," said Edith.

"Of course," I replied. "But we imposed them on the poor, and those who had no alternative but starvation."

"And increased the burden you imposed on them by adding your contempt," remarked Dr. Leete.

"I don't think I clearly understand," said Edith. "Do you mean that you permitted people to do things for you which you despised them for doing, or that you accepted services from them which you would have been unwilling to render them? You can't surely mean that, Mr. West?"

I was obliged to tell her that the fact was just as she had stated. Dr. Leete, however, came to my relief.

"To understand why Edith is surprised," he said, "you must know that nowadays it is an axiom of ethics that to accept a service from another which we would be unwilling to return in kind, if need were, is like borrowing with the intention of not repaying, while to enforce such a service by taking advantage of the poverty or necessity of a person would be an outrage like forcible robbery. It is the worst thing about any system which divides men, or allows them to be divided, into classes and castes, that it weakens the sense of a common humanity. Unequal distribution of wealth, and, still more effectually, unequal opportunities of education and culture, divided society in your day into classes which in many respects regarded each other as distinct races. There is not, after all, such a difference as might appear between our ways of looking at this question of service. Ladies and gentlemen of the cultured class in your day would no more have permitted persons of their own class to render them services they would scorn to return than we would permit anybody to do so. The poor and the uncultured, however, they looked upon as of another kind from themselves. The equal wealth and equal opportunities of culture which all persons now enjoy have simply made us all members of one class, which corresponds to the most fortunate class with you. Until this equality of condition had come to pass, the idea of the solidarity of humanity, the brotherhood of all men, could never have become the real conviction and practical principle of action it is nowadays. In your day the same phrases were indeed used, but they were phrases merely."

"Do the waiters, also, volunteer?"

"No," replied Dr. Leete. "The waiters are young men in the unclassified grade of the industrial army who are assignable to all sorts of miscellaneous occupations not requiring special skill. Waiting on table is one of these, and every young recruit is given a taste of it. I myself served as a waiter for several months in this very dining-house some forty years ago. Once more you must remember that there is recognized no sort of difference between the dignity of the different sorts of work required by the nation. The individual is never regarded, nor regards himself, as the servant of those he serves, nor is he in any way dependent upon them. It is always the nation which he is serving. No difference is recognized between a waiter's functions and those of any other worker. The fact that his is a personal service is indifferent from our point of view. So is a doctor's. I should as soon expect our waiter to-day to look down on me because I served him as a doctor, as think of looking down on him because he serves me as a waiter."

After dinner my entertainers conducted me about the building, of which the extent, the magnificent architecture and richness of embellishment, astonished me. It seemed that it was not merely a dining-hall, but likewise a great pleasure-house and social rendezvous of the quarter, and no appliance of entertainment or recreation seemed lacking.

"You find illustrated here," said Dr. Leete, when I had expressed my admiration, "what I said to you in our first conversation, when you were looking out over the city, as to the splendor of our public and common life as compared with the simplicity of our private and home life, and the contrast which, in this respect, the twentieth bears to the nineteenth century. To save ourselves useless burdens, we have as little gear about us at home as is consistent with comfort, but the social side of our life is ornate and luxurious beyond anything the world ever knew before. All the industrial and professional guilds have clubhouses as extensive as this, as well as country, mountain, and seaside houses for sport and rest in vacations."

NOTE. In the latter part of the nineteenth century it became a practice of needy young men at some of the colleges of the country to earn a little money for their term bills by serving as waiters on tables at hotels during the long summer vacation. It was claimed, in reply to critics who expressed the prejudices of the time in asserting that persons voluntarily following such an occupation could not be gentlemen, that they were entitled to praise for vindicating, by their example, the dignity of all honest and necessary labor. The use of this argument illustrates a common confusion in thought on the part of my former contemporaries. The business of waiting on tables was in no more need of defense than most of the other ways of getting a living in that day, but to talk of dignity attaching to labor of any sort under the system then prevailing was absurd. There is no way in which selling labor for the highest price it will fetch is more dignified than selling goods for what can be got. Both were commercial transactions to be judged by the commercial standard. By setting a price in money on his service, the worker accepted the money measure for it, and renounced all clear claim to be judged by any other. The sordid taint which this necessity imparted to the noblest and the highest sorts of service was bitterly resented by generous souls, but there was no evading it. There was no exemption, however transcendent the quality of one's service, from the necessity of haggling for its price in the market-place. The physician must sell his healing and the apostle his preaching like the rest. The prophet, who had guessed the meaning of God, must dicker for the price of the revelation, and the poet hawk his visions in printers' row. If I were asked to name the most distinguishing felicity of this age, as compared to that in which I first saw the light, I should say that to me it seems to consist in the dignity you have given to labor by refusing to set a price upon it and abolishing the market-place forever. By requiring of every man his best you have made God his taskmaster, and by making honor the sole reward of achievement you have imparted to all service the distinction peculiar in my day to the soldier's.

Chapter XV

*W*HEN, in the course of our tour of inspection, we came to the library, we succumbed to the temptation of the luxurious leather chairs with which it was furnished, and sat down in one of the book-lined alcoves to rest and chat awhile.[1]

"Edith tells me that you have been in the library all the morning," said Mrs. Leete. "Do you know, it seems to me, Mr. West, that you are the most enviable of mortals."

"I should like to know just why," I replied.

"Because the books of the last hundred years will be new to you," she answered. "You will have so much of the most absorbing literature to read as to leave you scarcely time for meals these five years to come. Ah, what would I give if I had not already read Berrian's novels."

"Or Nesmyth's, mamma," added Edith.

"Yes, or Oates' poems, or 'Past and Present,' or, 'In the Beginning,' or,—oh, I could name a dozen books, each worth a year of one's life," declared Mrs. Leete, enthusiastically.

"I judge, then, that there has been some notable literature produced in this century."

"Yes," said Dr. Leete. "It has been an era of unexampled intellectual splendor. Probably humanity never before passed through a moral and material evolution, at once so vast in its scope and brief in its time of accomplishment, as that from the old order to the new in the early part of this century. When men came to realize the greatness of the felicity which had befallen them, and

[1] I cannot sufficiently celebrate the glorious liberty that reigns in the public libraries of the twentieth century as compared with the intolerable management of those of the nineteenth century, in which the books were jealously railed away from the people, and obtainable only at an expenditure of time and red tape calculated to discourage any ordinary taste for literature.

that the change through which they had passed was not merely an improvement in details of their condition, but the rise of the race to a new plane of existence with an illimitable vista of progress, their minds were affected in all their faculties with a stimulus, of which the outburst of the mediaeval renaissance offers a suggestion but faint indeed. There ensued an era of mechanical invention, scientific discovery, art, musical and literary productiveness to which no previous age of the world offers anything comparable."

"By the way," said I, "talking of literature, how are books published now? Is that also done by the nation?"

"Certainly."

"But how do you manage it? Does the government publish everything that is brought it as a matter of course, at the public expense, or does it exercise a censorship and print only what it approves?"

"Neither way. The printing department has no censorial powers. It is bound to print all that is offered it, but prints it only on condition that the author defray the first cost out of his credit. He must pay for the privilege of the public ear, and if he has any message worth hearing we consider that he will be glad to do it. Of course, if incomes were unequal, as in the old times, this rule would enable only the rich to be authors, but the resources of citizens being equal, it merely measures the strength of the author's motive. The cost of an edition of an average book can be saved out of a year's credit by the practice of economy and some sacrifices. The book, on being published, is placed on sale by the nation."

"The author receiving a royalty on the sales as with us, I suppose," I suggested.

"Not as with you, certainly," replied Dr. Leete, "but nevertheless in one way. The price of every book is made up of the cost of its publication with a royalty for the author. The author fixes this royalty at any figure he pleases. Of course if he puts it unreasonably high it is his own loss, for the book will not sell.* The amount of this royalty is set to his credit and he is

* [This sentence and the one immediately preceding were added in the second edition.]

discharged from other service to the nation for so long a period as this credit at the rate of allowance for the support of citizens shall suffice to support him. If his book be moderately successful, he has thus a furlough for several months, a year, two or three years, and if he in the mean time produces other successful work, the remission of service is extended so far as the sale of that may justify. An author of much acceptance succeeds in supporting himself by his pen during the entire period of service, and the degree of any writer's literary ability, as determined by the popular voice, is thus the measure of the opportunity given him to devote his time to literature. In this respect the outcome of our system is not very dissimilar to that of yours, but there are two notable differences. In the first place, the universally high level of education nowadays gives the popular verdict a conclusiveness on the real merit of literary work which in your day it was as far as possible from having. In the second place, there is no such thing now as favoritism of any sort to interfere with the recognition of true merit. Every author has precisely the same facilities for bringing his work before the popular tribunal. To judge from the complaints of the writers of your day, this absolute equality of opportunity would have been greatly prized."

"In the recognition of merit in other fields of original genius, such as music, art, invention, design," I said, "I suppose you follow a similar principle."

"Yes," he replied, "although the details differ. In art, for example, as in literature, the people are the sole judges. They vote upon the acceptance of statues and paintings for the public buildings, and their favorable verdict carries with it the artist's remission from other tasks to devote himself to his vocation. On copies of his work disposed of, he also derives the same advantage as the author on sales of his books.* In all these lines of original genius the plan pursued is the same,—to offer a free field to aspirants, and as soon as exceptional talent is recognized to release it from all trammels and let it have free course. The remission of other service in these cases is not intended as a gift

* [This sentence was added in the second edition.]

or reward, but as the means of obtaining more and higher service. Of course there are various literary, art, and scientific institutes to which membership comes to the famous and is greatly prized. The highest of all honors in the nation, higher than the presidency, which calls merely for good sense and devotion to duty, is the red ribbon awarded by the vote of the people to the great authors, artists, engineers, physicians, and inventors of the generation. Not over a certain number wear it at any one time, though every bright young fellow in the country loses innumerable nights' sleep dreaming of it. I even did myself."

"Just as if mamma and I would have thought any more of you with it," exclaimed Edith; "not that it isn't, of course, a very fine thing to have."

"You had no choice, my dear, but to take your father as you found him and make the best of him," Dr. Leete replied; "but as for your mother, there, she would never have had me if I had not assured her that I was bound to get the red ribbon or at least the blue."

On this extravagance Mrs. Leete's only comment was a smile.

"How about periodicals and newspapers?" I said. "I won't deny that your book publishing system is a considerable improvement on ours, both as to its tendency to encourage a real literary vocation, and, quite as important, to discourage mere scribblers; but I don't see how it can be made to apply to magazines and newspapers. It is very well to make a man pay for publishing a book, because the expense will be only occasional; but no man could afford the expense of publishing a newspaper every day in the year. It took the deep pockets of our private capitalists to do that, and often exhausted even them before the returns came in. If you have newspapers at all, they must, I fancy, be published by the government at the public expense, with government editors, reflecting government opinions. Now, if your system is so perfect that there is never anything to criticise in the conduct of affairs, this arrangement may answer. Otherwise I should think the lack of an independent unofficial medium for the expression of public opinion would have most unfortunate results. Confess, Dr. Leete, that a free newspaper press, with all that it implies, was a redeeming incident of the old system when capital was in private hands, and that you have to set off the loss of that against your gains in other respects."

"I am afraid I can't give you even that consolation," replied Dr. Leete, laughing. "In the first place, Mr. West, the newspaper press is by no means the only or, as we look at it, the best vehicle for serious criticism of public affairs. To us, the judgments of your newspapers on such themes seem generally to have been crude and flippant, as well as deeply tinctured with prejudice and bitterness. In so far as they may be taken as expressing public opinion, they give an unfavorable impression of the popular intelligence, while so far as they may have formed public opinion, the nation was not to be felicitated. Nowadays, when a citizen desires to make a serious impression upon the public mind as to any aspect of public affairs, he comes out with a book or pamphlet, published as other books are. But this is not because we lack newspapers and magazines, or that they lack the most absolute freedom. The newspaper press is organized so as to be a more perfect expression of public opinion than it possibly could be in your day, when private capital controlled and managed it primarily as a money-making business, and secondarily only as a mouthpiece for the people."

"But," said I, "if the government prints the papers at the public expense, how can it fail to control their policy? Who appoints the editors, if not the government?"

"The government does not pay the expense of the papers, nor appoint their editors, nor in any way exert the slightest influence on their policy," replied Dr. Leete. "The people who take the paper pay the expense of its publication, choose its editor, and remove him when unsatisfactory. You will scarcely say, I think, that such a newspaper press is not a free organ of popular opinion."

"Decidedly I shall not," I replied, "but how is it practicable?"

"Nothing could be simpler. Supposing some of my neighbors or myself think we ought to have a newspaper reflecting our opinions, and devoted especially to our locality, trade, or profession. We go about among the people till we get the names of such a number that their annual subscriptions will meet the cost of the paper, which is little or big according to the largeness of its constituency. The amount of the subscriptions marked off the credits of the citizens guarantees the nation against loss in publishing the paper, its business, you understand, being that of a publisher purely, with no option to refuse the duty required. The subscribers to the paper now elect somebody as editor, who, if he accepts the office, is discharged from other service during his incumbency. Instead of paying a salary to him, as in your day, the subscribers pay the nation an indemnity equal to the cost of his support for taking him away from the general service. He manages the paper just as one of your editors did, except that he has no counting-room to obey, or interests of private capital as against the public good to defend. At the end of the first year, the subscribers for the next either reëlect the former editor or choose any one else to his place. An able editor, of course, keeps his place indefinitely. As the subscription list enlarges, the funds of the paper increase, and it is improved by the securing of more and better contributors, just as your papers were."

"How is the staff of contributors recompensed, since they cannot be paid in money."

"The editor settles with them the price of their wares. The amount is transferred to their individual credit from the guarantee credit of the paper, and a remission of service is granted the contributor for a length of time corresponding to the amount credited him, just as to other authors. As to magazines, the system is the same. Those interested in the prospectus of a new periodical pledge enough subscriptions to run it for a year; select their editor, who recompenses his contributors just as in the other case, the printing bureau furnishing the necessary force and material for publication, as a matter of course. When an editor's services are no longer desired, if he cannot earn the right to his time by other literary work, he simply resumes his place in the industrial army. I should add that, though ordinarily the editor is elected only at the end of the year, and as a rule is continued in office for a term of years, in case of any sudden change he should give to the tone of the paper, provision is made for taking the sense of the subscribers as to his removal at any time."

"However earnestly a man may long for leisure for purposes

of study or meditation," I remarked, "he cannot get out of the harness, if I understand you rightly, except in these two ways you have mentioned. He must either by literary, artistic, or inventive productiveness indemnify the nation for the loss of his services, or must get a sufficient number of other people to contribute to such an indemnity."

"It is most certain," replied Dr. Leete, "that no able-bodied man nowadays can evade his share of work and live on the toil of others, whether he calls himself by the fine name of student, or confesses to being simply lazy. At the same time our system is elastic enough to give free play to every instinct of human nature which does not aim at dominating others or living on the fruit of others' labor. There is not only the remission by indemnification but the remission by abnegation. Any man in his thirty-third year, his term of service being then half done, can obtain an honorable discharge from the army, provided he accepts for the rest of his life one half the rate of maintenance other citizens receive. It is quite possible to live on this amount, though one must forego the luxuries and elegancies of life, with some, perhaps, of its comforts." *

When the ladies retired that evening, Edith brought me a book and said:—

"If you should be wakeful to-night, Mr. West, you might be interested in looking over this story by Berrian. It is considered his masterpiece, and will at least give you an idea what the stories nowadays are like."

I sat up in my room that night reading "Penthesilia" till it grew gray in the east, and did not lay it down till I had finished it. And yet let no admirer of the great romancer of the twentieth century resent my saying that at the first reading what most impressed me was not so much what was in the book as what was left out of it. The story-writers of my day would have deemed the making of bricks without straw a light task compared with the construction of a romance from which should be excluded all effects drawn from the contrasts of wealth and poverty, education and ignorance, coarseness and refinement, high and low,

---

* [The preceding two paragraphs were added in the second edition.]

all motives drawn from social pride and ambition, the desire of being richer or the fear of being poorer, together with sordid anxieties of any sort for one's self or others; a romance in which there should, indeed, be love galore, but love unfretted by artificial barriers created by differences of station or possessions, owning no other law but that of the heart. The reading of "Penthesilia" was of more value than almost any amount of explanation would have been in giving me something like a general impression of the social aspect of the twentieth century. The information Dr. Leete had imparted was indeed extensive as to facts, but they had affected my mind as so many separate impressions, which I had as yet succeeded but imperfectly in making cohere. Berrian put them together for me in a picture.

Chapter XVI

*N*EXT morning I rose somewhat before the breakfast hour. As I descended the stairs, Edith stepped into the hall from the room which had been the scene of the morning interview between us described some chapters back.

"Ah!" she exclaimed, with a charmingly arch expression, "you thought to slip out unbeknown for another of those solitary morning rambles which have such nice effects on you. But you see I am up too early for you this time. You are fairly caught."

"You discredit the efficacy of your own cure," I said, "by supposing that such a ramble would now be attended with bad consequences."

"I am very glad to hear that," she said. "I was in here arranging some flowers for the breakfast table when I heard you come down, and fancied I detected something surreptitious in your step on the stairs."

"You did me injustice," I replied. "I had no idea of going out at all."

Despite her effort to convey an impression that my interception was purely accidental, I had at the time a dim suspicion of what I afterwards learned to be the fact, namely, that this sweet creature, in pursuance of her self-assumed guardianship over me, had risen for the last two or three mornings at an unheard-of hour, to insure against the possibility of my wandering off alone in case I should be affected as on the former occasion. Receiving permission to assist her in making up the breakfast bouquet, I followed her into the room from which she had emerged.

"Are you sure," she asked, "that you are quite done with those terrible sensations you had that morning?"

"I can't say that I do not have times of feeling decidedly queer," I replied, "moments when my personal identity seems an open question. It would be too much to expect after my experience that I should not have such sensations occasionally, but as for being carried entirely off my feet, as I was on the point of being that morning, I think the danger is past."

"I shall never forget how you looked that morning," she said.

"If you had merely saved my life," I continued, "I might, perhaps, find words to express my gratitude, but it was my reason you saved, and there are no words that would not belittle my debt to you." I spoke with emotion, and her eyes grew suddenly moist.

"It is too much to believe all this," she said, "but it is very delightful to hear you say it. What I did was very little. I was ᵥvery much distressed for you, I know. Father never thinks anything ought to astonish us when it can be explained scientifically, as I suppose this long sleep of yours can be, but even to fancy myself in your place makes my head swim. I know that I could not have borne it at all."

"That would depend," I replied, "on whether an angel came to support you with her sympathy in the crisis of your condition, as one came to me." If my face at all expressed the feelings I had a right to have toward this sweet and lovely young girl, who had played so angelic a role toward me, its expression must have been very worshipful just then. The expression or the words, or both together, caused her now to drop her eyes with a charming blush.

"For the matter of that," I said, "if your experience has not been as startling as mine, it must have been rather overwhelming to see a man belonging to a strange century, and apparently a hundred years dead, raised to life."

"It seemed indeed strange beyond any describing at first," she said, "but when we began to put ourselves in your place, and realize how much stranger it must seem to you, I fancy we forgot our own feelings a good deal, at least I know I did. It seemed then not so much astounding as interesting and touching beyond anything ever heard of before."

"But does it not come over you as astounding to sit at table with me, seeing who I am?"

"You must remember that you do not seem so strange to us as

we must to you," she answered. "We belong to a future of which you could not form an idea, a generation of which you knew nothing until you saw us. But you belong to a generation of which our forefathers were a part. We know all about it; the names of many of its members are household words with us. We have made a study of your ways of living and thinking; nothing you say or do surprises us, while we say and do nothing which does not seem strange to you. So you see, Mr. West, that if you feel that you can, in time, get accustomed to us, you must not be surprised that from the first we have scarcely found you strange at all."

"I had not thought of it in that way," I replied. "There is indeed much in what you say. One can look back a thousand years easier than forward fifty. A century is not so very long a retrospect. I might have known your great-grand-parents. Possibly I did. Did they live in Boston?"

"I believe so."

"You are not sure, then?"

"Yes," she replied. "Now I think, they did."

"I had a very large circle of acquaintances in the city," I said. "It is not unlikely that I knew or knew of some of them. Perhaps I may have known them well. Wouldn't it be interesting if I should chance to be able to tell you all about your great-grand-father, for instance?"

"Very interesting."

"Do you know your genealogy well enough to tell me who your forbears were in the Boston of my day?"

"Oh, yes."

"Perhaps, then, you will some time tell me what some of their names were."

She was engrossed in arranging a troublesome spray of green, and did not reply at once. Steps upon the stairway indicated that the other members of the family were descending.

"Perhaps, some time," she said.

After breakfast, Dr. Leete suggested taking me to inspect the central warehouse and observe actually in operation the machinery of distribution, which Edith had described to me. As we walked away from the house I said, "It is now several days that I have been living in your household on a most extraordinary footing, or rather on none at all. I have not spoken of this aspect of my position before because there were so many other aspects yet more extraordinary. But now that I am beginning a little to feel my feet under me, and to realize that, however I came here, I am here, and must make the best of it, I must speak to you on this point."

"As for your being a guest in my house," replied Dr. Leete, "I pray you not to begin to be uneasy on that point, for I mean to keep you a long time yet. With all your modesty, you can but realize that such a guest as yourself is an acquisition not willingly to be parted with."

"Thanks, doctor," I said. "It would be absurd, certainly, for me to affect any oversensitiveness about accepting the temporary hospitality of one to whom I owe it that I am not still awaiting the end of the world in a living tomb. But if I am to be a permanent citizen of this century I must have some standing in it. Now, in my time a person more or less entering the world, however he got in, would not be noticed in the unorganized throng of men, and might make a place for himself anywhere he chose if he were strong enough. But nowadays everybody is a part of a system with a distinct place and function. I am outside the system, and don't see how I can get in; there seems no way to get in, except to be born in or to come in as an emigrant from some other system."

Dr. Leete laughed heartily.

"I admit," he said, "that our system is defective in lacking provision for cases like yours, but you see nobody anticipated additions to the world except by the usual process. You need, however, have no fear that we shall be unable to provide both a place and occupation for you in due time. You have as yet been brought in contact only with the members of my family, but you must not suppose that I have kept your secret. On the contrary, your case, even before your resuscitation, and vastly more since, has excited the profoundest interest in the nation. In view of your precarious nervous condition, it was thought best that I should take exclusive charge of you at first, and that you should, through me and my family, receive some general idea of the sort of world you had come back to before you began to make the acquaintance generally of its inhabitants. As to finding a function for you in society, there was no hesitation as to what that would be. Few of us have it in our power to confer so great a service on the nation as you will be able to when you leave my roof, which, however, you must not think of doing for a good time yet."

"What can I possibly do?" I asked. "Perhaps you imagine I have some trade, or art, or special skill. I assure you I have none whatever. I never earned a dollar in my life, or did an hour's work. I am strong, and might be a common laborer, but nothing more."

"If that were the most efficient service you were able to render the nation, you would find that avocation considered quite as respectable as any other," replied Dr. Leete; "but you can do something else better. You are easily the master of all our historians on questions relating to the social condition of the latter part of the nineteenth century, to us one of the most absorbingly interesting periods of history; and whenever in due time you have sufficiently familiarized yourself with our instituttions, and are willing to teach us something concerning those of your day, you will find an historical lectureship in one of our colleges awaiting you."

"Very good! very good indeed," I said, much relieved by so practical a suggestion on a point which had begun to trouble me. "If your people are really so much interested in the nineteenth century, there will indeed be an occupation readymade for me. I don't think there is anything else that I could possiby earn my salt at, but I certainly may claim without conceit to have some special qualifications for such a post as you describe."

Chapter XVII

I FOUND the processes at the warehouse quite as interesting as Edith had described them, and became even enthusiastic over the truly remarkable illustration which is seen there of the prodigiously multiplied efficiency which perfect organization can give to labor. It is like a gigantic mill, into the hopper of which goods are being constantly poured by the train-load and shipload, to issue at the other end in packages of pounds and ounces, yards and inches, pints and gallons, corresponding to the infinitely complex personal needs of half a million people. Dr. Leete, with the assistance of data furnished by me as to the way goods were sold in my day, figured out some astounding results in the way of the economies effected by the modern system.

As we set out homeward, I said: "After what I have seen today, together with what you have told me, and what I learned under Miss Leete's tutelage at the sample store, I have a tolerably clear idea of your system of distribution, and how it enables you to dispense with a circulating medium. But I should like very much to know something more about your system of production. You have told me in general how your industrial army is levied and organized, but who directs its efforts? What supreme authority determines what shall be done in every department, so that enough of everything is produced and yet no labor wasted? It seems to me that this must be a wonderfully complex and difficult function, requiring very unusual endowments."

"Does it indeed seem so to you?" responded Dr. Leete. "I assure you that it is nothing of the kind, but on the other hand so simple, and depending on principles so obvious and easily applied, that the functionaries at Washington to whom it is trusted require to be nothing more than men of fair abilities to discharge it to the entire satisfaction of the nation. The machine which they direct is indeed a vast one, but so logical in its principles and direct and simple in its workings, that it all but runs itself; and nobody but a fool could derange it, as I think you will agree after a few words of explanation. Since you already have a pretty good idea of the working of the distributive system, let us begin at that end. Even in your day statisticians were able to tell you the number of yards of cotton, velvet, woolen, the number of barrels of flour, potatoes, butter, number of pairs of shoes, hats, and umbrellas annually consumed by the nation. Owing to the fact that production was in private hands, and that there was no way of getting statistics of actual distribution, these figures were not exact, but they were nearly so. Now that every pin which is given out from a national warehouse is recorded, of course the figures of consumption for any week, month, or year, in the possession of the department of distribution at the end of that period, are precise. On these figures, allowing for tendencies to increase or decrease and for any special causes likely to affect demand, the estimates, say for a year ahead, are based. These estimates, with a proper margin for security, having been accepted by the general administration, the responsibility of the distributive department ceases until the goods are delivered to it. I speak of the estimates being furnished for an entire year ahead, but in reality they cover that much time only in case of the great staples for which the demand can be calculated on as steady. In the great majority of smaller industries for the product of which popular taste fluctuates, and novelty is frequently required, production is kept barely ahead of consumption, the distributive department furnishing frequent estimates based on the weekly state of demand.

"Now the entire field of productive and constructive industry is divided into ten great departments, each representing a group of allied industries, each particular industry being in turn represented by a subordinate bureau, which has a complete record of the plant and force under its control, of the present product, and means of increasing it. The estimates of the distributive department, after adoption by the administration, are sent as mandates to the ten great departments, which allot them to the subordinate bureaus representing the particular industries, and these set the men at work. Each bureau is responsible for the task given it, and this responsibility is enforced by departmental oversight and that of the administration; nor does the distributive department accept the product without its own inspection; while even if in the hands of the consumer an article turns out unfit, the system enables the fault to be traced back to the original workman. The production of the commodities for actual public consumption does not, of course, require by any means all the national force of workers. After the necessary contingents have been detailed for the various industries, the amount of labor left for other employment is expended in creating fixed capital, such as buildings, machinery, engineering works, and so forth."

"One point occurs to me," I said, "on which I should think there might be dissatisfaction. Where there is no opportunity for private enterprise, how is there any assurance that the claims of small minorities of the people to have articles produced, for which there is no wide demand, will be respected? An official decree at any moment may deprive them of the means of gratifying some special taste, merely because the majority does not share it."

"That would be tyranny indeed," replied Dr. Leete, "and you may be very sure that it does not happen with us, to whom liberty is as dear as equality or fraternity. As you come to know our system better, you will see that our officials are in fact, and not merely in name, the agents and servants of the people. The administration has no power to stop the production of any commodity for which there continues to be a demand. Suppose the demand for any article declines to such a point that its production becomes very costly. The price has to be raised in proportion, of course, but as long as the consumer cares to pay it, the production goes on. Again, suppose an article not before produced is demanded. If the administration doubts the reality of the demand, a popular petition guaranteeing a certain basis of consumption compels it to produce the desired article. A government, or a majority, which should undertake to tell the people, or a minority, what they were to eat, drink, or wear, as I believe governments in America did in your day, would be regarded as a curious anachronism indeed. Possibly you had reasons for tolerating these infringements of personal independence, but we should not think them endurable. I am glad you raised this point, for it has given me a chance to show you how much more direct and efficient is the control over production exercised by the individual citizen now than it was in your day, when what you called private initiative prevailed, though it should have been called capitalist initiative, for the average private citizen had little enough share in it."

"You speak of raising the price of costly articles," I said. "How can prices be regulated in a country where there is no competition between buyers or sellers?"

"Just as they were with you," replied Dr. Leete. "You think that needs explaining," he added, as I looked incredulous, "but the explanation need not be long; the cost of the labor which produced it was recognized as the legitimate basis of the price of an article in your day, and so it is in ours. In your day, it was the difference in wages that made the difference in the cost of labor; now it is the relative number of hours constituting a day's work in different trades, the maintenance of the worker being equal in all cases. The cost of a man's work in a trade so difficult that in order to attract volunteers the hours have to be fixed at four a day is twice as great as that in a trade where the men work eight hours. The result as to the cost of labor, you see, is just the same as if the man working four hours were paid, under your system, twice the wages the other gets. This calculation applied to the labor employed in the various processes of a manufactured article gives its price relatively to other articles. Besides the cost of production and transportation, the factor of scarcity affects the prices of some commodities. As regards the great staples of life, of which an abundance can always be secured, scarcity is eliminated as a factor. There is always a large surplus kept on hand from which any fluctuations of demand or supply can be corrected, even in most cases of bad crops. The prices of the staples grow less year by year, but rarely, if ever, rise. There are, however, certain classes of articles permanently, and others temporarily, unequal to the demand, as, for example, fresh fish or dairy products in the latter category, and the products of high skill and rare materials in the other. All that can be done here is to equalize the inconvenience of the scarcity. This is done by temporarily raising the price if the scarcity be temporary, or fixing it high if it be permanent. High prices in your day meant restriction of the articles affected to the rich, but nowadays, when the means of all are the same, the effect is only that those to whom the articles seem most desirable are the ones who purchase them. Of course the nation, as any other caterer for the public needs must be, is frequently left with small lots of goods on its hands by changes in taste, unseasonable weather, and various other causes. These it has to dispose of at a sacrifice just as merchants often did in your day, charging up the loss to the expenses of the business. Owing, however, to the vast body of consumers to which such lots can be simultaneously offered, there is rarely any difficulty in getting rid of them at trifling loss.* I have given you now some general notion of our system of production, as well as distribution. Do you find it as complex as you expected?"

I admitted that nothing could be much simpler.

"I am sure," said Dr. Leete, "that it is within the truth to say that the head of one of the myriad private businesses of your day, who had to maintain sleepless vigilance against the fluctuations of the market, the machinations of his rivals, and the failure of his debtors, had a far more trying task than the group of men at Washington who nowadays direct the industries of the entire nation. All this merely shows, my dear fellow, how much easier it is to do things the right way than the wrong. It is easier for a general up in a balloon, with perfect survey of the field, to manoeuvre a million men to victory than for a sergeant to manage a platoon in a thicket."

* [The passage beginning "Of course the nation. . . . " was added in the second edition.]

"The general of this army, including the flower of the manhood of the nation, must be the foremost man in the country, really greater even than the President of the United States," I said.

"He is the President of the United States," replied Dr. Leete, "or rather the most important function of the presidency is the headship of the industrial army."

"How is he chosen?" I asked.

"I explained to you before," replied Dr. Leete, "when I was describing the force of the motive of emulation among all grades of the industrial army, that the line of promotion for the meritorious lies through three grades to the officer's grade, and thence up through the lieutenancies to the captaincy or foremanship, and superintendency or colonel's rank. Next, with an intervening grade in some of the larger trades, come the general of the guild, under whose immediate control all the operations of the trade are conducted. This officer is at the head of the national bureau representing his trade, and is responsible for its work to the administration. The general of his guild holds a splendid position, and one which amply satisfies the ambition of most men, but above his rank, which may be compared—to follow the military analogies familiar to you—to that of a general of division or major-general, is that of the chiefs of the ten great departments, or groups of allied trades. The chiefs of these ten grand divisions of the industrial army may be compared to your commanders of army corps, or lieutenant-generals, each having from a dozen to a score of generals of separate guilds reporting to him. Above these ten great officers, who form his council, is the general-in-chief, who is the President of the United States.

"The general-in-chief of the industrial army must have passed through all the grades below him, from the common laborers up. Let us see how he rises. As I have told you, it is simply by the excellence of his record as a worker that one rises through the grades of the privates and becomes a candidate for a lieutenancy. Through the lieutenancies he rises to the colonelcy, or superintendent's position, by appointment from above, strictly limited to the candidates of the best records. The general of the guild appoints to the ranks under him, but he himself is not appointed, but chosen by suffrage."

"By suffrage!" I exclaimed. "Is not that ruinous to the discipline of the guild, by tempting the candidates to intrigue for the support of the workers under them?"

"So it would be, no doubt," replied Dr. Leete, "if the workers had any suffrage to exercise, or anything to say about the choice. But they have nothing. Just here comes in a peculiarity of our system. The general of the guild is chosen from among the superintendents by vote of the honorary members of the guild, that is, of those who have served their time in the guild and received their discharge. As you know, at the age of forty-five we are mustered out of the army of industry, and have the residue of life for the pursuit of our own improvement or recreation. Of course, however, the associations of our active lifetime retain a powerful hold on us. The companionships we formed then remain our companionships till the end of life. We always continue honorary members of our former guilds, and retain the keenest and most jealous interest in their welfare and repute in the hands of the following generation. In the clubs maintained by the honorary members of the several guilds, in which we meet socially, there are no topics of conversation so common as those which relate to these matters, and the young aspirants for guild leadership who can pass the criticism of us old fellows are likely to be pretty well equipped. Recognizing this fact, the nation entrusts to the honorary members of each guild the election of its general, and I venture to claim that no previous form of society could have developed a body of electors so ideally adapted to their office, as regards absolute impartiality, knowledge of the special qualifications and record of candidates, solicitude for the best result, and complete absence of self-interest.

"Each of the ten lieutenant-generals or heads of departments is himself elected from among the generals of the guilds grouped as a department, by vote of the honorary members of the guilds thus grouped. Of course there is a tendency on the part of each guild to vote for its own general, but no guild of any group has nearly enough votes to elect a man not supported by most of the others. I assure you that these elections are exceedingly lively."

"The President, I suppose, is selected from among the ten heads of the great departments," I suggested.

"Precisely, but the heads of departments are not eligible to the presidency till they have been a certain number of years out of office. It is rarely that a man passes through all the grades to the headship of a department much before he is forty, and at the end of a five years' term he is usually forty-five. If more, he still serves through his term, and if less, he is nevertheless discharged from the industrial army at its termination. It would not do for him to return to the ranks. The interval before he is a candidate for the presidency is intended to give time for him to recognize fully that he has returned into the general mass of the nation, and is identified with it rather than with the industrial army. Moreover, it is expected that he will employ this period in studying the general condition of the army, instead of that of the special group of guilds of which he was the head. From among the former heads of departments who may be eligible at the time, the President is elected by vote of all the men of the nation who are not connected with the industrial army."

"The army is not allowed to vote for President?"

"Certainly not. That would be perilous to its discipline, which it is the business of the President to maintain as the representative of the nation at large. His right hand for this purpose is the inspectorate, a highly important department of our system; to the inspectorate come all complaints or information as to defects in goods, insolence or inefficiency of officials, or dereliction of any sort in the public service. The inspectorate, however, does not wait for complaints. Not only is it on the alert to catch and sift every rumor of a fault in the service, but it is its business, by systematic and constant oversight and inspection of every branch of the army, to find out what is going wrong before anybody else does.* The President is usually not far from fifty when elected, and serves five years, forming an honorable ex-

* [The passage beginning "His right hand. . . ." was added in the second edition.]

ception to the rule of retirement at forty-five. At the end of his term of office, a national Congress is called to receive his report and approve or condemn it. If it is approved, Congress usually elects him to represent the nation for five years more in the international council. Congress, I should also say, passes on the reports of the outgoing heads of departments, and a disapproval renders any one of them ineligible for President. But it is rare, indeed, that the nation has occasion for other sentiments than those of gratitude toward its high officers. As to their ability, to have risen from the ranks, by tests so various and severe, to their positions, is proof in itself of extraordinary qualities, while as to faithfulness, our social system leaves them absolutely without any other motive than that of winning the esteem of their fellow citizens. Corruption is impossible in a society where there is neither poverty to be bribed nor wealth to bribe, while as to demagoguery or intrigue for office, the conditions of promotion render them out of the question."

"One point I do not quite understand," I said. "Are the members of the liberal professions eligible to the presidency? and if so, how are they ranked with those who pursue the industries proper?"

"They have no ranking with them," replied Dr. Leete. "The members of the technical professions, such as engineers and architects, have a ranking with the constructive guilds; but the members of the liberal professions, the doctors and teachers, as well as the artists and men of letters who obtain remissions of industrial service, do not belong to the industrial army. On this ground they vote for the President, but are not eligible to his office. One of its main duties being the control and discipline of the industrial army, it is essential that the President should have passed through all its grades to understand his business."

"That is reasonable," I said; "but if the doctors and teachers do not know enough of industry to be President, neither, I should think, can the President know enough of medicine and education to control those departments."

"No more does he," was the reply. "Except in the general way that he is responsible for the enforcement of the laws as to all classes, the President has nothing to do with the faculties of medicine and education, which are controlled by boards of regents of their own, in which the President is ex-officio chairman, and has the casting vote. These regents, who, of course, are responsible to Congress, are chosen by the honorary members of the guilds of education and medicine, the retired teachers and doctors of the country."

"Do you know," I said, "the method of electing officials by votes of the retired members of the guilds is nothing more than the application on a national scale of the plan of government by alumni, which we used to a slight extent occasionally in the management of our higher educational institutions."

"Did you, indeed?" exclaimed Dr. Leete, with animation. "That is quite new to me, and I fancy will be to most of us, and of much interest as well. There has been great discussion as to the germ of the idea, and we fancied that there was for once something new under the sun. Well! well! In your higher educational institutions! that is interesting indeed. You must tell me more of that."

"Truly, there is very little more to tell than I have told already," I replied. "If we had the germ of your idea, it was but as a germ."

Chapter XVIII

T HAT evening I sat up for some time after the ladies had retired, talking with Dr. Leete about the effect of the plan of exempting men from further service to the nation after the age of forty-five, a point brought up by his account of the part taken by the retired citizens in the government.

"At forty-five," said I, "a man still has ten years of good manual labor in him, and twice ten years of good intellectual service. To be superannuated at that age and laid on the shelf must be regarded rather as a hardship than a favor by men of energetic dispositions."

"My dear Mr. West," exclaimed Dr. Leete, beaming upon me, "you cannot have any idea of the piquancy your nineteenth century ideas have for us of this day, the rare quaintness of their effect. Know, O child of another race and yet the same, that the labor we have to render as our part in securing for the nation the means of a comfortable physical existence is by no means regarded as the most important, the most interesting, or the most dignified employment of our powers. We look upon it as a necessary duty to be discharged before we can fully devote ourselves to the higher exercise of our faculties, the intellectual and spiritual enjoyments and pursuits which alone mean life. Everything possible is indeed done by the just distribution of burdens, and by all manner of special attractions and incentives to relieve our labor of irksomeness, and, except in a comparative sense, it is not usually irksome, and is often inspiring. But it is not our labor, but the higher and larger activities which the performance of our task will leave us free to enter upon, that are considered the main business of existence.

"Of course not all, nor the majority, have those scientific, artistic, literary, or scholarly interests which make leisure the one thing valuable to their possessors. Many look upon the last half of life chiefly as a period for enjoyment of other sorts; for travel, for social relaxation in the company of their life-time friends; a time for the cultivation of all manner of personal idiosyncrasies and special tastes, and the pursuit of every imaginable form of recreation; in a word, a time for the leisurely and unperturbed appreciation of the good things of the world which they have helped to create. But whatever the differences between our individual tastes as to the use we shall put our leisure to, we all agree in looking forward to the date of our discharge as the time when we shall first enter upon the full enjoyment of our birthright, the period when we shall first really attain our majority and become enfranchised from discipline and control, with the fee of our lives vested in ourselves. As eager boys in your day anticipated twenty-one, so men nowadays look forward to forty-five. At twenty-one we become men, but at forty-five we renew youth. Middle age and what you would have called old age are considered, rather than youth, the enviable time of life. Thanks to the better conditions of existence nowadays, and above all the freedom of every one from care, old age approaches many years later and has an aspect far more benign than in past times. Persons of average constitution usually live to eighty-five or ninety, and at forty-five we are physically and mentally younger, I fancy, than you were at thirty-five. It is a strange reflection that at forty-five, when we are just entering upon the most enjoyable period of life, you already began to think of growing old and to look backward. With you it was the forenoon, with us it is the afternoon, which is the brighter half of life."

After this I remember that our talk branched into the subject of popular sports and recreations at the present time as compared with those of the nineteenth century.

"In one respect," said Dr. Leete, "there is a marked difference. The professional sportsmen, which were such a curious feature of your day, we have nothing answering to, nor are the prizes for which our athletes contend money prizes, as with you. Our contests are always for glory only. The generous rivalry existing between the various guilds, and the loyalty of each worker to his own, afford a constant stimulation to all sorts of games and matches by sea and land, in which the young men take scarcely more interest than the honorary guildsmen who have served their time. The guild yacht races off Marblehead take place next week, and you will be able to judge for yourself of the popular enthusiasm which such events nowadays call out as compared with your day. The demand for '*panem et circenses*' preferred by the Roman populace is recognized nowadays as a wholly reasonable one. If bread is the first necessity of life, recreation is a close second, and the nation caters for both. Americans of the nineteenth century were as unfortunate in lacking an adequate provision for the one sort of need as for the other. Even if the people of that period had enjoyed larger leisure, they would, I fancy, have often been at a loss how to pass it agreeably. We are never in that predicament."

Chapter XIX

I N the course of an early morning constitutional I visited Charlestown. Among the changes, too numerous to attempt to indicate, which mark the lapse of a century in that quarter, I particularly noted the total disappearance of the old state prison.

"That went before my day, but I remember hearing about it," said Dr. Leete, when I alluded to the fact at the breakfast table. "We have no jails nowadays. All cases of atavism are treated in the hospitals."

"Of atavism!" I exclaimed, staring.

"Why, yes," replied Dr. Leete. "The idea of dealing punitively with those unfortunates was given up at least fifty years ago, and I think more."

"I don't quite understand you," I said. "Atavism in my day was a word applied to the cases of persons in whom some trait of a remote ancestor recurred in a noticeable manner. Am I to understand that crime is nowadays looked upon as the recurrence of an ancestral trait?"

"I beg your pardon," said Dr. Leete with a smile half humorous, half deprecating, "but since you have so explicitly asked the question, I am forced to say that the fact is precisely that."

After what I had already learned of the moral contrasts between the nineteenth and the twentieth centuries, it was doubtless absurd in me to begin to develop sensitiveness on the subject, and probably if Dr. Leete had not spoken with that apologetic air and Mrs. Leete and Edith shown a corresponding embarrassment, I should not have flushed, as I was conscious I did.

"I was not in much danger of being vain of my generation before," I said; "but, really"—

"This is your generation, Mr. West," interposed Edith. "It is

the one in which you are living, you know, and it is only because we are alive now that we call it ours."

"Thank you. I will try to think of it so," I said, and as my eyes
met hers their expression quite cured my senseless sensitiveness.
"After all," I said, with a laugh, "I was brought up a Calvinist
and ought not to be startled to hear crime spoken of as an ancestral trait."

"In point of fact," said Dr. Leete, "our use of the word is no
reflection at all on your generation, if, begging Edith's pardon,
we may call it yours, so far as seeming to imply that we think
ourselves, apart from our circumstances, better than you were.
In your day fully nineteen twentieths of the crime, using the
word broadly to include all sorts of misdemeanors, resulted from
the inequality in the possessions of individuals; want tempted
the poor, lust of greater gains, or the desire to preserve former
gains, tempted the well-to-do. Directly or indirectly, the desire
for money, which then meant every good thing, was the motive
of all this crime, the taproot of a vast poison growth, which the
machinery of law, courts, and police could barely prevent from
choking your civilization outright. When we made the nation
the sole trustee of the wealth of the people, and guaranteed to
all abundant maintenance, on the one hand abolishing want,
and on the other checking the accumulation of riches, we cut
this root, and the poison tree that overshadowed your society
withered, like Jonah's gourd, in a day. As for the comparatively
small class of violent crimes against persons, unconnected with
any idea of gain, they were almost wholly confined, even in your
day, to the ignorant and bestial; and in these days, when education and good manners are not the monopoly of a few, but
universal, such atrocities are scarcely ever heard of. You now
see why the word "atavism" is used for crime. It is because nearly
all forms of crime known to you are motiveless now, and when
they appear can only be explained as the outcropping of ancestral
traits. You used to call persons who stole, evidently without any
rational motive, kleptomaniacs, and when the case was clear
deemed it absurd to punish them as thieves. Your attitude toward
the genuine kleptomaniac is precisely ours toward the victim

of atavism, an attitude of compassion and firm but gentle restraint."

"Your courts must have an easy time of it," I observed. "With no private property to speak of, no disputes between citizens over business relations, no real estate to divide or debts to collect, there must be absolutely no civil business at all for them; and with no offenses against property, and mighty few of any sort to provide criminal cases, I should think you might almost do without judges and lawyers altogether."

"We do without the lawyers, certainly," was Dr. Leete's reply. "It would not seem reasonable to us, in a case where the only interest of the nation is to find out the truth, that persons should take part in the proceedings who had an acknowledged motive to color it."

"But who defends the accused?"

"If he is a criminal he needs no defense, for he pleads guilty in most instances," replied Dr. Leete. "The plea of the accused is not a mere formality with us, as with you. It is usually the end of the case."

"You don't mean that the man who pleads not guilty is thereupon discharged?"

"No, I do not mean that. He is not accused on light grounds, and if he denies his guilt, must still be tried. But trials are few, for in most cases the guilty man pleads guilty. When he makes a false plea and is clearly proved guilty, his penalty is doubled. Falsehood is, however, so despised among us that few offenders would lie to save themselves."

"That is the most astounding thing you have yet told me," I exclaimed. "If lying has gone out of fashion, this is indeed the 'new heavens and the new earth wherein dwelleth righteousness,' which the prophet foretold."

"Such is, in fact, the belief of some persons nowadays," was the doctor's answer. "They hold that we have entered upon the millennium, and the theory from their point of view does not lack plausibility. But as to your astonishment at finding that the world has outgrown lying, there is really no ground for it. Falsehood, even in your day, was not common between gentlemen and ladies, social equals. The lie of fear was the refuge of cowardice, and the lie of fraud the device of the cheat. The inequalities of men and the lust of acquisition offered a constant premium on lying at that time. Yet even then, the man who neither feared another nor desired to defraud him scorned false-hood. Because we are now all social equals, and no man either has anything to fear from another or can gain anything by de-ceiving him, the contempt of falsehood is so universal that it is rarely, as I told you, that even a criminal in other respects will be found willing to lie. When, however, a plea of not guilty is returned, the judge appoints two colleagues to state the opposite sides of the case. How far these men are from being like your hired advocates and prosecutors, determined to acquit or convict, may appear from the fact that unless both agree that the verdict found is just, the case is tried over, while anything like bias in the tone of either of the judges stating the case would be a shocking scandal."

"Do I understand," I said, "that it is a judge who states each side of the case as well as a judge who hears it?"

"Certainly. The judges take turns in serving on the bench and at the bar, and are expected to maintain the judicial temper equally whether in stating or deciding a case. The system is indeed in effect that of trial by three judges occupying different points of view as to the case. When they agree upon a verdict, we believe it to be as near to absolute truth as men well can come."

"You have given up the jury system, then?"

"It was well enough as a corrective in the days of hired advo-cates, and a bench sometimes venal, and often with a tenure that made it dependent, but is needless now. No conceivable motive but justice could actuate our judges."

"How are these magistrates selected?"

"They are an honorable exception to the rule which discharges all men from service at the age of forty-five. The President of the nation appoints the necessary judges year by year from the class reaching that age. The number appointed is, of course, ex-ceedingly few, and the honor so high that it is held an offset to the additional term of service which follows, and though a judge's appointment may be declined, it rarely is. The term is five years, without eligibility to reappointment. The members of the Supreme Court, which is the guardian of the constitution, are selected from among the lower judges. When a vacancy in that court occurs, those of the lower judges, whose terms expire that year, select, as their last official act, the one of their colleagues left on the bench whom they deem fittest to fill it."

"There being no legal profession to serve as a school for judges," I said, "they must, of course, come directly from the law school to the bench."

"We have no such things as law schools," replied the doctor, smiling. "The law as a special science is obsolete. It was a system of casuistry which the elaborate artificiality of the old order of society absolutely required to interpret it, but only a few of the plainest and simplest legal maxims have any application to the existing state of the world. Everything touching the relations of men to one another is now simpler, beyond any comparison, than in your day. We should have no sort of use for the hair-splitting experts who presided and argued in your courts. You must not imagine, however, that we have any disrespect for those ancient worthies because we have no use for them. On the contrary, we entertain an unfeigned respect, amounting almost to awe, for the men who alone understood and were able to expound the interminable complexity of the rights of property, and the relations of commercial and personal dependence involved in your system. What, indeed, could possibly give a more powerful impression of the intricacy and artificiality of that system than the fact that it was necessary to set apart from other pursuits the cream of the intellect of every generation, in order to provide a body of pundits able to make it even vaguely intelligible to those whose fates it determined. The treatises of your great lawyers, the works of Blackstone and Chitty, of Story and Parsons, stand in our museums, side by side with the tomes of Duns Scotus and his fellow scholastics, as curious monuments of intellectual subtlety devoted to subjects equally remote from the interests of modern men. Our judges are simply widely informed, judicious, and discreet men of ripe years.

"I should not fail to speak of one important function of the minor judges," added Dr. Leete. "This is to adjudicate all cases where a private of the industrial army makes a complaint of unfairness against an officer. All such questions are heard and settled without appeal by a single judge, three judges being required only in graver cases.* The efficiency of industry requires the strictest discipline in the army of labor, but the claim of the workman to just and considerate treatment is backed by the whole power of the nation. The officer commands and the private obeys, but no officer is so high that he would dare display an overbearing manner toward a workman of the lowest class. As for churlishness or rudeness by an official of any sort, in his relations to the public, not one among minor offenses is more sure of a prompt penalty than this. Not only justice but civility is enforced by our judges in all sorts of intercourse. No value of service is accepted as a set-off to boorish or offensive manners."

It occurred to me, as Dr. Leete was speaking, that in all his talk I had heard much of the nation and nothing of the state governments. Had the organization of the nation as an industrial unit done away with the states? I asked.

"Necessarily," he replied. "The state governments would have interfered with the control and discipline of the industrial army, which, of course, required to be central and uniform. Even if the state governments had not become inconvenient for other reasons, they were rendered superfluous by the prodigious simplification in the task of government since your day. Almost the sole function of the administration now is that of directing the industries of the country. Most of the purposes for which governments formerly existed no longer remain to be subserved. We

* [In the first edition there follows this passage which was deleted from the second edition:

"There must be need of such a tribunal in your system, for under it a man who is treated unfairly cannot leave his place as with us."

"Certainly he can," replied Dr. Leete. "Not only is a man always sure of a fair hearing and redress in case of actual oppression, but if his relations with his foreman or chief are unpleasant, he can secure a transfer on application. Under your system a man could indeed leave work if he did not like his employer, but be [he] left his means of support at the same time. One of our workmen, however, who finds himself disagreeably situated is not obliged to risk his means of subsistence to find fair play."]

have no army or navy, and no military organization. We have no departments of state or treasury, no excise or revenue services, no taxes or tax collectors. The only function proper of government, as known to you, which still remains, is the judiciary and police system. I have already explained to you how simple is our judicial system as compared with your huge and complex machine. Of course the same absence of crime and temptation to it, which make the duties of judges so light, reduces the number and duties of the police to a minimum."

"But with no state legislatures, and Congress meeting only once in five years, how do you get your legislation done?"

"We have no legislation," replied Dr. Leete, "that is, next to none. It is rarely that Congress, even when it meets, considers any new laws of consequence, and then it only has power to commend them to the following Congress, lest anything be done hastily. If you will consider a moment, Mr. West, you will see that we have nothing to make laws about. The fundamental principles on which our society is founded settle for all time the strifes and misunderstandings which in your day called for legislation.

"Fully ninety-nine hundredths of the laws of that time concerned the definition and protection of private property and the relations of buyers and sellers. There is neither private property, beyond personal belongings, now, nor buying and selling, and therefore the occasion of nearly all the legislation formerly necessary has passed away. Formerly, society was a pyramid poised on its apex. All the gravitations of human nature were constantly tending to topple it over, and it could be maintained upright, or rather upwrong (if you will pardon the feeble witticism), by an elaborate system of constantly renewed props and buttresses and guy-ropes in the form of laws. A central Congress and forty state legislatures, turning out some twenty thousand laws a year, could not make new props fast enough to take the place of those which were constantly breaking down or becoming ineffectual through some shifting of the strain. Now society rests on its base, and is in as little need of artificial supports as the everlasting hills."

"But you have at least municipal governments besides the one central authority?"

"Certainly, and they have important and extensive functions in looking out for the public comfort and recreation, and the improvement and embellishment of the villages and cities."

"But having no control over the labor of their people, or means of hiring it, how can they do anything?"

"Every town or city is conceded the right to retain, for its own public works, a certain proportion of the quota of labor its citizens contribute to the nation. This proportion, being assigned it as so much credit, can be applied in any way desired."

Chapter XX

*T*HAT afternoon Edith casually inquired if I had yet revisited the underground chamber in the garden in which I had been found.

"Not yet," I replied. "To be frank, I have shrunk thus far from doing so, lest the visit might revive old associations rather too strongly for my mental equilibrium."

"Ah, yes!" she said, "I can imagine that you have done well to stay away. I ought to have thought of that."

"No," I said, "I am glad you spoke of it. The danger, if there was any, existed only during the first day or two. Thanks to you, chiefly and always, I feel my footing now so firm in this new world, that if you will go with me to keep the ghosts off, I should really like to visit the place this afternoon."

Edith demurred at first, but, finding that I was in earnest, consented to accompany me. The rampart of earth thrown up from the excavation was visible among the trees from the house, and a few steps brought us to the spot. All remained as it was at the point when work was interrupted by the discovery of the tenant of the chamber, save that the door had been opened and the slab from the roof replaced. Descending the sloping sides of the excavation, we went in at the door and stood within the dimly-lighted room.

Everything was just as I had beheld it last on that evening one hundred and thirteen years previous, just before closing my eyes for that long sleep. I stood for some time silently looking about me. I saw that my companion was furtively regarding me with an expression of awed and sympathetic curiosity. I put out my hand to her and she placed hers in it, the soft fingers responding with a reassuring pressure to my clasp. Finally she whispered, "Had we not better go out now? You must not try yourself too far. Oh, how strange it must be to you!"

"On the contrary," I replied, "it does not seem strange; that is the strangest part of it."

"Not strange?" she echoed.

"Even so," I replied. "The emotions with which you evidently credit me, and which I anticipated would attend this visit, I simply do not feel. I realize all that these surroundings suggest, but without the agitation I expected. You can't be nearly as much surprised at this as I am myself. Ever since that terrible morning when you came to my help, I have tried to avoid thinking of my former life, just as I have avoided coming here, for fear of the agitating effects. I am for all the world like a man who has permitted an injured limb to lie motionless under the impression that it is exquisitely sensitive, and on trying to move it finds that it is paralyzed."

"Do you mean your memory is gone?"

"Not at all. I remember everything connected with my former life, but with a total lack of keen sensation. I remember it for clearness as if it had been but a day since then, but my feelings about what I remember are as faint as if to my consciousness, as well as in fact, a hundred years had intervened. Perhaps it is possible to explain this, too. The effect of change in surroundings is like that of lapse of time in making the past seem remote. When I first woke from that trance, my former life appeared as yesterday, but now, since I have learned to know my new surroundings, and to realize the prodigious changes that have transformed the world, I no longer find it hard, but very easy, to realize that I have slept a century. Can you conceive of such a thing as living a hundred years in four days? It really seems to me that I have done just that, and that it is this experience which has given so remote and unreal an appearance to my former life. Can you see how such a thing might be?"

"I can conceive it," replied Edith, meditatively, "and I think we ought all to be thankful that it is so, for it will save you much suffering, I am sure."

"Imagine," I said, in an effort to explain, as much to myself as to her, the strangeness of my mental condition, "that a man first heard of a bereavement many, many years, half a lifetime perhaps, after the event occurred. I fancy his feeling would be perhaps something as mine is. When I think of my friends in the world of that former day, and the sorrow they must have felt for me, it is with a pensive pity, rather than keen anguish, as of a sorrow long, long ago ended."

"You have told us nothing yet of your friends," said Edith. "Had you many to mourn you?"

"Thank God, I had very few relatives, none nearer than cousins," I replied. "But there was one, not a relative, but dearer to me than any kin of blood. She had your name. She was to have been my wife soon. Ah me!"

"Ah me!" sighed the Edith by my side. "Think of the heartache she must have had."

Something in the deep feeling of this gentle girl touched a chord in my benumbed heart. My eyes, before so dry, were flooded with the tears that had till now refused to come. When I had regained my composure, I saw that she too had been weeping freely.

"God bless your tender heart," I said. "Would you like to see her picture?"

A small locket with Edith Bartlett's picture, secured about my neck with a gold chain, had lain upon my breast all through that long sleep, and removing this I opened and gave it to my companion. She took it with eagerness, and after poring long over the sweet face, touched the picture with her lips.

"I know that she was good and lovely enough to well deserve your tears," she said; "but remember her heartache was over long ago, and she has been in heaven for nearly a century."

It was indeed so. Whatever her sorrow had once been, for nearly a century she had ceased to weep, and, my sudden passion spent, my own tears dried away. I had loved her very dearly in my other life, but it was a hundred years ago! I do not know but some may find in this confession evidence of lack of feeling, but I think, perhaps, that none can have had an experience sufficiently like mine to enable them to judge me. As we were about to leave the chamber, my eye rested upon the great iron safe which stood in one corner. Calling my companion's attention to it, I said:—

"This was my strong room as well as my sleeping room. In the safe yonder are several thousand dollars in gold, and any amount of securities. If I had known when I went to sleep that night just how long my nap would be, I should still have thought that the gold was a safe provision for my needs in any country or any century, however distant. That a time would ever come when it would lose its purchasing power, I should have considered the wildest of fancies. Nevertheless, here I wake up to find myself among a people of whom a cartload of gold will not procure a loaf of bread."

As might be expected, I did not succeed in impressing Edith that there was anything remarkable in this fact. "Why in the world should it?" she merely asked.

Chapter XXI

I t had been suggested by Dr. Leete that we should devote the next morning to an inspection of the schools and colleges of the city, with some attempt on his own part at an explanation of the educational system of the twentieth century.

"You will see," said he, as we set out after breakfast, "many very important differences between our methods of education and yours, but the main difference is that nowadays all persons equally have those opportunities of higher education which in your day only an infinitesimal portion of the population enjoyed. We should think we had gained nothing worth speaking of, in equalizing the physical comfort of men, without this educational equality."

"The cost must be very great," I said.

"If it took half the revenue of the nation, nobody would grudge it," replied Dr. Leete, "nor even if it took all save a bare pittance. But in truth the expense of educating ten thousand youth is not ten nor five times that of educating one thousand. The principle which makes all operations on a large scale proportionally cheaper than on a small scale holds as to education also."

"College education was terribly expensive in my day," said I.

"If I have not been misinformed by our historians," Dr. Leete answered, "it was not college education but college dissipation and extravagance which cost so highly. The actual expense of your colleges appears to have been very low, and would have been far lower if their patronage had been greater. The higher education nowadays is as cheap as the lower, as all grades of teachers, like all other workers, receive the same support. We have simply added to the common school system of compulsory education, in vogue in Massachusetts a hundred years ago, a half dozen higher grades, carrying the youth to the age of twenty-one and giving him what you used to call the education of a gentleman, instead of turning him loose at fourteen or fifteen with no mental equipment beyond reading, writing, and the multiplication table."

"Setting aside the actual cost of these additional years of education," I replied, "we should not have thought we could afford the loss of time from industrial pursuits. Boys of the poorer classes usually went to work at sixteen or younger, and knew their trade at twenty."

"We should not concede you any gain even in material product by that plan," Dr. Leete replied. "The greater efficiency which education gives to all sorts of labor, except the rudest, makes up in a short period for the time lost in acquiring it."

"We should also have been afraid," said I, "that a high education, while it adapted men to the professions, would set them against manual labor of all sorts."

"That was the effect of high education in your day, I have read," replied the doctor; "and it was no wonder, for manual labor meant association with a rude, coarse, and ignorant class of people. There is no such class now. It was inevitable that such a feeling should exist then, for the further reason that all men receiving a high education were understood to be destined for the professions or for wealthy leisure, and such an education in one neither rich nor professional was a proof of disappointed aspirations, an evidence of failure, a badge of inferiority rather than superiority. Nowadays, of course, when the highest education is deemed necessary to fit a man merely to live, without any reference to the sort of work he may do, its possession conveys no such implication."

"After all," I remarked, "no amount of education can cure natural dullness or make up for original mental deficiencies. Unless the average natural mental capacity of men is much above its level in my day, a high education must be pretty nearly thrown away on a large element of the population. We used to hold that a certain amount of susceptibility to educational influences is required to make a mind worth cultivating, just as a certain natural fertility in soil is required if it is to repay tilling."

"Ah," said Dr. Leete, "I am glad you used that illustration, for it is just the one I would have chosen to set forth the modern view of education. You say that land so poor that the product will not repay the labor of tilling is not cultivated. Nevertheless, much land that does not begin to repay tilling by its product was cultivated in your day and is in ours. I refer to gardens, parks, lawns, and, in general, to pieces of land so situated that, were they left to grow up to weeds and briers, they would be eyesores and inconveniences to all about. They are therefore tilled, and though their product is little, there is yet no land that, in a wider sense, better repays cultivation. So it is with the men and women with whom we mingle in the relations of society, whose voices are always in our ears, whose behavior in innumerable ways affects our enjoyment,—who are, in fact, as much conditions of our lives as the air we breathe, or any of the physical elements on which we depend. If, indeed, we could not afford to educate everybody, we should choose the coarsest and dullest by nature, rather than the brightest, to receive what education we could give. The naturally refined and intellectual can better dispense with aids to culture than those less fortunate in natural endowments.

"To borrow a phrase which was often used in your day, we should not consider life worth living if we had to be surrounded by a population of ignorant, boorish, coarse, wholly uncultivated men and women, as was the plight of the few educated in your day. Is a man satisfied, merely because he is perfumed himself, to mingle with a malodorous crowd? Could he take more than a very limited satisfaction, even in a palatial apartment, if the windows on all four sides opened into stable yards? And yet just that was the situation of those considered most fortunate as to culture and refinement in your day. I know that the poor and ignorant envied the rich and cultured then; but to us the latter, living as they did, surrounded by squalor and brutishness, seem little better off than the former. The cultured man in your age was like one up to the neck in a nauseous bog solacing himself with a smelling bottle. You see, perhaps, now, how we look at this question of universal high education. No single thing is so important to every man as to have for neighbors intelligent, companionable persons. There is nothing, therefore, which the nation can do for him that will enhance so much his own happiness as to educate his neighbors. When it fails to do so, the value of his own education to him is reduced by half, and many of the tastes he has cultivated are made positive sources of pain.

"To educate some to the highest degree, and leave the mass wholly uncultivated, as you did, made the gap between them almost like that between different natural species, which have no means of communication. What could be more inhuman than this consequence of a partial enjoyment of education! Its universal and equal enjoyment leaves, indeed, the differences between men as to natural endowments as marked as in a state of nature, but the level of the lowest is vastly raised. Brutishness is eliminated. All have some inkling of the humanities, some appreciation of the things of the mind, and an admiration for the still higher culture they have fallen short of. They have become capable of receiving and imparting, in various degrees, but all in some measure, the pleasures and inspirations of a refined social life. The cultured society of the nineteenth century,—what did it consist of but here and there a few microscopic oases in a vast, unbroken wilderness? The proportion of individuals capable of intellectual sympathies or refined intercourse, to the mass of their contemporaries, used to be so infinitesimal as to be in any broad view of humanity scarcely worth mentioning. One generation of the world to-day represents a greater volume of intellectual life than any five centuries ever did before.

"There is still another point I should mention in stating the grounds on which nothing less than the universality of the best education could now be tolerated," continued Dr. Leete, "and that is, the interest of the coming generation in having educated parents. To put the matter in a nutshell, there are three main grounds on which our educational system rests: first, the right of every man to the completest education the nation can give him on his own account, as necessary to his enjoyment of himself; second, the right of his fellow-citizens to have him educated, as necessary to their enjoyment of his society; third, the right of the unborn to be guaranteed an intelligent and refined parentage."

I shall not describe in detail what I saw in the schools that day. Having taken but slight interest in educational matters in my former life, I could offer few comparisons of interest. Next to the fact of the universality of the higher as well as the lower education, I was most struck with the prominence given to physical culture, and the fact that proficiency in athletic feats and games as well as in scholarship had a place in the rating of the youth.

"The faculty of education," Dr. Leete explained, "is held to the same responsibility for the bodies as for the minds of its charges. The highest possible physical, as well as mental, development of every one is the double object of a curriculum which lasts from the age of six to that of twenty-one."

The magnificent health of the young people in the schools impressed me strongly. My previous observations, not only of the notable personal endowments of the family of my host, but of the people I had seen in my walks abroad, had already suggested the idea that there must have been something like a general improvement in the physical standard of the race since my day, and now, as I compared these stalwart young men and fresh, vigorous maidens with the young people I had seen in the schools of the nineteenth century, I was moved to impart my thought to Dr. Leete. He listened with great interest to what I said.

"Your testimony on this point," he declared, "is invaluable. We believe that there has been such an improvement as you speak of, but of course it could only be a matter of theory with us. It is an incident of your unique position that you alone in the world of to-day can speak with authority on this point. Your opinion, when you state it publicly, will, I assure you, make a profound sensation. For the rest it would be strange, certainly, if the race did not show an improvement. In your day, riches debauched one class with idleness of mind and body, while poverty sapped the vitality of the masses by overwork, bad food, and pestilent homes. The labor required of children, and the burdens laid on women, enfeebled the very springs of life. Instead of these maleficent circumstances, all now enjoy the most favorable conditions of physical life; the young are carefully nurtured and studiously cared for; the labor which is required of all is limited to the period of greatest bodily vigor, and is never excessive; care for one's self and one's family, anxiety as to livelihood, the strain of a ceaseless battle for life—all these influences, which once did so much to wreck the minds and bodies of men and women, are known no more. Certainly, an improvement of the species ought to follow such a change. In certain specific respects we know, indeed, that the improvement has taken place. Insanity, for instance, which in the nineteenth century was so terribly common a product of your insane mode of life, has almost disappeared, with its alternative, suicide."

Chapter XXII

W E had made an appointment to meet the ladies at the dining-hall for dinner, after which, having some engagement, they left us sitting at table there, discussing our wine and cigars with a multitude of other matters.

"Doctor," said I, in the course of our talk, "morally speaking, your social system is one which I should be insensate not to admire in comparison with any previously in vogue in the world, and especially with that of my own most unhappy century. If I were to fall into a mesmeric sleep to-night as lasting as that other, and meanwhile the course of time were to take a turn backward instead of forward, and I were to wake up again in the nineteenth century, when I had told my friends what I had seen, they would every one admit that your world was a paradise of order, equity, and felicity. But they were a very practical people, my contemporaries, and after expressing their admiration for the moral beauty and material splendor of the system, they would presently begin to cipher and ask how you got the money to make everybody so happy; for certainly, to support the whole nation at a rate of comfort, and even luxury, such as I see around me, must involve vastly greater wealth than the nation produced in my day. Now, while I could explain to them pretty nearly everything else of the main features of your system, I should quite fail to answer this question, and failing there, they would tell me, for they were very close ciphers, that I had been dreaming; nor would they ever believe anything else. In my day, I know that the total annual product of the nation, although it might have been divided with absolute equality, would not have come to more than three or four hundred dollars per head, not very much more than enough to supply the necessities of life with few or any of its comforts. How is it that you have so much more?"

"That is a very pertinent question, Mr. West," replied Dr. Leete, "and I should not blame your friends, in the case you supposed, if they declared your story all moonshine, failing a satisfactory reply to it. It is a question which I cannot answer exhaustively at any one sitting, and as for the exact statistics to bear out my general statements, I shall have to refer you for them to books in my library, but it would certainly be a pity to leave you to be put to confusion by your old acquaintances, in case of the contingency you speak of, for lack of a few suggestions.

"Let us begin with a number of small items wherein we economize wealth as compared with you. We have no national, state, county, or municipal debts, or payments on their account. We have no sort of military or naval expenditures for men or materials, no army, navy, or militia. We have no revenue service, no swarm of tax assessors and collectors. As regards our judiciary, police, sheriffs, and jailers, the force which Massachusetts alone kept on foot in your day far more than suffices for the nation now. We have no criminal class preying upon the wealth of society as you had. The number of persons, more or less absolutely lost to the working force through physical disability, of the lame, sick, and debilitated, which constituted such a burden on the able-bodied in your day, now that all live under conditions of health and comfort, has shrunk to scarcely perceptible proportions, and with every generation is becoming more completely eliminated.

"Another item wherein we save is the disuse of money and the thousand occupations connected with financial operations of all sorts, whereby an army of men was formerly taken away from useful employments. Also consider that the waste of the very rich in your day on inordinate personal luxury has ceased, though, indeed, this item might easily be over-estimated. Again, consider that there are no idlers now, rich or poor,—no drones.

"A very important cause of former poverty was the vast waste of labor and materials which resulted from domestic washing and cooking, and the performing separately of innumerable other tasks to which we apply the coöperative plan.

"A larger economy than any of these—yes, of all together—is effected by the organization of our distributing system, by which the work done once by the merchants, traders, storekeepers, with their various grades of jobbers, wholesalers, retailers, agents, commercial travelers, and middlemen of all sorts, with an excessive waste of energy in needless transportation and interminable handlings, is performed by one-tenth the number of hands and an unnecessary turn of not one wheel. Something of what our distributing system is like you know. Our statisticians calculate that one eightieth part of our workers suffices for all the processes of distribution which in your day required one eighth of the population, so much being withdrawn from the force engaged in productive labor."

"I begin to see," I said, "where you get your greater wealth."

"I beg your pardon," replied Dr. Leete, "but you scarcely do as yet. The economies I have mentioned thus far, in the aggregate, considering the labor they would save directly and indirectly through saving of material, might possibly be equivalent to the addition to your annual production of wealth of one-half its former total. These items are, however, scarcely worth mentioning in comparison with other prodigious wastes, now saved, which resulted inevitably from leaving the industries of the nation to private enterprise. However great the economies your contemporaries might have devised in the consumption of products, and however marvelous the progress of mechanical invention, they could never have raised themselves out of the slough of poverty so long as they held to that system.

"No mode more wasteful for utilizing human energy could be devised, and for the credit of the human intellect it should be remembered that the system never was devised, but was merely a survival from the rude ages when the lack of social organization made any sort of coöperation impossible."

"I will readily admit," I said, "that our industrial system was ethically very bad, but as a mere wealth-making machine, apart from moral aspects, it seemed to us admirable."

"As I said," responded the doctor, "the subject is too large to discuss at length now, but if you are really interested to know the main criticisms which we moderns make on your industrial system as compared with our own, I can touch briefly on some of them.

"The wastes which resulted from leaving the conduct of industry to irresponsible individuals, wholly without mutual understanding or concert, were mainly four: first, the waste by mistaken undertakings; second, the waste from the competition and mutual hostility of those engaged in industry; third, the waste by periodical gluts and crises, with the consequent interruptions of industry; fourth, the waste from idle capital and labor, at all times. Any one of these four great leaks, were all the others stopped, would suffice to make the difference between wealth and poverty on the part of a nation.

"Take the waste by mistaken undertakings, to begin with. In your day the production and distribution of commodities being without concert or organization, there was no means of knowing just what demand there was for any class of products, or what was the rate of supply. Therefore, any enterprise by a private capitalist was always a doubtful experiment. The projector having no general view of the field of industry and consumption, such as our government has, could never be sure either what the people wanted, or what arrangements other capitalists were making to supply them. In view of this, we are not surprised to learn that the chances were considered several to one in favor of the failure of any given business enterprise, and that it was common for persons who at last succeeded in making a hit to have failed repeatedly. If a shoemaker, for every pair of shoes he succeeded in completing, spoiled the leather of four or five pair, besides losing the time spent on them, he would stand about the same chance of getting rich as your contemporaries did with their system of private enterprise, and its average of four or five failures to one success.

"The next of the great wastes was that from competition. The field of industry was a battlefield as wide as the world, in which the workers wasted, in assailing one another, energies which, if expended in concerted effort, as to-day, would have enriched all.

As for mercy or quarter in this warfare, there was absolutely no suggestion of it. To deliberately enter a field of business and destroy the enterprises of those who had occupied it previously, in order to plant one's own enterprise on their ruins, was an achievement which never failed to command popular admiration. Nor is there any stretch of fancy in comparing this sort of struggle with actual warfare, so far as concerns the mental agony and physical suffering which attended the struggle, and the misery which overwhelmed the defeated and those dependent on them. Now nothing about your age is, at first sight, more astounding to a man of modern times than the fact that men engaged in the same industry, instead of fraternizing as comrades and co-laborers to a common end, should have regarded each other as rivals and enemies to be throttled and overthrown. This certainly seems like sheer madness, a scene from bedlam. But more closely regarded, it is seen to be no such thing. Your contemporaries, with their mutual throat-cutting, knew very well what they were at. The producers of the nineteenth century were not, like ours, working together for the maintenance of the community, but each solely for his own maintenance at the expense of the community. If, in working to this end, he at the same time increased the aggregate wealth, that was merely incidental. It was just as feasible and as common to increase one's private hoard by practices injurious to the general welfare. One's worst enemies were necessarily those of his own trade, for, under your plan of making private profit the motive of production, a scarcity of the article he produced was what each particular producer desired. It was for his interest that no more of it should be produced than he himself could produce. To secure this consummation as far as circumstances permitted, by killing off and discouraging those engaged in his line of industry, was his constant effort. When he had killed off all he could, his policy was to combine with those he could not kill, and convert their mutual warfare into a warfare upon the public at large by cornering the market, as I believe you used to call it, and putting up prices to the highest point people would stand before going without the goods. The day dream of the nineteenth century producer was to gain absolute control of the supply of some necessity of life, so that he might keep the public at the verge of starvation, and always command famine prices for what he supplied. This, Mr. West, is what was called in the nineteenth century a system of production. I will leave it to you if it does not seem, in some of its aspects, a great deal more like a system for preventing production. Some time when we have plenty of leisure I am going to ask you to sit down with me and try to make me comprehend, as I never yet could, though I have studied the matter a great deal, how such shrewd fellows as your contemporaries appear to have been in many respects ever came to entrust the business of providing for the community to a class whose interest it was to starve it. I assure you that the wonder with us is, not that the world did not get rich under such a system, but that it did not perish outright from want. This wonder increases as we go on to consider some of the other prodigious wastes that characterized it.

"Apart from the waste of labor and capital by misdirected industry, and that from the constant bloodletting of your industrial warfare, your system was liable to periodical convulsions, overwhelming alike the wise and unwise, the successful cut-throat as well as his victim. I refer to the business crises at intervals of five to ten years, which wrecked the industries of the nation, prostrating all weak enterprises and crippling the strongest, and were followed by long periods, often of many years, of so-called dull times, during which the capitalists slowly regathered their dissipated strength while the laboring classes starved and rioted. Then would ensue another brief season of prosperity, followed in turn by another crisis and the ensuing years of exhaustion. As commerce developed, making the nations mutually dependent, these crises became world-wide, while the obstinacy of the ensuing state of collapse increased with the area affected by the convulsions, and the consequent lack of rallying centres. In proportion as the industries of the world multiplied and became complex, and the volume of capital involved was increased, these business cataclysms became more frequent, till, in the latter part of the nineteenth century, there were two years of bad times to one of good, and the system of industry, never before so extended or so imposing, seemed in danger of collapsing by its own weight. After endless discussions, your economists appear by that time to have settled down to the despairing conclusion that there was no more possibility of preventing or controlling these crises than if they had been drouths or hurricanes. It only remained to endure them as necessary evils, and when they had passed over to build up again the shattered structure of industry, as dwellers in an earthquake country keep on rebuilding their cities on the same site.

"So far as considering the causes of the trouble inherent in their industrial system, your contemporaries were certainly correct. They were in its very basis, and must needs become more and more maleficent as the business fabric grew in size and complexity. One of these causes was the lack of any common control of the different industries, and the consequent impossibility of their orderly and coördinate development. It inevitably resulted from this lack that they were continually getting out of step with one another and out of relation with the demand.

"Of the latter there was no criterion such as organized distribution gives us, and the first notice that it had been exceeded in any group of industries was a crash of prices, bankruptcy of producers, stoppage of production, reduction of wages, or discharge of workmen. This process was constantly going on in many industries, even in what were called good times, but a crisis took place only when the industries affected were extensive. The markets then were glutted with goods, of which nobody wanted beyond a sufficiency at any price. The wages and profits of those making the glutted classes of goods being reduced or wholly stopped, their purchasing power as consumers of other classes of goods, of which there was no natural glut, was taken away, and, as a consequence, goods of which there was no natural glut became artificially glutted, till their prices also were broken down, and their makers thrown out of work and deprived of income. The crisis was by this time fairly under way, and nothing could check it till a nation's ransom had been wasted.

"A cause, also inherent in your system, which often produced and always terribly aggravated crises, was the machinery of money and credit. Money was essential when production was in many private hands, and buying and selling was necessary to secure what one wanted. It was, however, open to the obvious objection of substituting for food, clothing, and other things a merely conventional representative of them. The confusion of mind which this favored, between goods and their representative, led the way to the credit system and its prodigious illusions. Already accustomed to accept money for commodities, the people next accepted promises for money, and ceased to look at all behind the representative for the thing represented. Money was a sign of real commodities, but credit was but the sign of a sign. There was a natural limit to gold and silver, that is, money proper, but none to credit, and the result was that the volume of credit, that is, the promises of money, ceased to bear any ascertainable proportion to the money, still less to the commodities, actually in existence. Under such a system, frequent and periodical crises were necessitated by a law as absolute as that which brings to the ground a structure overhanging its centre of gravity. It was one of your fictions that the government and the banks authorized by it alone issued money; but everybody who gave a dollar's credit issued money to that extent, which was as good as any to swell the circulation till the next crisis. The great extension of the credit system was a characteristic of the latter part of the nineteenth century, and accounts largely for the almost incessant business crises which marked that period. Perilous as credit was, you could not dispense with its use, for, lacking any national or other public organization of the capital of the country, it was the only means you had for concentrating and directing it upon industrial enterprises. It was in this way a most potent means for exaggerating the chief peril of the private enterprise system of industry by enabling particular industries to absorb disproportionate amounts of the disposable capital of the country, and thus prepare disaster. Business enterprises were always vastly in debt for advances of credit, both to one another and to the banks and capitalists, and the prompt withdrawal of this credit at the first sign of a crisis was generally the precipitating cause of it.

"It was the misfortune of your contemporaries that they had to cement their business fabric with a material which an accident might at any moment turn into an explosive. They were in the plight of a man building a house with dynamite for mortar, for credit can be compared with nothing else.

"If you would see how needless were these convulsions of business which I have been speaking of, and how entirely they resulted from leaving industry to private and unorganized management, just consider the working of our system. Overproduction in special lines, which was the great hobgoblin of your day, is impossible now, for by the connection between distribution and production supply is geared to demand like an engine to the governor which regulates its speed. Even suppose by an error of judgment an excessive production of some commodity. The consequent slackening or cessation of production in that line throws nobody out of employment. The suspended workers are at once found occupation in some other department of the vast workshop and lose only the time spent in changing, while, as for the glut, the business of the nation is large enough to carry any amount of product manufactured in excess of demand till the latter overtakes it. In such a case of over-production, as I have supposed, there is not with us, as with you, any complex machinery to get out of order and magnify a thousand times the original mistake. Of course, having not even money, we still less have credit. All estimates deal directly with the real things, the flour, iron, wood, wool, and labor, of which money and credit were for you the very misleading representatives. In our calculations of cost there can be no mistakes. Out of the annual product the amount necessary for the support of the people is taken, and the requisite labor to produce the next year's consumption provided for. The residue of the material and labor represents what can be safely expended in improvements. If the crops are bad, the surplus for that year is less than usual, that is all. Except for slight occasional effects of such natural causes, there are no fluctuations of business; the material prosperity of the nation flows on uninterruptedly from generation to generation, like an ever broadening and deepening river.

"Your business crises, Mr. West," continued the doctor, "like either of the great wastes I mentioned before, were enough, alone, to have kept your noses to the grindstone forever; but I have still to speak of one other great cause of your poverty, and that was the idleness of a great part of your capital and labor. With us it is the business of the administration to keep in constant employment every ounce of available capital and labor in the country. In your day there was no general control of either capital or labor, and a large part of both failed to find employment. 'Capital,' you used to say, 'is naturally timid,' and it would certainly have been reckless if it had not been timid in an epoch when there was a large preponderance of probability that any particular business venture would end in failure. There was no time when, if security could have been guaranteed it, the amount of capital devoted to productive industry could not have been greatly increased. The proportion of it so employed underwent constant extraordinary fluctuations, according to the greater or less feeling of uncertainty as to the stability of the industrial situation, so that the output of her national industries greatly varied in different years. But for the same reason that the amount of capital employed at times of special insecurity was far less than at times of somewhat greater security, a very large proportion was never employed at all, because the hazard of business was always very great in the best of times.

"It should be also noted that the great amount of capital always seeking employment where tolerable safety could be insured terribly embittered the competition between capitalists when a promising opening presented itself. The idleness of capital, the result of its timidity, of course meant the idleness of labor in corresponding degree. Moreover, every change in the adjustments of business, every slightest alteration in the condition of commerce or manufactures, not to speak of the innumerable business failures that took place yearly, even in the best of times, were constantly throwing a multitude of men out of employment for periods of weeks or months, or even years. A great number of these seekers after employment were constantly traversing the country, becoming in time professional vagabonds, then criminals. 'Give us work!' was the cry of an army of the unemployed at nearly all seasons, and in seasons of dullness in business this army swelled to a host so vast and desperate as to threaten the stability of the government. Could there conceivably be a more conclusive demonstration of the imbecility of the system of private enterprise as a method for enriching a nation than the fact that, in an age of such general poverty and want of everything, capitalists had to throttle one another to find a safe chance to invest their capital and workmen rioted and burned because they could find no work to do?

"Now, Mr. West," continued Dr. Leete, "I want you to bear in mind that these points of which I have been speaking indicate only negatively the advantages of the national organization of industry by showing certain fatal defects and prodigious imbecilities of the systems of private enterprise which are not found in it. These alone, you must admit, would pretty well explain why the nation is so much richer than in your day. But the larger half of our advantage over you, the positive side of it, I have yet barely spoken of. Supposing the system of private enterprise in industry were without any of the great leaks I have mentioned; that there were no waste on account of misdirected effort growing out of mistakes as to the demand, and inability to command a general view of the industrial field. Suppose, also, there were no neutralizing and duplicating of effort from competition. Suppose, also, there were no waste from business panics and crises through bankruptcy and long interruptions of industry, and also none from the idleness of capital and labor. Supposing these evils, which are essential to the conduct of industry by capital in private hands, could all be miraculously prevented, and the system yet retained; even then the superiority of the results attained by the modern industrial system of national control would remain overwhelming.

"You used to have some pretty large textile manufacturing establishments, even in your day, although not comparable with ours. No doubt you have visited these great mills in your time, covering acres of ground, employing thousands of hands, and combining under one roof, under one control, the hundred distinct processes between, say, the cotton bale and the bale of glossy calicoes. You have admired the vast economy of labor as of mechanical force resulting from the perfect interworking with the rest of every wheel and every hand. No doubt you have reflected how much less the same force of workers employed in that factory would accomplish if they were scattered, each man working independently. Would you think it an exaggeration to say that the utmost product of those workers, working thus apart, however amicable their relations might be, was increased not merely by a percentage, but many fold, when their efforts were organized under one control? Well now, Mr. West, the organization of the industry of the nation under a single control, so that all its processes interlock, has multiplied the total product over the utmost that could be done under the former system, even leaving out of account the four great wastes mentioned, in the same proportion that the product of those millworkers was increased by coöperation. The effectiveness of the working force of a nation, under the myriad-headed leadership of private capital, even if the leaders were not mutual enemies, as compared with that which it attains under a single head, may be likened to the military efficiency of a mob, or a horde of barbarians with a thousand petty chiefs, as compared with that of a disciplined army under one general—such a fighting machine, for example, as the German army in the time of Von Moltke."

"After what you have told me," I said, "I do not so much wonder that the nation is richer now than then, but that you are not all Croesuses."

"Well," replied Dr. Leete, "we are pretty well off. The rate at which we live is as luxurious as we could wish. The rivalry of ostentation, which in your day led to extravagance in no way conducive to comfort, finds no place, of course, in a society of people absolutely equal in resources, and our ambition stops at the surroundings which minister to the enjoyment of life. We might, indeed, have much larger incomes, individually, if we chose so to use the surplus of our product, but we prefer to expend it upon public works and pleasures in which all share, upon public halls and buildings, art galleries, bridges, statuary, means of transit, and the conveniences of our cities, great musical and theatrical exhibitions, and in providing on a vast scale for the recreations of the people. You have not begun to see how we live yet, Mr. West. At home we have comfort, but the splendor of our life is, on its social side, that which we share with our fellows. When you know more of it you will see where the money goes, as you used to say, and I think you will agree that we do well so to expend it."

"I suppose," observed Dr. Leete, as we strolled homeward from the dining hall, "that no reflection would have cut the men of your wealth-worshiping century more keenly than the suggestion that they did not know how to make money. Nevertheless, that is just the verdict history has passed on them. Their system of unorganized and antagonistic industries was as absurd economically as it was morally abominable. Selfishness was their only science, and in industrial production selfishness is suicide. Competition, which is the instinct of selfishness, is another word for dissipation of energy, while combination is the secret of efficient production; and not till the idea of increasing the individual hoard gives place to the idea of increasing the common stock can industrial combination be realized, and the acquisition of wealth really begin. Even if the principle of share and share alike for all men were not the only humane and rational basis for a society, we should still enforce it as economically expedient, seeing that until the disintegrating influence of self-seeking is suppressed no true concert of industry is possible."

Chapter XXIII

T HAT evening, as I sat with Edith in the music room, listening to some pieces in the programme of that day which had attracted my notice, I took advantage of an interval in the music to say, "I have a question to ask you which I fear is rather indiscreet."

"I am quite sure it is not that," she replied, encouragingly.

"I am in the position of an eavesdropper," I continued, "who, having overheard a little of a matter not intended for him, though seeming to concern him, has the impudence to come to the speaker for the rest."

"An eavesdropper!" she repeated, looking puzzled.

"Yes," I said, "but an excusable one, as I think you will admit."

"This is very mysterious," she replied.

"Yes," said I, "so mysterious that often I have doubted whether I really overheard at all what I am going to ask you about, or only dreamed it. I want you to tell me. The matter is this: When I was coming out of that sleep of a century, the first impression of which I was conscious was of voices talking around me, voices that afterwards I recognized as your father's, your mother's, and your own. First, I remember your father's voice saying, 'He is going to open his eyes. He had better see but one person at first.' Then you said, if I did not dream it all, 'Promise me, then, that you will not tell him.' Your father seemed to hesitate about promising, but you insisted, and your mother interposing, he finally promised, and when I opened my eyes I saw only him."

I had been quite serious when I said that I was not sure that I had not dreamed the conversation I fancied I had overheard, so incomprehensible was it that these people should know anything of me, a contemporary of their great-grandparents, which I did not know myself. But when I saw the effect of my words upon Edith, I knew that it was no dream, but another mystery, and a more puzzling one than any I had before encountered. For from the moment that the drift of my question became apparent, she showed indications of the most acute embarrassment. Her eyes, always so frank and direct in expression, had dropped in a panic before mine, while her face crimsoned from neck to forehead.

"Pardon me," I said, as soon as I had recovered from bewilderment at the extraordinary effect of my words. "It seems, then, that I was not dreaming. There is some secret, something about me, which you are withholding from me. Really, doesn't it seem a little hard that a person in my position should not be given all the information possible concerning himself?"

"It does not concern you—that is, not directly. It is not about you—exactly," she replied, scarcely audibly.

"But it concerns me in some way," I persisted. "It must be something that would interest me."

"I don't know even that," she replied, venturing a momentary glance at my face, furiously blushing, and yet with a quaint smile flickering about her lips which betrayed a certain perception of humor in the situation despite its embarrassment,—"I am not sure that it would even interest you."

"Your father would have told me," I insisted, with an accent of reproach. "It was you who forbade him. He thought I ought to know."

She did not reply. She was so entirely charming in her confusion that I was now prompted, as much by the desire to prolong the situation as by my original curiosity, to importune her further.

"Am I never to know? Will you never tell me?" I said.

"It depends," she answered, after a long pause.

"On what?" I persisted.

"Ah, you ask too much," she replied. Then, raising to mine a face which inscrutable eyes, flushed cheeks, and smiling lips combined to render perfectly bewitching, she added, "What should you think if I said that it depended on—yourself?"

"On myself?" I echoed. "How can that possibly be?"

"Mr. West, we are losing some charming music," was her only

reply to this, and turning to the telephone, at a touch of her finger she set the air to swaying to the rhythm of an adagio. After that she took good care that the music should leave no opportunity for conversation. She kept her face averted from me, and pretended to be absorbed in the airs, but that it was a mere pretense the crimson tide standing at flood in her cheeks sufficiently betrayed.

When at length she suggested that I might have heard all I cared to, for that time, and we rose to leave the room, she came straight up to me and said, without raising her eyes, "Mr. West, you say I have been good to you. I have not been particularly so, but if you think I have, I want you to promise me that you will not try again to make me tell you this thing you have asked to-night, and that you will not try to find it out from any one else,—my father or mother, for instance."

To such an appeal there was but one reply possible. "Forgive me for distressing you. Of course I will promise," I said. "I would never have asked you if I had fancied it could distress you. But do you blame me for being curious?"

"I do not blame you at all."

"And some time," I added, "if I do not tease you, you may tell me of your own accord. May I not hope so?"

"Perhaps," she murmured.

"Only perhaps?"

Looking up, she read my face with a quick, deep glance. "Yes," she said, "I think I may tell you—some time;" and so our conversation ended, for she gave me no chance to say anything more.

That night I don't think even Dr. Pillsbury could have put me to sleep, till toward morning at least. Mysteries had been my accustomed food for days now, but none had before confronted me at once so mysterious and so fascinating as this, the solution of which Edith Leete had forbidden me even to seek. It was a double mystery. How, in the first place, was it conceivable that she should know any secret about me, a stranger from a strange age? In the second place, even if she should know such a secret, how account for the agitating effect which the knowledge of it seemed to have upon her? There are puzzles so difficult that one cannot even get so far as a conjecture as to the solution, and this seemed one of them. I am usually of too practical a turn to waste time on such conundrums; but the difficulty of a riddle embodied in a beautiful young girl does not detract from its fascination. In general, no doubt, maidens' blushes may be safely assumed to tell the same tale to young men in all ages and races, but to give that interpretation to Edith's crimson cheeks would, considering my position and the length of time I had known her, and still more the fact that this mystery dated from before I had known her at all, be a piece of utter fatuity. And yet she was an angel, and I should not have been a young man if reason and common sense had been able quite to banish a roseate tinge from my dreams that night.

Chapter XXIV

I N the morning I went down stairs early in the hope of seeing Edith alone. In this, however, I was disappointed. Not finding her in the house, I sought her in the garden, but she was not there. In the course of my wanderings I visited the underground chamber, and sat down there to rest. Upon the reading table in the chamber several periodicals and newspapers lay, and thinking that Dr. Leete might be interested in glancing over a Boston daily of 1887, I brought one of the papers with me into the house when I came.

At breakfast I met Edith. She blushed as she greeted me, but was perfectly self-possessed. As we sat at table, Dr. Leete amused himself with looking over the paper I had brought in. There was in it, as in all the newspapers of that date, a great deal about the labor troubles, strikes, lockouts, boycotts, the programmes of labor parties, and the wild threats of the anarchists.

"By the way," said I, as the doctor read aloud to us some of these items, "what part did the followers of the red flag take in the establishment of the new order of things? They were making considerable noise the last thing that I knew."

"They had nothing to do with it except to hinder it, of course," replied Dr. Leete. "They did that very effectually while they lasted, for their talk so disgusted people as to deprive the best considered projects for social reform of a hearing. The subsidizing of those fellows was one of the shrewdest moves of the opponents of reform."

"Subsidizing them!" I exclaimed in astonishment.

"Certainly," replied Dr. Leete. "No historical authority nowadays doubts that they were paid by the great monopolies to wave the red flag and talk about burning, sacking, and blowing people up, in order, by alarming the timid, to head off any real reforms. What astonishes me most is that you should have fallen into the trap so unsuspectingly."

"What are your grounds for believing that the red flag party was subsidized?" I inquired.

"Why simply because they must have seen that their course made a thousand enemies of their professed cause to one friend. Not to suppose that they were hired for the work is to credit them with an inconceivable folly.[1] In the United States, of all countries, no party could intelligently expect to carry its point without first winning over to its ideas a majority of the nation, as the national party eventually did."

"The national party!" I exclaimed. "That must have arisen after my day. I suppose it was one of the labor parties."

"Oh no!" replied the doctor. "The labor parties, as such, never could have accomplished anything on a large or permanent scale. For purposes of national scope, their basis as merely class organizations was too narrow. It was not till a rearrangement of the industrial and social system on a higher ethical basis, and for the more efficient production of wealth, was recognized as the interest, not of one class, but equally of all classes, of rich and poor, cultured and ignorant, old and young, weak and strong, men and women, that there was any prospect that it would be achieved. Then the national party arose to carry it out by political methods. It probably took that name because its aim was to nationalize the functions of production and distribution. Indeed, it could not well have had any other name, for its purpose was to realize the idea of the nation with a grandeur and completeness never before conceived, not as an association of men for certain merely political functions affecting their happiness only remotely and superficially, but as a family, a vital union, a common life, a mighty heaven-touching tree whose leaves are its

---

[1] I fully admit the difficulty of accounting for the course of the anarchists on any other theory than that they were subsidized by the capitalists, but, at the same time, there is no doubt that the theory is wholly erroneous. It certainly was not held at the time by any one, though it may seem so obvious in the retrospect.

people, fed from its veins, and feeding it in turn. The most patriotic of all possible parties, it sought to justify patriotism and raise it from an instinct to a rational devotion, by making the native land truly a father land, a father who kept the people alive and was not merely an idol for which they were expected to die."

Chapter XXV

T HE personality of Edith Leete had naturally impressed me strongly ever since I had come, in so strange a manner, to be an inmate of her father's house, and it was to be expected that after what had happened the night previous, I should be more than ever preoccupied with thoughts of her. From the first I had been struck with the air of serene frankness and ingenuous directness, more like that of a noble and innocent boy than any girl I had ever known, which characterized her. I was curious to know how far this charming quality might be peculiar to herself, and how far possibly a result of alterations in the social position of women which might have taken place since my time. Finding an opportunity that day, when alone with Dr. Leete, I turned the conversation in that direction.

"I suppose," I said, "that women nowadays, having been relieved of the burden of housework, have no employment but the cultivation of their charms and graces."

"So far as we men are concerned," replied Dr. Leete, "we should consider that they amply paid their way, to use one of your forms of expression, if they confined themselves to that occupation, but you may be very sure that they have quite too much spirit to consent to be mere beneficiaries of society, even as a return for ornamenting it. They did, indeed, welcome their riddance from housework, because that was not only exceptionally wearing in itself, but also wasteful, in the extreme, of energy, as compared with the coöperative plan; but they accepted relief from that sort of work only that they might contribute in other and more effectual, as well as more agreeable, ways to the common weal. Our women, as well as our men, are members of the industrial army, and leave it only when maternal duties claim them. The result is that most women, at one time or another of their lives, serve industrially some five or ten or fifteen years, while those who have no children fill out the full term."

"A woman does not, then, necessarily leave the industrial service on marriage?" I queried.

"No more than a man," replied the doctor. "Why on earth should she? Married women have no housekeeping responsibilities now, you know, and a husband is not a baby that he should be cared for."

"It was thought one of the most grievous features of our civilization that we required so much toil from women," I said; "but it seems to me you get more out of them than we did."

Dr. Leete laughed. "Indeed we do, just as we do out of our men. Yet the women of this age are very happy, and those of the nineteenth century, unless contemporary references greatly mislead us, were very miserable. The reason that women nowadays are so much more efficient co-laborers with the men, and at the same time are so happy, is that, in regard to their work as well as men's, we follow the principle of providing every one the kind of occupation he or she is best adapted to. Women being inferior in strength to men, and further disqualified industrially in special ways, the kinds of occupation reserved for them, and the conditions under which they pursue them, have reference to these facts. The heavier sorts of work are everywhere reserved for men, the lighter occupations for women. Under no circumstances is a woman permitted to follow any employment not perfectly adapted, both as to kind and degree of labor, to her sex. Moreover, the hours of women's work are considerably shorter than those of men's, more frequent vacations are granted, and the most careful provision is made for rest when needed. The men of this day so well appreciate that they owe to the beauty and grace of women the chief zest of their lives and their main incentive to effort, that they permit them to work at all only because it is fully understood that a certain regular requirement of labor, of a sort adapted to their powers, is well for body and mind, during the period of maximum physical vigor. We believe that the magnificent health which distinguishes our women from those of your day, who seem to have been so generally sickly, is owing largely to the fact that all alike are furnished with healthful and inspiriting occupation."

"I understood you," I said, "that the women workers belong to the army of industry, but how can they be under the same system of ranking and discipline with the men, when the conditions of their labor are so different."

"They are under an entirely different discipline," replied Dr. Leete, "and constitute rather an allied force than an integral part of the army of the men. They have a woman general-in-chief and are under exclusively feminine régime. This general, as also the higher officers, is chosen by the body of women who have passed the time of service, in correspondence with the manner in which the chiefs of the masculine army and the President of the nation are elected. The general of the women's army sits in the cabinet of the President and has a veto on measures respecting women's work, pending appeals to Congress. I should have said, in speaking of the judiciary, that we have women on the bench, appointed by the general of the women, as well as men. Causes in which both parties are women are determined by women judges, and where a man and a woman are parties to a case, a judge of either sex must consent to the verdict."

"Womanhood seems to be organized as a sort of *imperium in imperio* in your system," I said.

"To some extent," Dr. Leete replied; "but the inner *imperium* is one from which you will admit there is not likely to be much danger to the nation. The lack of some such recognition of the distinct individuality of the sexes was one of the innumerable defects of your society. The passional attraction between men and women has too often prevented a perception of the profound differences which make the members of each sex in many things strange to the other, and capable of sympathy only with their own. It is in giving full play to the differences of sex rather than in seeking to obliterate them, as was apparently the effort of some reformers in your day, that the enjoyment of each by itself and the piquancy which each has for the other, are alike enhanced. In your day there was no career for women except in an unnatural rivalry with men. We have given them a world of their own, with its emulations, ambitions, and careers, and I assure you they are very happy in it. It seems to us that women were more than any other class the victims of your civilization. There is something which, even at this distance of time, penetrates one with pathos in the spectacle of their ennuied, undeveloped lives, stunted at marriage, their narrow horizon, bounded so often, physically, by the four walls of home, and morally by a petty circle of personal interests. I speak now, not of the poorer classes, who were generally worked to death, but also of the well-to-do and rich. From the great sorrows, as well as the petty frets of life, they had no refuge in the breezy outdoor world of human affairs, nor any interests save those of the family. Such an existence would have softened men's brains or driven them mad. All that is changed to-day. No woman is heard nowadays wishing she were a man, nor parents desiring boy rather than girl children. Our girls are as full of ambition for their careers as our boys. Marriage, when it comes, does not mean incarceration for them, nor does it separate them in any way from the larger interests of society, the bustling life of the world. Only when maternity fills a woman's mind with new interests does she withdraw from the world for a time. Afterwards, and at any time, she may return to her place among her comrades, nor need she ever lose touch with them. Women are a very happy race nowadays, as compared with what they ever were before in the world's history, and their power of giving happiness to men has been of course increased in proportion."

"I should imagine it possible," I said, "that the interest which girls take in their careers as members of the industrial army and candidates for its distinctions might have an effect to deter them from marriage."

Dr. Leete smiled. "Have no anxiety on that score, Mr. West," he replied. "The Creator took very good care that whatever other modifications the dispositions of men and women might with time take on, their attraction for each other should remain constant. The mere fact that in an age like yours, when the struggle for existence must have left people little time for other thoughts, and the future was so uncertain that to assume parental responsibilities must have often seemed like a criminal risk, there was even then marrying and giving in marriage, should be conclusive on this point. As for love nowadays, one of our authors says that the vacuum left in the minds of men and women by the absence of care for one's livelihood has been entirely taken up by the tender passion. That, however, I beg you to believe, is something of an exaggeration. For the rest, so far is marriage from being an interference with a woman's career, that the higher positions in the feminine army of industry are intrusted only to women who have been both wives and mothers, as they alone fully represent their sex."

"Are credit cards issued to the women just as to the men?"

"Certainly."

"The credits of the women, I suppose, are for smaller sums, owing to the frequent suspension of their labor on account of family responsibilities."

"Smaller!" exclaimed Dr. Leete, "oh, no! The maintenance of all our people is the same. There are no exceptions to that rule, but if any difference were made on account of the interruptions you speak of, it would be by making the woman's credit larger, not smaller. Can you think of any service constituting a stronger claim on the nation's gratitude than bearing and nursing the nation's children? According to our view, none deserve so well of the world as good parents. There is no task so unselfish, so necessarily without return, though the heart is well rewarded, as the nurture of the children who are to make the world for one another when we are gone."

"It would seem to follow, from what you have said, that wives are in no way dependent on their husbands for maintenance."

"Of course they are not," replied Dr. Leete, "nor children on their parents either, that is, for means of support, though of course they are for the offices of affection. The child's labor, when he grows up, will go to increase the common stock, not his parents', who will be dead, and therefore he is properly nurtured out of the common stock. The account of every person, man, woman, and child, you must understand, is always with the nation directly, and never through any intermediary, except, of course, that parents, to a certain extent, act for children as their guardians. You see that it is by virtue of the relation of individuals to the nation, of their membership in it, that they are entitled to support; and this title is in no way connected with or affected by their relations to other individuals who are fellow members of the nation with them. That any person should be dependent for the means of support upon another would be shocking to the moral sense as well as indefensible on any rational social theory. What would become of personal liberty and dignity under such an arrangement? I am aware that you called yourselves free in the nineteenth century. The meaning of the word could not then, however, have been at all what it is at present, or you certainly would not have applied it to a society of which nearly every member was in a position of galling personal dependence upon others as to the very means of life, the poor upon the rich, or employed upon employer, women upon men, children upon parents. Instead of distributing the product of the nation directly to its members, which would seem the most natural and obvious method, it would actually appear that you had given your minds to devising a plan of hand to hand distribution, involving the maximum of personal humiliation to all classes of recipients.

"As regards the dependence of women upon men for support, which then was usual, of course natural attraction in case of marriages of love may often have made it endurable, though for spirited women I should fancy it must always have remained humiliating. What, then, must it have been in the innumerable cases where women, with or without the form of marriage, had to sell themselves to men to get their living? Even your contemporaries, callous as they were to most of the revolting aspects of their society, seem to have had an idea that this was not quite as it should be; but, it was still only for pity's sake that they deplored the lot of the women. It did not occur to them that it was robbery as well as cruelty when men seized for themselves the whole product of the world and left women to beg and wheedle for their share. Why—but bless me, Mr. West, I am really running on at a remarkable rate, just as if the robbery, the sorrow, and the shame which those poor women endured were not over a century since, or as if you were responsible for what you no doubt deplored as much as I do."

"I must bear my share of responsibility for the world as it then was," I replied. "All I can say in extenuation is that until the nation was ripe for the present system of organized production and distribution, no radical improvement in the position of woman was possible. The root of her disability, as you say, was her personal dependence upon man for her livelihood, and I can imagine no other mode of social organization than that you have adopted, which would have set women free of man at the same time that it set men free of one another. I suppose, by the way, that so entire a change in the position of women cannot have taken place without affecting in marked ways the social relations of the sexes. That will be a very interesting study for me."

"The change you will observe," said Dr. Leete, "will chiefly be, I think, the entire frankness and unconstraint which now characterizes those relations, as compared with the artificiality which seems to have marked them in your time. The sexes now meet with the ease of perfect equals, suitors to each other for nothing but love. In your time the fact that women were dependent for support on men made the woman in reality the one chiefly benefited by marriage. This fact, so far as we can judge from contemporary records, appears to have been coarsely enough recognized among the lower classes, while among the more polished it was glossed over by a system of elaborate conventionalities which aimed to carry the precisely opposite meaning, namely, that the man was the party chiefly benefited. To keep up this convention it was essential that he should always seem the suitor. Nothing was therefore considered more shocking to the proprieties than that a woman should betray a fondness for a man before he had indicated a desire to marry her. Why, we actually have in our libraries books, by authors of your day, written for no other purpose than to discuss the question whether, under any conceivable circumstances, a woman might, without discredit to her sex, reveal an unsolicited love. All this seems exquisitely absurd to us, and yet we know that, given your circumstances, the problem might have a serious side. When for a woman to proffer her love to a man was in effect to invite him to assume the burden of her support, it is easy to see that pride and delicacy might well have checked the promptings of the heart. When you go out into our society, Mr. West, you must be prepared to be often cross-questioned on this point by our young people, who are naturally much interested in this aspect of old-fashioned manners." [1]

"And so the girls of the twentieth century tell their love."

"If they choose," replied Dr. Leete. "There is no more pretense of a concealment of feeling on their part than on the part of their lovers. Coquetry would be as much despised in a girl as in a man. Affected coldness, which in your day rarely deceived a lover, would deceive him wholly now, for no one thinks of practicing it."

"One result which must follow from the independence of women I can see for myself," I said. "There can be no marriages now except those of inclination."

"That is a matter of course," replied Dr. Leete.

"Think of a world in which there are nothing but matches of pure love! Ah me, Dr. Leete, how far you are from being able to understand what an astonishing phenomenon such a world seems to a man of the nineteenth century!"

"I can, however, to some extent, imagine it," replied the doctor. "But the fact you celebrate, that there are nothing but love matches, means even more, perhaps, than you probably at first realize. It means that for the first time in human history the principle of sexual selection, with its tendency to preserve and transmit the better types of the race, and let the inferior types drop out, has unhindered operation. The necessities of poverty, the need of having a home, no longer tempt women to accept as the fathers of their children men whom they neither can love

---

[1] I may say that Dr. Leete's warning has been fully justified by my experience. The amount and intensity of amusement which the young people of this day, and the young women especially, are able to extract from what they are pleased to call the oddities of courtship in the nineteenth century, appear unlimited.

nor respect. Wealth and rank no longer divert attention from personal qualities. Gold no longer 'gilds the straitened forehead of the fool.' The gifts of person, mind, and disposition; beauty, wit, eloquence, kindness, generosity, geniality, courage, are sure of transmission to posterity. Every generation is sifted through a little finer mesh than the last. The attributes that human nature admires are preserved, those that repel it are left behind. There are, of course, a great many women who with love must mingle admiration, and seek to wed greatly, but these not the less obey the same law, for to wed greatly now is not to marry men of fortune or title, but those who have risen above their fellows by the solidity or brilliance of their services to humanity. These form nowadays the only aristocracy with which alliance is distinction.

"You were speaking, a day or two ago, of the physical superiority of our people to your contemporaries. Perhaps more important than any of the causes I mentioned then as tending to race purification has been the effect of untrammeled sexual selection upon the quality of two or three successive generations. I believe that when you have made a fuller study of our people you will find in them not only a physical, but a mental and moral improvement. It would be strange if it were not so, for not only is one of the great laws of nature now freely working out the salvation of the race, but a profound moral sentiment has come to its support. Individualism, which in your day was the animating idea of society, not only was fatal to any vital sentiment of brotherhood and common interest among living men, but equally to any realization of the responsibility of the living for the generation to follow. To-day this sense of responsibility, practically unrecognized in all previous ages, has become one of the great ethical ideas of the race, reinforcing, with an intense conviction of duty, the natural impulse to seek in marriage the best and noblest of the other sex. The result is, that not all the encouragements and incentives of every sort which we have provided to develop industry, talent, genius, excellence of whatever kind, are comparable in their effect on our young men with the fact that our women sit aloft as judges of the race and reserve themselves to reward the winners. Of all the whips, and spurs, and baits, and prizes, there is none like the thought of the radiant faces which the laggards will find averted.

"Celibates nowadays are almost invariably men who have failed to acquit themselves creditably in the work of life. The woman must be a courageous one, with a very evil sort of courage, too, whom pity for one of these unfortunates should lead to defy the opinion of her generation—for otherwise she is free—so far as to accept him for a husband. I should add that, more exacting and difficult to resist than any other element in that opinion, she would find the sentiment of her own sex. Our women have risen to the full height of their responsibility as the wardens of the world to come to whose keeping the keys of the future are confided. Their feeling of duty in this respect amounts to a sense of religious consecration. It is a cult in which they educate their daughters from childhood."

After going to my room that night, I sat up late to read a romance of Berrian, handed me by Dr. Leete, the plot of which turned on a situation suggested by his last words, concerning the modern view of parental responsibility. A similar situation would almost certainly have been treated by a nineteenth century romanticist so as to excite the morbid sympathy of the reader with the sentimental selfishness of the lovers, and his resentment toward the unwritten law which they outraged. I need not describe—for who has not read "Ruth Elton?"—how different is the course which Berrian takes, and with what tremendous effect he enforces the principle which he states: "Over the unborn our power is that of God, and our responsibility like His toward us. As we acquit ourselves toward them, so let Him deal with us."

Chapter XXVI

I THINK if a person were ever excusable for losing track of the days of the week, the circumstances excused me. Indeed, if I had been told that the method of reckoning time had been wholly changed and the days were now counted in lots of five, ten, or fifteen instead of seven, I should have been in no way surprised after what I had already heard and seen of the twentieth century. The first time that any inquiry as to the days of the week occurred to me was the morning following the conversation related in the last chapter. At the breakfast table Dr. Leete asked me if I would care to hear a sermon.

"Is it Sunday, then?" I exclaimed.

"Yes," he replied. "It was on Friday, you see, when we made the lucky discovery of the buried chamber to which we owe your society this morning. It was on Saturday morning, soon after midnight, that you first awoke, and Sunday afternoon when you awoke the second time with faculties fully regained."

"So you still have Sundays and sermons," I said. "We had prophets who foretold that long before this time the world would have dispensed with both. I am very curious to know how the ecclesiastical systems fit in with the rest of your social arrangements. I suppose you have a sort of national church with official clergymen."

Dr. Leete laughed, and Mrs. Leete and Edith seemed greatly amused.

"Why, Mr. West," Edith said, "what odd people you must think us. You were quite done with national religious establishments in the nineteenth century, and did you fancy we had gone back to them?"

"But how can voluntary churches and an unofficial clerical

profession be reconciled with national ownership of all buildings, and the industrial service required of all men?" I answered.

"The religious practices of the people have naturally changed considerably in a century," replied Dr. Leete; "but supposing them to have remained unchanged, our social system would accommodate them perfectly. The nation supplies any person or number of persons with buildings on guarantee of the rent, and they remain tenants while they pay it. As for the clergymen, if a number of persons wish the services of an individual for any particular end of their own, apart from the general service of the nation, they can always secure it, with that individual's own consent, of course, just as we secure the service of our editors, by contributing from their credit-cards an indemnity to the nation for the loss of his services in general industry. This indemnity paid the nation for the individual answers to the salary in your day paid to the individual himself; and the various applications of this principle leave private initiative full play in all details to which national control is not applicable. Now, as to hearing a sermon to-day, if you wish to do so, you can either go to a church to hear it or stay at home."

"How am I to hear it if I stay at home?"

"Simply by accompanying us to the music room at the proper hour and selecting an easy chair. There are some who still prefer to hear sermons in church, but most of our preaching, like our musical performances, is not in public, but delivered in acoustically prepared chambers, connected by wire with subscribers' houses. If you prefer to go to a church I shall be glad to accompany you, but I really don't believe you are likely to hear anywhere a better discourse than you will at home. I see by the paper that Mr. Barton is to preach this morning, and he preaches only by telephone, and to audiences often reaching 150,000."

"The novelty of the experience of hearing a sermon under such circumstances would incline me to be one of Mr. Barton's hearers, if for no other reason," I said.

An hour or two later, as I sat reading in the library, Edith came for me, and I followed her to the music room, where Dr. and Mrs. Leete were waiting. We had not more than seated ourselves comfortably when the tinkle of a bell was heard, and a few moments after the voice of a man, at the pitch of ordinary conversation, addressed us, with an effect of proceeding from an invisible person in the room. This was what the voice said:—

Mr. Barton's Sermon.

"We have had among us, during the past week, a critic from the nineteenth century, a living representative of the epoch of our great-grandparents. It would be strange if a fact so extraordinary had not somewhat strongly affected our imaginations. Perhaps most of us have been stimulated to some effort to realize the society of a century ago, and figure to ourselves what it must have been like to live then. In inviting you now to consider certain reflections upon this subject which have occurred to me, I presume that I shall rather follow than divert the course of your own thoughts."

Edith whispered something to her father at this point, to which he nodded assent and turned to me.

"Mr. West," he said, "Edith suggests that you may find it slightly embarrassing to listen to a discourse on the lines Mr. Barton is laying down, and if so, you need not be cheated out of a sermon. She will connect us with Mr. Sweetser's speaking room if you say so, and I can still promise you a very good discourse."

"No, no," I said. "Believe me, I would much rather hear what Mr. Barton has to say."

"As you please," replied my host.

When her father spoke to me Edith had touched a screw, and the voice of Mr. Barton had ceased abruptly. Now at another touch the room was once more filled with the earnest sympathetic tones which had already impressed me most favorably.

"I venture to assume that one effect has been common with us as a result of this effort at retrospection, and that it has been to leave us more than ever amazed at the stupendous change which one brief century has made in the material and moral conditions of humanity.

"Still, as regards the contrast between the poverty of the nation and the world in the nineteenth century and their wealth now, it is not greater, possibly, than had been before seen in human history, perhaps not greater, for example, than that between the poverty of this country during the earliest colonial period of the seventeenth century and the relatively great wealth it had attained at the close of the nineteenth, or between the England of William the Conqueror and that of Victoria. Although the aggregate riches of a nation did not then, as now, afford any accurate criterion of the masses of its people, yet instances like these afford partial parallels for the merely material side of the contrast between the nineteenth and the twentieth centuries. It is when we contemplate the moral aspect of that contrast that we find ourselves in the presence of a phenomenon for which history offers no precedent, however far back we may cast our eye. One might almost be excused who should exclaim, 'Here, surely, is something like a miracle!' Nevertheless, when we give over idle wonder, and begin to examine the seeming prodigy critically, we find it no prodigy at all, much less a miracle. It is not necessary to suppose a moral new birth of humanity, or a wholesale destruction of the wicked and survival of the good, to account for the fact before us. It finds its simple and obvious explanation in the reaction of a changed environment upon human nature. It means merely that a form of society which was founded on the pseudo self-interest of selfishness, and appealed solely to the anti-social and brutal side of human nature, has been replaced by institutions based on the true self-interest of a rational unselfishness, and appealing to the social and generous instincts of men.

"My friends, if you would see men again the beasts of prey they seemed in the nineteenth century, all you have to do is to restore the old social and industrial system, which taught them to view their natural prey in their fellow-men, and find their gain in the loss of others. No doubt it seems to you that no necessity, however dire, would have tempted you to subsist on what superior skill or strength enabled you to wrest from others equally needy. But suppose it were not merely your own life that you were responsible for. I know well that there must have been many a man among our ancestors who, if it had been merely a question of his own life, would sooner have given it up than nourished it by bread snatched from others. But this he was not permitted to do. He had dear lives dependent on him. Men loved women in those days, as now. God knows how they dared be fathers, but they had babies as sweet, no doubt, to them as ours to us, whom they must feed, clothe, educate. The gentlest creatures are fierce when they have young to provide for, and in that wolfish society the struggle for bread borrowed a peculiar desperation from the tenderest sentiments. For the sake of those dependent on him, a man might not choose, but must plunge into the foul fight,—cheat, overreach, supplant, defraud, buy below worth and sell above, break down the business by which his neighbor fed his young ones, tempt men to buy what they ought not and to sell what they should not, grind his laborers, sweat his debtors, cozen his creditors. Though a man sought it carefully with tears, it was hard to find a way in which he could earn a living and provide for his family except by pressing in before some weaker rival and taking the food from his mouth. Even the ministers of religion were not exempt from this cruel necessity. While they warned their flocks against the love of money, regard for their families compelled them to keep an outlook for the pecuniary prizes of their calling. Poor fellows, theirs was indeed a trying business, preaching to men a generosity and unselfishness which they and everybody knew would, in the existing state of the world, reduce to poverty those who should practice them, laying down laws of conduct which the law of self-preservation compelled men to break. Looking on the inhuman spectacle of society, these worthy men bitterly bemoaned the depravity of human nature; as if angelic nature would not have been debauched in such a devil's school! Ah, my friends, believe me, it is not now in this happy age that humanity is proving the divinity within it. It was rather in those evil days when not even the fight for life with one another, the struggle for mere existence, in which mercy was folly, could wholly banish generosity and kindness from the earth.

"It is not hard to understand the desperation with which men and women, who under other conditions would have been full of gentleness and truth, fought and tore each other in the scramble for gold, when we realize what it meant to miss it, what poverty was in that day. For the body it was hunger and thirst, torment by heat and frost, in sickness neglect, in health unremitting toil; for the moral nature it meant oppression, contempt, and the patient endurance of indignity, brutish associations from infancy, the loss of all the innocence of childhood, the grace of womanhood, the dignity of manhood; for the mind it meant the death of ignorance, the torpor of all those faculties which distinguish us from brutes, the reduction of life to a round of bodily functions.

"Ah, my friends, if such a fate as this were offered you and your children as the only alternative of success in the accumulation of wealth, how long do you fancy would you be in sinking to the moral level of your ancestors?

"Some two or three centuries ago an act of barbarity was committed in India, which, though the number of lives destroyed was but a few score, was attended by such peculiar horrors that its memory is likely to be perpetual. A number of English prisoners were shut up in a room containing not enough air to supply one-tenth their number. The unfortunates were gallant men, devoted comrades in service, but, as the agonies of suffocation began to take hold on them, they forgot all else, and became involved in a hideous struggle, each one for himself, and against all others, to force a way to one of the small apertures of the prison at which alone it was possible to get a breath of air. It was a struggle in which men became beasts, and the recital of its horrors by the few survivors so shocked our forefathers that for a century later we find it a stock reference in their literature as a typical illustration of the extreme possibilities of human misery, as shocking in its moral as its physical aspect. They could scarcely have anticipated that to us the Black Hole of Calcutta, with its press of maddened men tearing and trampling one another in the struggle to win a place at the breathing holes, would seem a striking type of the society of their age. It lacked something of being a complete type, however, for in the Calcutta Black Hole there were no tender women, no little children and old men and women, no cripples. They were at least all men, strong to bear, who suffered.

"When we reflect that the ancient order of which I have been speaking was prevalent up to the end of the nineteenth century, while to us the new order which succeeded it already seems antique, even our parents having known no other, we cannot fail to be astounded at the suddenness with which a transition so profound beyond all previous experience of the race must have been effected. Some observation of the state of men's minds during the last quarter of the nineteenth century will, however, in great measure, dissipate this astonishment. Though general intelligence in the modern sense could not be said to exist in any community at that time, yet, as compared with previous generations, the one then on the stage was intelligent. The inevitable consequence of even this comparative degree of intelligence had been a perception of the evils of society, such as had never before been general. It is quite true that these evils had been even worse, much worse, in previous ages. It was the increased intelligence of the masses which made the difference, as the dawn reveals the squalor of surroundings which in the darkness may have seemed tolerable. The key-note of the literature of the period was one of compassion for the poor and unfortunate, and indignant outcry against the failure of the social machinery to ameliorate the miseries of men. It is plain from these outbursts that the moral hideousness of the spectacle about them was, at least by flashes, fully realized by the best of the men of that time, and that the lives of some of the more sensitive and generous hearted of them were rendered well-nigh unendurable by the intensity of their sympathies.

"Although the idea of the vital unity of the family of mankind, the reality of human brotherhood, was very far from being apprehended by them as the moral axiom it seems to us, yet it is a mistake to suppose that there was no feeling at all corresponding to it. I could read you passages of great beauty from some of their writers which show that the conception was clearly attained by a few, and no doubt vaguely by many more. Moreover, it must not be forgotten that the nineteenth century was in name

Christian, and the fact that the entire commercial and industrial frame of society was the embodiment of the anti-Christian spirit must have had some weight, though I admit it was strangely little, with the nominal followers of Jesus Christ.

"When we inquire why it did not have more, why, in general, long after a vast majority of men had agreed as to the crying abuses of the existing social arrangement, they still tolerated it, or contented themselves with talking of petty reforms in it, we come upon an extraordinary fact. It was the sincere belief of even the best of men at that epoch that the only stable elements in human nature, on which a social system could be safely founded were its worst propensities. They had been taught and believed that greed and self-seeking were all that held mankind together, and that all human associations would fall to pieces if anything were done to blunt the edge of these motives or curb their operation. In a word, they believed—even those who longed to believe otherwise—the exact reverse of what seems to us self-evident; they believed, that is, that the anti-social qualities of men, and not their social qualities, were what furnished the cohesive force of society. It seemed reasonable to them that men lived together solely for the purpose of overreaching and oppressing one another, and of being overreached and oppressed, and that while a society that gave full scope to these propensities could stand, there would be little chance for one based on the idea of coöperation for the benefit of all. It seems absurd to expect any one to believe that convictions like these were ever seriously entertained by men; but that they were not only entertained by our great-grandfathers, but were responsible for the long delay in doing away with the ancient order, after a conviction of its intolerable abuses had become general, is as well established as any fact in history can be. Just here you will find the explanation of the profound pessimism of the literature of the last quarter of the nineteenth century, the note of melancholy in its poetry, and the cynicism of its humor.

"Feeling that the condition of the race was unendurable, they had no clear hope of anything better. They believed that the evolution of humanity had resulted in leading it into a *cul de sac*, and that there was no way of getting forward. The frame of men's minds at this time is strikingly illustrated by treatises which have come down to us, and may even now be consulted in our libraries by the curious, in which laborious arguments are pursued to prove that despite the evil plight of men, life was still, by some slight preponderance of considerations, probably better worth living than leaving. Despising themselves, they despised their Creator. There was a general decay of religious belief. Pale and watery gleams, from skies thickly veiled by doubt and dread, alone lighted up the chaos of earth. That men should doubt Him whose breath is in their nostrils, or dread the hands that moulded them, seems to us indeed a pitiable insanity; but we must remember that children who are brave by day have sometimes foolish fears at night. The dawn has come since then. It is very easy to believe in the fatherhood of God in the twentieth century.

"Briefly, as must needs be in a discourse of this character, I have adverted to some of the causes which had prepared men's minds for the change from the old to the new order, as well as some causes of the conservation of despair which for a while held it back after the time was ripe. To wonder at the rapidity with which the change was completed after its possibility was first entertained is to forget the intoxicating effect of hope upon minds long accustomed to despair. The sunburst, after so long and dark a night, must needs have had a dazzling effect. From the moment men allowed themselves to believe that humanity after all had not been meant for a dwarf, that its squat stature was not the measure of its possible growth, but that it stood upon the verge of an avatar of limitless development, the reaction must needs have been overwhelming. It is evident that nothing was able to stand against the enthusiasm which the new faith inspired.

"Here, at last, men must have felt, was a cause compared with which the grandest of historic causes had been trivial. It was doubtless because it could have commanded millions of martyrs, that none were needed. The change of a dynasty in a petty kingdom of the old world often cost more lives than did the revolution which set the feet of the human race at last in the right way.

"Doubtless it ill beseems one to whom the boon of life in our resplendent age has been vouchsafed to wish his destiny other, and yet I have often thought that I would fain exchange my share in this serene and golden day for a place in that stormy epoch of transition, when heroes burst the barred gate of the future and revealed to the kindling gaze of a hopeless race, in place of the blank wall that had closed its path, a vista of progress whose end, for very excess of light, still dazzles us. Ah, my friends! who will say that to have lived then, when the weakest influence was a lever to whose touch the centuries trembled, was not worth a share even in this era of fruition?

"You know the story of that last, greatest, and most bloodless of revolutions. In the time of one generation men laid aside the social traditions and practices of barbarians, and assumed a social order worthy of rational and human beings. Ceasing to be predatory in their habits, they became co-workers, and found in fraternity, at once, the science of wealth and happiness. 'What shall I eat and drink, and wherewithal shall I be clothed?' stated as a problem beginning and ending in self, had been an anxious and an endless one. But when once it was conceived, not from the individual, but the fraternal standpoint, 'What shall we eat and drink, and wherewithal shall we be clothed?'—its difficulties vanished.

"Poverty with servitude had been the result, for the mass of humanity, of attempting to solve the problem of maintenance from the individual standpoint, but no sooner had the nation become the sole capitalist and employer than not alone did plenty replace poverty, but the last vestige of the serfdom of man to man disappeared from earth. Human slavery, so often vainly scotched, at last was killed. The means of subsistence no longer doled out by men to women, by employer to employed, by rich to poor, was distributed from a common stock as among children at the father's table. It was impossible for a man any longer to use his fellow-men as tools for his own profit. His esteem was the only sort of gain he could thenceforth make out of him. There was no more either arrogance or servility in the relations of human beings to one another. For the first time since the creation every man stood up straight before God. The fear of want and the lust of gain became extinct motives when abundance was assured to all and immoderate possessions were made impossible of attainment. There were no more beggars nor almoners. Equity left charity without an occupation. The ten commandments became well-nigh obsolete in a world where there was no temptation to theft, no occasion to lie either for fear or favor, no room for envy where all were equal, and little provocation to violence where men were disarmed of power to injure one another. Humanity's ancient dream of liberty, equality, fraternity, mocked by so many ages, at last was realized.

"As in the old society the generous, the just, the tender-hearted had been placed at a disadvantage by the possession of those qualities, so in the new society the cold-hearted, the greedy, and self-seeking found themselves out of joint with the world. Now that the conditions of life for the first time ceased to operate as a forcing process to develop the brutal qualities of human nature, and the premium which had heretofore encouraged selfishness was not only removed, but placed upon unselfishness, it was for the first time possible to see what unperverted human nature really was like. The depraved tendencies, which had previously overgrown and obscured the better to so large an extent, now withered like cellar fungi in the open air, and the nobler qualities showed a sudden luxuriance which turned cynics into panegyrists and for the first time in human history tempted mankind to fall in love with itself. Soon was fully revealed, what the divines and philosophers of the old world never would have believed, that human nature in its essential qualities is good, not bad, that men by their natural intention and structure are generous, not selfish, pitiful, not cruel, sympathetic, not arrogant, godlike in aspiration, instinct with divinest impulses of tenderness and self-sacrifice, images of God indeed, not the travesties upon Him they had seemed. The constant pressure, through numberless generations, of conditions of life which might have perverted angels, had not been able to essentially alter the natural nobility of the stock, and these conditions once removed, like a bent tree, it had sprung back to its normal uprightness.

"To put the whole matter in the nutshell of a parable, let me compare humanity in the olden time to a rosebush planted in a swamp, watered with black bog-water, breathing miasmatic fogs by day, and chilled with poison dews at night. Innumerable generations of gardeners had done their best to make it bloom, but beyond an occasional half-opened bud with a worm at the heart, their efforts had been unsuccessful. Many, indeed, claimed that the bush was no rosebush at all, but a noxious shrub, fit only to be uprooted and burned. The gardeners, for the most part, however, held that the bush belonged to the rose family, but had some ineradicable taint about it, which prevented the buds from coming out, and accounted for its generally sickly condition. There were a few, indeed, who maintained that the stock was good enough, that the trouble was in the bog, and that under more favorable conditions the plant might be expected to do better. But these persons were not regular gardeners, and being condemned by the latter as mere theorists and day dreamers, were, for the most part, so regarded by the people. Moreover, urged some eminent moral philosophers, even conceding for the sake of the argument that the bush might possibly do better elsewhere, it was a more valuable discipline for the buds to try to bloom in a bog than it would be under more favorable conditions. The buds that succeeded in opening might indeed be very rare, and the flowers pale and scentless, but they represented far more moral effort than if they had bloomed spontaneously in a garden.

"The regular gardeners and the moral philosophers had their way. The bush remained rooted in the bog, and the old course of treatment went on. Continually new varieties of forcing mixtures were applied to the roots, and more recipes than could be numbered, each declared by its advocates the best and only suitable preparation, were used to kill the vermin and remove the mildew. This went on a very long time. Occasionally some one claimed to observe a slight improvement in the appearance of the bush, but there were quite as many who declared that it did not look so well as it used to. On the whole there could not be said to be any marked change. Finally, during a period of general despondency as to the prospects of the bush where it was, the idea of transplanting it was again mooted, and this time found favor. 'Let us try it,' was the general voice. 'Perhaps it may thrive better elsewhere, and here it is certainly doubtful if it be worth cultivating longer.' So it came about that the rosebush of humanity was transplanted, and set in sweet, warm, dry earth, where the sun bathed it, the stars wooed it, and the south wind caressed it. Then it appeared that it was indeed a rosebush. The vermin and the mildew disappeared, and the bush was covered with most beautiful red roses, whose fragrance filled the world.

"It is a pledge of the destiny appointed for us that the Creator has set in our hearts an infinite standard of achievement, judged by which our past attainments seem always insignificant, and the goal never nearer. Had our forefathers conceived a state of society in which men should live together like brethren dwelling in unity, without strifes or envying, violence or overreaching, and where, at the price of a degree of labor not greater than health demands, in their chosen occupations, they should be wholly freed from care for the morrow and left with no more concern for their livelihood than trees which are watered by unfailing streams,—had they conceived such a condition, I say, it would have seemed to them nothing less than paradise. They would have confounded it with their idea of heaven, nor dreamed that there could possibly lie further beyond anything to be desired or striven for.

"But how is it with us who stand on this height which they gazed up to? Already we have well-nigh forgotten, except when it is especially called to our minds by some occasion like the present, that it was not always with men as it is now. It is a strain on our imaginations to conceive the social arrangements of our immediate ancestors. We find them grotesque. The solution of the problem of physical maintenance so as to banish care and crime, so far from seeming to us an ultimate attainment, appears but as a preliminary to anything like real human progress. We have but relieved ourselves of an impertinent and needless harassment which hindered our ancestors from undertaking the real ends of existence. We are merely stripped for the race; no more. We are like a child which has just learned to stand upright and to walk. It is a great event, from the child's point of view, when he first walks. Perhaps he fancies that there can be little beyond that achievement, but a year later he has forgotten that he could not always walk. His horizon did but widen when he rose, and enlarge as he moved. A great event indeed, in one sense, was his first step, but only as a beginning, not as the end. His true career was but then first entered on. The enfranchisement of humanity in the last century, from mental and physical absorption in working and scheming for the mere bodily necessities, may be regarded as a species of second birth of the race, without which its first birth to an existence that was but a burden would forever have remained unjustified, but whereby it is now abundantly vindicated. Since then, humanity has entered on a new phase of spiritual development, an evolution of higher faculties, the very existence of which in human nature our ancestors scarcely suspected. In place of the dreary hopelessness of the nineteenth century, its profound pessimism as to the future of humanity, the animating idea of the present age is an enthusiastic conception of the opportunities of our earthly existence, and the unbounded possibilities of human nature. The betterment of mankind from generation to generation, physically, mentally, morally, is recognized as the one great object supremely worthy of effort and of sacrifice. We believe the race for the first time to have entered on the realization of God's ideal of it, and each generation must now be a step upward.

"Do you ask what we look for when unnumbered generations shall have passed away? I answer, the way stretches far before us, but the end is lost in light. For twofold is the return of man to God 'who is our home,' the return of the individual by the way of death, and the return of the race by the fulfilment of the evolution, when the divine secret hidden in the germ shall be perfectly unfolded. With a tear for the dark past, turn we then to the dazzling future, and, veiling our eyes, press forward. The long and weary winter of the race is ended. Its summer has begun. Humanity has burst the chrysalis. The heavens are before it."

Chapter XXVII

I NEVER could tell just why, but Sunday afternoon during my old life had been a time when I was peculiarly subject to melancholy, when the color unaccountably faded out of all the aspects of life, and everything appeared pathetically uninteresting. The hours, which in general were wont to bear me easily on their wings, lost the power of flight, and toward the close of the day, drooping quite to earth, had fairly to be dragged along by main strength. Perhaps it was partly owing to the established association of ideas that, despite the utter change in my circumstances, I fell into a state of profound depression on the afternoon of this my first Sunday in the twentieth century.

It was not, however, on the present occasion a depression without specific cause, the mere vague melancholy I have spoken of, but a sentiment suggested and certainly quite justified by my position. The sermon of Mr. Barton, with its constant implication of the vast moral gap between the century to which I belonged and that in which I found myself, had had an effect strongly to accentuate my sense of loneliness in it. Considerately and philosophically as he had spoken, his words could scarcely have failed to leave upon my mind a strong impression of the mingled pity, curiosity, and aversion which I, as a representative of an abhorred epoch, must excite in all around me.

The extraordinary kindness with which I had been treated by Dr. Leete and his family, and especially the goodness of Edith, had hitherto prevented my fully realizing that their real sentiment toward me must necessarily be that of the whole generation to which they belonged. The recognition of this, as regarded Dr. Leete and his amiable wife, however painful, I might have endured, but the conviction that Edith must share their feeling was more than I could bear.

The crushing effect with which this belated perception of a fact so obvious came to me opened my eyes fully to something which perhaps the reader has already suspected,—I loved Edith.

Was it strange that I did? The affecting occasion on which our intimacy had begun, when her hands had drawn me out of the whirlpool of madness; the fact that her sympathy was the vital breath which had set me up in this new life and enabled me to support it; my habit of looking to her as the mediator between me and the world around in a sense that even her father was not,—these were circumstances that had predetermined a result which her remarkable loveliness of person and disposition would alone have accounted for. It was quite inevitable that she should have come to seem to me, in a sense quite different from the usual experience of lovers, the only woman in this world. Now that I had become suddenly sensible of the fatuity of the hopes I had begun to cherish, I suffered not merely what another lover might, but in addition a desolate loneliness, an utter forlornness, such as no other lover, however unhappy, could have felt.

My hosts evidently saw that I was depressed in spirits, and did their best to divert me. Edith especially, I could see, was distressed for me, but according to the usual perversity of lovers, having once been so mad as to dream of receiving something more from her, there was no longer any virtue for me in a kindness that I knew was only sympathy.

Toward nightfall, after secluding myself in my room most of the afternoon, I went into the garden to walk about. The day was overcast, with an autumnal flavor in the warm, still air. Finding myself near the excavation, I entered the subterranean chamber and sat down there. "This," I muttered to myself, "is the only home I have. Let me stay here, and not go forth any more." Seeking aid from the familiar surroundings, I endeavored to find a sad sort of consolation in reviving the past and summoning up the forms and faces that were about me in my former life. It was in vain. There was no longer any life in them. For nearly one hundred years the stars had been looking down on Edith Bartlett's grave, and the graves of all my generation.

The past was dead, crushed beneath a century's weight, and from the present I was shut out. There was no place for me anywhere. I was neither dead nor properly alive.

"Forgive me for following you."

I looked up. Edith stood in the door of the subterranean room, regarding me smilingly, but with eyes full of sympathetic distress. "Send me away if I am intruding on you," she said; "but we saw that you were out of spirits, and you know you promised to let me know if that were so. You have not kept your word."

I rose and came to the door, trying to smile, but making, I fancy, rather sorry work of it, for the sight of her loveliness brought home to me the more poignantly the cause of my wretchedness.

"I was feeling a little lonely, that is all," I said. "Has it never occurred to you that my position is so much more utterly alone than any human being's ever was before that a new word is really needed to describe it?"

"Oh, you must not talk that way,—you must not let yourself feel that way,—you must not!" she exclaimed, with moistened eyes. "Are we not your friends? It is your own fault if you will not let us be. You need not be lonely."

"You are good to me beyond my power of understanding," I said, "but don't you suppose that I know it is pity merely, sweet pity, but pity only. I should be a fool not to know that I cannot seem to you as other men of your own generation do, but as some strange uncanny being, a stranded creature of an unknown sea, whose forlornness touches your compassion despite its grotesqueness. I have been so foolish, you were so kind, as to almost forget that this must needs be so, and to fancy I might in time become naturalized, as we used to say, in this age, so as to feel like one of you and to seem to you like the other men about you. But Mr. Barton's sermon taught me how vain such a fancy is, how great the gulf between us must seem to you."

"Oh that miserable sermon!" she exclaimed, fairly crying now in her sympathy, "I wanted you not to hear it. What does he know of you? He has read in old musty books about your times, that is all. What do you care about him, to let yourself be vexed by anything he said? Isn't it anything to you, that we who know you feel differently? Don't you care more about what we think of you than what he does who never saw you? Oh, Mr. West! you don't know, you can't think, how it makes me feel to see you so forlorn. I can't have it so. What can I say to you? How can I convince you how different our feeling for you is from what you think?"

As before, in that other crisis of my fate when she had come to me, she extended her hands towards me in a gesture of helpfulness, and, as then, I caught and held them in my own; her bosom heaved with strong emotion, and little tremors in the fingers which I clasped emphasized the depth of her feeling. In her face, pity contended in a sort of divine spite against the obstacles which reduced it to impotence. Womanly compassion surely never wore a guise more lovely.

Such beauty and such goodness quite melted me, and it seemed that the only fitting response I could make was to tell her just the truth. Of course I had not a spark of hope, but on the other hand I had no fear that she would be angry. She was too pitiful for that. So I said presently, "It is very ungrateful in me not to be satisfied with such kindness as you have shown me, and are showing me now. But are you so blind as not to see why they are not enough to make me happy? Don't you see that it is because I have been mad enough to love you?"

At my last words she blushed deeply and her eyes fell before mine, but she made no effort to withdraw her hands from my clasp. For some moments she stood so, panting a little. Then blushing deeper than ever, but with a dazzling smile, she looked up.

"Are you sure it is not you who are blind?" she said.

That was all, but it was enough, for it told me that, unaccountable, incredible as it was, this radiant daughter of a golden age had bestowed upon me not alone her pity, but her love. Still, I half believed I must be under some blissful hallucination even as I clasped her in my arms. "If I am beside myself," I cried, "let me remain so."

"It is I whom you must think beside myself," she panted,

escaping from my arms when I had barely tasted the sweetness of her lips. "Oh! oh! what must you think of me almost to throw myself in the arms of one I have known but a week? I did not mean that you should find it out so soon, but I was so sorry for you I forgot what I was saying. No, no; you must not touch me again till you know who I am. After that, sir, you shall apologize to me very humbly for thinking, as I know you do, that I have been over quick to fall in love with you. After you know who I am, you will be bound to confess that it was nothing less than my duty to fall in love with you at first sight, and that no girl of proper feeling in my place could do otherwise."

As may be supposed, I would have been quite content to waive explanations, but Edith was resolute that there should be no more kisses until she had been vindicated from all suspicion of precipitancy in the bestowal of her affections, and I was fain to follow the lovely enigma into the house. Having come where her mother was, she blushingly whispered something in her ear and ran away, leaving us together.

It then appeared that, strange as my experience had been, I was now first to know what was perhaps its strangest feature. From Mrs. Leete I learned that Edith was the great-granddaughter of no other than my lost love, Edith Bartlett. After mourning me for fourteen years, she had made a marriage of esteem, and left a son who had been Mrs. Leete's father. Mrs. Leete had never seen her grandmother, but had heard much of her, and, when her daughter was born, gave her the name of Edith. This fact might have tended to increase the interest which the girl took, as she grew up, in all that concerned her ancestress, and especially the tragic story of the supposed death of the lover, whose wife she expected to be, in the conflagration of his house. It was a tale well calculated to touch the sympathy of a romantic girl, and the fact that the blood of the unfortunate heroine was in her own veins naturally heightened Edith's interest in it. A portrait of Edith Bartlett and some of her papers, including a packet of my own letters, were among the family heirlooms. The picture represented a very beautiful young woman about whom it was easy to imagine all manner of tender and romantic things.

My letters gave Edith some material for forming a distinct idea of my personality, and both together sufficed to make the sad old story very real to her. She used to tell her parents, half jestingly, that she would never marry till she found a lover like Julian West, and there were none such nowadays.

Now all this, of course, was merely the day-dreaming of a girl whose mind had never been taken up by a love affair of her own, and would have had no serious consequence but for the discovery that morning of the buried vault in her father's garden and the revelation of the identity of its inmate. For when the apparently lifeless form had been borne into the house, the face in the locket found upon the breast was instantly recognized as that of Edith Bartlett, and by that fact, taken in connection with the other circumstances, they knew that I was no other than Julian West. Even had there been no thought, as at first there was not, of my resuscitation, Mrs. Leete said she believed that this event would have affected her daughter in a critical and life-long manner. The presumption of some subtle ordering of destiny, involving her fate with mine, would under all circumstances have possessed an irresistible fascination for almost any woman.

Whether when I came back to life a few hours afterward, and from the first seemed to turn to her with a peculiar dependence and to find a special solace in her company, she had been too quick in giving her love at the first sign of mine, I could now, her mother said, judge for myself. If I thought so, I must remember that this, after all, was the twentieth and not the nineteenth century, and love was, no doubt, now quicker in growth, as well as franker in utterance than then.

From Mrs. Leete I went to Edith. When I found her, it was first of all to take her by both hands and stand a long time in rapt contemplation of her face. As I gazed, the memory of that other Edith, which had been affected as with a benumbing shock by the tremendous experience that had parted us, revived, and my heart was dissolved with tender and pitiful emotions, but also very blissful ones. For she who brought to me so poignantly the sense of my loss was to make that loss good. It was as if from her eyes Edith Bartlett looked into mine, and smiled consolation to me. My fate was not alone the strangest, but the most fortunate that ever befell a man. A double miracle had been wrought for me. I had not been stranded upon the shore of this strange world to find myself alone and companionless. My love, whom I had dreamed lost, had been reëmbodied for my consolation. When at last, in an ecstasy of gratitude and tenderness, I folded the lovely girl in my arms, the two Ediths were blended in my thought, nor have they ever since been clearly distinguished. I was not long in finding that on Edith's part there was a corresponding confusion of identities. Never, surely, was there between freshly united lovers a stranger talk than ours that afternoon. She seemed more anxious to have me speak of Edith Bartlett than of herself, of how I had loved her than how I loved herself, rewarding my fond words concerning another woman with tears and tender smiles and pressures of the hand.

"You must not love me too much for myself," she said. "I shall be very jealous for her. I shall not let you forget her. I am going to tell you something which you may think strange. Do you not believe that spirits sometimes come back to the world to fulfill some work that lay near their hearts? What if I were to tell you that I have sometimes thought that her spirit lives in me,—that Edith Bartlett, not Edith Leete, is my real name. I cannot know it; of course none of us can know who we really are; but I can feel it. Can you wonder that I have such a feeling, seeing how my life was affected by her and by you, even before you came. So you see you need not trouble to love me at all, if only you are true to her. I shall not be likely to be jealous."

Dr. Leete had gone out that afternoon, and I did not have an interview with him till later. He was not, apparently, wholly unprepared for the intelligence I conveyed, and shook my hand heartily.

"Under any ordinary circumstances, Mr. West, I should say that this step had been taken on rather short acquaintance; but these are decidedly not ordinary circumstances. In fairness, perhaps I ought to tell you," he added, smilingly, "that while I cheerfully consent to the proposed arrangement, you must not feel too much indebted to me, as I judge my consent is a mere formality. From the moment the secret of the locket was out, it had to be, I fancy. Why, bless me, if Edith had not been there to redeem her great-grandmother's pledge, I really apprehend that Mrs. Leete's loyalty to me would have suffered a severe strain."

That evening the garden was bathed in moonlight, and till midnight Edith and I wandered to and fro there, trying to grow accustomed to our happiness.

"What should I have done if you had not cared for me?" she exclaimed. "I was afraid you were not going to. What should I have done then, when I felt I was consecrated to you! As soon as you came back to life, I was as sure as if she had told me that I was to be to you what she could not be, but that could only be if you would let me. Oh, how I wanted to tell you that morning, when you felt so terribly strange among us, who I was, but dared not open my lips about that, or let father or mother"—

"That must have been what you would not let your father tell me!" I exclaimed, referring to the conversation I had overheard as I came out of my trance.

"Of course it was," Edith laughed. "Did you only just guess that? Father being only a man, thought that it would make you feel among friends to tell you who we were. He did not think of me at all. But mother knew what I meant, and so I had my way. I could never have looked you in the face if you had known who I was. It would have been forcing myself on you quite too boldly. I am afraid you think I did that to-day, as it was. I am sure I did not mean to, for I know girls were expected to hide their feelings in your day, and I was dreadfully afraid of shocking you. Ah me, how hard it must have been for them to have always had to conceal their love like a fault. Why did they think it such a shame to love any one till they had been given permission? It is so odd to think of waiting for permission to fall in love. Was it because men in those days were angry when girls loved them? That is not the way women would feel, I am sure, or men either, I think, now. I don't understand it at all. That will be one of the curious things about the women of those days that you will have to explain to me. I don't believe Edith Bartlett was so foolish as the others."

After sundry ineffectual attempts at parting, she finally insisted that we must say good night. I was about to imprint upon her lips the positively last kiss, when she said, with an indescribable archness:—

"One thing troubles me. Are you sure that you quite forgive Edith Bartlett for marrying any one else? The books that have come down to us make out lovers of your time more jealous than fond, and that is what makes me ask. It would be a great relief to me if I could feel sure that you were not in the least jealous of my great-grandfather for marrying your sweetheart. May I tell my great-grandmother's picture when I go to my room that you quite forgive her for proving false to you?"

Will the reader believe it, this coquettish quip, whether the speaker herself had any idea of it or not, actually touched and with the touching cured a preposterous ache of something like jealousy which I had been vaguely conscious of ever since Mrs. Leete had told me of Edith Bartlett's marriage. Even while I had been holding Edith Bartlett's great-granddaughter in my arms, I had not, till this moment, so illogical are some of our feelings, distinctly realized that but for that marriage I could not have done so. The absurdity of this frame of mind could only be equalled by the abruptness with which it dissolved as Edith's roguish query cleared the fog from my perceptions. I laughed as I kissed her.

"You may assure her of my entire forgiveness," I said, "although if it had been any man but your great-grandfather whom she married, it would have been a very different matter."

On reaching my chamber that night I did not open the musical telephone that I might be lulled to sleep with soothing tunes, as had become my habit. For once my thoughts made better music than even twentieth century orchestras discourse, and it held me enchanted till well toward morning, when I fell asleep.

Chapter XXVIII

*I*T's a little after the time you told me to wake you, sir. You did not come out of it as quick as common, sir."

The voice was the voice of my man Sawyer. I started bolt upright in bed and stared around. I was in my underground chamber. The mellow light of the lamp which always burned in the room when I occupied it illumined the familiar walls and furnishings. By my bedside, with the glass of sherry in his hand which Dr. Pillsbury prescribed on first rousing from a mesmeric sleep, by way of awakening the torpid physical functions, stood Sawyer.

"Better take this right off, sir," he said, as I stared blankly at him. "You look kind of flushed like, sir, and you need it."

I tossed off the liquor and began to realize what had happened to me. It was, of course, very plain. All that about the twentieth century had been a dream. I had but dreamed of that enlightened and care-free race of men and their ingeniously simple institutions, of the glorious new Boston with its domes and pinnacles, its gardens and fountains, and its universal reign of comfort. The amiable family which I had learned to know so well, my genial host and Mentor, Dr. Leete, his wife, and their daughter, the second and more beauteous Edith, my betrothed,—these, too, had been but figments of a vision.

For a considerable time I remained in the attitude in which this conviction had come over me, sitting up in bed gazing at vacancy, absorbed in recalling the scenes and incidents of my fantastic experience. Sawyer, alarmed at my looks, was meanwhile anxiously inquiring what was the matter with me. Roused at length by his importunities to a recognition of my surroundings, I pulled myself together with an effort and assured the faithful fellow that I was all right. "I have had an extraordinary dream, that's all, Sawyer," I said, "a most-ex-traor-dinary-dream."

I dressed in a mechanical way, feeling lightheaded and oddly uncertain of myself, and sat down to the coffee and rolls which Sawyer was in the habit of providing for my refreshment before I left the house. The morning newspaper lay by the plate. I took it up, and my eye fell on the date, May 31, 1887. I had known, of course, from the moment I opened my eyes that my long and detailed experience in another century had been a dream, and yet it was startling to have it so conclusively demonstrated that the world was but a few hours older than when I had lain down to sleep.

Glancing at the table of contents at the head of the paper, which reviewed the news of the morning, I read the following summary:—

"FOREIGN AFFAIRS.— The impending war between France and Germany. The French Chambers asked for new military credits to meet Germany's increase of her army. Probability that all Europe will be involved in case of war.—Great suffering among the unemployed in London. They demand work. Monster demonstration to be made. The authorities uneasy.—Great strikes in Belgium. The government preparing to repress outbreaks. Shocking facts in regard to the employment of girls in Belgium coal mines.—Wholesale evictions in Ireland.

"HOME AFFAIRS.— The epidemic of fraud unchecked. Embezzlement of half a million in New York.—Misappropriation of a trust fund by executors. Orphans left penniless.—Clever system of thefts by a bank teller; $50,000 gone.—The coal barons decide to advance the price of coal and reduce production.—Speculators engineering a great wheat corner at Chicago.—A clique forcing up the price of coffee.—Enormous land-grabs of Western syndicates.—Revelations of shocking corruption among Chicago officials. Systematic bribery.—The trials of the Boodle aldermen to go on at New York.—Large failures of business houses. Fears of a business crisis.—A large grist of burglaries and larcenies.—A woman murdered in cold blood for her money at New Haven.—A householder shot by a burglar in this city last night.—A man shoots himself in Worcester because he could not get work. A large family left destitute.—An aged couple in New Jersey commit suicide rather than go to the poor-house.—Pitiable destitution among the women wage-workers in the great cities.—Startling growth of illiteracy in Massachusetts.—More insane asylums wanted.—Decoration Day addresses. Professor Brown's oration on the moral grandeur of nineteenth century civilization."

It was indeed the nineteenth century to which I had awaked; there could be no kind of doubt about that. Its complete micro-cosm this summary of the day's news had presented, even to that last unmistakable touch of fatuous self-complacency. Coming after such a damning indictment of the age as that one day's chronicle of world-wide bloodshed, greed, and tyranny, was a bit of cynicism worthy of Mephistopheles, and yet of all whose eyes it had met this morning I was, perhaps, the only one who perceived the cynicism, and but yesterday I should have per-ceived it no more than the others. That strange dream it was which had made all the difference. For I know not how long, I forgot my surroundings after this, and was again in fancy moving in that vivid dream-world, in that glorious city, with its homes of simple comfort and its gorgeous public palaces. Around me were again faces unmarred by arrogance or servility, by envy or greed, by anxious care or feverish ambition, and stately forms of men and women who had never known fear of a fellow man or depended on his favor, but always, in the words of that sermon which still rang in my ears, had "stood up straight before God."

With a profound sigh and a sense of irreparable loss, not the less poignant that it was a loss of what had never really been, I roused at last from my reverie, and soon after left the house.

A dozen times between my door and Washington Street I had to stop and pull myself together, such power had been in that vision of the Boston of the future to make the real Boston strange. The squalor and malodorousness of the town struck me, from the moment I stood upon the street, as facts I had never before observed. But yesterday, moreover, it had seemed quite a matter of course that some of my fellow-citizens should wear silks, and others rags, that some should look well fed, and others hungry. Now on the contrary the glaring disparities in the dress and condition of the men and women who brushed each other on the sidewalks shocked me at every step, and yet more the entire indifference which the prosperous showed to the plight of the unfortunate. Were these human beings, who could behold the wretchedness of their fellows without so much as a change of countenance? And yet, all the while, I knew well that it was I who had changed, and not my contemporaries. I had dreamed of a city whose people fared all alike as children of one family and were one another's keepers in all things.

Another feature of the real Boston, which assumed the extraordinary effect of strangeness that marks familiar things seen in a new light, was the prevalence of advertising. There had been no personal advertising in the Boston of the twentieth century, because there was no need of any, but here the walls of the buildings, the windows, the broadsides of the newspapers in every hand, the very pavements, everything in fact in sight, save the sky, were covered with the appeals of individuals who sought, under innumerable pretexts, to attract the contributions of others to their support. However the wording might vary, the tenor of all these appeals was the same:—

"Help John Jones. Never mind the rest. They are frauds. I, John Jones, am the right one. Buy of me. Employ me. Visit me. Hear me, John Jones. Look at me. Make no mistake. John Jones is the man and nobody else. Let the rest starve, but for God's sake remember John Jones!"

Whether the pathos or the moral repulsiveness of the spectacle most impressed me, so suddenly become a stranger in my own city, I know not. Wretched men, I was moved to cry, who, because they will not learn to be helpers of one another, are doomed to be beggars of one another from the least to the greatest! This horrible babel of shameless self-assertion and mutual depreciation, this stunning clamor of conflicting boasts, appeals, and adjurations, this stupendous system of brazen beggary, what was it all but the necessity of a society in which the opportunity to serve the world according to his gifts, instead of being secured to every man as the first object of social organization, had to be fought for!

I reached Washington Street at the busiest point, and there I stood and laughed aloud, to the scandal of the passers-by. For my life I could not have helped it, with such a mad humor was I moved at sight of the interminable rows of stores on either side, up and down the street so far as I could see,—scores of them, to make the spectacle more utterly preposterous, within a stone's throw devoted to selling the same sort of goods. Stores! stores! stores! miles of stores! ten thousand stores to distribute the goods needed by this one city, which in my dream had been supplied with all things from a single warehouse, as they were ordered through one great store in every quarter, where the buyer, without waste of time or labor, found under one roof the world's assortment in whatever line he desired. There the labor of distribution had been so slight as to add but a scarcely perceptible fraction to the cost of commodities to the user. The cost of production was virtually all he paid. But here the mere distribution of the goods, their handling alone, added a fourth, a third, a half and more, to the cost. All these ten thousand plants must be paid for, their rent, their staffs of superintendence, their platoons of salesmen, their ten thousand sets of accountants, jobbers, and business dependents, with all they spent in advertising themselves and fighting one another, and the consumers must do the paying. What a famous process for beggaring a nation!

Were these serious men I saw about me, or children, who did their business on such a plan? Could they be reasoning beings, who did not see the folly which, when the product is made and ready for use, wastes so much of it in getting it to the user? If people eat with a spoon that leaks half its contents between bowl and lip, are they not likely to go hungry?

I had passed through Washington Street thousands of times before and viewed the ways of those who sold merchandise, but my curiosity concerning them was as if I had never gone by their way before. I took wondering note of the show windows of the stores, filled with goods arranged with a wealth of pains and artistic device to attract the eye. I saw the throngs of ladies looking in, and the proprietors eagerly watching the effect of the bait. I went within and noted the hawk-eyed floor-walker watching for business, overlooking the clerks, keeping them up to their task of inducing the customers to buy, buy, buy, for money if they had it, for credit if they had it not, to buy what they wanted not, more than they wanted, what they could not afford. At times I momentarily lost the clue and was confused by the sight. Why this effort to induce people to buy? Surely that had nothing to do with the legitimate business of distributing products to those who needed them. Surely it was the sheerest waste to force upon people what they did not want, but what might be useful to another. The nation was so much the poorer for every such achievement. What were these clerks thinking of? Then I would remember that they were not acting as distributors like those in the store I had visited in the dream Boston. They were not serving the public interest, but their immediate personal interest, and it was nothing to them what the ultimate effect of their course on the general prosperity might be, if but they increased their own hoard, for these goods were their own, and the more they sold and the more they got for them, the greater their gain. The more wasteful the people were, the more articles they did not want which they could be induced to buy, the better for these sellers. To encourage prodigality was the express aim of the ten thousand stores of Boston.

Nor were these storekeepers and clerks a whit worse men than any others in Boston. They must earn a living and support their families, and how were they to find a trade to do it by which did not necessitate placing their individual interests before those of others and that of all? They could not be asked to starve while they waited for an order of things such as I had seen in my dream, in which the interest of each and that of all were identical. But, God in heaven! what wonder, under such a system as this about me—what wonder that the city was so shabby, and the people so meanly dressed, and so many of them ragged and hungry!

Some time after this it was that I drifted over into South Boston and found myself among the manufacturing establishments. I had been in this quarter of the city a hundred times before, just as I had been on Washington Street, but here, as well as there, I now first perceived the true significance of what I witnessed. Formerly I had taken pride in the fact that, by actual count, Boston had some four thousand independent manufacturing establishments; but in this very multiplicity and independence I recognized now the secret of the insignificant total product of their industry.

If Washington Street had been like a lane in Bedlam, this was a spectacle as much more melancholy as production is a more vital function than distribution. For not only were these four thousand establishments not working in concert, and for that reason alone operating at prodigious disadvantage, but, as if this did not involve a sufficiently disastrous loss of power, they were using their utmost skill to frustrate one another's effort, praying by night and working by day for the destruction of one another's enterprises.

The roar and rattle of wheels and hammers resounding from every side was not the hum of a peaceful industry, but the clangor of swords wielded by foemen. These mills and shops were so many forts, each under its own flag, its guns trained on the mills and shops about it, and its sappers busy below, undermining them.

Within each one of these forts the strictest organization of industry was insisted on; the separate gangs worked under a single central authority. No interference and no duplicating of work were permitted. Each had his allotted task, and none were idle. By what hiatus in the logical faculty, by what lost link of reasoning, account, then, for the failure to recognize the necessity of applying the same principle to the organization of the national industries as a whole, to see that if lack of organization could impair the efficiency of a shop, it must have effects as much more disastrous in disabling the industries of the nation at large as the latter are vaster in volume and more complex in the relationship of their parts.

People would be prompt enough to ridicule an army in which

there were neither companies, battalions, regiments, brigades, divisions, or army corps,—no unit of organization, in fact, larger than the corporal's squad, with no officer higher than a corporal, and all the corporals equal in authority. And yet just such an army were the manufacturing industries of nineteenth century Boston, an army of four thousand independent squads led by four thousand independent corporals, each with a separate plan of campaign.

Knots of idle men were to be seen here and there on every side, some idle because they could find no work at any price, others because they could not get what they thought a fair price.

I accosted some of the latter, and they told me their grievances. It was very little comfort I could give them. "I am sorry for you," I said. "You get little enough, certainly, and yet the wonder to me is, not that industries conducted as these are do not pay you living wages, but that they are able to pay you any wages at all."

Making my way back again after this to the peninsular city, toward three o'clock I stood on State Street, staring, as if I had never seen them before, at the banks and brokers' offices, and other financial institutions, of which there had been in the State Street of my vision no vestige. Business men, confidential clerks, and errand boys were thronging in and out of the banks, for it wanted but a few minutes of the closing hour. Opposite me was the bank where I did business, and presently I crossed the street, and, going in with the crowd, stood in a recess of the wall looking on at the army of clerks handling money, and the cues of depositors at the tellers' windows. An old gentleman whom I knew, a director of the bank, passing me and observing my contemplative attitude, stopped a moment.

"Interesting sight, isn't it, Mr. West," he said. "Wonderful piece of mechanism; I find it so myself. I like sometimes to stand and look on at it just as you are doing. It's a poem, sir, a poem, that's what I call it. Did you ever think, Mr. West, that the bank is the heart of the business system? From it and to it, in endless flux and reflux, the life blood goes. It is flowing in now. It will flow out again in the morning;" and pleased with his little conceit, the old man passed on smiling.

Yesterday I should have considered the simile apt enough, but since then I had visited a world incomparably more affluent than this, in which money was unknown and without conceivable use. I had learned that it had a use in the world around me only because the work of producing the nation's livelihood, instead of being regarded as the most strictly public and common of all concerns, and as such conducted by the nation, was abandoned to the hap-hazard efforts of individuals. This original mistake necessitated endless exchanges to bring about any sort of general distribution of products. These exchanges money effected—how equitably, might be seen in a walk from the tenement house districts to the Back Bay—at the cost of an army of men taken from productive labor to manage it, with constant ruinous break-downs of its machinery, and a generally debauching influence on mankind which had justified its description, from ancient time, as the "root of all evil."

Alas for the poor old bank director with his poem! He had mistaken the throbbing of an abcess for the beating of the heart. What he called "a wonderful piece of mechanism" was an imperfect device to remedy an unnecessary defect, the clumsy crutch of a self-made cripple.

After the banks had closed I wandered aimlessly about the business quarter for an hour or two, and later sat a while on one of the benches of the Common, finding an interest merely in watching the throngs that passed, such as one has in studying the populace of a foreign city, so strange since yesterday had my fellow citizens and their ways become to me. For thirty years I had lived among them, and yet I seemed to have never noted before how drawn and anxious were their faces, of the rich as of the poor, the refined, acute faces of the educated as well as the dull masks of the ignorant. And well it might be so, for I saw now, as never before I had seen so plainly, that each as he walked constantly turned to catch the whispers of a spectre at his ear, the spectre of Uncertainty. "Do your work never so well," the spectre was whispering,—"rise early and toil till late, rob cunningly or serve faithfully, you shall never know security. Rich you may be now and still come to poverty at last. Leave never so much wealth to your children, you cannot buy the assurance that your son may not be the servant of your servant, or that your daughter will not have to sell herself for bread."

A man passing by thrust an advertising card in my hand, which set forth the merits of some new scheme of life insurance. The incident reminded me of the only device, pathetic in its admission of the universal need it so poorly supplied, which offered these tired and hunted men and women even a partial protection from uncertainty. By this means, those already well-to-do, I remembered, might purchase a precarious confidence that after their death their loved ones would not, for a while at least, be trampled under the feet of men. But this was all, and this was only for those who could pay well for it. What idea was possible to these wretched dwellers in the land of Ishmael, where every man's hand was against each and the hand of each against every other, of true life insurance as I had seen it among the people of that dream land, each of whom, by virtue merely of his membership in the national family, was guaranteed against need of any sort, by a policy underwritten by one hundred million fellow countrymen.

Some time after this it was that I recall a glimpse of myself standing on the steps of a building on Tremont Street, looking at a military parade. A regiment was passing. It was the first sight in that dreary day which had inspired me with any other emotions than wondering pity and amazement. Here at last were order and reason, an exhibition of what intelligent coöperation can accomplish. The people who stood looking on with kindling faces,—could it be that the sight had for them no more than but a spectacular interest? Could they fail to see that it was their perfect concert of action, their organization under one control, which made these men the tremendous engine they were, able to vanquish a mob ten times as numerous? Seeing this so plainly, could they fail to compare the scientific manner in which the nation went to war with the unscientific manner in which it went to work? Would they not query since what time the killing of men had been a task so much more important than feeding and clothing them, that a trained army should be deemed alone adequate to the former, while the latter was left to a mob?

It was now toward nightfall, and the streets were thronged with the workers from the stores, the shops, and mills. Carried along with the stronger part of the current, I found myself, as it began to grow dark, in the midst of a scene of squalor and human degradation such only the South Cove tenement district could present. I had seen the mad wasting of human labor; here I saw in direst shape the want that waste had bred.

From the black doorways and windows of the rookeries on every side came gusts of fetid air. The streets and alleys reeked with the effluvia of a slave ship's between-decks. As I passed I had glimpses within of pale babies gasping out their lives amid sultry stenches, of hopeless-faced women deformed by hardship, retaining of womanhood no trait save weakness, while from the windows leered girls with brows of brass. Like the starving bands of mongrel curs that infest the streets of Moslem towns, swarms of half-clad brutalized children filled the air with shrieks and curses as they fought and tumbled among the garbage that littered the court-yards.

There was nothing in all this that was new to me. Often had I passed through this part of the city and witnessed its sights with feelings of disgust mingled with a certain philosophical wonder at the extremities mortals will endure and still cling to life. But not alone as regarded the economical follies of this age, but equally as touched its moral abominations, scales had fallen from my eyes since that vision of another century. No more did I look upon the woful dwellers in this Inferno with a callous curiosity as creatures scarcely human. I saw in them my brothers and sisters, my parents, my children, flesh of my flesh, blood of my blood. The festering mass of human wretchedness about me offended not now my senses merely, but pierced my heart like a knife, so that I could not repress sighs and groans. I not only saw but felt in my body all that I saw.

Presently, too, as I observed the wretched beings about me more closely, I perceived that they were all quite dead. Their bodies were so many living sepulchres. On each brutal brow was plainly written the *hic jacet* of a soul dead within.

As I looked, horror struck, from one death's head to another, I was affected by a singular hallucination. Like a wavering translucent spirit face superimposed upon each of these brutish masks I saw the ideal, the possible face that would have been the actual if mind and soul had lived. It was not till I was aware of these ghostly faces, and of the reproach that could not be gainsaid which was in their eyes, that the full piteousness of the ruin that had been wrought was revealed to me. I was moved with contrition as with a strong agony, for I had been one of those who had endured that these things should be. I had been one of those who, well knowing that they were, had not desired to hear or be compelled to think much of them, but had gone on as if they were not, seeking my own pleasure and profit. Therefore now I found upon my garments the blood of this great multitude of strangled souls of my brothers. The voice of their blood cried out against me from the ground. Every stone of the reeking pavements, every brick of the pestilential rookeries, found a tongue and called after me as I fled: What hast thou done with thy brother Abel?

I have no clear recollection of anything after this till I found myself standing on the carved stone steps of the magnificent home of my betrothed in Commonwealth avenue. Amid the tumult of my thoughts that day, I had scarcely once thought of her, but now obeying some unconscious impulse my feet had found the familiar way to her door. I was told that the family were at dinner, but word was sent out that I should join them at table. Besides the family, I found several guests present, all known to me. The table glittered with plate and costly china. The ladies were sumptuously dressed and wore the jewels of queens. The scene was one of costly elegance and lavish luxury. The company was in excellent spirits, and there was plentiful laughter and a running fire of jests.

To me it was as if, in wandering through the place of doom, my blood turned to tears by its sights, and my spirit attuned to sorrow, pity, and despair, I had happened in some glade upon

a merry party of roisterers. I sat in silence until Edith began to
rally me upon my sombre looks. What ailed me? The others presently joined in the playful assault, and I became a target for
quips and jests. Where had I been, and what had I seen to
make such a dull fellow of me?

"I have been in Golgotha," at last I answered. "I have seen
Humanity hanging on a cross! Do none of you know what sights
the sun and stars look down on in this city, that you can think
and talk of anything else? Do you not know that close to your
doors a great multitude of men and women, flesh of your flesh,
live lives that are one agony from birth to death? Listen! their
dwellings are so near that if you hush your laughter you will
hear their grievous voices, the piteous crying of the little ones
that suckle poverty, the hoarse curses of men sodden in misery,
turned half-way back to brutes, the chaffering of an army of
women selling themselves for bread. With what have you stopped
your ears that you do not hear these doleful sounds? For me, I
can hear nothing else."

Silence followed my words. A passion of pity had shaken me
as I spoke, but when I looked around upon the company, I saw
that, far from being stirred as I was, their faces expressed a cold
and hard astonishment, mingled in Edith's with extreme mortifi-
cation, in her father's with anger. The ladies were exchanging
scandalized looks, while one of the gentlemen had put up his
eyeglass and was studying me with an air of scientific curiosity.
When I saw that things which were to me so intolerable moved
them not at all, that words that melted my heart to speak had
only offended them with the speaker, I was at first stunned and
then overcome with a desperate sickness and faintness at the
heart. What hope was there for the wretched, for the world, if
thoughtful men and tender women were not moved by things
like these! Then I bethought myself that it must be because I
had not spoken aright. No doubt I had put the case badly. They
were angry because they thought I was berating them, when God
knew I was merely thinking of the horror of the fact without
any attempt to assign the responsibility for it.

I restrained my passion, and tried to speak calmly and logically that I might correct this impression. I told them that I had not meant to accuse them, as if they, or the rich in general, were responsible for the misery of the world. True indeed it was, that the superfluity which they wasted would, otherwise bestowed, relieve much bitter suffering. These costly viands, these rich wines, these gorgeous fabrics and glistening jewels represented the ransom of many lives. They were verily not without the guiltiness of those who waste in a land stricken with famine. Nevertheless, all the waste of all the rich, were it saved, would go but ε. little way to cure the poverty of the world. There was so little to divide that even if the rich went share and share with the poor, there would be but a common fare of crusts, albeit made very sweet then by brotherly love.

The folly of men, not their hard-heartedness, was the great cause of the world's poverty. It was not the crime of man, nor of any class of men, that made the race so miserable, but a hideous, ghastly mistake, a colossal world-darkening blunder. And then I showed them how four fifths of the labor of men was utterly wasted by the mutual warfare, the lack of organization and concert among the workers. Seeking to make the matter very plain, I instanced the case of arid lands where the soil yielded the means of life only by careful use of the watercourses for irrigation. I showed how in such countries it was counted the most important function of the government to see that the water was not wasted by the selfishness or ignorance of individuals, since otherwise there would be famine. To this end its use was strictly regulated and systematized, and individuals of their mere caprice were not permitted to dam it or divert it, or in any way to tamper with it.

The labor of men, I explained, was the fertilizing stream which alone rendered earth habitable. It was but a scanty stream at best, and its use required to be regulated by a system which expended every drop to the best advantage, if the world were to be supported in abundance. But how far from any system was the actual practice! Every man wasted the precious fluid as he wished, animated only by the equal motives of saving his own crop and spoiling his neighbor's, that his might sell the better.

What with greed and what with spite some fields were flooded while others were parched, and half the water ran wholly to waste. In such a land, though a few by strength or cunning might win the means of luxury, the lot of the great mass must be poverty, and of the weak and ignorant bitter want and perennial famine.

Let but the famine-stricken nation assume the function it had neglected, and regulate for the common good the course of the life-giving stream, and the earth would bloom like one garden, and none of its children lack any good thing. I described the physical felicity, mental enlightenment, and moral elevation which would then attend the lives of all men. With fervency I spoke of that new world, blessed with plenty, purified by justice and sweetened by brotherly kindness, the world of which I had indeed but dreamed, but which might so easily be made real. But when I had expected now surely the faces around me to light up with emotions akin to mine, they grew ever more dark, angry, and scornful. Instead of enthusiasm, the ladies showed only aversion and dread, while the men interrupted me with shouts of reprobation and contempt. "Madman!" "Pestilent fellow!" "Fanatic!" "Enemy of society!" were some of their cries, and the one who had before taken his eyeglass to me exclaimed, "He says we are to have no more poor. Ha! ha!"

"Put the fellow out!" exclaimed the father of my betrothed, and at the signal the men sprang from their chairs and advanced upon me.

It seemed to me that my heart would burst with the anguish of finding that what was to me so plain and so all-important was to them meaningless, and that I was powerless to make it other. So hot had been my heart that I had thought to melt an iceberg with its glow, only to find at last the overmastering chill seizing my own vitals. It was not enmity that I felt toward them as they thronged me, but pity only, for them and for the world.

Although despairing, I could not give over. Still I strove with them. Tears poured from my eyes. In my vehemence I became inarticulate. I panted, I sobbed, I groaned, and immediately afterward found myself sitting upright in bed in my room in

Dr. Leete's house, and the morning sun shining through the open window into my eyes. I was gasping. The tears were streaming down my face, and I quivered in every nerve.

As with an escaped convict who dreams that he has been re-captured and brought back to his dark and reeking dungeon, and opens his eyes to see the heaven's vault spread above him, so it was with me, as I realized that my return to the nineteenth century had been the dream, and my presence in the twentieth was the reality.

The cruel sights which I had witnessed in my vision, and could so well confirm from the experience of my former life, though they had, alas! once been, and must in the retrospect to the end of time move the compassionate to tears, were, God be thanked, forever gone by. Long ago oppressor and oppressed, prophet and scorner, had been dust. For generations, rich and poor had been forgotten words.

But in that moment, while yet I mused with unspeakable thankfulness upon the greatness of the world's salvation and my privilege in beholding it, there suddenly pierced me like a knife a pang of shame, remorse, and wondering self-reproach, that bowed my head upon my breast and made me wish the grave had hid me with my fellows from the sun. For I had been a man of that former time. What had I done to help on the de-liverance whereat I now presumed to rejoice? I who had lived in those cruel, insensate days, what had I done to bring them to an end? I had been every whit as indifferent to the wretchedness of my brothers, as cynically incredulous of better things, as be-sotted a worshipper of Chaos and Old Night, as any of my fellows. So far as my personal influence went, it had been exerted rather to hinder than to help forward the enfranchisement of the race which was even then preparing. What right had I to hail a salva-tion which reproached me, to rejoice in a day whose dawning I had mocked?

"Better for you, better for you," a voice within me rang, "had this evil dream been the reality, and this fair reality the dream; better your part pleading for crucified humanity with a scoffing generation, than here, drinking of wells you digged not, and eating of trees whose husbandmen you stoned;" and my spirit answered, "Better, truly."

When at length I raised my bowed head and looked forth from the window, Edith, fresh as the morning, had come into the garden and was gathering flowers. I hastened to descend to her. Kneeling before her, with my face in the dust, I confessed with tears how little was my worth to breathe the air of this golden century, and how infinitely less to wear upon my breast its consummate flower. Fortunate is he who, with a case so desperate as mine, finds a judge so merciful.

*Postscript**

The Rate of the World's Progress.

To the Editor of the Boston Transcript: The Transcript of March 30, 1888, contained a review of *Looking Backward*, in response to which I beg to be allowed a word. The description to which the book is devoted, of the radically new social and industrial institutions and arrangements supposed to be enjoyed by the people of the United States in the twentieth century, is not objected to as depicting a degree of human felicity and moral development necessarily unattainable by the race, provided time enough had been allowed for its evolution from the present chaotic state of society. In failing to allow this, the reviewer thinks that the author has made an absurd mistake, which seriously detracts from the value of the book as a work of realistic imagination. Instead of placing the realization of the ideal social state a scant fifty years ahead, it is suggested that he should have made his figure seventy-five centuries. There is certainly a large discrepancy between seventy-five centuries and fifty

* [The "Postscript" was added in the second edition.]

years, and if the reviewer is correct in his estimate of the probable rate of human progress, the outlook of the world is decidedly discouraging. But is he right? I think not.

Looking Backward, although in form a fanciful romance, is intended, in all seriousness, as a forecast, in accordance with the principles of evolution, of the next stage in the industrial and social development of humanity, especially in this country; and no part of it is believed by the author to be better supported by the indications of probability than the implied prediction that the dawn of the new era is already near at hand, and that the full day will swiftly follow. Does this seem at first thought incredible, in view of the vastness of the changes presupposed? What is the teaching of history, but that great national transformations, while ages in unnoticed preparation, when once inaugurated, are accomplished with a rapidity and resistless momentum portioned to their magnitude, not limited by it?

In 1759, when Quebec fell, the might of England in America seemed irresistible, and the vassalage of the colonies assured. Nevertheless, thirty years later, the first President of the American Republic was inaugurated. In 1849, after Novara, Italian prospects appeared as hopeless as at any time since the Middle Ages; yet only fifteen years after, Victor Emmanuel was crowned King of United Italy. In 1864, the fulfillment of the thousand-year dream of German unity was apparently as far off as ever. Seven years later it had been realized, and William had assumed at Versailles the Crown of Barbarossa. In 1832, the original Anti-slavery Society was formed in Boston by a few so-called visionaries. Thirty-eight years later, in 1870, the society disbanded, its programme fully carried out.

These precedents do not, of course, prove that any such industrial and social transformation as is outlined in *Looking Backward* is impending; but they do show that, when the moral and economical conditions for it are ripe, it may be expected to go forward with great rapidity. On no other stage are the scenes shifted with a swiftness so like magic as on the great stage of history when once the hour strikes. The question is not, then, how extensive the scene-shifting must be to set the stage for the new fraternal civilization, but whether there are any special indications that a social transformation is at hand. The causes that have been bringing it ever nearer have been at work from immemorial time. To the stream of tendency setting toward an ultimate realization of a form of society which, while vastly more efficient for material prosperity, should also satisfy and not outrage the moral instincts, every sigh of poverty, every tear of pity, every humane impulse, every generous enthusiasm, every true religious feeling, every act by which men have given effect to their mutual sympathy by drawing more closely together for any purpose, have contributed from the beginnings of civilization. That this long stream of influence, ever widening and deepening, is at last about to sweep away the barriers it has so long sapped, is at least one obvious interpretation of the present universal ferment of men's minds as to the imperfections of present social arrangements. Not only are the toilers of the world engaged in something like a world-wide insurrection, but true and humane men and women, of every degree, are in a mood of exasperation, verging on absolute revolt, against social conditions that reduce life to a brutal struggle for existence, mock every dictate of ethics and religion, and render well-nigh futile the efforts of philanthropy.

As an iceberg, floating southward from the frozen North, is gradually undermined by warmer seas, and, become at last unstable, churns the sea to yeast for miles around by the mighty rockings that portend its overturn, so the barbaric industrial and social system, which has come down to us from savage antiquity, undermined by the modern humane spirit, riddled by the criticism of economic science, is shaking the world with convulsions that presage its collapse.

All thoughtful men agree that the present aspect of society is portentous of great changes. The only question is, whether they will be for the better or the worse. Those who believe in man's essential nobleness lean to the former view, those who believe in his essential baseness to the latter. For my part, I hold to the former opinion. *Looking Backward* was written in the belief that the Golden Age lies before us and not behind us, and is not far away. Our children will surely see it, and we, too, who are already men and women, if we deserve it by our faith and by our works.

Edward Bellamy

THE JOHN HARVARD LIBRARY

*The intent of
Waldron Phoenix Belknap, Jr.,
as expressed in an early will, was for
Harvard College to use the income from a
permanent trust fund he set up, for "editing and
publishing rare, inaccessible, or hitherto unpublished
source material of interest in connection with the
history, literature, art (including minor and useful
art), commerce, customs, and manners or way of
life of the Colonial and Federal Periods of the United
States . . . In all cases the emphasis shall be on the
presentation of the basic material." A later testament
broadened this statement, but Mr. Belknap's interests remained constant until his death.*

*In linking the name of the first benefactor of
Harvard College with the purpose of this later,
generous-minded believer in American culture the
John Harvard Library seeks to emphasize the importance of Mr. Belknap's purpose. The John Harvard
Library of the Belknap Press of Harvard University
Press exists to make books and documents
about the American past more readily
available to scholars and the
general reader.*